THE
BONDS
THAT
BREAK US

THE BOUND BY BLOOD SERIES

ERIN MAINORD

First published in the United States of America 2024 by Lake Country Press & Reviews.

Cataloging-in-Publication Data is on file with the Library of Congress.

ISBN: Hardcover: 979-8-9889859-3-8

Paperback: 979-8-9889859-4-5

Ebook: 979-8-9889859-5-2

Author website: https://www.erinmainord.com

Publisher website: https://www.lakecountrypress.com

Editor: Rebecca Puhl

Cover: Emily's World of Design

Formatting: Dawn Lucous of Yours Truly Book Services

Author photo: Kaitlyn Hull Photography

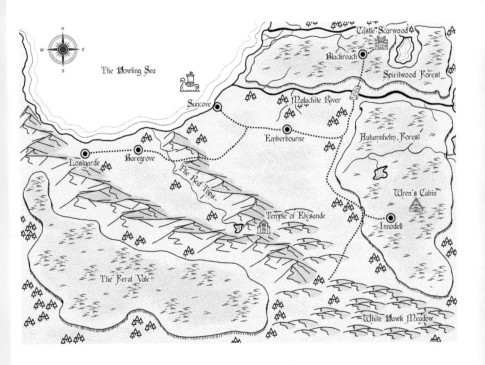

For those who have had to break away from toxic family bonds and find themselves for the first time... I'm so proud of you.

Dear Reader:

It means so much to me that you enjoyed the beginning of Sin and Wren's story enough to come back for a second bite. From the very bottom of my heart, thank you for taking a chance on me and allowing me to share my stories with you. Judging from the events of book 1, you can safely assume this second installment is also going to be an emotional rollercoaster, so you may want to buckle up.

That being said, the mental health of my readers is always my priority, and so here is the list of **content warnings** for what you will find inside The Bonds That Break Us.

Please note this list contains spoilers:

Alcohol consumption, breath play, death, descriptions of blood, explicit language, explicit sexual content, hand necklaces, mention of the death of a partner, talk and threats of genocide of fantasy creatures, violence.

Mental health matters.

You matter.

PLAYLIST

A Dangerous Thing: Aurora
Alkaline: Sleep Token
Bloodsport: Sleep Token
Chokehold: Sleep Token
Dangerous Hands: Austin Giorgio
Dirty Thoughts: Chloe Adams
Haunting: Halsey
I Don't Wanna Live Forever: ZAYN, Taylor Swift
In The Air Tonight: Natalie Taylor
Jealous Sea: Meg Myers
Just Pretend: Bad Omens
Shameless: Camila Cabello
Take Me Back To Eden: Sleep Token
Wicked Game: Theory of a Deadman

CHAPTER 1

The water bleeds scarlet.

Juice seeps into the current as if the bowels of the river hemorrhaged, drifting down the bank and over the loose rocks. Hooking a slender finger between my lips like a caught fish, I sweep a digit across my gums and spit a few more lingonberry seeds into the river.

It won't be the last time I spit red from my mouth.

I scrub at the stubborn mud slathering my cheeks and forehead, watching the clumpy brown soil wash into the shallow river. Somewhere deep in the thorn-infested bramble, a throaty whistle of a songbird floats out. Its chirps weave through the labyrinth of plump dewberries and squeeze through the arching shoots to pierce my ears with its mocking trill.

When the last of the dirt and grime is washed away, leaving my skin burning from the scratchy linen cloth, the bird flutters its tiny wings to perch on one of the many tangled canes. It peers at me with dark eyes, hopping on spindly legs and showing off its collection of brown and gray feathers.

Such a foolish animal, content to live its life nibbling on the seeds of grains and weeds, chirruping merrily, unaware of the danger watching through the lattice of branches above its head. In the overgrown guts of the forest, the hawk needs to survive as much as the sparrow. Swooping off its roost, the raptor dives through the dense canopy and buries curved talons in the squishy sides of its meal, taking off before any other predators can try to steal its afternoon snack.

I don't pity the dead thing. Bouncing from shrub to shrub, growing fat on tender grasses and swollen berries without a thought of self-preservation, ignorant to the perils lurking just out of sight. Something so eager to risk its life in exchange for minuscule pleasures chose its fate.

Deserves it too.

If it had been aware of the menace stalking from above and taken cover, the hawk's sensitive feet couldn't have pierced the prickly hedge. Instead, foolishness led to its feeble bones being crushed, and its stomach spilling out from feathered sides.

At least the hawk gets to eat, I think, turning back to my reflection rippling in the river, my image as clear as tumbled quartz. My long hair is littered with debris from tending to the gardens, my nose and chin beaming with red agitation from scrubbing off the mud. I slip into the river's cold viscera, gooseflesh blooming along my skin.

Two months ago, I was that sparrow. Snatched up in the jowls of a beast that prowled in shadows.

But despite my namesake bird, I have never been one to take kindly to a cage.

Unfortunate for him, really. He should have never let me go. Because now I have traded my gilded cage for a set of lethal, pointed teeth and an appetite to match.

I am prey no longer.

No.

I am the Wren.

"Your legs would be wise to find some knickers before devotion tonight."

Running my hands through my sopping tresses and wringing the ends in a death grip, I turn and meet the gray eyes of my bear-sized best-friend. "My *legs* are quite capable of thinking for themselves. It's you, I dare say, that struggles to think clearly around the high priestess, brother."

A mock shudder ripples down Eldridge's massive body, and he rubs his arms as if the mere mention of the elven priestess, Aeverie, burrows chills deep into his core. "Low blow, Wren. The woman's a damn nightmare. Only a godsdamned fool wouldn't piss themselves every time she smacks that stick around."

"Us educated folk call that a staff, Eldridge," I jest, wrapping a length of linen around myself and stepping out of the river.

He shoots me a pointed smirk. We both know I've received no more of an education than Eldridge has, each of us growing up in less than prosperous conditions, and spending the greater half of our lives with our adoptive mother.

"Yeah, *staff*," he says, making quotation marks with his fingers. "Will you still call it that when she's sticking it up my ass and displaying me in the yard like tanned leather?"

A laugh spurts out of me at the mental image. "I think that's exactly the kind of woman you need in your life—someone not afraid to shove a magical stick up your ass once in a while." I plunge my legs into my light-colored pants and pull on a sea-foam tunic while Eldridge chuckles at my remark, his arms folded, and looks off into the abyss of trees surrounding us while I dress.

"Well, she's also like a million years old, so if you're going to insist on finding me a Mate, maybe start looking a few centuries younger."

"Don't you know it's rude to comment on a lady's age, mister?"

Truth be told, neither of us knows how many years the priestess has walked the earth. I'm not even sure the average lifespan of one of their kind, other than that it is far greater than Eldridge and mine combined. I welcome Eldridge's humor and the smiles I pull from him so easily. Life has been startlingly different since we fled our Autumnhelm cabin and moved to The Feral Vale two months ago, when *he*...

My hands twist my hair into an obedient plait with more vigor than necessary, and I have to forcibly unclench my fingers to finish weaving the locks together. I haven't allowed myself to utter his name since the night Cosmina and I raced back to our cabin and rousted our family from their slumber. It was too dangerous for them to stay put, not when... not when *he* knew where my family resided. The family of the woman who doused his home in flames and stormed off with the squad that killed his guards and unleashed alchemist fire on his precious castle.

Life has been a constant weight on my chest since, every day trying its hardest to shove its complications into my lungs until they're packed to capacity, and I explode like an overinflated balloon. Eldridge's easy smiles and comforting scent make me feel just a little larger on the inside, like finding a crawl space in an abandoned home. An extra room to chuck the lumps of all the blackened memories I harbor, remnants of the fire that scorched all that I possessed.

All that I was.

But none of that matters now.

"Let's go. I don't want us to be late and have to watch as Madam Priestess bends you over her knee again," I tease, tugging at Eldridge's elbow to urge him forward. He snakes an arm around my waist, tucking me against his side, and the scent of wood and worn-in leather envelops me.

We traipse through the overgrown brush, stepping over thick roots and vining plants creeping across the forest floor. Growing up, I was told stories of what lurked beyond The Feral Vale, the expanse that bordered the desecrated city of Lostgarde. Legends claimed the kingdom feared the creatures that skulked in these woods, creatures that relied on the thick canopy of trees to survive, unable to withstand the sun's radiating light. So, Ephraim burned every tree and living foliage in the two closest cities, reducing Lostgarde and Baregrove to skeletal towns void of any verdant life. Without the trees' protective covering, the monsters that dwelled in the Vale could never emerge, trapped on the western coast of Aegidale. That's what the rumors had us believe anyway.

Now we know the kingdom was full of shit.

Eldridge walks ahead of me, taking the brunt of the jagged sticks and other thorny obstacles in our path. "For the elves supposedly having so much magic, you'd think they could spare some of it to trim down the fucking weeds once in a while," he huffs, taking a particularly pointy-looking branch to the calf.

I hold back a snort. "Maybe don't let them hear you referring to their plant life as *weeds*."

The Feral Vale is not what I expected. The monstrous beings the kingdom tells stories about aren't beasts at all, though the elves would be no more terrifying if they did have curved horns and claws filed into daggered points. Their magic is deeply rooted in what they call Source, as intertwined with the earth as the minerals mined from caves and the craggy floor of the sea. It's no wonder Ephraim feared their power—elven magic is ancient—and if I'm being blatant—downright petrifying.

If they simply had the numbers, the elves could take back their lost lands in a heartbeat.

Not lost—stolen.

But alas, the kingdom possesses more than enough bodies to keep the Vale's inhabitants in isolation, and ancient magic aside, elven skin is still as easily pierced by arrows as my own.

We break through the last of the wild herbage and step into the Vale's center. The heart of the forest is occupied by a plethora of stone buildings, some quaint and modest, others towering and looming. All irrevocably beautiful. The grass beneath our feet is silky, a sweeping green carpet stretching for miles in front of a mountainous backdrop of rocky cliffs and soaring peaks.

Passageways of stacked stone connect some of the shelters, an interlocked city of slab and mortar, while the grander ones sit alone, their tented roofs rivaling the mountains behind them for height. The grass floor weaves around several large lakes, adorned with floating gardens, some sprouting a variety of vibrant, leafy vegetables, others flavorful spices. Even after two months of living in the Vale, its beauty never fails to sweep the breath from my lungs.

While this hidden part of the isle has never failed to leave me wonderstruck, nothing is more resplendent than the southernmost temple, the Elven House of Worship.

And nothing is more frightening than Aeverie, the Elven High Priestess.

The elves hold their devotion ceremony at the start of each new week, a trek Eldridge and I use as an excuse to stick our noses in each other's business and exchange our latest theories on what Aeverie sees behind her milky sclerae. This trip is no different, and I am hoarse from laughter when we finally arrive.

The House of Worship greets us like the lady of a fine manor finding rain-sodden merchants at her door, seeking shelter from a furious storm. Its thick pillars, embellished with vining garlands and colorful budding flowers, peer down at us as if sentient, scrunching their noses as if they smell our humanity and expect our presence to litter their holy space with our tainted blood.

A line of bodies stretches down the steep stone steps from the arched entrance, a mix of elves, transcendents, and a few mundane. Sera hadn't been lying when she told the kingdom she spent the past decade compiling an army, collecting shifters and sympathizers like they were pretty ribbons she could sew into her finest dresses.

I spot Cosmina and the dark-haired transcendent woman she's been cozying up to by the long wooden table set up along the side of the temple. On it is a silver bucket overflowing with the roundest, most delicious-looking red apples, and a large barrel filled with water and hollowed out rocks for sipping it with. Food is rationed in the Vale, the elves having developed an ecosystem of sustainability, and now they must stretch their supplies further to accommodate the increased number of bodies and their hungry stomachs. And hungry they are because even the food tastes more scrumptious in the sweeping shadows of these woods.

I catch Cosmina's eye, and she waves frantically, pulling a more subtle nod from her friend, Blythe. Both of their lips are stained purple-black from the dewberry juice, signifying they've already bowed before the high priestess and received her blessing for this week.

Eldridge and I take our place in the throng of bodies

waiting to ascend the steps and enter the temple. When it is my turn to approach the lectern, Aeverie watches carefully, her stare as glacial as its color. Her skin is pulled tight across cheekbones set high in her face, just beneath the slender arches of her eyes. If I wasn't aware of the elves' long lifespans, I might think she were no older than forty.

Her cloudy pupils dart side-to-side, like tadpoles buried beneath a sheet of ice, taking in every inch of me. Most of the elves possess eyes so dark they border on black, having adapted to seeing in the naturally dusky expanse of the forest, but Aeverie's lack of irises is believed to be a gift from Source, granting the priestess the ability to see in both this realm and the next. A mane of dark brown hair is secured at the nape of her neck with a tightly pulled ribbon, and a crown crafted from blueberries and white flowers woven through branches sits on her head of silky hair.

I kneel as the high priestess dips two slender fingers into the jar on the lectern and pulls them out, sauced in berry extract. She presses them to my lips, leaving a sticky smear in their wake as she utters a blessing in her native tongue. The elves worship nature in place of gods, and the juice from the first berries of the harvest are collected and preserved to be used in the priestess's weekly blessing.

Aeverie studies me closely as I accept her favor and rise to my feet, tilting her head in a succession of rapid movements more animal than elf. I offer a curt nod and turn to leave through the open-air side of the temple, opposite where we entered.

The lively wind rushes through my nose and lungs, chasing out the closed-in feeling the priestess's presence always manages to invoke in me. I'm quite certain there's a seam ripper hidden behind her frosted eyes, ripping apart the sutures of my soul so she can inspect it layer by malignant layer. From the stoic expression permanently fixed upon her bony face, I can't tell if she finds my essence repulsive or as scintillating as the morning sun that rarely peeks its head through these trees. Perhaps she is merely cautious of a blood-witch residing in the sanctity of her home.

"*Fuck,* that woman shrivels my balls," Eldridge says, catching up to me after receiving his own weekly benediction.

I shoot him a sideways look, wiggling my eyebrows. "Arousing. You talk to all your friends like that, or am I special?"

His lopsided grin plucks a mirroring one from myself. "Oh, you're special alright, Wren. A *special* pain in my hairy red ass." He tugs me against him with one tree-trunk sized arm and ruffles his hand through my hair, unraveling some of my snowy braid.

I shove him away, my tongue darting out to lick away the residual juice glazing my lips, and we stumble our way towards where the rest of our family has joined Cosmina and Blythe, the two of us chortling like imbeciles. Galen bounds towards me, blond curls bouncing erratically, and throws two boyish arms around my waist. I lean forward and plant a kiss on my nephew's soft golden tresses, noting both our mothers' absences—Zorina and Morrinne must be on dinner duty.

Everyone has their roles to play in the Vale, and we were promptly assigned ours upon arrival. Cosmina and I tend to the gardens and surrounding landscape, while Zorina and Blythe work in helping to sort food into rations for each family. Eldridge and Theon were assigned to maintenance and repairs of the private houses and communal buildings, and Morrinne looks after a group of young ones, essentially a nanny while their parents are occupied with performing their duties to the Vale. A special dinner service is offered on devotion nights, each of us taking a turn in the weekly preparation on a rotating schedule.

"What's this—no love for your favorite uncle?" Eldridge asks, arms spread out wide in front of him. A shy smile blooms across Galen's face as he leaps into Eldridge's arms, a slew of giggles bubbling out of his mouth as Eldridge leans back, lifting him well off the ground.

"I'm starving. Sera invited us to have dinner with her tonight," Cosmina says, arching an eyebrow at me.

I mirror her with one of my own. I don't trust Sera any more than my sister does, but at the moment, it's Sera's arrangement with the elves that secures our refuge. Hungry to take back their rightful lands, Sera's army provides them with more man-power than they've had in ages. I have no doubt they are itching to meet the kingdom with an elaborate show of magic and teeth.

"It's in our best interest to accept the offer," I answer begrudgingly.

"I don't care if she's serving food from Slaine's ass crack, I'm hungry, and if there's food with our names on it somewhere else, why are we here and not there?" Eldridge asks, smirking through that overgrown reddish-orange bush he calls a beard.

I grab the braided part of his facial hair, the twisted plait going all the way to his stomach, and give it a small tug, urging him to follow. "I was thinking the same thing."

After all, what can go wrong with having dinner with the mother of the man that ruined my life?

CHAPTER 2

Sera's house is nestled along the farthest valve of the Vale's heart, and far too close to the rocky cliff overhanging the turbulent Howling Sea for my comfort. *House* is hardly the appropriate term for the rustic dwellings the elves reside in. The walls are constructed of piled stone, stacked together with a mix of sand and limestone cement, and arched roofs tent overhead to keep out the cold and precipitation. There are small windows and chimneys for ventilation, each house supplied with a hearth to warm the buildings' wintry guts, clouds of smoke always puffing into the sky.

Sera sits with her back to us, the tips of her dark brown hair brushing the rolled slumps of her shoulders. The mouthwatering scent of seasoned game and roasting vegetables fills my nose, and my stomach makes a sound of protest, now hours past digesting the small lunch I ate this afternoon.

A group of about ten sits on worn-away rocks and overturned logs around the fire, and a few more pace around it, chatting amongst themselves.

"Look at that, our old friend has decided to join us for dinner," Cosmina says loud enough for my ears only.

Seated across the fire and the game it smolders, the flames

licking his deep blue eyes like the sea itself was ablaze, is the Legion Commander.

I roll my bottom lip between my teeth, my own fire tunneling into my veins. Cathal's eyes flash to mine as if he heard the quickening of my pulse. Given his transcendent ears, maybe he did.

A forced smile creeps across his face when he spots us. "If it isn't my two favorite sisters," Cathal calls, sitting upright and spreading out his arms as if welcoming old friends.

It isn't the first I've seen him in these woods, but I've kept a wide berth between us. I would have been content to never again speak to the man who viewed me as nothing more than a shiny weapon to wield, but living in a forest whose space is finite, we were bound to cross paths soon enough.

"Who the hell invited the Legion ass-rat?" Eldridge gripes, suddenly *very* close to me.

Sera looks over her shoulder and waves us forward, ushering for us to find seats while two women turn over the spits of game searing in the heat and smoke of the fire. I plop on the ground next to Cosmina, stretching out my legs and leaning most of my weight on one elbow, assuming a casual position. Theon clasps a hand onto Galen's shoulder and steers him out of earshot, quizzing him on the medicinal properties of berries and vegetation found here. Eldridge paces back and forth behind Cosmina and me, every bit the agitated wolf.

His vehement energy provokes my own wrath, now simmering in my gut like a bubbling cauldron, but I find the sensation comforting. After months of feeling as hollow as the rocks and shells the elves drink from, the anger careening through my blood feels like an old friend. Familiar. Safe.

"Cathal has agreed to be on his best behavior, hasn't he?" Sera says, crossing her legs and fixing the commander with a barbed stare.

"Only the best for the wicked sisters," he answers, leaning forward again and propping his elbows on parted knees.

"I asked Cathal and your family to join me tonight so we may address the allegations being whispered behind closed doors," Sera continues, her words edged in steel.

Blythe, who had been hanging back, sits down cross-legged behind Cosmina. She gathers my sister's sweeping black hair and begins to idly braid it down her back.

"What allegations?" I ask.

"I am not ignorant to the rumors spreading that I have no plans to move on the kingdom, and I want to make it *sparkling* clear that that could not be further from the truth."

Cosmina's eyes skate to mine, assessing my reaction. I haven't exactly been forthcoming about the extent of my relationship with the Black Art, but my sister doesn't miss much. Darkness clung to me after we fled from Scarwood. I couldn't rid myself of the anger that overcame me like a horde of starved leeches, biting and sucking out every last remnant of joy from my flesh. Too fervent a reaction to learning that the warlord, whose heart was said to be as black as his namesake title, betrayed me... Why would I have gotten so upset over an outcome that was too damn easy to predict?

Because he had been so much more than that to me.

And I had been so much less to him.

Cosmina never asked about the extent of the Black Art and my relations during my time at Scarwood. When I was his prisoner, and later, when I stayed of my own volition, agreeing to aid his kingdom in exchange for his help finding my sister. She doesn't know about all the softly spoken words he whispered to me in the shadows, nor the ones I pledged to him while she lay rotting away in iron bracelets beneath my feet.

May she never learn what her captor and I did in the dark.

But the way she watches me now, gauging my reaction to

the mention of the impending war that's been hanging over all our heads like the fattest, darkest storm clouds... I'm certain she knows I've been keeping secrets of my own.

Eldridge huffs, working his one hand to crack the knuckles of the other. "For Slaine's sake, Sera, you can hardly fault the lot of them for thinking that. It's not as if we're winning any wars sitting here telling stories 'round the damn campfire, are we?"

"For once, I agree with the overgrown *mutt*," Cathal mutters, a sneer peeking out from the scruff strangling half his face.

"Insulting your own kind, Commander? Or I should say, *ex*-commander, since you led your entire army to slaughter. I always did wonder how you managed to sleep at night. I'd think the weight of their deaths would be too much, even for a brute like me," Eldridge muses, pursing his lips.

Cathal chuckles, and one of the women tending to the food hands him a steaming plate: a mouthwatering slab of herb seasoned venison and eggplant, with a small helping of plump red berries on the side. "Never insulted my kind, only yours, mutt. I *know* who my parents are. The blood in these veins is pure predator, and proud of it."

Before Cathal captured and turned me over to his degenerate friends, I had shared too much information about my family, including that Eldridge's father abandoned him, leaving him and Zorina to be raised by their mundane mother. It isn't surprising Eldridge reacted so passionately when Galen's father abandoned his sister and nephew, or that Morrinne welcomed them both into her home after Eldridge had asked her to stretch the logs of her cabin for two more bodies.

"Shut your mouth, Cathal, or I will shut it for you," I warn from behind clenched teeth.

Cathal flicks his tongue across his top lip and waves me forward. "Let's see it, sweetheart."

"Enough!" Sera demands, now helping to plate and hand out the rest of the meals to the others around the fire.

I reach for mine eagerly, grateful for the hot food to appease the deep rumbling in the pit of my stomach.

"We extended an offer of negotiation to the Black Art, and we will honor that. If we do not hear from the kingdom soon, I'll send a pigeon to inquire if they are ready to discuss treaty lines, and a warning to heed if they are not."

"Come now, Sera. Do you hear yourself?" Cathal snickers. "Because the fucker that booby trapped an entire city to light up every shifter on the isle is going to wake up one morning and say, 'Hm, I think I'll negotiate a peace treaty today.'"

"How much time do you intend for us to wait?" Blythe asks, leaning around my sister to direct her question to Sera.

"We give them one more week and then send the pigeon."

"We need to be sending them the heads of their royal fucking guards," Eldridge growls from behind me, huffing like an annoyed bear. "They've made it more than clear that the only negotiating they're interested in is asking if we want their blades in our throats or our guts. They held Cosmina captive for months. Tried using Wren as a weapon against us. I am tired of being on the losing end of this fucking war."

"*We* are not on the losing end of anything. Do not cite Cathal's shortcomings as my own," Sera snaps, spearing Eldridge with a glare.

"If you want to discuss shortcomings so badly, Sera, why don't we start with your godsdamned son?" Cathal says, jabbing his fork towards her and wiping his hand over his mouth, bits of roasted eggplant peppering his thick beard.

The very marrow in my bones runs cold at the mention of him. I stab my own fork into the venison with more force than necessary, juice splashing my chin as I pop a meaty bite between my lips and chew so hard my jaw clicks.

Cosmina reaches over and strokes the side of my arm. My sister doesn't miss much. Never has.

"You would be wise to remember I am your connection to the Vale, Cathal, and I can have them toss you out of here as quickly as I negotiated your welcome. My patience is thin these days, and I am growing tired of the ramblings of sweaty old men."

I nearly choke on my mouthful of food, and Blythe buries a snicker in the back of Cosmina's shoulder. If anything, Sera is likely a handful of years *older* than Cathal, but her rounded face and springy skin suggest otherwise. Whatever salves she's slathering on herself at night, I need to get my hands on some. The stress of the past few months has taken a bite out of me, leaving my eyes heavy from nights of restless sleep, and my neck and shoulders rigid from batting away intrusive thoughts like rabid hounds snapping at my heels.

Cathal erupts into laughter. "Keep that fire, girl, all the way until we put Singard's head on a fucking spike. Soon all of Aegidale will know who really runs this isle."

My food turns to acid in my stomach at the sound of his name. I've refused to say it since that night.

Cathal springs to his feet, throws his head back, and unleashes an ear-splitting howl. "It's time we take back this damn land and show that Black Art piece of shit who holds the real power here—US GODSDAMNED WOLVES!" He rubs his hands over one another and drops his eyes to mine, now bright with perverse excitement. I raise my chin as he sinks onto a knee to meet my deadpan stare. "Don't worry, sweetheart. Cathal will take care of him for what he did to you."

I spit in his face. "They should have let you roast in that fire like the pig you are."

The night Sera set alchemist fire to the castle, after Cosmina and I rousted our family from their beds, we met her group on their ship near the sandbars outside Innodell. There are no words to describe the extent of my gratitude for Cornelius pulling my sister from the dungeon before igniting the inferno, just as none could convey my disappointment when I learned he had done the same for Cathal. Given Cornelius's absence tonight, I assume he is also on the dinner shift. Pity. I would have liked to thwack him upside the head again for releasing him. Some monsters should remain in captivity.

Others should be rotting away slowly in the depths of Hell.

And given the dreams I've had of sucking my blade dry after cleaving Singard Kilbreth in two, I've deemed there's a third option for creatures like me. Not even Hell could keep the wrath I feel for the Black Art confined. It would find a way to slither free through every crack and crevice until it hunted Sin down. Punctured his flesh and burrowed deep in his bones, flooding his bloodstream with the tears of my weeping heart.

There is no fortress strong enough to shield him from my venom.

Cathal chortles and runs a hand across his unkept beard. "Little late for that now, sweetheart."

"Get out of my face, Cathal, or I'll tear your heart from your chest like I did every one of your pathetic, flunky soldiers."

Eldridge's knee brushes my shoulder as he steps up behind me, and with a half-smile, Cathal's gaze slowly crawls upwards like a horde of spindly spiders. "It appears I've upset the mule." He rises to his feet, the top of his thick, dark hair coming to Eldridge's shoulders, and he cocks his head to the side. "I love thinking about how pissed you must be that she fucked me and *still* won't go near you."

I'm on my feet immediately, one hand splayed across

Eldridge's brawny chest and the other out in front of me to warn Cathal not to take a step closer. From my periphery, I see Sera's attention snap to us, but I don't dare take my eyes off the former Legion commander.

"It's fine, Sera. No one's fighting today," I say around clenched teeth, though I'm sure the look on my face contradicts my statement.

The elves abide by a strict no violence inside the Vale code of conduct, apart from sparring and running drills. I've seen the elves spar, many of their weapons adorned with jewels and sigils—magic siphons—that enchant their swords and bows with their ancient incantations. The transcendents are allowed to participate in their own training practices as well, but the second a sparring match turns tail from friendly, their welcome to the Vale expires. And no one enforces that rule more than Sera, who frequently reminds us all she will not hesitate to toss anyone out that threatens her arrangement with the elves. An arrangement I don't fully understand.

"No fighting in the Vale," Eldridge agrees, crossing his arms and leaning forward towards Cathal. "She said nothing about me hauling you out of it and tossing you to the fucking pits. Wouldn't even kill you; I'd let the wolves finish tearing you apart."

Lies. If Eldridge unleashed his temper long enough to take even one swing at Cathal, I have no doubt the years of resentment would come pouring out of him like an erupting volcano. Cathal would be pummeled until twin pools of crimson regret pooled in his sunken eye sockets, and the bones in his face splintered far beyond recognition.

I'd feel bad for the wolves that would surely come to lap up the remains. No animal deserves to eat such tarnished meat.

Sera sidles up to Cathal, pressing the front of her left shoulder to his chest. She raises her hand to his cheek, one nail lengthening into a yellow-tinged claw, and traces it gingerly over his jawline. "Play nicely, sunshine," she whispers, her tone almost... *sultry.*

I think I actually cringe and dare a glance at Eldridge, nearly chuckling at the disgust contorting his face. There is no way Sera and Cathal have *that* kind of relationship. Absolutely not. Weren't they just insulting one another?

Cathal catches Sera's hand and turns it around to softly kiss the backs of her knuckles. "Fine, but if I back down, you best make it worth my while."

I almost puke.

She slips her hand out from under his and walks past, gently brushing against him as she does. "We both know the rules, Cathal," she trills.

Paying one final glance to Eldridge and me, he turns his back on us and plops back down on the overturned log. Sauntering away as if he made the decision to back down, not because Sera cock-baited him with whatever game of debauchery she's playing, and certainly not because Eldridge could launch him into the next realm with one well-placed punch to his thick skull.

The deep blow of a horn rends the air.

The signal sends each of us scrambling to our feet, reaching for our weapons, code of pacifism be damned. My own hand quickly grasps for the athame tucked in my waistband. A war horn only has one meaning in these lands.

Invasion.

CHAPTER 3

In the blink of an eye, the peaceful forest shifts into the feared menace the kingdom spread stories about. Elves armed with enchanted swords, spears, and bows storm from their stone dwellings, fastening armor to their arms and chests. They pack into tight uniform rows until the heart of the Vale is threaded with soldiers.

Accessing Source is as natural as breathing for some elves, Aeverie explained. Those more bonded with Source apprentice under the arcane leaders. The others join the sparring rings young, training to wield steel in place of magic. Light reflects in the facets of the gems welded into their weaponry, the elven warriors blessed by the power of their ancient magic.

Sera's army of transcendents, spread out amongst the houses along the western perimeter, rush to her post where she begins shouting orders for them to report to their positions. Eldridge grabs my arm and motions for me to follow, but I pause at the thundering of two approaching horses.

"With us, wanderers," Aeverie calls from her perch atop one of the steeds, the massive animal making her petite frame appear even more bony and frail. Though if anyone mistook the high priestess's appearance as a measure of strength, they'd be in for a grave surprise when she set her sights on them.

Wanderers is what the elves continually refer to transcendents as, though I'm still not sure where the term originated. Long white robes billow out from Aeverie as she approaches, only a simple tunic underneath, but something tells me armor would benefit her very little.

"What do we know?" Sera asks, shoving her hands into pre-laced leather gauntlets. Transcendents don't wear plated armor, nothing that might restrict their ability to shift at a moment's notice, and the few pieces they do don are often fastened with easily unstrung ties and laces.

Vox, the rider of the second horse, peers down at us through crow feather eyes. "Soldiers. Only five spotted, but likely more behind them," the elven commander answers in a voice as cold and biting as death. Deep brown leathers cover him from head to toe, twin lengths of shined chainmail extending from either shoulder to his upper chest.

My breath hitches when his piercing stare shifts to me, his near black irises filling my chest with frigid sea-water. His long blond hair is pulled into tight braids on either side of his head, perfectly pointed ears peeking through, and if I wasn't so jaded towards the opposite sex right now, I might say he is stupidly handsome. "It appears they are in pursuit of the bloodwitch."

Cosmina's hand curls around my elbow instinctively. No one was ignorant to the risk they were taking by sheltering me in the Vale. Of course the kingdom wouldn't be content to allow a bloodwitch, let alone one that publicly announced intention to ally against them and then set fire to their castle, walk away unscathed. It was only a matter of time until they searched every acre of the isle and realized the only stones left unturned were those beyond The Feral Vale. And yet, it's not fear that sends my heart thumping against my ribcage like an overzealous rabbit.

It's something much hungrier.

A wrath so sentient it hammers my nerves into dinner plates and floods my mouth with a floral-coated tang.

Saliva washes out my mouth with the subtle savor of hyacinths—blood-tipped and rain-soaked—a flavor I'll never forget.

The taste of Singard Kilbreth's black, traitorous blood.

"Best not to keep them waiting then. Please lead the way, Commander," I say, entranced in his heavy stare as if his very gaze is hypnotic. Perhaps another elven power to add to their impressive list. Or maybe he really is just so irritatingly handsome that the struggle to look away is entirely mundane.

"Should Wren be hidden?" Eldridge asks, then grumbles when Vox shakes his head.

Confusion knits Cosmina's eyebrows together. "Won't seeing her prompt them to attack?"

"If they're courageous enough to step foot beyond our borders, they already know she's here. Keeping her hidden will serve little more than to insult their intelligence," Aeverie supplies.

Blythe snorts, her muscular brown shoulders shrugging beneath the thin straps of her top. "Not exactly hard to do."

"I did not declare war on Singard Kilbreth to *hide* when he finally found me. Secure your weapons," I spit, orange magic licking my fingertips. I swear Aeverie's glacial eyes, always so stoic, widen at the display. I tuck my dagger into my pants and run a hand along my hair to smooth the strands that have frayed loose from their braid. Don't want to look disheveled when I finally serve up the Black Art's grisly heart on a platter.

"With me then," Vox says, motioning with his chin for me to mount his horse. "I have our own waiting for my order should there be more soldiers close behind. Until then, it's wise we don't frighten them off with the sound of an approaching army." The scouts' war horn is enchanted to only carry the sound the direction it is blown; in this case, towards the Vale's heart and away from the soldiers. It is likely they have no idea the elves have even been made aware of their not so sneaky arrival.

I cock my head to the side, the movement feeling almost feral. "I like the way you think, Commander." Vox doesn't speak much outside of training sessions, but if his reputation precedes him, he doesn't want to scare the invaders off because he has no intention of allowing them to leave these woods alive.

And that's a battle tactic I have no qualm getting behind.

Vox offers a leather clad hand and steadies me as I hoist myself onto the back of his dapple-gray horse, and Sera quickly readies another from the hitching post.

"We should bring one more body so we're not outnumbered," Vox says, scanning some of Sera's transcendents. A few of them I recognize from the night she infiltrated Scarwood just a couple months prior.

Eldridge pulls his shirt over his head, revealing his wide sun-kissed chest dotted with soft red hair, and a soft stomach that suggests he enjoys the baked goods Zorina pedals from the kitchen as much as he enjoys hauling lumber around. His arms are swollen with the kind of muscles one only achieves through repetitive lifting of heavy weight, and combined with his towering height, Eldridge is not a force to tempt lightly. "Already behind you," he says, his lips twisting into a too-eager grin. His hands drop to his pants, unfastening the clasps and tugging them down.

I avert my eyes and lean forward. "And that's our cue, Commander," I whisper near his ear.

With a crack of the reins, his horse takes off. Aeverie and Sera catch up to us a few moments later, and I look over my shoulder to find Eldridge bounding after us on four furred legs, his canine head held low as he races towards us.

Our horses dart through the forest like fired arrows, rounding thick trunks and skidding across tapestries of damp foliage. Even the trees are more beautiful in the Vale, a variety of deep green needle-shaped leaves and low-hanging mosses, with sky-punching height and silvery white bark. The setting sun casts warm beacons through the verdant canopy, illuminating our ride to the border in a blood-orange haze.

Both elves pull their horses to a startling halt, and my hands cinch around Vox's trim waist. Eldridge's paws dig into the forest floor, and he shifts his weight to slow his body in a graceful stop. He always has been more graceful in this form.

Aeverie throws up a hand, a warning for us to remain quiet as she tilts her head, her pointed ears hearing something far outside the range of my own. Vox dismounts, and I follow after him, my weight hitting the ground with an embarrassingly loud thud after the commander's quiet leap.

The elves are predators in their own right—lithe and nearly silent. I don't fully comprehend their magic, *their Source,* but their ability to pussyfoot across a floor covered in crunchy, organic material is reason enough for me to sleep lightly these nights. Anything that can move at their speed, and supposedly tap into the very earth's power, is a threat as far as I'm concerned. I've taken plenty of blows from mages bending the collective, but something tells me a punch coming from the earth's essence would hurt a whole lot fucking worse.

It made me wary that I've been unable to latch my collective onto theirs to sift through their intentions, one of my greatest strengths stripped from my magical tool-belt. I suspect this Source isn't rooted in the collective at all, but something far more ancient, and far more terrifying than I care to consider.

Eldridge sidles up to me as we follow Vox and Aeverie through the woods on foot, Sera on my other side. Without a sound, Vox unsheathes the long sword strapped to his back, the garnet-colored stones embedded in the hilt catching the last rays of sunlight in their faceted surfaces. My palms heat, and Sera readies herself with a dagger in each hand, while Aeverie merely follows after the elven commander with steady grace, as if she was walking into the temple for worship, and not approaching an enemy invader.

A moment later, Vox motions for us to back farther into the camouflage, away from the game trail made worn from foot traffic. We take cover behind a few trees, Eldridge dipping his giant head low to the ground next to my crouched legs.

And then I hear them.

Their footsteps aren't quiet as the group approaches, whispering amongst themselves in voices too low for me to decipher their words. For a brief moment, my heart lodges in my throat as I wonder who has been sent here and if... if *he* would have come with the men he ordered. The thought only stokes the flames licking my heart, and I channel the sudden onset of rage to fuel the magic simmering in my hands.

It happens so fast.

I barely catch sight of the first set of heads as they round into view before Vox is behind them, his blond braids flying out around him, as he moves at inhuman speed. The others must barely glimpse his form because they startle, looking around themselves like they *thought* they saw something, and then all five of their chins jerk upwards as if they were grabbed by the throat.

Aeverie steps out from behind the tree her back was flattened against, one hand outstretched in front of her as she approaches the men clawing at their necks, strangled sounds rasping from their lips. She does not move with haste. In fact, her steps seem even more measured than usual as she slowly glides towards them with as much leisure as if she were about to pour herself a steaming cup of tea and kick her feet up in relaxation. Perhaps for elves, choking the life out of your enemies is the means to a tranquil afternoon. Vox kicks each of them to their knees and has them all disarmed in the span of a few seconds.

I share a look with Eldridge. I've had enough practice reading his canine features to recognize the hint of surprise in his furred eyebrows, and the glint of amusement in his gray eyes. Vox, now in front of the group, slams the needle point of his sword into the squishy ground and leans against it, one hand still wrapped around the crystal infused hilt. Sera takes a step forward, her twin daggers still firm in her grip, but maintains an appropriate distance.

Vox exchanges a glance with the high priestess, and the men at his feet suck in sharp breaths, the pressure on their jugulars suddenly gone. Judging by their stillness, their bodies are still caught in a state of paralysis, courtesy of Aeverie's magic. "You're foreigners," Vox says, a hint of a snarl in his voice.

It's then I take in the soldiers' uniforms. They each wear a deep blue padded gambeson coat, buckled securely against their frames with a sword and shield emblem cross-stitched on the side of their arms.

"Baelliarah," Sera supplies. "I spent several years there during my recruiting. I recognize the crest."

Aegidale hasn't been at war with Baelliarah since Ephraim invaded their nation after a surge of our transcendents fled there for refuge, seeking protection from the previous Black Art's incriminating laws against their kind. A war that resulted

26

in as much bloodshed from mundane soldiers as the shifters. Baelliarah's king has a distaste for monarchies governed by mages, and he was eager to lend his troops to see to their protection. The war was bloody and cruel, and ended with Aegidale reclaiming their transcendents and escorting them back to the isle that would continue to discriminate against them. Ephraim had no sympathy for the transcendents—he simply didn't want them allying with his closest neighbor across the sea and risk them invading his isle nation. This was when Dusaro still served as the Black Hand, and his only son had earned his reputation as the heartless reaper of souls as he sailed across the Howling Sea and reclaimed what was never his.

"Bold of you to encroach on elven land. I offer you the opportunity to explain what is behind your courageousness," Aeverie says, her voice like dripping honey and not at all matching the sharpness of her angled features.

The one in the center spits at her feet, but the others take in Aeverie and Vox's whetted features and pointed ears with widened eyes. Baelliarah is a mostly mundane land; it is unlikely they've ever seen elves before. Hell, I live on this island and the only thing I knew of them were the rumors the kingdom spread to incite fear and cover up the fact they were too damn frightened of their magic to openly war with their kind. Instead, the kingdom incinerated the Vale's nearby cities and spread stories that the elves couldn't emerge in sunlight. In actuality, the elves simply had no reason to leave the protection the forest provided them. Not when they were so outnumbered.

Vox reclaims his sword and lifts the chin of the spitter with the tip of his blade. "My priestess asked you a question."

"Your priestess can rot in Hell."

Vox chuckles, licking his lips in pregnant pause. Then, as if the action bores him entirely, he beheads the spitter in one clean slice of his blade. The headless corpse collapses to the ground, blood spurting from the now gaping hole in his neck. My mouth dries at the sight of it.

Fuck.

Ever since I fought side by side with the Black Art as we devastated Legion's forces, when I took my first kill followed by hundreds more, the desire to kill again has picked at me like starved vultures. Desire lashes through me as Vox kicks the corpse away, and the scent of its pooling blood pets my tongue.

"Hey, hey, hey! We didn't come here to hurt anyone, I swear. We were sent here to take a look around, that's it!" the soldier to the left of his fallen friend exclaims. Two others nod their heads in rapid succession, while the third can't take his eyes off his friend's headless body, tremors rocking through him.

"Sent by who?" Vox queries.

The one who spoke hesitates, but it only takes Vox lifting his sword to send the words fumbling free from his mouth. "King Varil! He sent us."

The commander pauses, his sword inches from the man's neck. "And what business does Baelliarah's king have with sending five measly men here?"

"He wanted us to scout. Get a lay of the land before Aegidale invades our nation."

"What do you mean 'invades our nation?'" Sera asks, stepping up next to Aeverie.

The soldier blinks at her, his gaze flickering between Sera and the tip of Vox's sword, the veins in his neck bulging as he struggles to maintain his composure. "We know the Black Art intends to invade Baelliarah with a bloodwitch. We were ordered to get in and get out, record as much detail as we could about the layout of the Vale. That's all, I swear."

"Since when does Singard want to invade Baelliarah?" Sera asks.

"What is this you speak of a bloodwitch?" Aeverie interrupts, clasping her hands together at her waist, her paralytic hold on the men not faltering.

"Your leader is rumored to have a bloodwitch working at his disposal. King Varil has been made aware of Kilbreth's plans to use her in his conquest to seize our land, using his... his *pet* as a means to destroy us all."

My lips pull back involuntarily, and Eldridge, now standing, bumps a furry shoulder into mine.

"Why would your king send you to our vale if he believes Singard is planning an invasion? The elves have not been in communication with our regent in many years, but I suspect your Varil is well aware of that fact if he was confident enough to send you to our sacred part of the isle," Aeverie says, a hiss creeping into her voice.

"Because we've been informed the bloodwitch is in the Vale."

My breath catches, and Sera shoots me a worried look to where I remain just out of the soldiers' lines of sight.

They know.

He knows.

It was only a matter of time until the Black Art finished scouring the isle looking for me. Once they checked every mountain pass and wooded trail, there would only be one place large enough to house the army Sera had boasted about to him. The Feral Vale.

Vox looks over his shoulder, waiting for Aeverie's command. It is becoming clear that while the commander draws the metal, it is the high priestess that gives the orders to wield it. They pause for a brief moment as if exchanging unspoken words, perhaps they *are* communicating in some unseen elven way, and then Vox slowly turns his head forward again.

"You've been most helpful. Unfortunately for your friends, we have not benefited from their silence."

The snapping sound that follows could have been mistaken for crunching branches if not for the three soldiers who suddenly slump forward, their necks twisted in unnatural angles. Aeverie's long fingers twitch against her waist, but that is the only indication she flexed her power at all.

"Fuck. Fuck, okay. Hey, let's talk about this. I'll tell you whatever you want to know," the chatty soldier chokes out, lifting his palms towards us.

"Does this King Varil have plans to invade preemptively?" Vox asks, staring down his slender nose at the begging man.

"I'm not aware of any plans to invade, but that might change after the meeting." He continues without having to be prompted. "Our king is meeting with your Black Art in three days, at the receiving center in Blackreach. Varil is going to attempt to negotiate. Kilbreth gets rid of the bloodwitch, we don't seize the isle. If he fails to agree to these terms, then my nation will attack, but that's all I know, I swear. Please, just let me go."

"We are not unreasonable people," Aeverie says, drawing her robes closed around her. The boredom in her tone suggests the altercation before her is now nothing more than a nuisance. "You provided us with valuable information, it is only fair we pay you the same respect. Return to your king and tell him should he again find himself bold enough to step a toe into our woods, it won't be Singard Kilbreth he needs to worry about."

Relief settles across his face, and he blows out a long breath. "Thank you, ma'am. Thank you." He bows his head low in respect, his pant leg soaked.

I step out from behind the tree and walk over to where he kneels in his piss. Vox gives me a curious look but doesn't caution my advance.

"Who told your king that the Black Art was working with a bloodwitch?" I ask.

The chatterer raises his head to meet my stare. "I don't have that information, ma'am. All I know is that your Black Art has one, and she's deranged, not right in the head. If your kind isn't on good terms with your kingdom, then you might want to consider preparing before he unleashes his pet on you too."

I lean down and softly brush the backs of my knuckles against his cheek. "She sounds like a monster," I whisper.

He nods under my fingers, but his eyes round when a smile surely too wide for my face stretches my mouth. "What is your name?" I ask.

"Darius, ma'am," he answers, his bottom lip trembling slightly as if he senses the energy shifting around us, circling us like a cyclone.

I nod slowly, the smile vanishing from my mouth. "Do you know what my favorite thing about monsters is, Darius?"

His lips part as he searches my expression, sweat beading across his bushy eyebrows and his forehead creasing into thin lines. He shakes his head. "What is that, ma'am?"

"No matter how much they eat, they're always so hungry."

I swipe my knife from my waist and slit his throat.

CHAPTER 4

I didn't have to kill him. We could have let him flee back to Baelliarah with the ominous message to his king. It would have been easy.

But nothing has ever been easy for me—why start now? He was an enemy. Allowing just one adversary to live is a threat to us all in the future—one more risk to my family. I want to believe that is the reason for the vicious necklace I bestowed upon him, but the swelling of my breasts and the hunger in my gut calls me a liar.

I murdered him for one reason alone.

Because he insinuated I belonged to the Black Art.

I plop my stained fingertips between my lips and suck the blood off them. I barely register Darius's limp body collapsing at my feet, or the elven commander wrapping an arm of tightly corded muscle around my front, pinning my back to his chest. Somewhere, I faintly hear the thump of two feet hitting the ground as Eldridge shifts into his human form, his bellows drowning out the ringing in my ears.

I killed him. I killed him and *enjoyed* it.

I snap out of my haze as someone jerks me backwards, and Eldridge engulfs my line of sight. He's reaching for me while Vox pulls me backwards, his arm banded around my waist. I snarl over my shoulder, baring my teeth at the commander, and to my surprise, he bares his right back.

"Don't try that with me," he hisses through still clenched teeth, tightening his hold.

Eldridge calls my name, and I snap forward again. He ducks so he's eye-level with me and places a hand on each of my shoulders. His eyes search both of mine, looking for recognition in my own, and he wrestles one of my hands free from Vox and places it on his bare chest.

"You shouldn't be touching her when she's not stable," Vox snaps from behind me.

A low growl thunders from somewhere deep in Eldridge's throat. "Give her to me."

I wrap my free hand around the arm still banded across my front. I make no move to harm him—the commander has only ever treated me with respect—but I am not a rabid animal that needs taming.

"I assure you I'm perfectly in control of my power, Commander," I say, then forcibly relax my lips that were still curled into a snarl. "I slaughtered half a Legion army. One loose-lipped soldier isn't going to be my demise."

Vox's sharp jaw clenches, mulling my words over in his mouth as if tasting them for lies. With a nod so quick I almost miss it, he releases me. I step towards Eldridge, but when he tries to pull me towards him, I shoot him a look that stops him in his tracks. I am not in the mood to be touched. I may be in control, but that doesn't negate the adrenaline licking at my nerves like they're made of the finest mead coin can buy.

"What the hell were you thinking, Wren?" Eldridge asks, crossing his arms across his chest. His braided beard hangs past his folded forearms, resting against the soft orange-red hair of his stomach. A trail of hair that leads to his...

"You're naked."

A beat of silence passes between us, and then a deep laugh spills from his lips. "Well, sorry, I didn't exactly have time to collect some clothes after I was forced to shift because you sliced a fucking guy's head off."

"I didn't; Vox did that," I say, thrusting my thumb over my shoulder where Vox is standing next to the decapitated corpse. "I just gifted the last one a pretty necklace." I smile sweetly.

"It would have been wise to send him back with our message to Varil," Vox scolds. "Why did you take his life?"

I shrug my shoulders. "He called me the Black Art's pet. I didn't like that."

Sera filled the others in on what happened. Cosmina's face fell when she saw me return, as if she knew immediately what I had done. I guess it didn't require much imagination when she saw the blood splattered on my cheeks and forehead. A part of me, albeit a very small part, burns with shame at my impulsiveness. But why should we have spared Darius's life and not the others? They invaded these lands to feed information to a king hell-bent on locating me. It isn't hard to guess what his course of action would have been when the rumors of the bloodwitch hiding in the Vale were proven to be true. Not that it matters much now. When none of Varil's soldiers return, the same message as the one we would have sent with Darius will still be heard loud and clear.

We bite.

"No one else thinks this is oddly convenient for us?" Cornelius asks, cocking an eyebrow as if we've all lost our damn minds to not see the giant trap laid out in front of us.

He and the others from our interrupted dinner party met

us in the conservatory near Sera's house. Morrinne, Zorina, and Galen sit sidled up to one another on the wooden bench next to the towering arbor with long green vines woven through the latticework, vibrant blooming flora erupting across the grid like the goddess of renewal and flourishment puked all over it. Cosmina and Blythe sit cross-legged at the base of the arch, across from where Theon and Eldridge pace back and forth, while Vox and Aeverie hang close to where Sera sits in her metal framework chair.

"Convenient, sure. But I'm not risking someone else getting the chance to sink their teeth into Kilbreth's neck before I do," Cathal huffs from where he straddles an over-turned log, one leg on either side of the thick trunk.

A low growl rumbles free from my chest, and Cathal's blue eyes flash to mine. "I'm sorry, sweetheart. Did you want to be the one to kill him? It seems all that time being the Black Art's lapdog has worked up your appetite. But know that when that time comes, and it will, it's going to be my blade that shreds that bastard's heart."

My knife is at his throat before I register what I'm doing— the blood magic making my body strike out instinctively. I shove him backwards off the log and sit on his chest, pinning his arms to the ground with my knees. I have no doubt Cathal could push me off easily if he wanted to, but he doesn't. Instead, he grins widely, either because he knows I could clot every ounce of his blood with half a thought, or because he likes the view of me on top of him. I press the tip of my dagger into his flesh, just enough to cut if he tries to make a sudden movement.

When I speak, my voice is a raw, feral thing. "Singard. Is *mine.*"

I rise to my feet and step away, not wanting to be near Cathal any longer than I must.

"Let us remember we are striving for a peace treaty first," Sera cautions. "If Sin has agreed to meet with King Varil, it's crucial we know the outcome of it. Baelliarah's involvement affects all of us."

"Again, it all seems a little too coincidental," Cornelius volleys. "For all we know, those guards were sent by Singard to lead us into a trap, knowing we'd come." His words earn a few encouraging nods from Morrinne and Zorina.

"It would be ill advised to get too close to the receiving center, but with our hearing, we don't need to," Vox explains. "The capital is a two-day voyage and that is *if* Source bestows us with favorable weather. We'll sail for Blackreach tomorrow and wait until Baelliarah docks. Then we close in at a safe distance. The fewer of us the better. Sera and I will go. And you," he nods at Eldridge, "should come too. In the unlikely event we find ourselves in combat, we need strength on our side."

Eldridge nods and mutters an agreement. Tucking my dagger back into my pants, I say, "I'm coming too."

The elves have a few ships docked along the sea line, and fortunately for us, they are cloaked with illusive magic, making the ships and everyone aboard them invisible. Ghosts on the water. They cloaked us when Cosmina and I gathered the rest of our family and sailed with Sera and her strike force to the Vale after setting fire to Scarwood. It worked for us then, and it'll work for us now.

"It is not necessary for you to accompany us," Vox says, his tone forged from steel. I'm beginning to think the elven commander is wary of my blood magic.

Cathal rights himself on the ground and leans his elbows onto his now propped up knees. "The bloodwitch gets to join in on the fun and I don't?" he asks incredulously.

"It's safer for you here, Wren," Eldridge says, crossing the distance between us. His words are laced with concern, and it's that knowledge that prevents me from ordering him to back off.

"Whether it's a trap or not, the kingdom knows I'm here. If anything, leaving the Vale might throw them off."

I look between them as Eldridge and Vox appear to consider my words, while Sera's expression remains tight-lipped and stern. She isn't convinced, and honestly, she shouldn't be. But it is Vox who nods and says, "Very well."

My family and I take our leave and head back to our house on the opposite side of the Vale's heart. I pack a bag before flopping into bed, stuffing my leather satchel with a few pairs of clean clothes and some basic toiletries to keep my hair, face, and body clean. The kingdoms are meeting in three days, which means we're already late.

First light, we sail for Blackreach.

CHAPTER 5

The boat isn't large. With just one mast and two white sails, the open-deck is spacious enough for the four of us and our rations with some additional room for us to move about. Fortunately, the skies have remained clear since we departed yesterday morning, and the wind has been strong enough to keep us trudging through the deep sea at an appreciative pace.

We're anchored out a couple miles from the coast of the isle's capital. Varil's ship should arrive soon, and we'll move in closer, within Vox's hearing threshold, later tonight or early tomorrow. For now, the four of us sit on the white inlaid bench seating and eat our evening meal—sandwiches constructed with cured meat and leafy vegetables from the Vale's gardens, kept fresh in the ice box on board.

Blackreach beams with a soft orange glow from the thousands of lanterns tucked into window sills and sconces illuminating the streets. Rearing up behind the city, the castle turrets spear the mauve-tinted sky, the stone-gray towers looming over the prosperous capital. The sight of the castle turns my meal to acid in my belly.

Only a couple of months ago, I rained vengeance across those streets and flooded their alleys with rebellion blood. And when my magic was swollen with their limp collectives, I returned to that castle and devoured the Black Art last, savoring his softly-spoken words and gentle touches. Until his affectionate fingers lengthened into claws and sunk into my chest, shredding the tenderness from my soul and hanging me out to dry.

I haven't told the others of Sin's transcendence. Not yet. I won't jeopardize their safety if there's the faintest chance the Black Art will enter into negotiation with Sera and her people. I agreed to safe-guard Sin's secret so long as he didn't declare war on the shifters. I'm quite certain that me setting fire to his turret and pledging fealty to his enemy is grounds for our agreement to expire, but until Sin makes that clear, I won't risk my family's safety.

Nevertheless, the guilt from keeping this knowledge from them settles like a log in my gut. I've never kept secrets from them, and now I harbor two.

Varil's ship docked this morning, and we moored ours nearby without arousing suspicions from the patrolling guards, our ship invisible under the cloaking magic. Our boat might as well be a child's toy compared to Baelliarah's impressive vessel with flapping onyx sails that boasts their sword and shield crest. When the first few passengers step off, the guards make haste to greet them. We're much too far for my ears to decipher what is being said, but Vox watches them intently.

"They're saying His Grace is ready to receive them. The emissary is sending for Varil now," Vox translates.

A moment later, a stocky man with a head of freshly clipped dark hair and a groomed beard disembarks. King Varil wears a tan leather tunic embellished with golden thread, and a long brown cloak collared with cream-colored furs. It's summer, but the waters are gelid, and even in the warmer months, Aegidale is constantly harassed by squalls blown in by the sea breeze. Even so, the king's furred hat, its bloody tint hinting it once belonged to a red fox, is surely providing him more warmth than is comfortable. Varil does not dress in his furs for the weather—he dresses to display his wealth.

Varil, his light-haired emissary, and six others clad in plated armor follow after Aegidale's guards towards the receiving center, leaving the docks bare minus the four of us and our invisible boat.

"They're far enough we can disembark, but we must remain hidden. The magic is tethered to the boat so as soon as your feet touch the docks, you are visible," Vox cautions.

"We need to get to the tree line," I say, eyeing the stretch of the Spiritwood forest skirting across the coast.

Vox nods, and I exchange pointed glances with Sera and Eldridge. There's no denying that Blackreach is the most dangerous city for a shifter to be caught in. Then again, it's the same for a bloodwitch or elf. Any of us found skulking around the city would raise immediate suspicion, but tailing the Black Art's private guards to his location... that is nothing short of treason.

"Let's try really hard not to get caught, okay?" I chirp.

"Agreed. It's crucial we learn what they're up to and report it back to the Vale. I have no desire to find myself being held captive by my son," Sera grumbles, but the creases around her round eyes seem to deepen, far away in her thoughts.

I shrug a shoulder. "And I'm not in the mood to kill your son today, but should we find ourselves in his company, perhaps I'll reconsider."

The words are bitter on my tastebuds, and even as I flick

my tongue against the roof of my mouth and savor the thought of drinking the Black Art dry until his very bones are as hollow as his heart, I'm not sure I meant what I said. I killed Darius without hesitation because he was an enemy soldier who would surely be tasked with killing me upon returning to his nation. Varil would have sent him to his death in time. I simply made it quick for him.

But Sin and I have history. A lot of it.

He swore promises to me, then cleaved through them like they were nothing more than spoiled carcasses for his disposal. Built me up just to peel me apart, layer by layer, and crunch them under his boots. Images of me seated in his throne with my strappy-heeled foot hooked over his shoulder, whirling around in lavish ball gowns while he skimmed warm fingers down my back... they all lash through my mind with the sting of a riding crop.

Sparks ignite in my palms, renewing my wrath.

Singard Kilbreth betrayed me. And I can't help but wonder if that betrayal has seeped into his bones and sweetened his blood like a smooth, honeyed wine. I lick my lips at the thought.

There's only one way to find out.

We cross into the tree line in under a minute, though speeding across the docks without cover felt like an eternity. We don't slow once we're in the woods, bounding through the forest that runs parallel to the capital city, towards the small clearing that is used to welcome and vet travelers. The receiving center, they call it. Far enough from the castle to be considered neutral ground, but close enough that more guards can be quickly summoned should affairs ever go awry.

A large, wooden framed gazebo with a slanted steel roof comes into view between the interconnected labyrinth of branches. Star jasmine vines around the four cedar pillars, their flowers like tiny yellow pinwheels hugging the supports, and more drape across the space under the awning like celebratory banners.

Having taken a shorter route by beelining through the trees, we arrive before Varil and the rest of the guards. Vox could have heard from a little farther away, but I wanted to be as close as possible without being seen. We're near enough now my ears might be able to barely make out their words, but Sera and Eldridge will be able to hear clearly now too. Transcendent hearing is not as attuned as the elves', but still has a far greater range than my own.

A single line of kingdom soldiers spans the far side of the outdoor shelter. Enough to provide a solid defense, but not so threatening as to spook traveling guests unnecessarily.

"No sign of Kilbreth yet," Vox murmurs, his dark eyes peering through the lattice of leave-riddled branches.

"No, but I can smell him," Sera says.

I swallow the lump in my throat, my skin suddenly itching as if a nest of spiders fell from the tree and skittered down my spine and legs.

"They're coming," Eldridge announces from my right.

Sure enough, Varil and the escorting kingdom guards arrive at the shelter a moment later. None of them appear to be interested in making small talk, and I can almost taste the tension in the air from here. They're anxiously waiting for Sin to make his appearance.

They're not the only ones.

Eldridge stiffens at my side, his burly shoulders pulling back further, and just as I'm about to ask what's wrong...

I see him.

The Black Art steps into the shelter, several more guards at his flank. Every hair on my body snaps to attention as my gut flips inside out and threatens to spill the contents of my breakfast on Eldridge's shoes. There has not been a single day, *not one day,* I haven't seen Sin's face in my mind since setting fire to his castle and storming off with his enemy two months ago. But seeing him in the flesh—his burnt umber skin still flush with life, his heart beating steadily in his chest while mine lays shattered in a thousand pieces behind my ribs—undoes me. I slip my hand into Eldridge's, and he squeezes it, a silent reminder we're in this together.

Sin meets Varil in the center of the gazebo and they shake hands cordially, though there is no welcoming smile on Sin's face. Varil's back is to me, but judging from the rigidness of his shoulders under his furs, he is mirroring the Black Art's stern expression.

"What are they saying?" I ask, working to keep my voice low.

"Singard denies intentions to invade Baelliarah and is asking Varil to reveal his source of information. Varil is, in turn, denying him that knowledge," Eldridge recites for my ordinary ears.

Sera shakes her head and fiddles with the dagger at her waist. "Who would be trying to spark a war between nations? If Singard is telling the truth, that is."

I almost laugh. If there's anything I learned from my time with the Black Art, it's that his word is shit.

"What are they saying now?" I prod, watching as Sin subtly widens his stance, and his hands lazily curl and uncurl at his sides. I look to Eldridge when he ignores me, and his lips pull down at the corners. I elbow him in the ribs. "Tell me!"

"They're talking about you."

Oh.

"Varil is asking about the bloodwitch. Singard just told him that..." he trails off.

"Fucking tell me, Eldridge!"

Sera steps up next to me, the dagger on her hip brushing mine. "Sin told him that you're dead," she fills in. Then turning to meet my stare, "He said he killed you."

Pride wracks through me, dislodging all remnants of humility. "He said *what?*"

She puts up a hand to quiet me, her forehead creasing as she strains to listen further. "He said you turned on him and that he 'put you down,'" she says, eyes narrowing.

"Why would he say that?"

"Likely to ease tensions," Vox chimes in from behind us. "If Baelliarah fears a bloodwitch, they may attack in anticipation. If he convinces Varil you're dead, that may be enough to get him to turn his ship around and mind their own business while Kilbreth repairs the damage to his own nation."

Air hisses through my teeth, and my hand instinctively reaches for the blade at my waist. "I'd like to see him try to *put me down.*"

I turn my attention back to the meeting, ignoring Varil entirely now and dragging my eyes down Sin's leather surcoat, wishing they were knives shredding his skin. Even after I'm gone, Sin is using me as a pawn in his dealings, luring his enemy into a false sense of—

Varil's head snaps violently to the side, his eyes going glassy and vacant as he collapses. Sin scurries backwards, orange magic birthing to life in his palms as he throws his hands up, assessing the shelter for the assailant. Except... there is none. Every guard from both nations has their weapons drawn immediately, and they turn in small circles, looking for the invisible killer.

"What in the fucking gods' names just happened?" Eldridge breathes at my side.

Before any of us can get another word out, soldier after soldier slumps to their knees as if pierced with a phantom sword, their bodies contorting at inhuman angles as their final breaths whoosh from their lungs, blood flying from their chests as if summoned by the gods themselves. The few guards remaining pivot around the room, spinning to locate the blight responsible for this, while Sin casts a ward around the gazebo.

It might as well be made from paper.

The Black Art's shield does nothing to stop the assault, as two more guards' guts are ripped open, their meat oozing out of them and dripping to the stone floor. The final remaining guard looks at Sin, and his sword clatters to his feet as he raises his palms, believing the Black Art must be responsible for the sudden attack. But the panic on Sin's face confirms he is mistaken, and the final guard arches backwards, his chest puffing out involuntarily before the seams of his skin are stretched too tight, and his carcass erupts into a bloody feast, organs cascading into the ruby pool that is now the receiving center.

It all happened so fast. One minute there were two leaders discussing war, the next, every guard lay decimated in a glistening pool of cardinal syrup. All except Sin. The Black Art slowly approaches the center of the floor with measured steps, his forearms blazing with fiery gloves, and his face twisted into something monstrous.

My heart thrums erratically in my chest, desperately trying to squeeze between my ribs like a hummingbird trapped in a gilded cage. We have to help him. *We have to help him!*

My body moves of its own volition, but Sera promptly grabs my elbow before I make it two steps forward. She shakes her head at me violently and points to her ears. With everyone dead around him, Sin is surely listening intently for the ghost, and I'm huddled with his enemies just out of sight.

Fuck.

But we can't just watch Sin be ripped limb by limb by some wicked phantom on a murderous rampage. Though... haven't I spent the past couple months fantasizing about this very moment? When I would finally witness the Black Art choking on his own vile black blood? Yes, but I'll be damned before I stand by and allow another to claim my kill. It will be *my* chalice cupped under his dripping throat, and from *my* chalice that I drink him dry.

But Sera's right. We can't just barge out there and reveal our hand. Because as convoluted as it may feel in this moment, Sin and I are enemies.

And this is war.

I steer my attention back to the gruesome sight before me. The bloodshed does not stoke her appetite—*my* appetite. I've stopped referring to my power as if it were something sentient, something that lives and breathes apart from me. No longer do I fear releasing some heinous version of myself that'll pound my heart flat with bloody fists and mold me into some abominable terror. My hands curl at my sides, and I narrow my eyes, willing the invasive coppery scent out of my nose, off my tongue.

I do not cower from the darkness that hums in my veins.

Not anymore.

Sin's head jerks to his right, and his body follows, his glowing palms facing out. A tall, slender man impeccably dressed in a black coat and trousers stops a few yards from the shelter. His dark brown hair is combed forward, a few pieces curled down over his left eyebrow, and his fair skin appears as if it hasn't been kissed by sunlight in years. Hands stuffed deep in his pockets, he takes a few steps forward, the ends of his lips curled into a facetious grin.

Sin's arm snaps forward, his fiery magic spiraling towards the strange man who throws his hand out, halting the destructive cast between them. The Black Art's brows knit together, and even with the distance between us, I take note of the corded muscles bulging in his forearms as he tries to overtake the stranger's ward. A ward that isn't wavering.

The attacker's face is smooth, not a single line of concentration scarring his forehead or mouth, even as he wields enough power to match the Black Art's goddess-blessed magic. He looks almost bored as he flicks his wrist to the right and Sin's massive body follows, thumping as he crashes into the stone floor, the blood of the deceased splattering his hair and clothing. The clacking of the mysterious mage's polished shoes is loud enough for even my hearing to detect as he approaches Sin, who recovered quickly, now already back on his feet. The mage says something, and Sin's lips part in what is undeniably a snarl.

"What is he saying?" I demand, panic raising my voice.

"He's mocking him. Monologuing some shit about how he's waited a long time to get this close to the Black Art," Eldridge supplies, his head cocked towards me, and his ear angled towards the altercation.

"Is he going to try to kill him?"

The men circle each other slowly, sizing the other up like two wolves about to brawl for the title of alpha. Physically, Sin is much larger—his shoulders wider and his entire body more muscular than his slender opponent, but their magics aren't as unbalanced as their statures.

"I don't know. Singard just threatened him but he's... being careful. Trying to bait him into giving information before he strikes."

Ever the strategist. Sin is likely keeping a damper on his own power still. Because behind this one mage is likely a leader that sent him. A leader with an army, coin, and a hit list with Sin's name scrawled at the top of it. But even so, Sin's ward did nothing to protect the guards in the shelter. This is no common foot soldier, and certainly no common mage.

Sin takes a measured step towards him before stumbling, his narrow eyes widening and his chin pointed up as if being grabbed by the throat.

"He's choking him," I blurt out.

"Good riddance," Eldridge sneers, and I resist the urge to deck him. He doesn't deserve it, and Sin has more than earned my family's malicious wishes.

Sera inches forward next to me, her lips pursed slightly as she watches her son struggle to breathe. I look to her, then to Vox, panic setting in. "We need to help him!"

The commander snarls. "That isn't our fight out there."

"I don't care who's fight it is, he's going to kill him!"

I don't waste another second before batting my way through the brush and racing for the Black Art.

CHAPTER 6

I make it halfway before a brick wall slams into me, sending me flying forward. I yelp as my stomach absorbs the blow, my teeth rattling within my jaw. I look over my shoulder and catch Vox's blond braids swinging wildly as he leans forward, wrestling my arms behind me.

"What the fuck are you doing? Get off me!" I buck my hips to try to dislodge his weight, not wanting to use magic against the elven commander, not if he's just trying to protect me against this threat we don't understand.

"I'm sorry about this," Vox grits through his teeth. *Sorry about wha—*

Metal bites my exposed palm, and before I can wield my collective, pain lances through my hand and shoots up my arms, turning my blood to lightning. I roar with thunder.

Sera's boots step into view, and I raise my head to watch as she carefully strips leather gloves I don't recall her wearing from her hands, tiny silver fragments clinging to the fabric.

My eyes widen in horror. Iron shavings.

Vox sliced my hand, and she dumped iron fragments into the wound.

Fire licks at my nerves, searing them into frayed edges, and

I screech through clenched teeth as the toxic metal tunnels into my bloodstream. Where the *fuck* is Eldridge?

"Have you brought me a snack, dear Sera?" A voice asks from somewhere close by.

"Enough, Alistair," she snips. "You've had your fun."

Straining against Vox's weight still pinning me on my stomach, I roll my head to assess the tall, finely-dressed male. Alistair carries himself forward, grinning down at me with a delirious glint in his dark brown eyes. "Oh... *oh,*" he coos, his nostrils flaring. "Aren't you sweet."

Something tells me he isn't referring to my charming personality. I bare my teeth.

"And perhaps a bit sour," he adds, grin widening.

Alistair spins on his heels but not fast enough to block Sin's punch, which sends him flying halfway around again. Neither Sera or Vox make a move to intervene, and Sin strikes him two more times before Alistair manages to throw a ward out that knocks the Black Art back several steps. One look at Alistair's more slender build and there's no way he can take Sin on hand-to-hand. But his magic...

A tempest of swirling smoke materializes, obstructing them both from my view as it envelops them in a ravenous hold. My vision grows bleary as the iron continues to dilute my blood with its toxins, but I force my eyelids open, searching for Sin in the thick fog and finding nothing but all-consuming gray. It's too dense.

A roar punctures the tornado, and the wind vanishes a moment later. Sin kneels on the ground, twin iron daggers protruding from either side of his lower abdomen, and his arms tethered behind his back. Alistair wrings his hands together, though not a drop of blood stains his alabaster palms, despite the pooling of it beneath Sin's dark surcoat.

He buried those blades into Sin with magic. Bound his hands with it too.

Vox slides off me and pulls me up by my elbows, my feet scrambling to plant themselves beneath my weight. As soon as everything stops spinning around me, I'm planting my knife in Sera's gut and strangling Vox with her innards.

Alistair steps away, his sights set on me. I dare another glance at Sin whose long hair is obscuring his face as he stares at the ground, likely trying to undo the magical bindings at his back before the iron seeps too far into his bloodstream and renders him helpless. Or before he bleeds out from the double daggers pierced through his flesh.

Gritting my teeth, I square myself towards the mage sauntering towards me. No longer are his features twisted in dark amusement, but rather they are bright with fascination. As if he is studying an oddity, a treasured relic. Vox's breath, usually silent, slips through his lips with urgency. Sera's attention hasn't veered an inch from Alistair since she attacked me, her rounded eyes now slivered in scrutiny.

"Where is Eldridge?" I direct the question over my shoulder, not taking my eyes off Alistair.

"Your friend is fine," Vox answers. "Incapacitated at the moment, but nothing he won't recover from."

I cock my head to the side and back in a quick, almost feral movement. "And who *the fuck* are you?"

Alistair's brown eyes spark to life again, but he doesn't smile this time, his expression much more serious than when he was antagonizing the Black Art minutes prior. "I am Alistair."

"I gathered that much." I arch my eyebrow, hoping I look stronger than I feel. My thighs tremble as if zapped by lightning, and my back goes glacial cold, the iron wringing the warmth from my body. In another minute, I won't be able to stand at all.

He swoops in closer and angles his head to the side to level his dark brown eyes with mine. Up close, I see the golden hues that ring his pupils, courtesy of the magic expulsion, the bleeding of colors reminiscent of the shimmering sand that breezes across the sandbars skirting Innodell and settles just inside the mud caves. I will strength into my legs, internally shouting for my knees not to collapse. Not yet. As if he hears the wobbling of my legs, Alistair's eyes drop. My muscles ache too much for me to follow his gaze, but his stare hardens my blood into a frozen cardinal sheet as he slowly sweeps it up my body. Not sexually, but as if he's mesmerized.

His attention fixates on something near my waist, and his nostrils flare widely. Alistair tilts his head back, eyes closing, and inhales deeply. His sharp cheekbones almost quiver with the movement, or perhaps that's me shaking, my control over my body slipping further. Mustering the last of my strength, I tilt my head down to see what caught his interest so consumingly.

I don't feel the hand cradled against my belly anymore, the poisonous shavings having chilled my essence to ice. My shirt is drenched, a dark puddle pooling beneath my bleeding palm, and I smack my lips as if someone placed a coin under my tongue.

Goddess above.

My head flops to the side, my eyelids fluttering to remain open, and a pressure builds in my armpits as Vox supports my failing muscles. Alistair tilts his head back down, and when he opens his eyes again, the golden rings have consumed half his irises.

"You're a bloodwitch." My words come out slurred, but the devious glint that sparks in his eyes confirms he hears me.

He nods slowly and slinks towards me. Instinct lashes at my muscles to move, *to run,* but they remain wedged in ice.

Come now. Move. Move!

When Alistair's heaving chest is but an inch from mine, his lips split, revealing a set of pointed, white teeth. "You smell fucking delicious."

He springs for me.

And everything goes black.

⁂

Gentle rocking cradles me. Calming. Tranquil.

Stabbing.

I let out a long groan as sentience floods into me, and I become aware of the knots that have replaced my muscles. My eyes open, and a red braided rope swings in front of my face, my head throbbing as I instinctively track the side-to-side movement. Eldridge speaks my name. Again. And again. I bat his hand away as he grips my biceps and gives me a shake, the force of it rattling my skull.

I mumble his name, and he lets out a sigh of relief. Large hands frame my face, and he tucks my head under his chin, his stocky fingers twisting into the back of my hair.

"Are you okay?" I ask him, forgetting my own pain for the moment. "Did they hurt you?"

Eldridge's posture stiffens, his shoulders rising an inch and his jaw tics in a slow, rhythmic cadence. He lifts his head, and I follow his gaze to Vox, who watches from where he leans against the boat, studying us intently.

We're back on the boat.

"You set us up," I spit, my legs trying to gain leverage to

stand, but Eldridge gives my shoulder a gentle push and his head a quick shake.

"We did nothing we knew Eldridge wouldn't make a full recovery from," Vox answers for him.

"Piss off, tree fucker," he grumbles under his breath but shoots a wink in my direction. "The other one may be small, but she's quick. As soon as you took off, he nearly split me in two with some fucking magic vines, and she had an iron dagger in me a second later."

"All of which, we healed you from the moment we could," the elven commander reminds bitterly, clicking his tongue.

I shake my head to clear the fog, almost as thick as the dark cottony clouds hovering above our heads, the sky a haze of lilac and gray. "How long have I been out?"

"A day and a half," Eldridge grumbles. "We'll be back at the Vale by morning."

"I apologize for the delay in your recovery," says Vox. "I had to siphon the iron from your blood, and I can only do it in short bursts so as to not drain my own reserves too far. It is likely you'll experience some bouts of dizziness for a day, but your wound is closed, and the iron has been lifted from your bloodstream."

I eye Vox suspiciously. "You some kind of healer now, Commander?"

"Elves are all kinds of things, blood mage."

He steps away from the boat's edge and heads towards the enclosed compartment.

"Sera?" I ask.

"She's asleep in the cabin. With Alistair."

"With—he's with us?" I crane my neck to look towards the cabin, but it's a futile attempt to see anything. The small covered portion of the boat has a few windows, all currently covered with hides to keep the warmth inside and the crisp sea air out. "What in Elysande's name is going on, Eldridge? They attacked us," I blurt, the memories of everything that happened piecing together more clearly now. "Sera and Vox and... Alistair! He lunged for me." Right before it all went black, but judging from the blood that appears to still be very much *inside* my body, I assume the bloodwitch was unsuccessful in securing another afternoon snack. As if he hadn't been absolutely *gorged* on the mess he made of the receiving center.

"I don't like it any more than you, but..." he fumbles for words, trying them on and committing to none. "Aside from hurting you, which I may still slit their necks for," he says, casting a glance over his shoulder, knowing Vox is likely listening to our conversation from inside, "their plan wasn't entirely a bad one. In fact, it worked pretty damn well."

I scowl at the hint of admiration coloring his tone. "What plan?" I ask hesitantly.

His eyes, the same stormy gray as the swollen clouds dotting the sky, brighten with a deep, wicked amusement. "To capture the Black Art."

CHAPTER 7

Deep water has always made me uneasy. That discomfort swells even more now as I peer out at the Howling Sea, the water a glistening cerulean blue in this sun-blessed hour. We arrived back at the Vale an hour or so ago, and I wasted no time hauling myself off the boat and back to my family's house, filling them in on all I knew. Which wasn't a lot.

It wasn't just my need to vent about what transpired during our trip that had me nearly tripping myself as I rushed off the boat, not bothering to collect my satchel or help offload the trunks. No. It was more than that. As eager as I was to see my family, I was more inclined to *not* see him.

Sin. Daggered and chained in the boat's hold.

Our prisoner.

They moved him off the ship, but I was long gone before they retrieved him from below deck. Closing my eyes, I blow out a long sigh, steadying myself against the waves crashing through my stomach with the same turbulence as the sea before me. Sera and the others are meeting in the conservatory to discuss next steps, and are likely wondering where I've wandered off to right about now. I turn my back to the foreboding water and make my way there, curiosity hurrying me along.

How *does* one proceed after capturing the Black Art of Aegidale?

"Well, I for one, think this is hilarious." Cathal claps his hands together, then cups the sides of his mouth, unleashing a hair-splitting howl of approval.

"It will not be hilarious when the kingdom sends their entire godsforsaken army after us!" Morrinne grabs the hems of her skirts with one hand and stalks towards Sera, a curled finger pointed at her chest. "You can play your games with your own people, fight your wars with the kingdom and your *spineless* son, but you do not make decisions when it comes to what affects *my daughter.*"

Sera clicks her tongue and folds her moonbeam arms across her chest. "Would you have preferred I wait for the kingdom to come to the Vale and burn it down, then? They know she's here already. We extended a grace period for Sin to come to terms with our proposal, and that period has expired. We cannot face them head on—we would be naïve to believe we could. This is not a war we will win with magic and steel alone. We need *leverage.*"

I've been tracing the grains of the wooden table with my finger for half an hour, listening as the group argues amongst themselves. Without our knowledge, Sera had conspired with the elves—spun them a plan for how to secure the Black Art in our custody with the help of her longtime friend, the male bloodwitch. Alistair has apparently traveled in and out of the Vale for a decade, popping in to occasionally do biddings for the elves and seeing to Sera's well-being. I don't fully understand the complexities of their relationship, but given that Alistair appears similar in age to myself, I presume Sera is a motherly figure to him. I chew on my lip, rolling it between my teeth as that thought sinks into my gut. Did abandoning Sin as a child leave a gaping chasm in her heart? Was Alistair merely a tourniquet for her?

I hope she faces suffering each day for what she has done. No one, not even Sin, deserves to be neglected by the one person who should be a lifetime guarantee for them.

Sera claims she didn't inform the rest of us about their plan —woven between Vox, Aeverie, and herself—because she knew the others would caution that it was too dangerous to try to capture the Black Art. And she isn't wrong. The plan sounds ludicrous, even to me. No amount of persuasion would have led me to believe we could actually pull this off.

When Baelliarah's men invaded the Vale, Sera contacted Alistair through a scrying spell, alerting him of Sin's forthcoming meeting with Varil. The remaining pieces fell into place, snapping together like some macabre puzzle.

I finger the silky white flowers springing from the clay vase on the table, admiring the silver veins threading through their leaves. My attention still on the bouquet, I say, "It was one thing for them to pinpoint my location. We were well aware that was inevitable, and you all accepted me being here knowing they would eventually come for the bloodwitch. But I'm not just a bloodwitch anymore; I'm the bloodwitch that killed every guard present at that meeting and captured our regent. And I'm pretty sure that is a whole lot worse."

Alistair picks at the threads of his dark waist-coat, his attire far too formal for the conservatory. Too elegant for anywhere in the Vale, actually. "We've barely just met and you're already trying to claim my accomplishments as your own?" he asks, his deep voice teasing but underlined with annoyance.

I squeeze too hard and crumble the delicate petal between my thumb and forefinger. "Am I mistaken that the kingdom has no record of you, Alistair? Sin acted as if I was the first bloodwitch he's encountered. When no one returned from the receiving center that morning and Dusaro finds the *massacre* you committed, *and his son missing,* who do you think he's going to blame? Who would be powerful enough to sneak in undetected and capture the Black Art from his own home? A bloodwitch. And goodie for him, he happens to know one who already threatened him and his son. They'll be here in days," I add, settling back into my seat and burying my hands in my armpits.

"Then it's a very good thing there are two of us, isn't it?" Alistair's smile stretches into something devious, out of place amongst the delicate flowers weaving through the latticework fences framing the conservatory. "I'll admit, I'm not used to sharing my meals, but I'll make an exception." The wink he shoots me is pure mischief, and I can't tell if he's teasing me, or merely attempting to make me uncomfortable.

Calloused hands wrap around my shoulders, and a quick glance behind me reveals their owner. Eldridge squeezes my shoulders, gently rolling them forward and back, releasing the tension, and a sigh falls from my lips.

Vox paces between the small rounded tables set up across the indoor garden, his footfalls silent against the stone. "I have every mage in our ranks working to establish a barrier now. A taxing endeavor, but it will prevent anyone not invited from entering the Vale. As Sera stated, it is no secret we are vastly outnumbered. The barrier will prevent them from overwhelming us with manpower. It, however, will do nothing to stop this forest from igniting should they decide to smoke us out."

"And what is our brilliant plan when they decide to do just that?" I ask, leaning into Eldridge's deep, massaging knuckles.

"Dusaro will not set fire to this Vale," Sera asserts, turning away from Morrinne to face me. "Baelliarah will be learning soon enough that their king is dead, if they haven't already. War has already been declared between nations, intentional or not. The last thing Dusaro will want is for Baelliarah and its new king to learn that Aegidale is without its ruler as well. This isle will be surrounded with enemy ships the minute they learn our kingdom is vulnerable. They'll already be watching us, and burning an entire forest that borders the western half of our nation puts off a lot of smoke. Not exactly subtle for keeping your enemy out of your domestic dealings."

I lean forward, tenting my fingers against the sides of my head. Sera makes a valid argument, though it is counting on Dusaro acting from a place of logic and reason, not fire and wrath. *Literally.*

A puff of air escapes my lips, and I shake my head against my hands. "Regardless, they'll still be here in a few days. Even if just to... *negotiate*," I emphasize the word, still not certain Dusaro won't start chucking torches into the forest as soon as he's within throwing distance.

Cathal snickers, but it is Vox that answers. "We will be ready for them when they come. Until then, Kilbreth will be kept under constant surveillance. Aeverie is with him now."

I swallow thickly. "Where is he being kept?"

"He's in one of the spare houses. Aeverie will need to be relieved from her watch soon, as she's exhausted herself already." The smooth white skin of the commander creases between his fair-colored brows, and his lips form around words that don't come out.

"What is it?" I press.

"Aeverie healed him to keep him from bleeding out, or dying from iron poisoning. He is bound in iron still, but without it in his bloodstream, it is wise that only the strongest of us rotate out for his watch. It would be our downfall to underestimate someone with goddess-blessed magic in their veins."

Oh. Fuck. Me.

"I have to help the others fortify the barrier," he continues. "The wanderers are no match for magic of his kind."

Cathal scoffs, but Sera nods in agreement. Vox is right. Transcendents are excellent in illusive magics, but cloaking spells aren't going to prevent Sin from slaughtering us all in our beds.

"Are you asking me to keep watch over the Black Art tonight?" I ask, already knowing the answer.

"I'd volunteer, princess, but apparently I'm not trusted enough to not eat our guest," Alistair chimes in.

Eldridge grumbles at my rear, but it does nothing to stop Vox's prompt nod. I huff once without laughter, and smack my palms against the table. "Fine. But first, I'm going to need a stiff fucking drink. Maybe twelve."

CHAPTER 8

The night is still, almost unnaturally so. As if even the stars hushed the summer breeze and trembling branches, turning their ears towards the spare stone house to hear the words left unspoken between us.

I hover outside the door, the unassuming building occupying a small lot along the northern side of the Vale's heart. Aeverie slipped out when she heard me arrive and merely bid me a quick nod before heading towards the temple. Vox informed me I would be relieved at first light so I may snag some sleep of my own. My injuries, while healed, have left me achy and tired. I suppose if I need a burst of energy overnight, I can always bleed the Black Art for a little snack. No one said I had to return him in the same condition I received him.

I almost chuckle at the thought but bite it back, knowing he would place the voice as my own. I want to *see* his face when he beholds me for the first time. After I blindly followed him to the cliffside he hurled me over, not even bothering to look over the edge and watch as my arms desperately tried to take flight before I smacked into the earth below.

Except, I never plummeted to rock. Singard forgot something important before he cast me aside so quickly and left me for figurative death. A wren is not a flightless bird.

I push open the door and step inside.

Goddess above.

Sin kneels in the center of the room, both of his arms stretched outward and shackled to two pillars supporting the structure, while another set of manacles bind his ankles together. His chest is bare and two large garnet scars adorn his abdomen where Alistair's iron daggers were buried. Aeverie healed his injuries, but left the visual reminder of them— perhaps as a reminder of the strength he is up against.

Sin doesn't look up as I step into the one-room dwelling, vacant aside from one dark-cushioned chair in the corner of the room. If he's awake or asleep, I can't tell. His head is tilted forward, his long black hair obscuring his face, spilling over his shoulders and grazing the hard planes of his chest. A pair of black trousers hang low on his waist, just beneath the twin scars marring the perfect V-shaped muscles of his obliques.

The door wafts shut behind me. I take pleasure in watching as every muscle in his body tightens as my scent rushes into his nose.

Sin remains motionless as I cross the room and sit in the single chair, crossing one leg over the other and interlocking my fingers in my lap. He doesn't look up, but his chest rises and falls faster now, and his pulse, thrumming in the pressure point of his neck, does not escape my notice. Even cuffed in iron and kneeling before me, the Black Art exudes a current— like the force of his ire may swell at any moment and flood the house entirely.

The reaper in chains. What a fascinating change of tides.

"Look at me." I don't know where I find the strength to command my voice with such certainty while my every nerve sparks and crackles with heat.

Sin obeys. His inky curtains split around his face as he rolls his head back to look at me, his narrow, serpentine eyes slicing into mine. Whatever I planned on saying catches in my throat as I lock gazes with the man I was tangled up with just months before, and suddenly, I wish he were looking anywhere else.

Tears bite at my eyes, and my nails prick my palms. I imagined this moment a thousand different ways, when I would finally have my chance for revenge against the man who imprisoned my sister, then lied to my face about it. But as he peers up at me, heat swirling in his verdant irises, it is nothing but hurt that tunnels through my veins. "I trusted you," is all I manage to whisper, hating how my voice cracks on the last word.

His face betrays no emotion, and I divert my eyes to one of the stacked stone pillars in the room. A sharp pang tugs at the outer casing of my heart, twisting and fraying the strings holding it together until my very essence bleeds from my aching chest.

"I gave you everything. Everything that I possibly could, I gave you. You told me not to trust you but... but I did. Wholeheartedly." The words keep spilling from my lips, matching the tears that have now welled over my ducts and stream down my cheeks. I wipe them away with the back of my hand and stand, my skin crawling with the need to sprint as far from here as I can. I pace to the side of the room and press my palms against the cool stone, staring down at my boots. From my periphery, I catch him assessing me from head to toe.

"Scanning for weapons I might slit your throat with?" I don't look at him when I ask, but I feel his eyes snap back to mine. It would be easy to kill him. Too easy, like wounded prey writhing in my trap. I slip my blade from my pants as I turn towards him, stalking closer. When I'm mere inches away, I begin to circle him, letting the soles of my boots drag a second too long across the floor with each step. I lean over him when I complete my orbit, tilting his chin up with the smooth side of my blade.

"Every single day since that night, I've imagined how good it would feel to make you hurt. It *plagues* me, thinking about it." I laugh quietly, and when he doesn't respond, I tighten my grip on the hilt, nudging the dagger a little further against the bronze skin of his neck. He doesn't recoil, but his breathing slows, or perhaps he's stopped breathing altogether now. "Want to know a secret, *Your Grace?* Sometimes when I'm all alone and it's late at night, I touch myself to the thought of bleeding every drop from your body. I've found bliss at the thought of you begging me to stop, to grant you mercy when you showed none."

A touch of pressure and my knife slips into his flesh. Desire settles low in my belly at the sight of the thin red necklace now adorning his neck. I chuckle again, and Sin's heady stare meets my own. Smoldering. Intoxicating. But not a drop of fear scorns his face. He's calling my bluff, and I don't blame him.

I'm not going to kill him.

I rise to my full height, taking my dagger with me. "As much as I'd like to say our time together has had no effect on me, that's not entirely true. It seems you *have* influenced me in one way after all, Your Grace, because like you, I am not satisfied with merely taking what I want. No. I rather enjoy the suffering. The *hunt*."

I bring the knife to my lips, and holding his stare captive, swirl my tongue around the blade, tasting his torment. My chest rattles with perverse delight, and I wrap my lips around the flat edge of the dagger, inviting his essence fully into my mouth. A deep moan spills from my lips before I lower the weapon to my side. "Just know, my sweet Blackheart, when I'm done chasing you, I will devour you. Bones and blood and soul."

Tucking the blade back into my pants, I quickly heal the shallow cut on his neck. Iron resists magic, so any deeper of a cut and his flesh wouldn't close at my touch. I turn my back to him and head for the corner of the room when, in a voice so quiet I'm not sure he intends for me to hear it at all, he whispers, "I know."

I slump into the far corner and sit with one leg outstretched and the other tucked against my chest, the chair opposite me offering a comfort I'm not inclined to feel at the moment.

I close my eyes. I don't dare long for sleep, but I refuse to look at him a moment longer. Even if I desired sleep, those two words echoing through my skull would surely frighten it away.

I know.

CHAPTER 9

When the fiery red dawn bathes the woods in a bloody glow, Vox relieves me from my post.

"Get some sleep. The earliest they could be here by horseback is tonight, but it would be foolish to come at that hour. It is probable they will be here by morning though, so go."

I heed the commander's advice and head straight for my family's house, turning down the stewed plum porridge Zorina offers, and crawl into my bed. Heavy phantom strings tug at my eyelids, trying to force them to close. I don't fight them any longer, desperate to forget all of this for a few hours.

For the first time in months, no monsters follow me into the undulating darkness of my dreams.

*   *   *

Cosmina is here when I wake, sitting on the edge of my bed with her feet tucked under a spare blanket. Her pale blue eyes meet mine over the top of the leather-bound romance book she's reading. She says nothing as she rises and retrieves a tea tray with a covered platter from the table in the corner. Lifting the lid reveals a plate of fire-roasted muskrat, creamed corn, a pile of leafy greens, and a slice of thick, crusty bread. My stomach groans in response.

I shovel the dinner into my mouth, the savory flavors coating my throat and belly with warmth and spice. Cosmina is quiet while I eat, and when I swallow the remaining bits of food and down the cup of water she brought me, she leans in and pats my mouth with a linen napkin. She tends to me as if I am ill, and I suppose in a way, I am.

"Thank you," I finally bring myself to say. I reach for the napkin and finish cleaning my face myself.

Cosmina leans back against the foot of the bed and picks up the knitting project she started last week from the footstool next to her. Her needles find their places in the yarn immediately, as if they never left their positions at all. "I don't like that Vox had you on watch last night. We came here to keep you out of danger, not thrust you in the face of it again," she says matter-of-factly. Pursing her lips, she tilts her head to gain a different perspective of the design she's knitting.

"I didn't come here to stay out of danger, sister. I came here to prepare for war. And as I intend on being on the winning side of that war, it is necessary I do my part in ensuring we have the upper hand. If right now that means guarding the Black Art, then guarding the Black Art is what I will do."

Cosmina raises one thin, dark eyebrow and rolls her bottom lip between her teeth. "Are we ever going to talk about that?"

I fold my cloth napkin and drape it over my now empty plate. I don't need to ask what 'that' she's referring to. "There's nothing to talk about."

"You endured a lot to see to my safety, and I'm certain it was awful to have your trust in our regent betrayed."

"We knew he couldn't be trusted; that was nothing new," I state firmly.

"Yes. But you did anyway." She doesn't speak it as a question.

I swing my legs over the bed and walk to the mirror propped against a large brown trunk. Unthreading my braid, I say, "A foolish mistake."

"Cut it out, Wren."

The sharpness of her tone has my shoulders tensing. I always hate when Cosmina grows stern with me. Something about it reminds me of my mother, even though my chosen sister is nothing like the wicked woman that birthed me.

She continues when I don't. "I saw the look on your face when I told you it was Singard that was responsible for my capture. You blanched like you were to be physically ill, like I shattered something inside you. Pardon my forwardness, sister, but that is not the reaction to someone learning that a certain ruler they've already hated has betrayed them. The hurt in your eyes was enough to burn out the sun."

The last of my braid unravels, and I comb my hands through the tresses, taming the tangles that have nested there. "If you're suggesting something, Cosmina, then out with it."

She sets her project on the bed and stands, folding her arms tightly across her frail chest. "All I'm saying, is if there was more to your relationship with the Black Art than a mere *platonic* alliance, you needn't be fearful of telling me."

I spin on my heel, facing her. "And if that were true, what would that make of me? If I *foolishly* allowed myself to grow affectionate towards a monster, someone who hurt you and would undoubtedly do it again? To Zorina? Eldridge?"

The creases around her eyes soften, and she closes the gap between us. She doesn't hesitate reaching for my folded arms, wrapping her tiny hands around my forearms. "It would make you many things, Wren. Most of all, it would make you human. But it would never make you not my sister."

I divert my gaze, tears pricking the corners of my eyes. My head shakes, but she catches my stare with her own, forcing me to look at her again. "Whatever history you have with the Black Art, no one has to know if you don't want them to. But know that it will never change anything between us."

She doesn't wait for my answer before she unfolds my arms and pulls me against her, wrapping her slender fingers into my hair and tucking my forehead to her bony shoulder. I soak the front of her blue tunic as she brushes her hands through my locks, unable to hold back the storm any longer. With no one but my sister to hear the pain that has tinted my blood to the darkest black, I whisper my hidden truth.

"I loved him."

CHAPTER 10

The shrill cry of the war horn has my sisters and I rushing to secure our blades to our belts and thighs, and we scurry outside. Cosmina slept in my bed last night, and this morning Morrinne woke us with steaming bowls of creamy oats drizzled with honey. We barely finished our breakfast before the alarm rings out, alerting us that the moment we prepared for has arrived.

The kingdom is here.

Vox is at our door within minutes of the warning call, motioning for me to hop onto the back of his onyx horse. I mount the steed and hold onto his leather armor, fighting the urge to shove him off the horse and trample him with it. He has not apologized for his deceit, nor would I forgive him if he did.

Cosmina and Eldridge are on the back of our family's borrowed horse a moment later, and the four of us head for the perimeter. Several others, the small team chosen to first greet whoever the kingdom sent on their behalf, fall into a gallop around us. With Sin gone, the Black Hand will have temporarily taken his place, and a brick falls into my stomach as I imagine the pressure Ileana must be facing right now.

The wailing call of the horn sounds twice more as we race for the perimeter. I catch sight of Sera's dark head bobbing to my right, and Aeverie beyond her. Several other armor-clad men and women fill in around us, the hooves of our horses pounding the earth in singular purpose. We veer around the final turn of the forested expanse, and our horses pull to a sharp stop at the border. The barrier the elves put up is invisible, but any mage can feel the vibration humming in the collective like they've stumbled onto one of the earth's vital pressure points.

Magic drags its jagged teeth down my forearms and nips at my palms as I dismount our horse and step towards the barrier, towards the menacing presence waiting for me on the opposite side.

Dusaro's inky hair is tied loosely down his back, twin braids twisted into either side of his head. His deep bronze skin is slightly swollen under his eyes, and dark stubble covers the bottom half of his sharp jaw. I don't so much as nod in greeting as I inch my toes towards the perimeter, but Vox offers a curt salutation as he steps up next to me. A quick sweep of my surroundings shows Aeverie still seated in her saddle, ten or so guards spread around us, and Sera, who approaches the border on foot from Vox's other side.

"Morning, husband," Sera trills. "I must say, I'm a little surprised it's taken you this long to find your way here."

Dusaro dismounts from his all-white steed, his black riding cloak fanning out behind him before the hem settles against the backs of his knee-length riding boots. There's about twenty of them here, none I recognize apart from Dusaro. Ileana is likely being sheltered in the castle for her protection, an arrangement I'm sure she is *just loving,* and Aldred is probably seeing directly to her protection. Capturing the Black Art was a declaration of war by the elves and transcendents alike, and with Baelliarah now sticking its nose in business it doesn't belong in, it is more critical than ever that the Black Hand be kept safe from harm.

"Where's my son?" Dusaro asks, not taking Sera's bait.

"I assure you *our* son is perfectly safe... for the moment." Sera shrugs one pale, rounded shoulder and widens her stance slightly.

"I am not here to play anymore of your pathetic, silly games, Seraphine. That *thing,*" Dusaro jerks his chin to where I stand, "slaughtered fifteen of my men, and twelve from our closest nation, a hostile one at that. You are providing shelter to someone who murders without remorse."

"Do not lecture me with talk of murdering without remorse, Dusaro," Sera snips, one hand finding the dip of her hip.

He shifts forward, and several of his guards mirror the motion behind him. "Give me. My son."

Vox cocks his head to the side, his braids tight against his scalp. "Should I assume you're ready to negotiate terms then, Lord Kilbreth?"

Dusaro bristles at the suggestion. "Careful, elf. You declared a war you are not fit to fight. Return me my son, and *maybe,* we can discuss reparations you may pay to us for this horrendous crime."

The commander tsks quietly to himself, shaking his head with each click of his tongue. "I'm afraid that won't do. No worries. I have enough iron on hand to keep Singard contained for a very long time. And should we run out," Vox does that quick flick of his head to the side again, "well, we have plenty of wildlife to feed."

Vermillion flames ignite in Dusaro's palms, his magic pressing against the barrier, my own collective slithering through my veins in response.

"If I have not made myself clear, the second you set so

much as a spark to these trees is the same moment you fail your operation. There will not even be a body to retrieve." I steal a glance at Vox, the sudden deepening of his voice, his dark irises like swirling black orbs in his face, so unnatural. Inhuman.

"Do you expect me to take you at your word that my son is even alive and that your bloodhound didn't already make a meal out of him?"

I smile at Dusaro, certain my lazy demeanor will stoke his temper more than if I bared my teeth at him. He scoffs at my grin, sucks in a whoosh of air, then spits at my feet. My lips only widen in response.

"Your kind never get any cleverer with your nicknames, do you?" A husky voice says at my rear. A glance over my shoulder confirms the tone belongs to Alistair, but I hardly register the other bloodwitch as my attention falls on the man at his side.

Sin approaches with Alistair, his wrists and ankles still bound with unforgiving iron. The Black Art locks eyes with his father immediately, but it's not relief that swarms his face. Sin's downward eyes narrow further as Dusaro appraises him, taking in the pink scars on his bare abdomen, and Sin's chin tilts towards his chest.

Shame.

The emotion simmers low in my belly, and I drop my hold on Sin's collective, not realizing I had latched onto it. I look back to the brigade in front of me, just as Dusaro shifts his scowling face back to Vox and Sera.

"Dusaro, is it?" Alistair coos. "I possess many skills, Dusaro, but modesty has never been one of my strengths. But you want to know what I am really... *fucking...* good at?" He pauses for an extended beat, tension swelling in his silence. "Killing," he finishes. Even with my back to him, the smile in his words is unmistakable.

Dusaro's nose scrunches, and he shields his face for a moment as if the mere sight of Alistair assaults him. "You're like her," he growls when he lowers his arm, his lips twisted in disgust. It's then I remember noticing the canines Alistair had sharpened and shaped into unnatural points when he smiled at me before.

I turn to look at the pair behind me again and catch Eldridge shuffling closer to me. Alistair throws a wink in my direction.

"You could say that, though I have a feeling Wren's appetite is not as insatiable as my own." When his lips split again, I take better notice of his carnivorous teeth. He must file them. *Pretentious, much?*

Sin doesn't respond, his eyes shuffling between the guards on the other side of the barrier, scanning. Something to his left snags his attention, but I can't bring myself to look away while Alistair is so close to him.

"You raise a hand to him, and I swear on every damn god in the heavens and the ones in Hell, I'll burn you all alive," Dusaro warns.

Alistair chuckles, the sound throaty, breathless. "Not to worry, I don't use my hands much." He flashes those teeth again, but my focus is fixed on Sin and the panic welling in his eyes. Surely he can't believe Sera would actually allow Alistair to hurt him... right? Though, whatever fraction of trust I may have placed in Sin's mother was devastated when she and Vox incapacitated me.

"We're wasting time," Sera interjects, laying her hands straight at her sides and squaring her shoulders to Dusaro's. "Our terms are quite simple. You run back to your castle and draft up new treaty lines on your pretty parchment, and we keep the Black Art stable. You set fire to these trees, we set fire to him." Small stature aside, Sera's controlled tone carries weight.

Dusaro chuckles and wipes a hand down his face, smearing the laugh from his mouth. "You're not going to hurt your own son, Sera. You couldn't possibly hurt him anymore than you already—"

"Father. *No*." It's the first I've heard him speak clearly since being brought here. When I look at Sin again, the panic in his face has morphed into something more savage, more animal. *He's furious*. He drills his heated stare into Dusaro's, his top lip curling when he says in a voice colder than the winter sea, "I am giving you an order. Do. *Not*," he snarls the word, "hurt her."

I catch Sera whipping back to Dusaro in my periphery, but my eyes are locked on Sin, unable to pull them away. Like there's an invisible tether tugging me towards him.

"He's not going to hurt me, son," Sera says, her words glazed with condescension at Dusaro's expense.

Dusaro chortles again, but whatever he says next grows silent as the weight of Sin's stare falls on me, knocking the breath from my lungs. He looks at me like he's searching for something buried beneath my skin, beneath my bones, deep in my ethereal matter. Realization clicks into place before I can react, and suddenly, I don't think he was telling his father not to hurt Sera. The fury melts from his face, and in its place, for a brief moment before he rips his gaze away and shouts something beyond me, I glimpse remorse.

Sound roars back into my ears, and I whip my head in the direction Sin bellowed. I catch sight of Vox drawing his swords from his back and Sera slinking back from the border, her hands reaching for the knives looped on her waist. A flash of red gleams in my periphery as Eldridge rushes to hunker as close to the border as he can, but none of it registers as I behold Dusaro watching me, scrutinizing me. His chin is lifted slightly, his head angled to the side, and a slow smile crawls across his mouth, revealing a set of white teeth that gleam against the dark copper of his skin.

I will enough sense back to myself to scan his body, but he reaches for no weapons. His hands are empty at his sides, but metal brushes leather all around me as swords are slid from their holsters on both sides of the border.

An ear-splitting howl has me ducking and covering my head instinctually, the sound so piercing, so wrathful, like a vengeful spirit of the woods. When the echo of the roar fades, I drop my arms and gasp at the sight before me. A second later, I'm flattening myself to the ground to avoid the giant black paws leaping over my head.

CHAPTER 11

The earth rumbles beneath me like a starved stomach about to swallow me whole. Another roar thunders in my ears, this one higher pitched, *pained*. I roll myself over and scramble to my feet, but Alistair plants a hand into my chest and shoves me backwards before charging the border, fire igniting from his hands all the way to his shoulders.

Swords clank against one another in a metallic dance, blood spritzes onto the damp leaves and surrounding trees, and shouts I don't discern rend the air. None of it matters. Nothing except...

Sin's massive furred body is slumped against the ground, a feather fletched bolt protruding from the side of his gut. His floral scented sap leaks from the wound, pooling around the arrow and dampening his midnight fur.

I fling myself at him, my hands hovering above the bolt, unsure if I should yank the arrow out or leave it in to slow the bleeding. Fuck. *Fuck!*

Gold wisps sprout from my fingertips, and I place my palms to his side, but his collective is limp in my mind, folding like a freshly cracked yolk. Whoever shot a bolt of this size was no standard archer.

This was fired from an arbalest.

My magic does nothing to clot the wound—the tip buried inside his stomach is surely iron, negating my attempts at healing. I scoot over to where his dark head rests against the soft ground, and I lean over him, cradling his face. "Listen to me. It's alright. You're going to be alright."

His yellow-green eyes roll up to meet mine, and even set in a furred feline face, Sin has never looked more human. And then his eyes begin to close.

I shove my fingers into the silky fur of his chest, shaking him, calling his name. "Do not close your eyes. Wake up. Sin. SINGARD! Fucking bastard, you are not dying today!" The tang of magic sours my tongue, and a stampede of footfalls rush our direction. A dense cloud of pewter smoke wafts around us, and faintly, I hear the pounding of hooves against earth in the distance. The fighting has stopped, but I'm hardly aware. I don't even know who won.

"Move out of the way, out of the way!" Sera orders, elbowing her way through the bodies crowding around where I cling to Sin. Her hands flutter around his face, and she dips her nose to his head. "My sweet boy," she whispers.

I don't think. I shove her backwards so hard her shoulders connect with the ground, and I curl my body over Sin's, baring my teeth at her. "He wasn't enough for you when you thought he was human, you do not get to sob over him now that you know the truth."

Her dark green eyes go wide as she sits up, but she doesn't reach for him again. Aeverie pushes the others aside and kneels down, hovering a hand over his stomach, Sin's chest rising and falling slower now. Too slowly.

"Vox!" shouts the high priestess. He's at her side at once. "Get him to the temple immediately. We need to remove the bolt and lift the iron from his system. Clot the blood before he loses too much. Quickly now. Fetch a cart, we don't have much time."

The commander shares a look with Eldridge, then mounts his horse and takes off in a gallop. Eldridge hops onto Aeverie's steed and hurries off after him, but not before he shoots me a look sharp enough to wound. I should have been appalled when I saw Sin shift into a beast before my eyes. Called him a traitor to his own kind, taken my knife and sliced his throat myself.

I did none of those things. Because when the opportunity I had envisioned a thousand times was upon me, every ounce of hatred I felt for the Black Art dissipated, replaced only by the need to save his life. Maybe the need stemmed from guilt. That bolt was meant for me, *my* heart. And Sin used the last of his power to shift under iron, to take that arrow to his own gut, even though it meant revealing his most guarded secret. But it was precisely my lack of surprise that told all.

Eldridge's gray eyes pierce me with an accusation as cold as the tumultuous storm brewing behind them.

Liar.

It is evening when I enter the temple. Eldridge never returned after helping Vox transport Sin's body to the healing ward, and I have no doubt it was me he was avoiding. I promised Zorina I would send him home once I found him, but that's assuming he listens long enough for me to try to explain why I lied to him.

Not lied exactly, but by omission, perhaps. I didn't tell him Sin is a transcendent. I didn't tell anyone. Partly because of the deal I made with the Black Art: I safeguard his secret so long as he doesn't declare war on shifter-kind. I was protecting my family. At least, that's what I reminded myself each night as I struggled to sleep, when the pressure of keeping this from everyone sat on my chest with the weight of a war hammer.

Sometimes I believed it enough to slip into an ignorant slumber. But every time I woke, drenched in a cold sweat despite the summer temperature, I remembered the other reason I hadn't told anyone. Remembered my betrayal, my shame. Sin never pretended to be something he wasn't. He looked me dead in the eyes and told me not to trust him, and I did it anyway.

I *chose* to love a monster.

And that is my most heinous crime of all.

When Alistair threatened him in the receiving center, I chose to help Sin. And today, when he used the last of his power to break the iron manacles the only way he could— shifting into his second skin and revealing his shame—I chose him again.

My footsteps clack loudly against the stone tiles of the temple—too loudly for a sacred space. I pass several waist-height pillars topped with busts of men and women carved from marble. Elves, judging from the shape of the ears. Descriptions are etched into the stone pillars beneath their detailed faces, and I make a mental note to come back when I have more time, curious to learn more about our hosts' ancient history.

The healing wing is in the back corner of the open-air temple, and as I round the corner at the end of the corridor, Aeverie steps out. She closes the door behind her before I glimpse anything, or *anyone,* inside.

"How is he?" I ask. I had wanted to visit immediately, but Vox sent word that Aeverie required several hours undisturbed to mend the injury. Sin was the only one who needed to be transported to the temple; a few others were injured but nothing that couldn't be promptly healed. No casualties on our side from the scrap earlier, but a few arrows found their way into kingdom soldiers' necks, courtesy of the elven archers positioned in the trees near the border. Aeverie is a skilled healer, Vox assured me, but it did nothing to calm my nerves that tangled together like a pit of restless snakes.

Her face remains stoic as she answers in a matter-of-fact tone. "The bolt pierced deep, barely missing vital organs. He lost a lot of blood. Too much for any man, but given the Black Art has both wanderer and goddess-blessed magics in his veins, he'll recover." Her left eyebrow arches slightly, and I can't decide if the movement is meant to be inquisitive or accusatory. "I lifted the iron from his blood, which was rather taxing, so I must rest now. He needs time to heal, and I cannot assist more until my own reserves replenish."

"How long will that take?"

"A few days. I replenish fast, but not as quickly as I once did. Don't tell the others, but I am not as youthful as I may appear." Nothing about her expression suggests she is teasing, but I sense the amusement in her words.

"Your secret is safe with me, Madam Priestess." I offer her a playful wink, and she nods once. I glance at the door behind her. "I would like to see him."

"As you wish, but enter at your own risk. I cannot restrain him in iron if I expect my magic to heal him, now can I? While his physical body is weak still, I would not underestimate him. Though, considering the reason for his injury, perhaps you have reason to believe the Black Art will not harm you." She fixes me with that icy stare again, the whites of her irises swirling like an unforgiving blizzard. If the priestess really can see into the next realm, I wonder just how far she can see into *me*.

"He's unrestrained entirely?" I balk. "Madam Priestess, forgive me, but what's to stop him from sneaking out of here the moment you leave?"

"The room is spelled to prevent him from exiting. You needn't worry about him getting out, just be certain that you want to go in."

I nod, then bow my head in respect as she steps around me, swiftly gliding out of sight. I don't hesitate pushing open the door. If he's awake, his transcendent ears heard our conversation, and he already knows I'm here. Delaying entrance will make him think I'm nervous, and I will not give him the satisfaction of thinking he has that effect on me.

The room is large enough to hold a few beds, though only one is present. There's a tall wooden shelf displaying a variety of leather-bound books, all appearing to be in pristine condition as if they've never been read, or only ever handled with immense care. Against the far wall is a small circular table with a white pitcher and a few matching cups arranged atop a decorative woven place setting. A couple cushioned chairs are set up around the space, and a plush tan rug lays on the floor next to the bed where the sleeper might rest their feet in the morning.

Sin sits on the bed by his pillow, his legs bent at the knees and one arm draped casually across them, no headboard to separate his back from the stone wall. I use the opportunity to assess him, allowing my gaze to slide across his bare chest and abdomen. A large white bandage covers a good portion of the right side of his stomach, and the pink lines from Alistair's daggers stand out against the deep tan of his skin.

I walk to the shelf and select a book at random, my fingers tracing over the smooth leather spine. He raises a hand and combs it through his hair, then turns his attention to me.

I forgot the intensity of his stare. The green of his eyes is dotted with yellow flecks, his magic still irritated as it works to further heal him. It's not the vibrancy of his irises I'd forgotten, but the *heat*. My cheeks warm under his careful assessment, coloring to what I'm sure is a rosy glow, and my pulse quickens as if each second his gaze is fixed on mine is a tick of a broken pendulum, counting the erratic cadence of my pounding heart.

"Wren." He whispers my name in a voice so low that if it weren't for his intense focus on me, I'd think he murmured it to himself.

Something crashes at my feet, and I startle as the book I'd been holding lays partially open on the floor. I scoop it up and press it against my chest as if it were my personal shield. "How are you feeling?" The words rush from my mouth too quickly, my lips eager to distract from my blunder.

"We need to stop them. We can't let them make it back."

His voice is so low and void of emotion that it takes me a moment to realize what he means. He wants us to stop Dusaro and the surviving guards from retreating to the castle, to where his father will have to decide what to do about the public sighting of his son's transcendence. About their Black Art shifting into the very thing they've been instructed to hate, encouraged to slaughter without remorse.

I snap the book shut and lower it from my chest, remembering I don't need nor want a barrier between me and the man highest on my hit list. "They cannot intervene. The elves leaving the Vale would be an outright declaration of war."

Sin leans forward, his raised knees dropping out a little further. "The elves brought themselves into this the moment they agreed to house my manipulating mother and absolutely ruthless ex-girlfriend."

A mocking laugh falls from my lips. "I was never your girlfriend." I slide one of the cushioned chairs next to the foot of the bed and sit, crossing one leg over the other.

His eyes drop to my folded legs for a second before meeting mine again. "Close enough."

"Do Black Arts even have *girlfriends?*" I air-quote the word he used. "Shouldn't you be courting eligible ladies and sipping wine on balconies under star-filled skies?"

He shrugs one bare shoulder. "I seem to recall us spending a night on a balcony once."

Oh, that smug son-of-a—

One second I'm seated in the chair, the next I'm leaning over him in the bed, my fingers twisted in his long dark hair, pulling his head back to expose his pretty throat. "Do *not*..." I hiss the word, "*ever*... speak of what we did. You do not have the privilege. Not here, not while you're on my territory."

My other hand skirts around my waist until my fingers are brushing the hilt of my dagger, expecting, *waiting,* for him to make another sarcastic remark, but his jaw clenches hard, his eyebrows knitting together in the center of his forehead. He almost looks... troubled. Conflicted.

He'd look better with his throat painted crimson.

I release him and approach the small table with the white pitcher and cups, pouring myself some tea. Warming the beverage with magic, I bring it to my nose. It smells faintly of gardenias with a hint of something spicy, like mahogany. I take a sip, savoring the floral and woodsy notes on my tongue, before lowering it to the small saucer and sitting back down in the chair, not offering to pour Sin a cup.

"Oh sorry, did you want one?" I ask with feigned sweetness, arching an eyebrow to further my point.

He leans over the bed, stretching the white bandage wrapped around his trim waist, and pulls out a fat bottle with a slender neck from somewhere next to him. "I wore an iron bolt as a belt today, I think I'll stick with something a tad stronger." He pops the cork and takes a deep pull before moving into a more upright position against the wall, bottle still firmly grasped in his hand. Closing his eyes, he blows out a heavy sigh. "Why are you here, Wren?"

I fiddle with the handle of my cup, spinning it in a slow circle around the saucer. "I agreed to follow Sera. She was already established here in the Vale so it only made sense that—"

"No," he interrupts with a lazy shake of his head. "Why are you here, in my room?"

"Oh."

The beginnings of a smile tugs up one side of his mouth, but it's gone in an instant. "You have no reason to care if I am well, nor do I think you desire my company. I'd suspect you came to finish me off yourself, but seeing as you haven't pulled that knife you're hiding in your pants on me yet, I'm beginning to think that's not it either. So tell me, why has my little witch come to see me?"

"*Don't* call me that," I hiss. "And because regardless of how much I'd like to have seen you die today, you didn't. As long as you remain alive, you're leverage, so it's in my best interest to see that you're recovering. A dead man doesn't serve us well in war. Not yet, anyway."

Sin chortles softly to himself and raises the bottle to his mouth again, wrapping his lips around the neck and dumping a more than healthy amount of liquor down his gullet. He winces slightly when he lowers it again, the movement having stretched the area under his bandage, but he wipes the pain from his face a second later.

"Is that why you ordered me not to die? Admittedly I was a bit out of it, but I'm pretty certain you called me a fucking bastard in the same breath."

"You deserve to be called a lot worse."

"Aye." He tips the neck of the bottle in my direction as if making a toast.

His agreement surprises me. "You owe me an explanation."

"I owe you a lot of things, little witch."

I ignore the nickname. If whatever alcohol in that bottle is loosening his lips, I'll let it slide. "Give me that." I motion to the liquor.

Sin holds it out for me, and I take a swig, the liquid courage burning as it slides down my throat and settles in my chest. "When were you going to tell me that you were holding my sister in your dungeon while you played with me upstairs like some kind of pet?"

"I wasn't. I was going to release her after I sent you home."

He told me that before, but for some reason, I wanted to hear him say it again. To confirm that he really never intended to admit to my face what he had done. "Fucking coward," I spit, shaking my head.

Sin waves two fingers towards himself, and I toss him the bottle. After another deep pull, he says, "You didn't tell them."

"About us?"

"About me," he clarifies. "I may have been half dead, but I still saw the surprise in their faces when I shifted. And the shock on yours. You didn't tell them what I am."

"We had a deal," I remind him. "I would never jeopardize my family's safety. If that meant keeping a secret from them..." I shrug a shoulder, as if keeping that secret hadn't burdened me with guilt every day since.

"I suppose I thought your setting my castle on fire was your charming way of telling me to go fuck myself with that deal," he says, no amusement in his tone.

"Why would you do it? Reveal what you are in front of everyone—my family, your mother? It was foolish."

Incredulity raises one of his thick eyebrows, and he stares

down at me as he wraps his lips around the slender neck of the bottle again. The liquid sloshes as he lowers it, the bottle teetering back and forth in the loose grip of his thumb and forefinger. "It wasn't exactly a choice. Shifting forms was the only way I was breaking out of that iron."

"You didn't need to do it publicly!"

"*Fuck,* Wren. They tried to kill you with an arbalest! I saved your life."

I jump to my feet, the chair screeching backwards against the floor, and storm to his spot on the bed. "I never asked you to. I never asked for you to be in my life, and I certainly never wanted you in it."

Tension rolls off both of us and hovers like a dense fog in the room, thick enough to choke. I lean over him, the end of my braid falling over my shoulder and brushing his bare chest.

Sin tilts his head back to look up at me. We're too close, only a few inches between our faces, our bodies, and my every nerve sparks like flint. "You showed up at my castle, little witch. *Not* the other way around," he growls, the sound rumbling deep in his chest.

"You tried to take everything from me." The words come out so low, so restrained, my lips trembling as they exaggerate the shape of the letters. A hot tear drips onto my cheek, the salt burning my eyes as more pool there, the anger now physically spilling out of me. "But you couldn't even stop there. Now my entire family knows the secrets I've kept from them. Eldridge isn't talking to me." I sniff loudly, snot running in my nose as the tears fall harder now, my wrath and pain too immense to keep trapped inside any longer.

Sin's eyes bear into mine, burning straight through my tears and red-stained vision. "What was I supposed to do—let you die?" he asks, his jaw barely moving. Much angrier now.

I swallow hard and step away from him. My lungs swell as

air rushes back into them, the added distance between us a reminder to breathe. "It would have been a better fate than ever having to look at you another day."

I'm gone before he can respond, slamming the door shut behind me. When I reach the end of the corridor, I hear the sound of glass shattering from the room.

I smile to myself, knowing there was still half a bottle's liquor remaining when he smashed it. Now even the drink won't let him hide from what he's done.

CHAPTER 12

Dusaro and the surviving soldiers will reach Blackreach tonight, assuming they've been taking advantage of every daylight hour, and possibly some nighttime ones too. It's been two days since I confronted Sin in his glorified prison cell. Aeverie reported this morning that he's almost made a full recovery in that time. Apparently, an iron bolt is no match against a high priestess's healing magic.

Shame.

I twist my hand around the vegetable stalk, exposing the decaying leaves that haven't fallen off, and clip the brown free with my garden shears. Cosmina works quietly at my side, patting plant food made from fruit peels and other organic matter around the vegetation to encourage its growth.

I would have been content for him to live the rest of his days bound to that room by Aeverie's spell, but the high priestess has agreed to allow Sin to address the clan publicly tonight. Whether I wanted him to or not, Sin did shift, revealing his most guarded secret in front of an army of witnesses. He didn't hesitate. Not when it really mattered. Not when it came to protecting me.

Dusaro will be forced to address the Black Art's ancestry, as well as his disappearance, when he returns to Scarwood. There are too many surviving witnesses for him to ignore it, too many bodies to make murdering them himself a viable solution.

"Big changes are on the horizon," Cosmina says, now offering water to the freshly fed plants. She wears a large woven sun hat that shields half her face, though few rays make it through the canopy of interlocking branches for it to serve any real purpose other than fashion.

I grumble an agreement. "Baelliarah will be itching to invade when they hear their king has been slain. And if they learn Aegidale is fighting their own civil war, they'll be humping our coasts in a matter of weeks. But the kingdom brought this on themselves—to Hell with all of them, anyway."

She turns to face me, adjusting the wide brim of her tan hat to better see me. "This affects all of us, Wren. Your feelings towards him are valid, but Baelliarah will not take the time to decipher which parts of the isle are worthy of being attacked. This is not good for *any* of us."

I sit back on my knees, tossing my shears to the freshly turned soil and run a hand across my forehead. Only facets of sunlight may make it to the forest floor, but the summer air is still hot and thick with humidity. Sweat beads down my neck, my back, and I wonder how my sister isn't overheating in that ridiculous hat.

Feelings towards *him,* she said. Not the kingdom, not the guard. Him.

"Have you seen Eldridge?"

"Zorina said he's been in the woods, running off the steam. You know how he gets; don't take it personally."

"I lied to him. To all of you." I stand, trying to pat the dirt from my thighs but end up smearing the mud into the dark fabric of my leggings instead.

Cosmina mirrors me, plucking a large yellow flower from one of the plants and bringing it with her. "You had your reasons for keeping the Black Art's secret. Maybe ones I don't understand, but I know you, and if you thought it was necessary to keep, then I trust your judgment." She reaches towards me and pins the sunshine flower in my hair just behind my right ear, a smile equally as vibrant blooming on her face at the sight of me wearing it.

And with that easy grin, one birthed from something as simple as pinning a flower in her sister's soil-ridden hair, the last of my resolve fractures, and I burst into tears. "Can I... would you like to know the full story?"

My sister's grin fades into something somber, but she forces the corner of her lips up. "Tell me everything."

✳

The Sacred Ridge Mountains span the northern and eastern borders of the Vale. A cave nestled into the foot of the northern face, not far from the border, leads to a hollowed-out space in the sediment. *The Spirit's Nest*, the elves call it.

The heart of the cavern is occupied by a large pool of water, a naturally occurring hot spring that heats the interior of the mountain and provides shelter to the elves during the harsh winters. A series of caves tunnel through the subterranean shelter, some leading off to private dens for sleeping, and others to work spaces with desks for spinning and looms for weaving. Stairs carved into the rock spiral to several stories above our heads, each story wrapping around the central hot spring like a giant corkscrew. In addition to being used for shelter in the winter, the cavern serves as a prime meeting location, the interior large enough to house the Vale's inhabitants, and the hollow rock provides great acoustics for addressing everyone at once.

After I laid my broken pieces before her, Cosmina and I joined the rest of our family, aside from Eldridge, in the large chamber. Morrinne tucks Cosmina and me against either hip, wrapping an arm around each of our shoulders. Theon and Zorina sit cross-legged on one of the fur rugs still draped on the floor since winter. During the frigid months, each den is supplied with ample rugs, blankets, and down-filled pillows, Blythe told me. More hot springs, smaller ones, are dotted through the interconnected caves too, ideal for more intimate groups or families.

Cathal and Sera stand with their arms across their chests next to the dais. Crafted from the same gray rock as the mountain, faint glimmers of white and purple faceted crystals wink from deep in the sediment. The rest of the elves fill the heart of the cavern, some standing, some sitting in groups, and some even sinking into the springs. A sea of heads loom over the constructed walls from stories above me, thousands of eyes dark as polished obsidian staring towards the platform where Aeverie waits, hands clasped against her waist. Her flowing white robes fan out around the dais, the scalloped edges brushing the ends of the raised step, and her dark hair is piled high in a bun that mirrors the ringed shape of the cavern.

Her head snaps to the tunnel opening, and the room falls silent, only the rattling of chains filling the space as Vox leads the shackled Black Art to the dais. Sin's bronze cheeks have a slight glow to them again, his eyes brighter than they were two days ago, and he walks with no sign of strain, though I don't doubt he'd mask any pain in a room full of his enemies. He's wearing a dark blue tunic with a plunging neckline and fitted black pants that mold to his muscled thighs a little too snugly. The elves are lankier creatures, their muscles built for endurance rather than strength, and the size of their clothing reflects it.

If Sin is still weakened by traces of the iron in his bloodstream, he doesn't show it as he stops before Aeverie and meets her gaze atop the stone dais. Vox takes a few steps to the side, and Morrinne's hand gives my arm a slight squeeze. The smell of sulfur permeates my nose, and my stomach turns inside out, though I'm not confident the reaction is entirely due to the stench of the hot springs.

"You have my gratitude for healing me," Sin breaks the unnatural silence.

Aeverie doesn't react, not so much as a muscle feathers in her cheeks as she stares down her slender nose at him. "Your father tried to have one of ours assassinated," she finally responds, her arms straight as boards at her sides.

One of ours. In times of war, choosing a side is necessary for survival. Clinging to some in-between ground will only result in resentment from both sides, and neither will claim you when the time comes. The elves have claimed me, out of their loyalty for Sera and whatever promises she has made them in exchange for their shelter. Still, the phrasing tastes like ash on my tongue. I do not take well to being *possessed*.

Sin shuffles his feet, and the sound of clanging metal fills the room, the room that now feels far too stuffy despite its size. "As certain as I am that you would love to pin that on me, I had no knowledge of an attempt on Wren's life. I caught a glimpse of the crossbow in the bush, and as soon as I confirmed it was her they were lining up in their sights, I... I acted."

Aeverie slams the butt of her staff into the dais, the assortment of gems tethered with braided rope bouncing with the movement. "You are a wanderer," she states without question.

"Like your mother. And the rest of her comrades we are providing refuge for."

Sin doesn't move, but his posture stiffens, his shoulders pulling back a hair. "Yes." His voice is low, almost too low to hear if it weren't for the echo in the cavern.

"Singard," a soft voice calls from my left. Sera steps forward, away from Cathal's side, shaking her head slightly. "You could have told me."

He angles himself towards her, and even in profile, I see the fire in his eyes, stoked from hearing his mother's voice. His hands clench at his sides, and I swear I see a glimmer of claws at the ends of his knuckles. "You never asked," he growls. "Do not pretend to harbor affection for me now that you think this has given you an advantage. This has changed nothing."

"This has changed everything," Sera disagrees, willing steel into her tone. "The Black Art is blessed with both magics. Never before has that happened. Never before have we had that kind of *leverage*. I always knew you were special, Singard, but I never imagined this. How could I have?"

"Just because he can physically turn does not make him one of us, Sera," Cathal says from behind them both, gritting his teeth. "He doesn't have the spirit, and he never will."

Sin's attention whips to where Cathal stands, and a low growl rumbles from somewhere deep in his chest. "So courageous when I'm bound by wrist and foot. Last I saw you, you were drowning in your own piss and blood in my dungeon."

Cathal huffs out a dry laugh, but it is unamused. "Say what you want about me, Kilbreth, but I only ever hunt down my enemies. You're the one slaying your own kind."

"Cathal!" Sera throws up her hand, palm facing the Legion commander, but Sin takes a step towards him, the chain between his wrists flexing as he curls his hands.

"Such an eager mouth when you're hiding behind women

ten times stronger than you. First Wren, now her." Sin tsks softly to himself.

A wicked smile erupts across Cathal's face. "You're right about half of that, Kilbreth. I have been behind both of them, but I sure as hell wasn't hiding. And if you were there, you'd know it isn't me that has the eager mouth. I just can't decide whose lips I like better around my cock—the witch's, or your *mother's.*"

Goddess above.

Well, at least one good thing has come from this meeting. If Sin somehow negotiates his freedom, Cathal is a dead man. Because despite the conflict between Sin and me, something tells me *no one*—and especially not Cathal—makes a comment like that to him and gets away unscathed.

Sin runs his tongue across the front of his teeth, the movement almost feral, and his jaw clenches as he swallows the wrath I have no doubt is requiring all of his self-control to not unleash. His fingers curl and uncurl at his sides, and this time, I'm certain I spot claws protruding from his last knuckles.

Oh, he's pissed. Cathal, you stupid motherfucker.

I smile to myself at the internal pun.

Sera turns on her heels and storms back to where Cathal stands, still wearing that lazy grin. He raises both his hands as if to placate her. "Come now, Seraphine, he should at least *know* about—"

She slaps him across the face. Cathal's cheek instantly reddens where she struck him, and his lips pull back in a snarl, but she promptly silences him with a look I can't see.

Aeverie slams her staff into the dais three times. "Enough of this nonsense." The words slither off her tongue, her presence bloating the cavern air like a cobra's swollen belly. "The Black Art and I have more pressing matters to discuss."

Sin angles himself back to the high priestess and dips his

head. She waves a delicate hand, prompting him to plead his case.

"My father and my men will return to Scarwood tonight. It is likely Lord Kilbreth will delay a public address, but he won't be able to for long. Too many guards witnessed my shifting. Rumor will spread, and my father will address it before too many hear from mouths that are not his own.

"It is custom for the Black Hand to assume the duties of the Art in the event they become ill, killed, or deemed unfit to rule. Ileana is fair, but she lacks experience in these kinds of dealings and will resort to my father's judgment to guide her decisions. And if you know Lord Kilbreth, you know he will order every single soldier to the Vale immediately, torches in hand. He will not hesitate to burn every tree in this forest, and murder every man, woman, and child."

Sin pauses, allowing his words to sink in. Aeverie's expression remains firm, except for the slight rolling of her bottom lip between her teeth. "It was the kingdom that instigated that attack," she reminds him.

"That will not matter to them. You declared war when you captured the Black Art. Coming to negotiate was merely an attempt to secure my freedom easily, but have no doubt, they would have attacked as soon as I was across the boundary had you released me. My father has no interest in negotiating with *elves,*" he growls the word, "or shifters, and therefore, Ileana will not either. It was foolish to ever think Dusaro Kilbreth would enter into a bargain with you, *not* that you've made it clear why you are helping the transcendents in the first place."

The high priestess pins one hand behind her back and using her staff as a walking stick, begins to pace the dais. "You are much younger than I, Singard Kilbreth, but this land belonged to elves far before you or your father or his father were ever born. When your kind discovered this isle, we were content to keep to the western half, and we resided there peacefully for centuries. It wasn't until *Ephraim Whytworthe's,*" she hisses the name, "paranoia became too much that he scorched our lands and shooed us into the Vale, like we were some kind of diseased species needing to be locked in a cage.

"Ironic to me," she muses, pressing her thin lips together as she approaches the edge of the platform, "that you consider us the ones to have antagonized by allying with the wanderers whom you also oppressed with your arrogant, entitled thinking, when it was your Black Art that trapped us here." Aeverie leans forward, extending the bottom half of her staff to tilt Sin's chin upward, forcing him to meet her gaze. "So yes, *Singard Kilbreth,* when your mother sought a base to house her growing army of wanderers, we agreed. Because no one deserves to have what is rightfully theirs stripped away from them simply because they are outnumbered and lack the coin to acquire more resources. For decades, Ephraim and your father refused to hear our negotiations, so the time has come we will ask no longer. We will simply take, like we have done with you."

Sin lifts his chin from the staff, and Aeverie returns it to her side, the crystals swaying from their ropes. "Tell me, Madam Priestess, how you plan on reclaiming the land you so passionately believe belongs to you when your home is reduced to ash, and the smoke too dense to make anywhere within miles and miles inhabitable?"

"That's where you come into the picture, Black Art," she responds, drawing out the last consonant. "I don't think Lord Kilbreth will be in favor of smoking us out, so long as it is your lungs he will also fill with smoke and ash."

I slip out of Morrinne's arm and take a few steps to my right for a better view of Sin's profile. His tongue slips out to slowly lick his bottom lip, and he shakes his head, a slight smile on his mouth, but it is void of amusement. "You must think highly of my father, Priestess, if you believe he would allow something so insignificant to stand in the way of preserving his power. My father hates transcendents—wanderers, as you call them—more than anything in this life. He has carried the weight of my secret for many years. It will be a relief for him to be rid of such a burden."

"I have been around plenty long enough to know when I am about to hear a proposal. What do you intend to suggest, Singard Kilbreth?" Aeverie plants her staff in front of her and leans forward, draping her forearms across the top of it.

"Your distaste for my father and kingdom is warranted, but I am the Black Art. Even now in the depths of this cavern, the kingdom's armies respond to *me*. They act to protect me and me alone. When my father returns, he will persuade Ileana to lead our army here, and likely feed her half-truths so she believes I am being kept elsewhere. I don't expect you to trust me, Priestess, but you should at least have the sense to know my father is ruthless and nothing will stand in his path for revenge. Even me," he adds, his voice a dark hum in the cavern.

Aeverie titters, the dry laughter stale, and her blanched eyes pull down at the corners. "I am impressed by the authenticity in your voice, Singard Kilbreth, but I have endured a great many years and become wise to the deceptions of mortal men."

"He's telling the truth," Sera calls from her place by Cathal, though she's a few feet farther from him than she was before. "Remember that I am still technically married to the man. I spent many years at Dusaro's side and witnessed his cruelty firsthand. Protecting our son is not enough for him. It never has been."

A low growl rumbles deep in Sin's chest, but he otherwise ignores his mother's statement. "Forgive me, High Priestess, but I have endured enough years myself to know I mustn't allow my pride to be the means to my end. You have young to protect. If you are truly interested in preserving your race, I suggest you begin with protecting the ones already here. Otherwise, your kind will soon be extinct, and this will all be a moot point anyway."

Aeverie thumps the butt of her staff against the hard sediment at her feet. "I will not be fearmongered into standing down and allowing the kingdom to continue their oppressive, manic dictatorship! The time to take our place has come, as the Ancients have always predicted."

"Your Ancients cannot protect you against kingdom steel!" Sin bellows, his calm mask slipping against Aeverie's stubbornness. "I mean no disrespect towards your faith, Priestess, but this is not a war that can be won from the whispers of ghosts and shadows."

Vox clears his throat loudly and closes the distance between himself and Aeverie, but angles his body so his back isn't completely turned to Sin. Even shackled by wrist and ankle, with enough motivation, Sin's goddess-blessed magic allows him to shift, even under iron's negation. And iron would do nothing to stop the Black Art from using his weight to wrap his shackled hands around the commander's throat. Not that he'd get far with the high priestess standing but a few feet away from them.

"Forgive me, Madam Priestess," Vox intercedes, "but I think it too grave a risk to remain here and hope Dusaro or the Hand agrees to compromise. They never have before, and I am inclined to believe the Black Art when he says his father does not harbor enough affection to care if he is lost in the form of collateral damage. Some may argue it would be seen as an honorable death, dying for the greater cause."

"The greater cause being *burning our home*," Aeverie supplies, her white eyes slitting.

Sin nods, his jaw clenched tight and his fingers curled into his palms, though it appears he has retracted his claws. "Ileana will act in my absence, but I need to speak with her and let her know what is going on. To tell her to stand down. She'll listen to me, but only to me."

Aeverie's eyes round, and she tsks sharply. "What do you mean to suggest?"

"I need to meet with her."

"Nonsense. We'll send a messenger and—"

"No," Sin cuts her off. "She won't believe anything that doesn't come from me directly. She's smart; she'll assume it's a trap, as she would be wise to do. This will only work if I meet with her face-to-face."

Vox spins to face Sin, his hand reaching to brush the hilt of the weapon at his waist instinctively. "Do you think that low of us elves to believe we are incapable of common sense? That we would allow you to return to Scarwood that easily?"

Sin shakes his head. "I never said I would have to return alone. There is a signal shared exclusively between the Art and Hand, should one find themselves in peril and need to alert the other. There is an old church just over the bridge in the outskirts of Black-reach. It's been abandoned for years since a fire gutted it, but it hasn't been high on our list of reconstruction efforts. If I light the lantern in the bell tower, I'm certain she'll come. With my absence, she'll be looking for the signal every night. It is part of her duties."

"And bring the entire army with her," Vox sneers.

"No army—far too risky. She will come alone. I give you my word."

I roll my eyes. As if the Black Art's *word* carries any weight in a room—well, cavern—filled with his enemies.

"I do not expect you to trust me, but if you wish to live to see another moon cycle, this is your only choice."

"You wish to take one of our boats?" Aeverie asks, raising a thinning dark brow.

"No. We will need to travel by horse. With Varil's death, there will be a swarm of guards posted at the docks, and our ships will be on constant patrol expecting Baelliarah troops. We will need to use that distraction to sneak in through the city's gates. By all means, send an escort with me, but it will have to be small. The more bodies, the more likely we get caught."

"How convenient for him," Cathal huffs.

Sera shoots him a sideways glare before turning her attention to Aeverie. "I'll go with him," she volunteers.

A deep growl cuts her off, and it takes me a moment to realize that sound is coming from Sin's chest. "Not her," he bites out, letting his eyes rake over his mother. "Anyone but her."

"I'll go," a raspy voice says from the tunnel's entrance. A pale figure steps out of the cave, and I grit my teeth as Alistair comes into view. He's once again dressed in a pressed black jacket and formal pants, and I roll my eyes at the ridiculously inappropriate attire.

We're in a cave for Goddess's sake.

Alistair saunters farther into the cavern, shoving his hands deep into his trouser pockets. "No offense to the rest of you, but I think this is a job best suited to a bloodwitch. Someone the almighty Black Art can't push around."

Sin shoots him a smile that's all teeth but doesn't object. "Be my guest."

"We should send another so he's outnumbered," Vox advises the priestess. "I would offer, but it is best I am here in case Lord Kilbreth returns with more."

Don't do it, Wren. Keep your mouth shut.

"I'll go too," I say, ignoring the furious whispers of Morrinne and my sisters and stepping forward.

Fuck me.

Alistair's brown eyes sweep to find me in the crowd and brighten as soon as they find the source of my voice. He claps his hands and rubs his palms together. "Oh, this is shaping up to be quite the adventure after all. I've only ever encountered one of our kind before and that was a long time ago. And never a female," he adds, cocking his head to the side and flashing those white teeth sharpened to unnatural points.

"Wren," Cosmina speaks up louder from behind me.

I angle my head so my jaw is parallel to my shoulder, but I can't meet her eyes. Not right now. "I have to go," I murmur, loud enough for only my sisters and family to hear before turning to capture Sin's burning stare with my own. "I will not risk *His Grace* fooling us with any of his tricks and slipping away. The only way he is getting away from us is if I slit his throat and burn him to ash before we return."

Alistair releases a low chuckle and licks his full lips. "I can help with that, princess."

"Bite me," I spit in his direction, not forgetting the way he savagely murdered every guard in the receiving center without a second's hesitation.

"Oh, I can help with that too."

Sin bares his teeth in a low hiss, but I refuse to look at him again, to even acknowledge I heard him at all. What I do with other men is none of his concern. In fact, maybe I need to make that point *very* clear during this trip.

"You should stay," Sin rasps in a graveled voice.

His words shatter the self-control I was using to not look at him, and I burrow my eyes into his, willing heat and rage into them and hoping it's potent enough to scorch him. "I'm going," I say slowly, accentuating each syllable.

"Not without me, you're not."

I whip around at the familiar voice and find Eldridge stepping out from a shadowed corner. My heart threatens to swell too large for my chest, and I resist the urge to run to him, to tell him how sorry I am. How much his friendship means to me, and that I hate myself for keeping those secrets from him.

Eldridge inhales and puffs out his chest, his massive height and body too large for such a crowded space. "If Wren's going, you'll have to make room for one more."

CHAPTER 13

Saying goodbye to my family was about as easy as I expected it to be—which was not easy at all. My sisters tried convincing me all last night to change my mind, but I think they both knew their attempts were fruitless. Morrinne, on the other hand, called me a *stubborn young thing*, but the crushing hug she gave me immediately following the scolding made it seem more like a compliment than anything. And when she buried her hand in my hair and pecked my forehead with a motherly kiss, she told me how proud she was. Her *little warrior,* she called me that time.

In the morning, I meet Eldridge in front of our house and find him stretching his burly arms above his head and leaning to the side.

"Did all that snoring last night throw your back out, old man?" I tease, slinging the leather strap of my saddle bag over one arm. His rhythmic breathing has always been comforting to me, a reminder that even on the nights I feel the loneliest, I am never truly alone. But I don't dare tell him that, or his head would grow too large to fit through another doorway ever again.

He straightens and buries an elbow into my ribs. "As a matter of fact, I did. And if you keep talking like that, I'll have to throw your back out too." Faster than I can react, he slips behind and tackles me. He knocks me forward but bands an arm around my waist to keep me from crashing face-first into the ground. And when the fingers clutching my side begin to tickle, I can't help the burst of laughter that booms out of me, even as I swat his hands and demand he release me.

I was eager to explain myself after leaving the cavern, to tell him why I felt obligated to keep the Black Art's secret. But regardless of my desire—no, my *need*—to keep my family safe, Eldridge would have forgiven me anyway. As gruff and brutish as he may appear on the outside, his heart is as soft as the peeling bark of winter's trees.

At least, it always has been towards me.

Eldridge slips his other arm underneath me and tickles the spot just beneath my armpit, my attempts to displace him with my weight failing to knock him back even an inch. "Come now, Wren, is this all the fight you have?" he teases, his arms like steel holding me against his front.

Someone loudly clears their throat behind us, and I jerk my head up to see Alistair and Sin approaching on two bridled steeds. The sound came from Alistair, who ditched his formal wear for a deep gray tunic and dark riding pants, his wavy brown hair freshly swept forward with the help of a holding agent, a few pieces curled down around his left eye. Next to him, mounted on a horse a shade darker than Alistair's light brown one, the Black Art's eyes lock onto where Eldridge's sun-kissed hands grip my sides.

"While I'm not one to discourage any from indulging in their pleasures, may I suggest you two continue this... *romping*... once we make camp tonight," Alistair says with a devious spark in his eyes and a crooked smirk.

I bring my hands down on top of Eldridge's and smack the backs of them. "You heard him—stop romping me."

Eldridge reluctantly uncurls his arms from around me, and I step out of his reach. I notice Sin's stare is still trained on my friend, tracking him as if Eldridge were a threat looming too close to his territory. Except in this case, *I'm* the territory.

I roll my eyes to no one in particular.

Oh, please.

"Ready your horses. Blackreach is a three-day journey, and that's if we hurry. And we *will* be hurrying," Sin says, not lifting his gaze from Eldridge.

"Why isn't he still chained? I thought we were escorting him, as in, throwing him on the back of a horse kind of thing," Eldridge asks.

"Make no mistake in thinking the journey we're about to make is not without great risk. If we are spotted, my men will be on us immediately, and they will not wait for an order before doing everything they can to put each of you down. In the event we find ourselves in that situation, or one similar, you're not going to want me *hindered*," Sin growls the last word, as if to emphasize that even the iron is merely an irritating obstacle to him, not a complete barrier between the threat he poses and us.

Alistair scoffs and stares off pointedly, as if insulted by the thought of anyone being able to *put him down.*

"You imprisoned my pack sister, then used Wren to do your bidding as your personal slave. I'd like to do a lot more than *hinder* you," Eldridge snarls, leaning towards the Black Art, his head dipping slightly. A habit I've noticed he's picked up from spending so much time in his animal form.

I move to Eldridge's side and place a hand on his forearm, taking note of how Sin's jaw clenches harder when I do. "We both would, but we're wasting time standing out here arguing. And if I have to listen to the three of you bickering, then none of this will matter anyway because I'll kill all of you myself before we ever make it to the godsdamned church."

Alistair curls his fingers into mock claws and swipes the air, making the sound of a pissed-off cat. "You heard the princess—time to put your cocks away, boys. We have grown-up business to attend to now."

I motion over my shoulder with my chin. "Let's ready our horses," I say to Eldridge, giving his arm a slight squeeze before turning my back on all of them. But not before I glimpse the burning indignation flaming in Sin's green irises, as if the forest itself caught fire.

I head towards where the horses are tethered to the hitching post, blowing out a long breath. *This is going to be the longest week of my life.* Eldridge's heavy footfalls sound behind me, and with my face hidden from view, I can't help but smile knowing how much my hot-tempered friend is sure to irritate Sin on our journey.

In fact, I hope he drives him fucking mad.

✦

Correction: this has been the longest *day* of my life, but not for the reasons I was expecting. Eldridge and Sin exchanged several more remarks, all of which Alistair was all too eager to encourage, but they've been mostly quiet for the past few hours. It isn't the tension between the men that has my shoulders in knots and my stomach threatening to dispel its contents.

It's *him.*

Being this close to the Black Art—so close I can *taste* his peppery steel scent in the air—has me fighting back tears for reasons I don't understand. Every fiber of my being wants to steer my horse into his, tackle him to the ground, and bleed his source from his body until he aches as much as I do. In the months I spent in the Vale, my hurt quickly shifted into wrath. My thoughts consumed with revenge, dreaming up ways I could make Sin suffer as he did to me. But now that he's finally within reach of my blade, that fury has deepened into something much darker, and infinitely more sorrowful.

As much as I don't want to acknowledge the effect his proximity has on me, how vulnerable his presence makes me feel—I can't deny that merely the sight of him pangs my chest like someone taking a hammer to the brittle cage shielding my heart.

The Black Art didn't just wrong me.

He *hurt* me.

And somehow that is far worse.

The sun provides us with light well into the evening hours, but when the buttery glow dims to a raging inferno, we make camp. We clung to the outskirts of Lostgarde and Baregrove, not wanting to chance any kingdom guards that may be on patrol spotting Sin, especially with the lack of tree cover in the barren cities. When we cleared them, we dove into the forest at the base of The Red Tops, the verdant canopy bright against the vermillion-tinged rock of the mountain range.

The four of us dismount at the first patch of forest floor we find that is mostly barren of boulders and exposed roots and lay out our bedrolls.

"The skies are clear so we needn't craft shelter to get through the night," Sin says, rummaging through some of the contents of his saddle bag and pulling out a waterskin.

Eldridge sifts through his own bag and pulls out a container of dried, salted venison and a few oat balls. "I wouldn't be crafting anything before we eat anyway. I'm fucking starving."

He hands me a portion of the food he gathered, and we sit down on his bedroll. I don't hesitate to dive in, eager to satisfy the roaring beast in my belly with the thick strips of meat and sticky oats that cling to my ribs and fill me with a sense of renewed fullness.

Alistair raises his hands above his head and leans at the waist in one direction, then the other. "Have anything to drink in that bag?" he asks me, motioning to my satchel with his chin.

I hold up my leather receptacle and shake it, sloshing the contents. "I brought a waterskin, same as you."

He laughs softly and shakes his head, making those loose curls fall even further into his left eye. "Not the kind of drink I was referring to. Have anything... *sweeter*?" The wink he shoots me sends warmth to my cheeks, not because of his light flirting, but because of his insinuation.

"I did not bring blood if that's what you're asking. Unlike you, I'm not a deranged animal."

Sin's hunkered down on his own makeshift bed, sharpening his dagger with a whetstone, but his expression is too intense for him to be focused on the activity alone.

The other bloodwitch walks to where Eldridge and I rest and squats before me so his eyes are almost at my level. "We're all animals, princess, but those like you and I... we're different. Predators." He emphasizes his point by flashing a smile that is nothing shy of *predatory*.

"Did you really file your teeth into points to try to intimidate people?" I ask, biting off a chunk of the meat and zeroing in on those jagged canines.

Alistair's body blocks most of my view, but I don't miss the movement behind him. Sin's watching us. Intently. Alistair rocks on his heels and licks his lips, and out of my periphery, I notice Eldridge's posture stiffening. "It's always worked for me before."

I shrug my shoulders in exaggerated indifference. "Seems to me you're overcompensating for something." Eldridge snorts, and I shoot him a sideways grin before turning my attention back to the male bloodwitch. "Look, I'm not judging, we all have our talents. For some of us, those talents just run a bit... *deeper*."

Alistair scoffs, but the suddenly more serious expression on his face isn't one of anger. He leans farther forward, and Eldridge inches closer to us as he does. In a husky voice, he rasps, "Make your fun, but only one of us has ever experienced true pleasure, princess."

Sin rises to his feet and begins crossing the camp towards us, but I don't tear my eyes away from Alistair's.

I sneer and shake my head. "Do not speak to me on matters you know nothing about. That includes my *pleasures*."

He cups my jaw with his hand and trails his thumb over the sensitive skin of my lips. "Have you ever drank from someone while you fucked them? Because I have... many, many times and gods," he grips my bottom lip harder, "it is fucking divine. I can only imagine how sweet *you* taste, darling bloodwitch."

I bite down, catching his thumb between my perfectly flattened teeth. He bleeds into my mouth, coating my tongue with a mix of sweet and sour like sugar-dusted cranberries. Alistair swears but doesn't rip his hand away. Instead, his eyes glaze over and fixate where my teeth graze his digit.

I spit his finger out and move to shove him away, but before my hands reach his chest, he stumbles backwards. Sin stands behind him, looking like a towering shadow from one of my many nightmares, one hand firmly grasped around his arm. Alistair snarls and tries to shake Sin off, but his grip only tightens.

"Get your hand off me," he says slowly, enunciating each word through clenched teeth.

"Keep your hands off her," Sin warns, his voice low and guttural. Something about the way he says it births a fire deep in my gut, betraying my thoughts to cut off both their arms and beat them to death with them.

Alistair's eyes flicker between Sin's hand and his menacing stare. The bloodwitch's fingers curl into his palms and the tang of magic grazes my tongue, just as the Black Art gives a subtle shake of his head. At this hour, I barely make out the soft blue aura around Sin, but judging from the rustic taste in my mouth, Alistair tried burning him with magic, an attack Sin anticipated and met with a ward.

I jump to my feet and shove a finger into Alistair's lanky chest. "I watched you slaughter every single person in that receiving center like they were toys for you to play with. Do not ever insinuate that you and I are anything alike. And *you*," I spin on my heel and drive that same finger into Sin's much harder chest and stalk towards him, forcing him to break his hold on Alistair. I shake my head slowly, clenching my teeth to hold in the slew of vulgar things I'd like to call him. "You have no right to involve yourself in anything that I do. You made it perfectly clear you care very little about my well-being when you imprisoned my sister, manipulated me into doing your bidding, and then lied to me about all of it. What I do, and *who* I do, is none of your concern. Do. Not. Make that mistake again."

A muscle feathers along Sin's jaw as he stares down at me, his mouth twitching slightly as if grinding his teeth together to hold in his own words. A hand presses against the small of my back, and I turn to see Eldridge looming behind me, his attention fixed on both of the assholes in front of us. I allow him to steer me away, and I reach for the waterskin I left on his bedroll. Taking a deep pull, I swish the liquid around and spit out the bloody water, ridding my mouth of all taste of Alistair.

"I'm tired, so all of you kindly shut the fuck up so I can get some sleep," I grumble.

Eldridge leans in so his lips are near my ear and whispers in a voice only for me. "Did he taste as horrible as he smells?" He wrinkles his nose, and I can't resist the curling of my lips in response.

I wipe my mouth with the back of my hand. "Worse."

CHAPTER 14

The pearly glow of the moon bathes the four of us in silver. A quick look around confirms none of the others have roused yet. Eldridge is snoring flat on his stomach, Alistair still as stone on his back, and Sin asleep on his side facing the rest of us.

I throw off the light blanket I packed, and careful not to make a sound, gather the soap and few toiletries I brought. Might as well use the alone time to get a head start preparing for another achingly long ride. I shove my feet into my black boots and slip away from the camp, heading for the nearby river we intentionally stayed close to. My thighs burn in protest as I walk through the woods, the full day of riding yesterday leaving my legs and back sore.

The river is calm and mostly quiet, aside from the trilling of nighttime insects and the sound of water cresting the pebbled banks. In this sun-abandoned hour, the soft roar is peaceful. Serene. Especially in contrast to the turmoil of the past few days.

Bending over, I tug off my boots and disrobe before wading in, sighing deeply as the algid water gets my blood pumping, and my eyes become less heavy despite the lack of sleep. I had been too consumed with thoughts of what today would bring to rest for more than a few hours, and even then, the sleep was fitful as I wrestled with dreams of monsters and men alike.

I don't know why I insisted on accompanying Alistair and Sin to the capital city. It is dangerous, and under no circumstances do I put it beneath the Black Art to be leading us into a trap. The plan he fed the high priestess of him and Ileana sharing some secret signal could be just a ruse for him to draw the entire kingdom to where Eldridge, Alistair, and I will be, where they would outnumber us thousands to one.

Not that I care much of what happens to the bloodwitch who has chosen to indulge in his violent cravings rather than resist them.

When I fled Scarwood, I thought I was joining an initiative determined to destroy the Black Art once and for all. And yet here I am, rushing to escort him so he may convene with his Hand, convince her not to attack the elves, and therefore save his own neck. I should be trying to convince the others to kill him now, before there is even a chance Sin can escape. Before he can flee back to the castle and declare war himself, before he can ignite every tree in the Vale, before he can plunge a dagger deep into my back.

No. *Never again.*

I grit my teeth as I splash water onto my neck and shoulders, lathering the soap I brought onto my arms and allowing the river to cleanse my skin. I bury my fingers in my hair, scrubbing my head with more of the soap, my fingernails biting into my scalp with a little too much force.

I won't be so blind this time.

I am not the same girl I was when I left. That Wren was still fanning her feathers, spreading her wings and teetering on the edge of the branch, frightful of taking that first leap. Worried she would step off and her wings would fail, sending her tumbling to an untimely demise.

Not anymore.

This Wren has learned she is capable of so much more than merely flapping her wings and treading air so she does not plummet to her death.

No. This Wren can *soar*.

Dunking my head under the water, I gather my hair and scrub it clean before snapping upright, my wet hair smacking against my back. With a final splash of water on my face, I turn towards the bank, my eyes scanning the grassy ledge where I left my night shirt and leggings.

What the—

I'm certain I left them draped over that rock, but the worn stone beams back at me with not so much as a scrap of fabric littering its surface. Had an animal come by and snagged them when my back was turned, perhaps smelling hints of the soap I had carried with me and mistaking it for food?

I wade towards the ledge, my eyes still scanning for my clothes. Perhaps a breeze blew them farther into the trees.

"Looking for something?" a low voice asks from somewhere in the dark expanse of the woods.

Fuck. Me.

I bare my teeth in instinct, recognizing that deep voice all too well. "I thought you were asleep."

Sin emerges from the darkness, looking like a shadow himself, and leans against one of the thick-barked trees, crossing his arms across his chest and planting one foot on the trunk behind him. "Perhaps I heard you sneak off." He shrugs a shoulder. "Or maybe..." his eyes burn into mine, even the shadows unable to hide the intensity of his irises shining with vicious, wicked beauty, "I haven't been able to stop staring at you all night and knew the exact moment you woke and slipped out of camp."

I blow out a sharp sigh and cant my head to the side, my

arms instinctively crossing over my chest even though I'm still deep enough in the river that the water obscures my breasts from his view. "It wasn't enough for you to steal months of my sister's life from her, you had to steal my clothing too?"

The grin disappears from his face, his posturing suddenly more tense than it was a moment ago. "I wanted to talk to you. You weren't going to listen to me on your own, so I had to force you to pause. Unless you despise my company so much you'd rather walk back to camp naked than listen to me." The corner of his lip raises slightly, but the heat in his eyes does nothing to warm the skin that is further chilling each minute I remain undressed at this sunless hour.

"I would rather pluck my eyes out of my head than listen to what you have to say. Now. Give. Me. My. Clothes."

Sin cocks his head to the side, a challenge. "No."

"You have a lot of fucking nerve trying to trap me in whatever this is," I motion first to my disrobed self, then to where he stands guarding my clothing, "after everything you've done to me."

His fingers drum on his arms, and he arches an eyebrow. "And you don't? Insisting on coming along with us? You shouldn't be here, Wren." Angrier now.

My breath hitches, his audacity snatching the words from my mouth for a moment. I capture my bottom lip between my teeth and shake my head slowly, exaggerating my dark amusement. "Afraid I'll see through your scheme to lead us all into a trap? Ruin your plan to turn on us and the elves the *second* you have the opportunity?"

The faint moonlight shining on his face highlights the tightening of his jaw as he says slowly, "I'm not leading you into a trap, but that doesn't change that it's dangerous to be out here with us."

"Right, you prefer to fuck people before you betray them,

how could I forget? Haven't had time to bed all the elves yet, have—"

"I was wrong to do what I did," he interjects. "But I have never claimed to be *good,* Wren. Whatever version of me you wanted to see, that is on you, not me."

"Forgive me for thinking you had a heart buried somewhere. That perhaps you were wronged so deeply by those you cared about, those you loved, that it convinced you that you were something you aren't. Clearly, I was wrong."

His fingers stop drumming. "I never asked you to *fix* me. At least I never tried to change you. I saw all of you—the parts that were tender and sweet, and the parts that were ruthless. And I wanted all of it. I wanted all of *you.*"

"How dare you say that to me when you did what you did? You didn't have to betray me, Singard. You. Chose. To betray me. And I am not so naïve to believe you're not itching to do it again. To burn down the entire Vale while you're at it."

He lunges off the tree, closing the distance between us in measured steps. "The entire reason I left with you three was to ensure that does not happen. I will do everything I can to make sure no one touches the Vale."

"It houses your enemies—why *wouldn't* you want to burn it down?"

His face hardens into a mask of fury, and his lips pull back just enough to reveal teeth when he growls, "Because *you* are in the Vale. And Goddess help whoever tries touching it."

Somehow I don't think he's referring to just the Vale anymore.

"I knew when you left that night, whatever we had was damaged beyond repair. I hurt you, and I cannot expect your forgiveness, nor will I ask for it. But that does not mean I am willing—that I am *capable*—of watching others try to harm or touch what once was mine."

Tears sting my eyes, his words threatening to open the valve of emotions I've kept locked up tight, but I will it to hold strong. "I was never y—"

My words halt as Sin begins unfastening the buttons of his black shirt, the fabric falling open to reveal his muscular chest, inch by inch. "What in the gods' names are you doing?"

"You're not the only one that needs to wash up." He shrugs out of his shirt, dropping it next to his feet.

I stare at him in disbelief. He can't be serious. Fire blazes in my chest. "You are *not* getting in here with me."

He waves his hand. "By all means, get out." The smirk he flashes is pure wicked, through and through.

His words fan the flames in my chest, setting it ablaze as wrath claws its way up my throat with white-hot pokers. I set my jaw and wade towards the bank. "Fine. I will." I hold his stare as I step out of the river, the frigid water coating my skin in a sheet of ice, and my nipples hardening in response. Sin's narrow eyes round for a second before he promptly wipes the surprise from his face. His tongue clicks against the roof of his mouth, and he drags it across the front of his teeth.

I shove my shoulder into his chest as I brush past him, but it does little more than sway his body an inch. I don't make it a step past him before a hand vices around my bicep, pulling me to a halt. My lips part, and a deep huff slips through as I glare at that hand with enough venom to stop his heart.

If only.

"I'll give you your clothes," Sin concedes, his tone clipped.

"Keep them," I say, yanking my arm out of his grasp, knowing damn well he could have kept me pinned there if he really wanted to.

"You're not walking back to camp naked. *Wren*," he growls my name. "Your clothes are behind the tree. Put them on."

I feign concentration, pursing my lips and cocking my

head. "No, no—finders, keepers and all that, right? Plus, I don't think Eldridge or Alistair will mind the view, so really, what's the harm?"

Sin snarls in what is unmistakably a warning. "I will pin you down and dress you myself before I let you walk back there like this." His eyes dip to my chest for a fleeting second before gluing back to my face where wet strands of hair cling to my cheeks.

He reaches for me again, but I dip around him, snatching his button-down shirt from the ground. Sin's eyes darken, but he makes no move to stop me as I slip my arms through it and fasten the lower few buttons, the hem brushing my mid thighs. I smile with forced sweetness. "I suggest you keep your pants close, or you might just find yourself without them when you get out."

I turn my back on him and head back to camp, clad only in his shirt. When I'm out of view, I inhale deeply, his familiar scent of sword oil cut with a peppery sweetness overwhelming me with more feelings than I could possibly know how to sort through.

CHAPTER 15

The others are still asleep when I return to camp. I use the silence to gather my thoughts, brushing and braiding my hair while I do. The heat in my chest has ebbed, leaving confusion in its wake.

I never asked you to fix me, Sin had said. I knew what he had endured, had foolishly believed that underneath his traumas and learnt wickedness, his heart was... not good, but salvageable. He told me not to trust him. He *told* me. And I ignored it all, averting my eyes from the truth because my heart longed to thrum to a different tune. A heinous, hateful lullaby.

I reach for my bag, my hand accidentally connecting with my waterskin. It thumps to the ground, and Eldridge stirs, his eyes fluttering open.

I wince. "Sorry!"

Eldridge rubs a hand down his face before dropping it and sitting upright. "We leaving?"

"Soon. I just washed in the river. You should probably do the same," I say, pinching my nose and waving my other hand in front of it.

He shoots me a vulgar gesture and takes a deep pull of his own waterskin, his eyes narrowing over the top of it. Pulling it away, he says, "What are you wearing?"

Heat rushes to my face before I can will it away, and I turn my head to the side to try and mask the involuntary reaction. "I misplaced my clothes at the river. I had to borrow someone else's," I rush to say. *Not a lie, but...*

Eldridge runs a hand down his long, braided beard. "Is that —is that Singard's shirt?"

"Yes, I guess, but I don't care what I'm wearing so long as it's clean. Which this," I say, pulling a pinch of the fabric away from me and inhaling, ignoring the flutter in my belly that Sin's scent involuntarily instills in me, "is not. Go wash so I can change."

He eyes me warily for a moment but gathers his bathing supplies and a clean set of clothes in his hands. The noise rouses Alistair from his slumber, and he slowly sits up, wiping the sleep from his eyes.

"I'll have food waiting for you when you get back," I tell him.

"Make it quick, I want us leaving before the sun crests."

I whip around at the sound of Sin's voice and cross my arms as he nears camp. He's dressed only in his black pants, his long, wet hair clinging to his bare chest. Eldridge grumbles in response and mutters something too low for me to hear, but the look Sin shoots his way tells me it was colorful. The Black Art angles himself towards me, and I mirror without thinking. It's then I notice he's carrying a wad of something in one of his hands, which he tosses at me.

I catch the few clumps of fabric and the anger that dulled earlier rears its head again as I recognize my clothing.

"I thought you might want these back," Sin says, a facetious smirk on his lips.

My fingers twist into the clothing, clenching them against my body. Eldridge releases a low growl, and when I force myself to look at him, accusation is heavy in his storm-colored eyes.

"Misplaced them?" he asks, echoing what I had told him earlier. Behind him, Alistair lets out a low whistle, the tune suggesting an alternate reason for the Black Art's and my swapped clothing.

"He took them while I was washing."

My defense does nothing to soften Eldridge's stance, and he thrusts a finger towards Sin. "Why were you bathing with him?"

His tone has my hand finding my hip, and I hitch my weight to the side. "I wasn't! I didn't even know he was there, *not* that it is any of your business who I do and do not bathe with."

Eldridge's stare sweeps over me, his features twisting into disgust as he studies Sin's shirt on me. Hurt swells in my chest. "You're so much smarter than this, Wren, but you'd never know it as you've made it your sole mission to make a fool of yourself."

Another growl, but the gravel in this one undoubtedly belongs to Sin. "*Careful.*"

Eldridge's words bite into me, the sting spreading from my cheeks, to my chest, and settling deep in my gut. I open my mouth, but no words come out. With a final shake of his head, Eldridge heads for the river behind us, keeping a wide berth between Sin and himself. It's for the best. Eldridge's temper would surely get himself into trouble if he decided to raise a hand to the Black Art.

The unrestrained, *unhindered* Black Art.

Sin takes to adjusting the saddle on his horse, his lips not fully hiding his amusement. I stalk towards him. "Continue to meddle in my private relationships, and you'll find out how quickly my dagger *meddles* with your scrotum."

Sin tightens the straps along the horse's underside, then leans forward to rest his elbows on the seat. "I simply returned what belonged to you, Wren. Speaking of which, you have something that belongs to me." He arches an eyebrow, and his eyes drop pointedly to the shirt I still wear, the sleeves extending past my hands a few inches and extra fabric bunching around my hips and waist.

I pull my braid over my shoulder and play with the ends of my hair a moment, feigning deliberation. "Mm, I think I'll keep it." Accepting it is not worth any more of my waning energy to argue with him, I turn and head back to my supplies. "Keep your hands off my stuff," I call over my shoulder. He grumbles something much too low for me to decipher, but I swear it contains Eldridge's name.

After changing into a clean tunic and pants, Alistair and I secure the supplies for travel. As promised, I leave a generous portion of food out for Eldridge who takes a while to return, much to Sin's annoyance. When my friend does return, he accepts the dried meat, apple, and waterskin I left for him, but says nothing to me as we mount our horses and continue our trek across the deserted plains southeast of Baregrove, clinging to the forest that borders the base of The Red Tops. Alistair leads our group with Eldridge at the rear, and Sin and I travel side-by-side in the center where everyone can easily keep eyes on our prisoner at all times.

It feels silly to think of Sin as a prisoner when no iron binds his wrists and twin swords are strapped across his back. Not his personal weapons, but the elves allowed him to borrow ones that are close to what he usually wields. As uneasy as it may make all of us, arming Sin is a necessary risk. Should we find ourselves overwhelmed by any lurking parties clutching a hit list with Sin's name on it, or more of Baelliarah's soldiers that may have been smuggled in, Sin would be more of a hindrance without a means to defend himself.

We'd make faster time if we clung to the road, but we can't risk traveling merchants or anyone traversing the road catching sight of us and recognizing the Black Art.

Sin was right when he said this journey is not one without peril, without risks. If we are seen, kingdom troops will chase us from coast to coast, flanking us until we are circled on all sides. Sin may not be leading us into a trap right now, but if we are caught and surrounded by his soldiers, why *wouldn't* he have us imprisoned—or killed—on sight?

Because you are in the Vale. And Goddess help whoever tries touching it.

I haven't been able to shake his words from earlier, turning them over in my mind like I could make them fit into some convoluted puzzle. At least a puzzle would have a clear picture, something tangible to analyze and make sense of, not just words spat between two enemies before the sun had even risen.

Enemies. Despite my ill feelings towards Sin, enemies doesn't feel like the right word to describe our relationship.

I wanted to forget.

Since leaving Scarwood, *so badly* I wanted to forget that Sin and I were ever something more. I fought it with every breath of my lungs and every thump of my heart, but no amount of anger I mustered could replace the pain. His betrayal split my chest wide open, leaving its meaty contents strewn about to be devoured.

He broke my fucking heart.

For months, I wanted nothing more than to break him in return. But as I steal the occasional glance of him at my side, watching as he scans the forest ahead for any sign of disturbance, it isn't anger I feel. It's something deeper. Darker. Infinitely more complicated.

The terrain is more treacherous through this part of the forest, our horses having to slow to keep their footing across sprawling exposed roots and shifting rocks. I notice how different the foliage in these woods is compared to Autumnhelm's. The forest I once called home was abundant with colorful, edible flowers, plump berries for the picking, and a variety of thriving plants that pestled nicely into seasonings and spices. These woods are thicker in vegetation, but the bushes are void of fresh fruit, and the trees are needled—lacking the wide, veiny leaves that made great insulation for the more tender plants Morrinne and I nursed in our garden. The garden outside our cabin, the one my family and I were forced to abandon.

Because *he* knew where they lived.

And not a fiber in my body trusted Sin not to hurt them.

We stop to water ourselves and our horses only a few times, and we keep those breaks short. Just long enough to relieve ourselves, satisfy our hunger and thirst, and let the horses rest their legs. Alistair and Eldridge have occupied themselves with conversation along the way, some of which I piped in on but stopped doing when I noticed Eldridge wasn't responding much to anything I said. Sin has spoken only a few words since leaving this morning, and all of them were reserved for terrain conditions to watch out for up ahead.

Eventually we're forced to leave the cover of the forest as we approach the eastern half of the isle, not far from White Hawk Meadow, the vast valley that plays host to the Rut each year.

"We need to make haste into Autumnhelm so we're out of sight from the road. Once we're back in tree covering, we can stop for the night," Sin says, nodding towards the very *open* plain separating us from my native woods.

My gut twists and churns at being so close to the forest I spent years traversing, familiarizing myself with every landmark for miles. *My* woods. My home. Morrinne's cabin isn't farther than a few miles out. I'd suggest we press on so we can spend the night sheltered instead of on the forest floor, but I keep quiet for two reasons. One, Sin suggests we settle near the kingdom outpost along the road so we can observe their patrols and guard rotation. And two, the thought of inviting the Black Art into the home he chased us from sinks into my stomach like a heavy, jagged stone.

"I already can't feel my legs or my balls, what's another hour of riding?" grumbles Eldridge, who runs the knuckles of his closed fist along his thigh.

"I can't say I *tried* feeling my balls with all of you around, but good to know I probably can't," Alistair says over his shoulder, bearing a sprightful smirk.

I roll my eyes and adjust my stance in my saddle, my own thighs burning with exhaustion. Sin's gaze sweeps over to where I absentmindedly knead my own leg. "You holding up okay?"

I may have shot a sarcastic remark if it weren't for his tone, which is surprisingly genuine and void of his usual smugness. I offer a curt nod instead.

After scanning for any travelers or patrolling soldiers, the four of us cross the expanse of beaten ground separating the road from the rolling hills that look down on White Hawk. None of us speak, the roar of hooves a thunderous storm between us as we push our horses faster, hurtling across the plains with more speed than the finest bone-tipped spear could muster. Despite the sun setting behind us, sweat beads down my back, my clothes clinging to my slick skin. There are several rivers that traverse these woods, I remind myself. A cold dip is almost within reach.

My lungs feel lighter the moment we slip past the tree line, the forest once again offering shelter from wandering eyes. But a pang of sorrow thuds in my chest as I behold the familiar foliage of the woods I grew up in—the trees Eldridge and Zorina ran through together in the middle of the night, the plants I gathered for crafting salves, the plump berries I smashed into jams and jellies.

I glance over my shoulder at Eldridge who looks far off, his gray eyes distanced, and I wonder if he is plagued by his own memories.

"Pull back on your speed; the outpost is just up ahead," Sin interrupts my reminiscing. "We can make camp farther in, then walk to the perimeter for observation. There's likely to be a guard rotation sometime in the night. Rest tonight because tomorrow we make haste to the other end of these woods, then when the guards are in their rotation, we can slip across the bridge and make it to the church before daybreak."

Alistair nods but flashes a fleeting glance over his shoulder. "Yeah, okay, but don't think you're getting anywhere near that outpost without us."

"The fewer of us that go for observation, the less chance we have of being seen," Sin argues.

"Agreed. Gingersnap will come with me to observe, and blondie can guard you at camp and make sure you don't find yourself sniffing anywhere near your little kingdom friends."

"I inherited this gorgeous hair from my mother. If you're jealous, just say it," Eldridge snickers at my rear.

"Why don't Eldridge and I observe, and you and Sin stay at camp?" I query.

"Not a chance, blondie."

I spread my arms in question, even though his back is to

me. But as if hearing my protest, Alistair continues, "I don't trust you and Eldridge together anymore than I trust Kilbreth. Don't take it personally—there's very few people I trust."

An agreeing huff falls from my lips. "You and me both."

"Quiet," Sin growls, his head dipped forward, eyes scanning the woods to our left. "The outpost should be half a segment from that break." He points to where the tree line dips in towards us, creating a divot in the verdant barrier. "Let's make camp inward, then you two can come back for observation after dark."

Alistair hops off his horse and heads for the divot.

"Get back on your horse, *witch*," Sin warns through clenched teeth. "They have a spyglass and there's enough light left that they can see you from here."

Alistair dismisses him with a backwards wave of his hand. "I'm just taking a look; they're not going to see me. Pull the godsdamned spear out of your ass, Kilbreth."

I dismount and follow him to the perimeter, inciting another frustrated growl from Sin. Alistair's shoulders knit together as I approach, and I feel the tension rolling off him as I sidle up next to him.

In a voice low enough for only my ears, he says, "Tell me, blondie, what do you see out there?"

My shoulder brushing his, I pull back the low-hanging branches and search the road in the distance, the beaten dirt path stretching as far as my naked eyes can see. Barren. "I don't see anything."

"Exactly," he bites back, his tone more hostile than it had been moments before. "Where the fuck is this outpost?"

"What do you see?" Eldridge calls to us. "Careful, or they'll spot your giant-ass head, Alistair."

"Maybe we're in the wrong spot. Not where Sin thought we were," I suggest.

Air hisses through his teeth. "He's the fucking Black Art. He knows where his own godsdamned outposts are."

I turn to look at him, but Alistair's already spinning on his heels and heading straight for Sin. My legs jump into motion, catching up with him a second later.

"Get off your horse," he snarls, his shoulders slumping forward as he beelines for the Black Art.

"Come again?" The words slide off Sin's tongue already coated in venom. He stares down at the bloodwitch at my side, his chin lifted slightly, challenging him.

"What's going on, Alistair?" Eldridge asks, shifting in his saddle and dropping the reins, preparing to dismount if needed.

"Where's the outpost, Kilbreth? Because it sure as shit isn't out there like you said," he hisses, pointing a long finger in the direction he and I came from.

Sin's eyes flash to mine, an unspoken question. I nod and cross my arms across my chest. "There's nothing for miles."

The muscles along his jaw feather, and he blows out a sigh that's half growl and rubs a hand across the bottom of his chin. "My father must have altered the routes."

Something like a snort erupts from beside me, and Alistair shakes his head with exaggerated slowness. "He's leading us into a trap. I'll admit, Kilbreth, I didn't trust you, but I didn't think you were dumb enough to try this with two blood-witches in your escort. Clearly I overestimated you."

"I said it before: I'm not leading you into a trap, *witch*. If the outpost isn't there, then it was reassigned. I had no way of knowing that, but if we leave now, we can make it to Mesa Pointe before dark and scope it out from the higher vantage point."

"Why didn't you want us to check it out before making

camp? Didn't want us catching you in your lies before you were ready, was that it?"

"He couldn't have known, Alistair," I placate. "He's been in the Vale. Dusaro probably redeployed the guards." Not that I want to be quick to defend Sin, but despite the circumstance, I don't think this is the workings of a trap. And dumb as it probably makes me, a part of me believed the Black Art when he promised his word to me at the river.

Sin's slivered eyes narrow further, and his hands tighten on the reins. His voice is lower when he addresses Alistair again. "I have two swords strapped on my back and more skill than all of you combined in wielding them. Your magic is rooted in bloodshed, witch, and given you haven't had the time to slaughter a small town today, even *that* is inferior to mine. *You* are inferior. If I wanted you dead, I wouldn't need a trap to do it. Now get on your horse, we are heading to Mesa Pointe. Continuing to delay us accomplishes nothing other than keeping us out in the open longer than necessary and pissing me off. And to be curt, I don't think Wren or Eldridge would mind very much at all if I silenced your ramblings permanently. So, I'll say it once more: *move.*"

Alistair holds his stare for an extended beat before spitting on the ground and mounting his horse. He waves his hand and in a biting tone, says, "After you, Black Art."

CHAPTER 16

Mesa Pointe is single-handedly the worst place the four of us could be, second only to Castle Scarwood itself. While a tiring climb for the horses up the craggy hillside, the peak is mostly level—a soft green blanket of tall, tender grasses swaying with the sea breeze that rips through them violently, no trees to caution its turpitude.

Flat. Open.

Exposed.

Sin is the first to dismount upon cresting the peak. He rummages through his saddle bag, pulls out a spyglass, and approaches the cliffside. Placing the glass to his eye, he tilts his head towards where the outpost was supposed to be located, surveying what remains of the abandoned station.

The rest of us follow suit and dismount. Eldridge takes out more of the dried meat and wordlessly hands me a few strips and a chunk of stale bread. I accept them with a nod, and neither of us hesitates silencing the hunger in our bellies with the provisions. Alistair leans against his horse, his arms folded across his chest and his head tilted down slightly. I don't need to follow his gaze to know who he watches so intently.

"You have a right to be suspicious of him, we all do, but I

don't think Sin had any way of predicting this," I murmur to Alistair.

"He's the Black Art, he is more than aware of what precaut—"

"*Fuck.*"

Sin's growl has all of us turning towards him. His fingers are interlocked across the back of his head, the spyglass at his feet, his stance so charged I'm certain it'd feel like I was shocked by lightning if I reached out and touched him.

"Something wrong with your master plan, *Your Grace?*" asks the bloodwitch at my side.

Sin's fingers tighten in his hair for a moment, before he drops his arms to his sides and turns around. "There's no outpost anymore because it's no longer needed." He speaks the words through clenched teeth, opening his eyes that had fluttered shut with annoyance.

"Speak clearly," Eldridge huffs, taking a step towards him, which also shadows half of my body behind his burly one.

I take a step to the side. "Explain."

"Quickly," Alistair adds, his fingers drumming his crossed forearms.

"They don't need an outpost along the road when no one is getting into Blackreach unnoticed. The bridge. They're on the fucking bridge."

I hurry to the cliffside, swiping the spyglass from the ground, and peer towards the bridge connecting the isle to the capital city. The overpass that was vast and open the last I'd seen it, is now occupied with armed guards posted at both entrances, and a few more dotted along the bridge itself. "They're inspecting everyone that enters or leaves," I say, interrupting the others' bickering.

"Yes, thank you for that enlightening observation, princess. We'd be terribly lost without your guidance."

I whirl towards Alistair. "I was thinking out loud so that we may come up with another plan. Kindly take your rotten attitude and choke on it."

Eldridge steps up next to me, staring off in the direction of the bridge. "Even if we swim across farther down, there's bound to be more of them on the other side. Your father has the place swarming with them. Fucking pests," he adds before throwing his head back and guzzling down half the contents of his waterskin, probably wishing it contained something much stronger right about now.

Sin folds both arms across his chest, the cords of muscles there pulling tight under the rolled-up sleeves of his dark shirt. "We're still getting to that church—you all just aren't going to like how."

I take a bite of the stale bread, my jaw clenching as I try to chew the hardened flour while Sin elaborates.

"There's a network of tunnels beneath the city. There's an entrance to the east," he says, pointing out over the cliff to our right, "near the bank of the Malachite. It connects to another opening in an alley that's not far from the church. It's not the preferred plan, and it certainly isn't going to be a pretty one, but it's our only option."

"Tunnels don't sound so bad—what, you scared of rats, Black Art?" Eldridge asks, his tone mocking.

Sin runs a hand through his long hair, and another squall rips his mane to the side. "Rats will be the least of your concerns down there. The tunnels aren't just dens for vermin. They're for sewage."

"Oh, for fuck's sake," Alistair exclaims, storming away from his horse. "I'm not crawling through some godsdamned shit tunnels because *you* fucked up the plan!"

"*Careful,* witch," growls the Black Art. "I am still the

authority of this isle and so long as you're living on it, your place is beneath me."

Alistair's mouth falls open, an expression equal parts amused as it is furious twists his features, and he stalks towards Sin who doesn't so much as give half an inch. "You're cautioning me?" he asks in disbelief. "The last I checked, you were our prisoner, Black Art. You'd be wise to remember that."

Sin stares at the bloodwitch with enough heat in his eyes to kindle a fire. His jaw is clenched, the muscles of his arms rigid beneath the shirt pulled tight across his shoulders. "Do not counsel me on wisdom as you arrogantly approach *your prisoner,* who has no shackles to bind their hands from strangling you, and no iron to stop me from exploding the empty space where your brain should be. I made a deal with your priestess, and I intend to honor my word in relaying our message to my Hand. That does not mean I will hesitate to crack your *fucking spine in half* and drop the pieces in front of her." The snarl in his words is beyond his usual authoritative tone. It's harder, rawer, more... beast-like. More *transcendent.*

I lay a hand on Alistair's arm, and Sin's eyes drop to track the movement, another growl slipping through his chest. "Back off, Alistair," I say with a nip of my own in my words. "We either take his word and go through the tunnels, or we don't relay the message at all, and his fucking kingdom comes and burns the godsdamned Vale down."

"They're not going to burn the Vale while Baelliarah is scouting," Eldridge objects. "That's like drawing a giant fucking sign that says, *'Hey, over here! We're in the middle of a civil war, so come beat our asses while we're distracted.'*"

Sin snorts an exasperated breath through his nose. "My father would surely surprise you, then." He takes a few steps back, his eyes glued to Alistair again, before turning and approaching the horses. "Let's make camp. We need to rest now so we can hit the tunnels before sunrise."

"It's bound to get cold up here overnight, and without a fire, I suggest we're in for a cozy night together," I say, smiling with mock enthusiasm.

Alistair mutters something vulgar, then rummages through his saddle bag and tosses a couple provisions to the ground, seemingly making room. "Make your fucking camp, I'm going to inspect where that outpost was and see if anything of value was left behind." He starts to mount his horse but halts suddenly, the muscles in his neck bulging as if he's being restrained.

I whip towards Sin and find his stance widened, his right hand splayed open at his side, fingers curled up. "Let him go," I murmur. "It's clear we all need to blow off some steam after enjoying each other's lovely company the past couple days." My tone is lighthearted, but my words are laced with intent.

If Alistair continues antagonizing the Black Art, neither Eldridge nor I will be able to stop Sin from *cracking his spine in half,* as he so affectionately promised. While I don't particularly care if the male bloodwitch lives or dies, I don't feel like explaining to the high priestess why four of us left entrusted with the mission, and only three returned. Not to mention, Sera seems to hold Alistair near to her heart, and considering her alliance with the elves, I needn't find myself ousted from the Vale while two kingdoms' armies are actively hunting the white-haired witch.

A gasp of air rushes from Alistair's throat the same second Sin's hand snaps closed. My own chest swells with relief, and Eldridge's shoulders lower in my periphery. Alistair growls something too low for me to hear, mounts his horse, and takes off down the hill.

"Fucker better be discreet," Eldridge grumbles.

The three of us begin unpacking our supplies, laying out our bedrolls and blankets, and I hand Sin a couple of the food storage containers, noting he still hasn't eaten. Eldridge makes a motion of sniffing himself under the arms and recoils. "I guess it doesn't matter if I smell like shit given we're about to be covered in it."

Sin sits on his bedroll with his knees bent and his arms resting loosely over them, a strip of jerky in his hand. "No one forced you to come."

Eldridge's eyes flash to mine for a second, then drop to his hands as he lays out a change of clothes.

"Why are you looking at me?" I ask, my voice thick with annoyance.

He doesn't look up, but his lips press together tightly, thinning at the seam. With a slight shake of his head, he says, "You know why."

"*You* insisted on coming. I didn't ask you to," I remind him, irritated that he's implying it is somehow my fault that he's in this situation.

His head whips towards mine. "You didn't have to, Wren! But you just had to go and get in the middle of things again, and we both know I wasn't going to let you come out here with these two fucks alone. Which by the way, I neglected to thank you for. So thank you, Wren, for getting both of us out here risking our necks for people that are not our own."

I rush towards him, jabbing a finger into his chest and pushing him back an inch. He rolls his head to the side and licks his lips in a lazy, annoyed demeanor, before blowing out a breath and meeting my stare again. "We are out here to ensure that that fucking army," I point the index finger of my other hand in the direction of the capital, "an army with *iron*, Eldridge, doesn't storm across the isle and slaughter all of us. That *is* protecting our own."

Eldridge snaps my hand to my side and erases the distance my finger put between us, pressing his chest against mine and tilting his head down to look at me. I can't see anything past Eldridge's boxy frame, but I hear as Sin rises to his feet. And if my ears don't betray me, that was a low growl I just heard.

"Then why does it feel like you've only been protecting him?"

Pain lashes through me, liquid fire curdling around my ribs.

"You knew what he was, that he was a fucking transcendent for godsfucking sake, Wren, and you told no one! That was literal gold we could have used against him, and you kept your mouth shut."

"I did that for you. For all of us! I made a deal with Sin, one that protected not just you, not just your sister, and Theon, and Morrinne, but *all* of your kind, and that deal required my silence. You are all a part of me, and I always protect what is mine. So don't you *dare* wag your finger at me and claim that I have chosen him over you."

The air between us drops to a dangerous temperature, and Eldridge's stormy eyes narrow as he searches both of mine. His arms are rigid at his sides, but even now with our rage a firestorm between us, I know he would never hurt me. No matter how pissed he may be. Still, I *feel* Sin hovering just behind Eldridge, almost as if the tether that once linked us lingers inside me, a shadow of what once bound me to him in more ways than one.

"He tortured Cosmina, and you still came back from the river wearing his shirt. He had your fucking clothes in his hands, Wren. How do you expect me to interpret that?"

My fingers curl into my palms, my nails digging into the sensitive flesh there, but I don't register the pain. "I already told you... he took my clothes," I seethe.

"And before?" he presses, dipping his head to lower himself to my eye-level.

My hand finds my hip, and I shift my weight to that side. "Excuse me?"

"Did you fuck him?"

My breath hitches, and my cheeks warm but not from embarrassment. From indignation. I flick my tongue over my bottom lip and capture it with my teeth next, shaking my head in disbelief. A part of me remembers Sin is lingering just beyond him, likely struggling not to intervene, but I don't have the emotional capacity to care how he perceives our argument. This isn't about him. It's about Eldridge and me. My best friend.

Who right now is really pissing me off.

"Answer the question, Wren. When you were running around as the Black Art's lapdog, while our sister rotted away in a dungeon cell, were you fucking him?"

I turn my head so he's forced to look at the side of my face as tears burn in my eyes. "That's not fair. That's not fair, Eldridge, and you know it."

An unrelenting force, he doesn't give an inch, the tension rolling off him penetrating my body, my soul. "Did. You. Fuck. Him?"

My heart shatters. All the hurt, the betrayal, the hatred at myself for the secrets I kept, explodes inside of me, splattering my bones with my pain. Gritting my teeth, I turn back to Eldridge and rise to my toes as I angle my head up towards his. "Yes, I fucked him," I growl, my words low and heavy and lethal. "And you want to know something else? I liked it, Eldridge."

Pain licks his eyes, but his stance doesn't soften, his jaw still clenched tight and his shoulders raised. And in this moment, I hate him. I hate all of him. For allowing his jealousy to slip between us, and for allowing his hatred of Sin to build a barrier between us. But mostly for his judgment. His insinuation that I made the choices I did with the knowledge that the same man that captured my sister, also captured my heart.

My voice is pure steel when I stand as high on my toes as I can, my lips grazing the underside of his clenched jaw. "I. Fucking. Loved. It."

We stay like this for an extended beat, two, three. Neither of us moving, breathing, the silence between us full of unspoken words. I will strength into my jaw to keep my lips from trembling against the underside of his, to hold firm under the crushing weight of his judgment.

Until finally, his shoulders sag, and he lets out a long breath through his nose. He steps backwards, the space between us only a few feet but there might as well be an ocean between us. His mouth falls open, but with a shake of his head, he quickly shuts it and turns his back on me.

Turning into Sin.

Judging from the sudden flexing of every muscle along Eldridge's neck and arms, he had been too distracted to notice just how close Sin hovered behind him, watching. Waiting. I'm certain no matter how furious Eldridge was with me, he'd never raise a hand to me, and vice versa, but the Black Art does not know my friend the same as I.

Eldridge halts as he turns into Sin, his left shoulder brushing the Black Art's, both of their heads tilted towards the other. Their stares clash for a moment, wrestling for dominance, both of their chests puffed and the lines of their necks pulled tight. I flex my collective, ready to intervene should one of them make a move against the other. Despite how furious I am at both of them, I am not allowing two overgrown men to fight because I have flared their tempers.

A storm brews between them. Eldridge like thunder, loud

and booming, while Sin is quicker, lethal, lightning incarnate. *Goddess above, just compare lengths already.*

I breathe a silent sigh of relief as Sin, ever so subtly, shifts his weight to allow Eldridge to pass. He skulks to the opposite side of camp, looking out towards the river rushing in the distance. Blinking back the tears, I turn towards the cliffside, ignoring Sin's stare that practically demands I look at him. He reaches for my wrist as I pass him, to force me to pause, but I yank it out of his reach. I don't need words for him to read the message in my body language, my scent.

This is your fault.

I brush past him and look out over the cliff, desperate to fill my head with images of anything other than the look on Eldridge's face as I buried words sharper than any blade into his gut, his heart.

But when I peer over the cliff, it's not relief I find.

It's hunger.

Splayed across the bridge in a sea of crimson are the bodies of every guard posted there. And standing before them, arms spread out in front of the fallen soldiers, in front of his *feast,* is Alistair.

CHAPTER 17

We're on our horses immediately, flying down the foothills towards the bridge, not bothering to stay amongst the trees this time. We need the advantage of flat ground to reach Alistair fast enough, fast enough to—

What? Certainly, not to save any of them.

They were all dead.

I didn't need the spyglass to make out their crumpled bodies scattered across the bridge like they were nothing more than piles of trash to be burned. Leaning forward, urging my horse into a violent gallop, we cover the open distance in a few minutes.

The others had said nothing as I looked over the cliff and let loose a snarl, one that had Sin at my side a second later. Sin's eyes turned to ice when he beheld the bloody scene, but the wrath that emanated from him in that moment was smoldering. No words were exchanged between us. They didn't have to be.

Eldridge sprang into action when he heard us tossing the supplies back into the bags and mounting the steeds without properly cinching the saddles, hopping onto his own horse after seeing the massacre in the distance.

Red stains my sight.

Alistair's sinewy form grows larger as we ride up on him, his back towards us as he kneels next to one of the fallen soldiers, his mouth leeched to their limp forearm. Sin is off his horse first, Eldridge close behind him, both of them storming towards the bloodwitch. I want to follow, to swing my leg over the saddle and sink to my feet, but my bones thicken, the marrow swelling and clotting in its hard casings, turning my limbs to stone.

The scent of their suffering somersaults into my nose, petting my tongue, their essence swirling down my throat and settling low in my belly. Hunger burns bright in my gut, and my lips part in a nefarious snarl. I clench my thighs tighter around the horse, molding myself here, willing my curled fingers to relax before my knuckles tear through the thin skin there.

Hearing the Black Art behind him, Sin making no effort to quiet his approach and Eldridge following close behind, Alistair leaps up and spins towards him. Alistair's eyes gleam with the vibrancy of every star in the sky, his usual dark brown irises now gilded orbs, the collectives of every guard fueling his magic. These men were mundane, so the effect won't be as strong as if he had taken the lives of fellow mages, but Alistair is still a hell of a lot more powerful than he was before he left camp.

My hunger turns virile, and slowly, my head tilts up, allowing the blood-misted air easier access into my nose, through my parted lips. So, so hungry.

No.

Starved.

The Black Art connects one punch to the side of Alistair's jaw before the bloodwitch snaps out of his blood-crazed haze and bares his teeth at Sin, not bothering to even touch the part of his face Sin's fist left battered. Alistair retaliates with an assault of destruction magic, an attack Sin catches with a ward sprung to life between his hands, but his arms tremble beneath the weight of Alistair's strengthened power.

Hands clamp down on the back of Sin's shoulders. The Black Art whips around, instinct triggering the need to protect his rear, magic simmering to a dangerous height in his opened hand. Recognition crosses his face, and he halts before releasing the lethal orb on Eldridge, but the show of power does nothing to stop my friend from twisting his fingers into Sin's shirt and jerking him towards him. A low growl rumbles in Eldridge's chest, and it's met with a feral snarl from the Black Art.

My vision tunnels to the scene unfolding behind them both. Alistair's arm is outstretched at his side, his palm towards the sky, his fingers curling in on them themselves as if...

Fuck me.

My legs absorb the impact when I slide off my horse too quickly to dismount properly, and I run towards the blood-witch. Sin and Eldridge are battling in a war of obscenities, seemingly forgetting about Alistair altogether as my ears register my name on their lips, but I'm too distracted to process their words. Though it doesn't require imagination to know what they're shouting about.

The area around Alistair's outstretched hand turns rouge as if the air itself were on fire. My eyes track the magic, following it to its lifeless source, one clad in kingdom armor. Blood sprays from the fallen soldier's gut like a turbulent geyser, solidifying mid-stream into a cardinal whip. The blood-witch turns back to the arguing pair, the blood whip in his hand dripping with the guard's spilled juice, twisting and curling around Alistair's body as if were one of his own limbs.

I don't think. I act.

Magic pools into my hands, warming them to a fevered heat, my own collective stirring and restless from the bloodshed. I barely notice as Sin's attention jerks to mine as I skid to a stop, a shimmering gold ward pulled taut between my hands.

Alistair's shoulder pulls back a split second before his hand comes tunneling forward, towards Sin. The whip cracks as it connects with my shield—no, *my arm*—and my teeth sink into my tongue. My own sweet syrup bleeds into my mouth, and I bare my crimson splattered teeth, a hiss slithering out from behind them. Alistair is quick to call the weapon back, but I'm quicker.

My collective latches onto the whip before he can react, and I pull, drawing source from the blood materializing it. The scourge bracelets my arm and coils around my waist, hovering inches from brushing my tunic. Alistair scowls at me, flipping his palms upward as he tries to pull more magic from the blood, but Sin is faster.

The Black Art buries his shoulder into the bloodwitch's chest, his arms banding around his center, and carries him to the ground. The howl that escapes Alistair confirms there are flames in Sin's hands. I step towards them, and a large hand grips my bicep with enough strength to halt me. I turn towards Eldridge, but his words are lost in the deafening ring in my ears, the chaotic cadence of my pounding heart. Gritting my teeth, I jerk my arm free, heat tunneling in my veins.

When I turn back to the fight before me, Alistair has regained the grip on his collective, and with a feral shout, shoves the Black Art off him with a destructive surge. Sin grunts as his back takes most of the blow but within seconds, his hands are planted on the ground, and he heaves himself upright. He grabs one of the swords at his back, the metal sliding smoothly from its leather scabbard, and running his hand along the blade, he shrouds the weapon with a blue casing: a magical barrier to prevent Alistair from ripping it from his hands with a phantom wind.

Alistair's veins may be swollen with blood magic, but they'll split under steel like any others.

He lets out a dark chuckle as he focuses on the Black Art, crimson flames roaring to life in his hands, flickering in his golden eyes like crackling fire. Sin swipes first, but I have trained with the warlord enough times to recognize a false charge when I see one. He's baiting Alistair, the mage whose slender form suggests he's never wielded steel before. He's never had to.

A beast doesn't need a blade when it has its claws and teeth.

The bloodwitch reacts to the false start, hitting Sin with a rush of the smoldering magic. It heaves him backwards again, the sword still clutched in Sin's hand while his other searches for purchase in the dirt, stopping his fall.

Dark amusement flares in my mind. I recognize this trick. It wasn't that long ago the Black Art intentionally weakened his shield so my magic would make contact. He's baiting Alistair to come closer, and the bloodwitch is too arrogant to notice the giant trap he's heading towards.

But this isn't Sin's fight. Not anymore.

I devoted years, decades, stifling my wrath. Warring with the monster inside me, intent on thinking that part of me was somehow sentient, a ghost haunting my every thought and desire. But it was never me and *her*. It was me and my own resentment towards those who harmed me, who tried to weaponize me for their cause. It was me and the self-assurance my mother stole. Me and Cathal who tried to break and berate me. Me and Sin who... who helped me see the bloodwitch was not something I needed to cower from as if she were something horrid that crawls out of legends to spook children in their beds. I lost years of my life trying to tame what I thought was an insatiable beast in my heart, and here Alistair stands, wicked pleasure sparking in his eyes, the embodiment of everything I swore I never was, and never would be.

This was never the Black Art's fight.

It is mine.

Sin recovers his balance, his knees digging into the dirt and his hand tightening further around the hilt of his blade. Baiting the bloodwitch's focus to his weapon clad hand while he calls forth his power in the other. Somewhere behind me, I hear Eldridge holler to me, shouting for me to get back, to stay out of it. But his pleas are fruitless. My blood trills with purpose, with excitement, and hastening my steps, I erase the remaining distance between us.

Sin raises his weapon, and my boot comes down on the Black Art's shoulder, forcing him to lower his hand. He shouts something to me, but I don't hear him. Don't make sense of his words. They don't matter. Eldridge's warnings at my rear don't matter. The slain guards adorning the bridge like stripped wood don't matter. Not anymore.

But I matter.

And Goddess strike me dead before I allow some sharpened teeth, arrogant asshole tarnish the legacy of the bloodwitch in my presence.

Sin's shoulder twists under the sole of my boot, and his large hand cups my calf, but he's too late. Alistair's golden gaze is heady with lust when it meets mine, and his tongue darts out to lap up the already drying blood on his lips.

"Did you want to play too, princess?"

I crack the whip across his face.

CHAPTER 18

A long, jagged laceration mars Alistair's cheek when he pulls his hand away. The flesh around the tear is already swollen, red and puffy, but no tears dot the bloodwitch's eyes. No. When Alistair steers his gaze back to mine, something far more ancient winks back at me.

My lips turn up as I admire the torn flesh upon his cheek, the way the skin split apart like crushed fruit when my whip bit his face. I clench my thighs together, but it does nothing to stop the pulsing of my sex, the sight of the bloodwitch battered and bruised going straight to my core. I always did love the way the caster's high affected me, but it is nothing compared to the effects of wielding blood magic. I didn't create the blood whip, but I sure as hell cracked it across Alistair's arrogant face all the same, and that rush of power throbs painfully between my legs.

Time moves in slow, steady beats, as if the magic froze everything in place except for Alistair and myself. But then the pounding of my blood ebbs from my ears, and sound and time come stampeding back. Sin is on his feet mere seconds after my assault, stepping in front of me and angling his body to shield most of mine from the bloodwitch. I swallow my amusement down with the rest of my dark thoughts. Eldridge sidles up to my other side a moment later, but I never lower my eyes from Alistair's.

Dropping his hand to his side, he lets out a low, dark chuckle, and his stare shifts to the Black Art whose sheer mass is now blocking most of me from his view. I step to the side, the whip curling delicately around my torso like a snake.

"Can't fight your own battles, Your Grace?" Alistair's voice is thick with mockery, then deepens into a booming laugh. He turns his head and spits, his hand instinctively reaching for his face, but he promptly drops it to his side again when he catches himself.

Sin's body is a current, tension rolling off him in waves, and long claws now protrude from his last knuckle joints.

"Easy, Alistair," I coo, my voice sticky sweet. "As much as I love the lack of symmetry, I'm happy to give you a matching lash on the other cheek."

"*Back away, Wren,*" Sin warns in a low growl, but his focus is trained entirely on the bloodwitch before him.

Eldridge is silent at my side, but he angles himself so that he's facing me, not Alistair. Preparing to stop me should I make another lunge for him. My head whips to the side, and I bare my teeth at my friend, but he doesn't give an inch.

"So. Fucking. Impulsive." Sin sounds almost tired when he speaks, but his words are laced with fury. He runs a hand through his long black hair, the cords of muscle in his forearm taut as he struggles to restrain his temper. And I know damn well he is itching to strangle Alistair with his bare hands.

"We needed the route clear. I wasn't climbing through some godsdamned underground shit pipes so we could sneak around your precious guards."

"There's bound to be a guard exchange in a few hours, and you just notified them that someone breached their city. You didn't want to sneak around—well, we don't have a fucking choice now."

"Oh, hush up about it. We'll be in and out before they even notice. Let's get to the church, call your little assistant lady, and we'll be on our way."

Sin closes the already too-small distance between them, only a hair's breadth remaining between their chests. I'm certain the only thing keeping his hands from wringing the life out of Alistair is him not wanting me to intervene again. Which I would, partly because Alistair is fueled with blood magic and far more powerful than he was before killing the guards, and partly because I just really want to make him bleed some more. My throat goes dry at the thought.

"We have to signal just before dawn—*that* is our agreement, and when she'll be looking for the lantern. But Dusaro will be alerted of this," Sin jabs a finger to the massacre behind Alistair, "before then, and Ileana won't be able to leave the castle without arousing suspicion."

"Not to break up your pissing contest here, but we need to move," Eldridge adds gruffly, eyeing the murder scene splayed across the bridge. "We don't know when the next rotation is, but I do know we don't want to be anywhere near here when it happens."

Sin closes his eyes and blows out a long breath. "Fucking *bloodwitch*." He growls the word, as if the taste of it in his mouth is vile.

My eyes narrow. I recall a time when he rather enjoyed the taste of bloodwitch on his tongue. "We can hunker down in the church. You said it's been abandoned since the fire, so let's rest there tonight, then signal Ileana tomorrow," I say, allowing the Black Art's *bloodwitch* comment to go ignored for now. "Hopefully by then they'll be too busy sniffing around the gates, they won't notice or care if the Black Hand takes leave for a moment."

Silence weighs heavy between us, and I take controlled breaths through my mouth, stopping myself from inhaling through my nose. Now is not the time for blood-controlled thoughts to be clouding my mind with images of daggers and debaucherous deeds.

A curt nod of his head and Sin backs away from Alistair. The air lightens around us when he does, but when the Black Art turns and captures my gaze with his, my lungs constrict painfully. His green irises glow faintly with a yellow hue from the magic expulsion, and the sight of them sends a flutter low in my belly. He reaches for me, and I sidestep, angling the whip away from him.

An exasperated sigh. "Your arm, Wren."

Oh.

Fuck.

I was too distracted before, but now that the tension has ebbed, I register the sharp, throbbing ache where Alistair's whip wound around my arm before I caught it. The flesh is peeled away in ribbons, bracelets of muscle and meat wrapping my forearm from wrist to elbow. I close my eyes, needing to distract myself from my ruined flesh to focus on my collective, and I release my hold on the weapon, returning it to the ether.

Eldridge and Alistair mutter something to each other about the horses, and they brush past us towards them. Opening my eyes, I study the wound on my arm, the blood magic like fire in my flesh. I'll be able to heal some of the laceration, enough to ward off infection, but wounds birthed from blood magic are a difficult beast to tame. Magic rooted in suffering has a special way of burrowing deep in the flesh and grinding its red-tipped claws into the meat.

"Let me see it," Sin demands again, but I keep my ruined arm near my chest.

"We need to move. I can heal it later." The half-truth rolls off my tongue with confidence, but I know I'll need Aeverie's ancient magic to heal an injury like this. Aeverie or...

Sin glances behind me towards the others mounting the horses, then back to me. "We're not far from the church. Especially since our path was just cleared, but as soon as we get there, I'm tending to it." His tone implies there is no room for negotiation. Perhaps he has forgotten who is escorting who.

"As you wish, Blackheart."

I turn towards the horses, but not before I catch the desiderating look on his face when I use the nickname I gave him months prior. My hips sway a little farther to each side as I approach my mount, the heat of the Black Art's stare burning a hole through my back.

CHAPTER 19

For a temple dedicated to the goddess of the arcane, the church is more secluded than I was expecting, though I suppose that is precisely the reason the Black Art and Hand chose it as their secret meeting point. The sanctuary is a two-story square building, its sides constructed of split logs, the wood a drab gray, and a dark red tented roof on top. Strips of wood have been hammered across the windows, the glass having shattered from the fire. Dark patches of burnt wood dot the exterior walls like tender bruises, the front door hangs slightly ajar on its hinges, and much of the grass around the building has receded—the little that remains now scraggly yellow-brown blades. Towering over the roof is the bell tower, complete with cutouts in the stone walls that serve as windows, and a private roof of the same red brick pitched over top.

Sin led us through a labyrinth of side alleys, leaving a wide berth between us and the main roads, which he said were occupied with guards even at this midnight hour. Still, we hid our faces behind the thick riding cloaks we packed, and clung deep to the shadows while we hurried through the capital. We find the church at the end of a cobblestone road, only a few streets away from the receiving center where we captured the Black Art.

"She even going to notice a little light up there?" Eldridge asks, peering up at the looming bell tower. "We're not exactly sidled up to the castle here."

Sin raises a dark eyebrow and shoots him a dubious look. "Would you rather we be rubbing elbows with the castle packed full of people who want to kill you?"

Eldridge grumbles and raises his hands to suggest he concedes his point.

"She'll see it because she'll have been looking for it every night since I've been gone. But it's inconspicuous enough that others won't blink twice. Churches light lanterns all the time, and the city is riddled with them."

We dismount and tether our horses around the back, away from any passing eyes that may notice four unattended steeds loitering around an abandoned church. There is a door behind the building—a back entrance—and I head towards it, pulling the hood of my cloak down.

Sin clears his throat, and when I look over my shoulder, he's staring at me, uncertainty brimming in his eyes. "Before we go in there, there's something I need to tell you." He's addressing all of us, but his stare doesn't waver from mine.

"Out with it, then."

But before he can answer, a deep groan startles me from behind, the sound far too reminiscent of an old wooden door being opened. I whip around just as a dark male figure steps through the threshold, his form obscured by gray robes, and his face shielded by a matching hood.

"Greetings, Your Grace. I have been anticipating your arrival." A man's voice, aged and worn. His head pulls back slightly, as if whatever face hidden within that dark expanse has settled its sights on me. "I see you brought friends. What a treat this is."

My dagger is at his throat a second later. He isn't tall, rather only a few inches taller than myself, and to my surprise, he offered no resistance as I slipped behind him, wrapped my arm around his chest, and pointed the tip of my blade to his neck. I yank his hood down, revealing a fair-haired male, his sandy hair streaked with ribbons of silver, and the lines around his eyes and mouth suggesting he's around sixty. He is rigid beneath my weapon, but his arms remain firmly at his sides, though his eyes have fixed on Sin.

In the time it took me to slip around the strange man, Alistair birthed fiery orbs in both palms, and Eldridge pulled the long sword from his back. The sword he now points at the Black Art.

But if Sin even notices Eldridge, he doesn't show it. His eyes are still glued to mine, his expression softened, but his body stiff, the muscles in his arm twitching under his fitted shirt. Bile coats my mouth, my stomach turning inside out as the reality of our situation weighs in it like swallowed stones. Images of my frail sister limping into view, one arm strung across Cornelius's shoulders, blinks behind my eyes, and an all too familiar word burns into my mind.

Betrayal.

"It's not what you think, Wren," Sin murmurs, his voice too soft for the intensity of the situation.

I inch my blade closer to the man's jugular. "Who is he?"

"His name is Gerard. He is one of the high priests. This is his station."

"You said this place was abandoned," Eldridge says, taking a step closer to Sin, leading with his sword.

"I *lied*," the Black Art growls, the word lingering on his tongue.

"Thanks for pointing that one out, mate," Alistair mocks, flicking his head to the side, the flames roaring higher in his upturned palms.

My fingers twitch on the blade, and despite me ordering my hand to hold steady, it trembles as hurt swells in my chest. Tears prick my eyes, but I force them back, along with the urge to chuck my knife into the Black Art's throat.

Sin takes a step towards me, and I bare my teeth. "There was little trust between us, and I am certain you would have not agreed to come here if you knew the shrine was still being tended. That is the only reason I did not tell you. Lower your weapon, Wren. He's not going to hurt you. I... I'm not going to hurt you." His voice is low, pained almost, but still underlined with his usual gruffness. Another step, and this time, he carefully reaches an arm towards both of us but stops several feet away.

"It is against the code for me to harm you, my Lady, but I have no desire to anyway. Nor do I suspect I could do much damage to someone who is clearly more qualified to engage in a tussle than myself," Gerard speaks, the bob of his throat brushing my knife.

I pull him against me tighter, inciting a low groan from him.

"Gerard serves Adelphia first. I would not have brought us here if I thought for a second that it would put you in danger. Adelphia chose me at the Rite. To harm the one who has been goddess-blessed would be a most egregious sin for any high priest, but especially the one who directly serves as Adelphia's Hand here."

The high priest shifts under my weight and clears his throat. "His Grace speaks with sincerity, my Lady. Loyalty to the one chosen by the goddess is my duty, and one I do not perceive lightheartedly. So long as the one touched by Adelphia invites you here, you are safe inside her temple. At least, from my hand, that is."

Alistair yawns loudly. "What do you say, blondie, which one should we send to meet their beloved goddess first?"

Sin's jaw is clenched, his stare burrowing into mine, ensnaring me in his hold as he takes another measured step. "Neither of us are going to hurt you, Wren."

A scowl paints my face as his words pestle salt into my gaping chest. "You said I wouldn't have believed you because there wasn't trust between us. This is a far cry from earning it, Singard."

He dips his head once and swallows tightly. "I know."

I glance at Eldridge, then Alistair, surveying their reactions before capturing Sin's eyes again. "Do not betray me again."

I shove the high priest towards him and storm into the house of worship.

CHAPTER 20

Gerard shows us around the church without requesting an explanation for why the missing Black Art has shown up outside his shrine seeking shelter. Nor does he elaborate on what prompted him to be expecting Sin's arrival, as he said upon opening the door. Though, I suppose it is in the high priest's best interest that he be kept in the dark—the less information he has, the less danger he'll be in should he find himself questioned by kingdom guards.

The temple is more elegant inside than its damaged exterior suggested, though the fire has left much of it in dire need of repair. A few wooden benches with low rise backs line the main hall, though depressions in the floor suggest this entire room was once filled with seating. The floor is soft beneath my feet, much of the wood having separated from the heat, and remnants of dirt and dead grasses speckle the boards. Aside from the deep bruising of the walls where smoke and ash claimed the supports as their own, the inner walls are made bright with a few paintings of the temple's namesake goddess. Some depict Adelphia overseeing the Rites, others show her blessing faceless figures with her power, and a few are merely portraits of her clad in form-hugging gowns. Based on the prominence of it, the goddess favors a shimmery ice blue for her fair complexion. The art is void of burn marks, suggesting Gerard had them brought in after the sanctuary's devastation to preserve the goddess's presence in her shrine.

A dais occupies the far side of the room, Adelphia's likeness preserved in a bronze statue resting atop the platform. Her palms face inward with mere inches between her copper hands, a cradle for the goddess's magic. Deep lines are carved into the metal to outline her gown, and soft ringlets of hair rest on her rounded shoulders. Stacked plates of votive candles frame the back corners of the dais, the flames lit and dancing merrily in their containers.

Gerard leads us up a creaky staircase tucked around one of the side walls to the second story, which is mostly a few empty storage rooms, the high priest's personal quarters, and another narrow stairwell that leads to the bell tower.

The others head outside to haul our bags to the upstairs rooms after Gerard finishes the short tour, but I take a seat near the front of the nave, basking in the warm glow of the candlelight and trying to make sense of the actions brought forth by the goddess of the arcane. Blessing a mage with transcendence in their blood has never happened before—why now? Surely she would have felt the blend of the Black Art's magics in his veins when she assessed his worth during the Rite, and definitely when she bled her own power into his. And yet, she stands by idly in whatever heavens may or may not exist, and bears witness as people of this isle slit shifter throats in her name.

A dark form moves into my periphery, casting me in sudden shadow. Sin hovers next to the bench, his black shirt pulled tight across his chest by his crossed arms, the cords of muscle there prominent. The soft firelight warming his reddish-brown skin sends a memory barreling to the front of my mind. It wasn't that long ago, the night of the celebratory gala after we defeated Legion, that I found His Grace sitting in his velvet-backed throne after I parted with Cornelius. I drank in his image, my very blood heady with need to consume him whole, but it was the Black Art that feasted that night, between my thighs, kneeling beneath me as I sat upon his throne.

"Will you walk with me?" he asks, voice gentler than usual.

I regard him for a moment, still not having forgiven him for hiding the reality of our accommodations from us. While not leading us into a trap per se, Sin didn't disclose we would have company, and when you're hiding from an army that outnumbers you thousands to one, company doesn't bode well for us. At least Gerard seems genuine. I pried into his collective while he gave us the impromptu tour, and nothing I experienced felt reminiscent of deceit. Though, I have been wrong before.

I don't answer but rise to my feet. He motions with his chin for me to follow. Sin leads us out the back door where we tethered the horses and pulls a bundled-up piece of cloth and a tall, slender bottle from his saddle bag. There's a small bench with a metal framework backing pushed against the rear entrance, and I take a seat, patting my leggings to send the dirt flying off. The back of the church bleeds into the Spiritwood Forest, so unless the towering oak trees report us to the guards, we're safe from wandering eyes back here.

The bench groans softly as the Black Art sits next to me, one of his spread knees brushing mine on the too-small seat. His eyes dip to my injured arm, and he reaches towards me, one of his inky eyebrows arching upwards. I hold out my arm, and he immediately cups my wrist with one of his large hands, his grip firm but gentle as he guides my arm to drape across his lap. He grazes two fingers from his other hand across the underside of my forearm, careful to avoid skimming the parts of my flesh that have split open.

I healed myself a little before we left the bridge, enough to take the burn away, but closing a wound birthed from blood magic is better suited to someone with a larger power source, someone like the high priestess.

Her or... the Black Art, whose face has twisted into something dark as he beholds the extent of my injury. "Weak stomach, Your Grace?" I ask.

His lips twitch but not in amusement. "You shouldn't have intervened. I told you to stay back."

"Perhaps in our time apart you have forgotten, Your Grace, but it's not often I heed the warnings of men."

His fingers press into the skin next to the start of the winding laceration, and I hiss. "I haven't forgotten, and look where it got you." He glances up at me through his long lashes, accusation heavy in his eyes.

I jerk my arm to pull it away, but he catches it, pinning it against his thigh.

"I do not need you to tend to me, and especially not if you are going to fault me for—"

A deep growl cuts me off. "I do not fault you for any of it. Only in that you have made it impossible to focus on the mission at hand. And that *fucking bloodwitch,*" Sin bares his teeth and doesn't finish the thought, his words bleeding into a snarl.

"That's twice now you've used that phrase to emphasize your hatred. I see our time together has done nothing to soften your opinion of my kind."

His eyes capture mine again, binding my stare in an impenetrable trap. "You and Alistair are nothing alike."

I shake my head. "That may be true, but our magics are sourced from the same dark well. I would be lying if I said I didn't find hunger in the aftermath of what Alistair did."

The Black Art's stare might as well be fire, setting me

ablaze everywhere he drags his gaze, flickering between my eyes, my mouth, the lines of my neck. "You do not need to feel shame for reacting to your body's desires. Your magic craves blood... power... control. It is not so different from my own. It's how you choose to react to those wants that separates you from Alistair."

I lean towards him, my head tilting to the side, suddenly too aware of everywhere my arm brushes against his lap. He reaches for the bottle he set at his feet, pops the cork from its slender neck, and hands it to me. "Drink up. Neither of us are going to enjoy this."

I grab the bottle and take a heavy swig of the sweet whiskey, its smooth finish coating my tongue in velvet. "Will it hurt you to heal the wound?" I ask.

He brings the cloth to my mouth and guides it between my teeth. "Only in spirit. It pains me to see you hurting, and especially at my hand."

The balled-up cloth dries my mouth as I close my lips around it. Sin scoots himself closer to me, laying my arm flat across his legs and wrapping his hands around it fully. "I'll be as gentle as I can."

That's the only warning I get before golden light appears beneath his palms, illuminating my flesh in a sickly yellow glow.

The pain is blinding.

My teeth sink into the cloth, and I turn my head away as a sharp hiss slips through my mouth. I think Sin mutters a curt apology, but the blood pounding in my ears tunes him out, and his words are lost to the wringing of my tendons as they try to twist and buck themselves free of the dark magic.

Fucking Alistair. *Fucking bloodwitch.*

The strained laughter that spurts from my mouth surprises me as much as it does Sin, and I giggle further at his puzzled expression. Spitting out the cloth, I say, "I'm beginning to share in your dislike for bloodwitches, Blackheart."

The ends of his lips twist up, and his eyes darken as he inclines his head towards me. "Careful how you speak of them, little witch. I happen to be rather fond of one."

My breath hitches at the use of the nickname. The Black Art may have begun referring to me as his *little witch* in condescension months ago, but it quickly grew into a term of endearment, and one that set my nerves on fire at that. In the best way possible.

But that was then. Things are different now.

We are different now.

"Blood magic is like poison; it turns the meat rancid if left in it too long. I need to lift it before closing the wound fully."

"Just do it," I rasp, the pain slithering its way through the mental barrier I put up.

Sin doesn't hesitate. His magic bleeds into my own, coursing through my body like an avalanche, swelling my veins with his chilled touch, and leaving a frosty finish everywhere his collective brushes mine. My breath catches again as our collectives join fully and his consciousness melds with my own, the seams of our minds overlapping until I'm not sure where mine ends and his begins.

My back arches as he steers his magic into the wound, sinking his mental claws into my flesh and locking them around the catalyst. My arm hollers with the pressure, the remnants of the whip's grip weakening as Sin lifts it from my flesh, my entire body warming with fever. Too hot.

Too fucking hot!

Agony lashes through me once more as he tears it free, the last of Alistair's toxic magic slipping through my tendons and returning to the ether. Sin works quickly, fusing my skin back together in a perfect seam and erasing the scar with a few more intentional touches. Sweat beads across my neck, my body burning up and ice cold at the same time, and my balance gives way.

Sin catches me before I fall from the bench, his arms wrapped around my waist to hold me steady against his side. I want to shrug him off, to recoil from his touch, but despite the warmth emanating from him, his touch is a balm to the firestorm slowly fading within me. We stay like this for a few minutes, both of us silent apart from my labored breathing, the tips of his fingers gently rubbing circles on my bicep.

When the last of the embers burn out, I sit upright, Sin's hands lingering for what feels like a couple seconds longer than necessary before falling to hang loosely over his knees as he leans his weight forward.

My voice is strained when I whisper, "Thank you."

"I know it wasn't pleasant."

My eyes flash to his. "I've been through worse."

If I thought the Black Art capable of remorse, it glimmers in his eyes now, his pupils ringed with a yellow hue from the magic expulsion. And suddenly, the air between us shifts— heavier, thicker, wringing the breath from my lungs as he searches my face. I'm not sure what he's looking for, but his voice is husky when he finally speaks. "I'm sorry," he whispers.

His words are weighted, and the small creases around his downturned eyes have me uncertain if he's referring to the pain I just suffered at the expense of his healing, or something more. I open my mouth to speak, but my mind dumps the thoughts before I manage to say anything. Something in his stare ensnares me, capturing my own as if caught in a trance. His breathing shifts heavier, and his eyes snag on my lips for the briefest of moments before he fleets them up to mine again.

I snap my head forward again, shattering his invisible hold, and instead watch as the branches of the mighty oaks sway, the summer wind tousling their leaves like tangled manes. The sky has blackened since we've been out here, the moonlight our own personal lantern as we sit in the quiet, listening to the dancing grasses and the thrumming of our own hearts.

I startle when Sin's voice breaks the silence. "How is she?" He murmurs the question, his voice a fleeting caress in my ear.

My throat swells, and I swallow the lump that forms in it. I don't need to ask who he's referring to. "She is well." A choked laugh spills out of me, and I look down at my hands that have clasped together and settled on my lap. "More than well, actually. My sister has always had an affinity for nature, and she possesses the greenest thumb anyone's ever had. And now she's living in a forest straight out of a fairytale with new herbs and flowers to discover. I dare say Cosmina is thriving."

He scratches the underside of his jaw which is now blanketed in a light scruff. "And you?" he asks, voice thick.

I capture my bottom lip and roll it between my teeth before letting out a short exhale. "I have lost the only home I have ever known. Forced my family from their only source of comfort and put them all in danger in the process. Eldridge hates my guts, and I don't blame him. He has every right to be angry with me, and I was unnecessarily cruel to him."

"Eldridge pinned you into a corner he knew you couldn't get out of," Sin growls. "He knew what he was doing when he asked you that."

When he demanded to know if Sin and I had been intimate while Cosmina lay rotting beneath our feet. "It doesn't matter. I didn't have to answer him the way I did."

"When you told him you loved it when I fucked you?"

His question stops me short, and I whip my head towards him, willing away the warmth staining my cheeks. I'm expecting one of his signature smirks to be plastered on his mouth, but his expression is reserved, only a sliver of amusement peeking out in the slight raise of one of his cheekbones. "Do not. Go there. In fact, never think of me that way again." I thrust the words at him and clench my thighs together so my right one no longer brushes his.

He tracks the movement, his own fingers curling slightly against his leg. "Why did you intervene with Alistair? I had it under control. You put yourself at unnecessary risk."

His abrupt change of topic has me furrowing my brow for a moment. "Why did you shift in front of your father and an entire kingdom brigade?" I shoot back. *And he means to caution me on unnecessary risks?*

Sin shakes his head and runs a hand through his long hair. "They weren't trying to wound you, Wren—they were aiming to plant that bolt right into your heart. They were trying to kill you," he says, voice harder now.

I shrug my shoulders, sharpening my eyes to slivered points. "Sounds to me like they would have done you a giant favor, then. Taken out your enemy and your vicious ex-lover in one shot."

Wrath shadows his face, and he leans towards me. My own breath catches as the warmth from his trails a lazy finger down my throat. "Do not mistake my past indiscretions to mean I do not care about you, Wren."

I smile sweetly. "I don't have to. Your current ones make that very clear, Your Grace, without me having to bring forth the past."

I don't fully mean it. He could have allowed his soldier to bury that arrow into my heart and strip the final breath from my lungs. But he didn't. He dug into the deepest source of his magic and used it to shift under iron, to break his bindings and emerge in his other form, the one he kept hidden from everyone.

Everyone, except me.

I am not so ignorant as to be unaware how much the Black Art put at risk to save my life, shielding me with his body to take that fatal arrow meant for my own. But even so, it does not erase the pain he inflicted when he kept my sister imprisoned and lied to my face about it.

He inches closer, his steel and peppercorn scent wafting into my nose, petting my tongue. My mouth waters involuntarily, and my thighs press together tighter. I turn my head to look away, but he catches my jaw with one of his hands and steers it back towards him. Without a word, he leans forward and presses his forehead to mine, the strands of his inky hair curtaining either side of my face.

"I'm sorry," he whispers again. He uttered these words earlier, but they are different now. Tenderer. Absolute.

His warmth wraps around me, enveloping me in his scent and setting every frayed nerve on fire.

Familiar.

That's what the Black Art feels like, his hand still cupping my jaw, his forehead pressed to mine with our eyes closed. And as much as I may hate to admit it, a part of me has yearned to feel this again, whatever it is, however wrong it may be. It does not erase what he has done, but his apology lodges deep in my throat, stealing any words I might have said.

He tilts his head back and softly brushes his mouth where his forehead had just been, his lips skimming for a moment before he releases my jaw and rises to his feet. And without another word, the Black Art slips back into the church, the door creaking shut between us.

CHAPTER 21

Sleep is fitful. Gerard instructed us to sleep in the mostly empty storage rooms upstairs, adjacent to his private quarters. Eldridge and I laid out our bedrolls in the room nearest to the high priest's, while Sin and Alistair settled in the one closest to the stairs. Alistair had a few snide remarks to make when Sin insisted on sleeping nearest the exit, but I have no doubts as to why the Black Art chose that one. Perhaps it was foolish to believe that Sin merely wanted to be near the exit to better hear should anyone try sneaking into the temple, but I did. Ever the strategist, even here, even now.

But it isn't fear of someone slipping into the church that leaves me restless and waking after only a few hours.

Do not mistake my past indiscretions to mean I do not care about you, Wren.

Faded red curtains are drawn shut over the open window to block out the faint glow of dawn, but they also keep the fresh air locked outside. And right now, fresh air is exactly what I need to rid myself of the Black Art's words that haven't stopped echoing in my mind since he uttered them.

Careful not to disturb Eldridge, I crawl out from my blanket and reach for my bag that stores my cloak and extra shirts in case it is chilly outside at this early morning hour. The leather bag sighs as I grasp it, and daring a glance at Eldridge to confirm the sound didn't wake him, I slip it around my arm and tiptoe out of the room. I'm confident a full-on war could break out in front of the church right now and even that wouldn't be loud enough to penetrate Eldridge's rhythmic snoring, but I don't want to chance it.

I pause to deliberate while my eyes adjust to the swallowing darkness in the hallway. I could slip out the back entrance, but despite the bordering tree cover, the sun will be blessing the undeserving capital with its light soon enough, and being outside at all, especially alone, feels too exposing.

The gleam of a black silver-veined metal fixed to a door farther down the hall catches my eye. I briefly remember Gerard gesturing to it during our tour, mentioning it led to the bell tower. Clutching my bag against my side, I head for the door, pushing it open as quietly as the old, groaning wood allows me to, and close it softly behind me.

A spiraling metal staircase winds several stories above my head. Over a decade spent living in the Autumnhelm Forest has left me physically fit, but even so, glass fills my lungs by the time I round the top platform, my chest heaving as I bend forward to place my hands on my knees, catching my breath. *At least there aren't any fucking staircases in the woods.*

The belfry is much larger on the inside than it appeared looking up at it from the ground. The platform is square-shaped with four arching windows carved into the stone tower overlooking Blackreach, and in the center of it all, rigged to a wooden mechanism through a labyrinth of braided ropes, is a massive, coppery bell. Dangling from the center is the bell's tongue, the clapper a lighter shade of brown-red than the rest of the chime. It is typical for church bells to be rung at midday, so if Gerard continues to ring this bell despite the temple being closed to the public, I'll be long gone by then.

There's a bench on the platform at the front side of the bell, and a small circular table beside it. Apparently I'm not the only one who finds comfort being up here. The city is sweeping from this vantage point. City streets running perpendicular to one another, the buttery gleam of the sun's first rays polishing the cobblestones into shimmery, gilded gems. It is too far to make out any of the signs, but the circular clearing in the center of the capital is impossible to miss. It was only months ago I met Bennett Langston in that market center, when he first informed me that the kingdom his family so loyally served was dutifully planning their next war. The one that would outlaw transcendents completely.

The one that would make my family *illegal*.

I promised the Black Art I would keep his secret so long as he kept his militant paws off transcendent-kind, and I held up my part—deceived my family even—to keep that knowledge hidden. And for what? Sin shifted—he *chose* to shift—in front of his own guard. Though, I suppose *chose* isn't a fair word. That iron bolt was meant for me, and bloodwitch aside, my heart is meaty and tender and would have accepted that fatal arrow as hungrily as anyone else's.

But it didn't get the chance.

The memory of Sin leaping over me flashes in my mind, his muscled legs finding purchase in the dirt as he shielded me with his body, taking the iron bolt into his flesh and bone. It was single-handedly the worst decision he could have made for himself. Which is why he didn't.

He made it for me.

A gust of wind rips through the open-air belfry, and my shoulders shudder with the icy nip. I reach a hand into the bag I set at my feet, my fingers curling around a soft bundle of fabric. I punch my arms into the openings of the shirt and pull it shut around me, but immediately note the extra fabric at my waist does not belong to the shirt-jacket I was expecting.

His scent rips through the seam of my lips a second later. Sword oils and peppercorn and something deeper, woodsier, like cedar, wrestle for my focus, teasing my tongue with his mouthwatering aroma. This is the shirt I swiped from the Black Art when he hid my clothes the second morning of our trip. The one I refused to give back to him out of spite. I stuffed it in my bag as a personal trophy, intent on returning it eventually, maybe, but now that I note just how much it smells like him, feels like him... perhaps I'll hold onto it a bit longer.

It wasn't long ago Sin and I painted these streets red with Legion blood, and I inhaled the perfume of their suffering, their abandon, deep into my lungs. It was intoxicating, thrilling, arousing. As if their torment settled deep into my core, the sounds of their dying breaths feeding my sex with every anguished, gasping pant.

I have not allowed myself to remember the details of what the Black Art and I did in his study that night, how we devoured and lapped at each other as if our very skin were petrified from honey. Months endured through which I dismissed my unyielding attraction to him, my hunger that was growing more painful with each passing day, and when the battle concluded, I was nothing short of *starved*.

I bury my nose in the collar, inviting Sin's scent farther into my body, and my hand slides under the waistband of my leggings. I work it down my legs, between my thighs, and pull my underwear to the side, the tips of my fingers skimming my sex greedily. While I hate admitting that the Black Art's proximity has any effect on me, the wetness pooling beneath my hand makes it impossible to deny. I swirl the pads of my pointer and middle fingers through my slick, my hips arching into them as my thumb rubs deep circles against my clit.

My other hand clutches Sin's shirt tighter, desperate to feel some part of him, as I dive a finger into my eager pussy. A low moan spills from my lips, and my hips rock faster, inviting a second finger into my heat.

When you told him you loved it when I fucked you?

Sin's words echo in my mind, and if possible, I grow wetter at the sound of his raspy voice in my head. His arrogance filled me with ire before, but right now, with the Black Art not around to witness my body's betrayal, it's exactly his confidence that has me moving my fingers in and out faster, an insurmountable pressure building within. It's been too long since I've found release, and Sin's closeness has stoked the fire that's been climbing to a dangerous height in my core, in my cunt that's now gripping my fingers for dear life. *It's not as if his confidence comes unwarranted,* I think, remembering the night on my balcony when Sin fingered me into one of the best orgasms of my existence.

I pull in a deep breath, his peppery steel scent gliding down my throat, and I come undone on my fingers. I'm suddenly grateful for the height of the tower because the moans that slip from my mouth are louder now, forceful, as I clench and unclench, my fingers glazed in my own glistening slick. When I ride out the last of the euphoric waves, stars winking in and out of my vision, I clutch Sin's shirt tighter still. The stars blink one final time, thrusting me into a darkness as black as the night sky.

*

It is mid-morning when consciousness finds me, the daytime sun highlighting the city in a citrine glow. I didn't mean to doze off up here, but after my body released the tension tightly coiled around my every nerve, exhaustion quickly seeped in to fill the space. The others are likely still asleep after having traveled so far the day before, and then unexpectedly through the night, courtesy of Alistair's spontaneous murder spree.

I slip my bag over my shoulder and head for the stairs. Descending them is much easier on my tired body than climbing them, and I reach the second story of the temple within a minute or so. I open the door that leads back to the storage rooms, careful to make sure the wood doesn't creak too loudly and wake the others. I can use this opportunity to change, and maybe the high priest has a basin and some water we can use for washing in his quarters when he—

A large hand clamps across my mouth, and an arm snakes around my waist, pinning my back against a hard body. A pair of lips find my ear before I can make a sound or grasp my magic, and a nose skims across my lobe.

"I need you to be very quiet, little witch," Sin murmurs in a voice like satin.

I go still. Too still, assessing my situation. My back is pinned firmly between Sin's hands and his front, ensnared in his trap. Every instinct hollers at me to flex my magic, conjure a ward around me, but something about the Black Art's grip has me ignoring them all. His hand viced around my waist doesn't feel violent but rather... *possessive.*

"Walk with me," he whispers again in my ear, his tone commanding.

I allow him to steer me down the hall, and when he sees I'm trusting him enough to blindly go with him, he drops his hand from my mouth. He leads us past the stairs that descend to the entrance level, and just as we pass, voices carry up from the ground floor. My eyes widen, and I turn to look at Sin over my shoulder, but he gives me a slight shake of his head and snaps my face forward again, his fingers twisting into the unbound hair at my nape. Not hard enough to hurt me, but enough to keep me from trying to look behind myself again.

Ice beads down my spine like buttons of a fine gown, every muscle cinching as Sin and I sneak down the long hallway, conscious of our footsteps. There are only a few rooms up here, and Sin steers us past the final door, gently pushing me farther down the corridor. We come to a dead end, a wall adorned with a large glacial blue tapestry with a gold embroidered border.

My vision bleeds the colors together as he whirls us around so I'm facing the stairwell, and he backs us up—*into* the tapestry. I duck my head around the quilted art he holds to the side, and he releases the blanket so it swings closed in front of us, sealing us into a very dark, very *tight* compartment.

The space is barely large enough for one adult body, but Sin and I manage to squeeze both of us in, though not without consequence. I am painfully aware of everywhere his body touches mine, my back pinned against his chest, his long, silky hair brushing my shoulders. He has one hand cinched around my left bicep and the other on my stomach, pressing me more firmly against his front. It's not his fault—there just isn't enough room for both of us without him pulling me against his chest, melding our bodies into one.

"What is going on?" I ask in a voice low enough for only him to hear.

"My father is having the city turned inside out. They would have found the guards at the bridge early this morning, so it seems they've been given orders to search every building in Blackreach. He will assume the bridge was my mother's doing... or *yours*," he adds darkly.

"It *was* our doing."

"It was Alistair's doing," he growls. "Regardless, they showed up a few minutes ago and you were nowhere to be found." His tone is chastising, his lips skimming the tip of my ear that peeks through my tangled hair.

"Where is Eldridge?" I demand. If we're here in a hidden space sized only for one—*two* if one person presses their ass so far into the other's crotch they're practically in their pants—then where are the others?

"There's a crawl space beneath the floorboards on the main level. Gerard got them both in there before the guards came in. It's a lot bigger than this space, but well, we can't exactly sneak down there while my men scour around, looking for the white-haired witch with a plentiful bounty on her head, can we?" His voice is playful, but there's a hardness to his words as if they were forged from steel.

A shaky breath rattles free before I can stop it, and I smash my lips together to keep it from happening again. Sin's body stills behind me, and his tone is gentler when he murmurs in my ear, "He is safe."

I nod wordlessly, grateful for his understanding. Eldridge and I may be fighting, but he's my best friend. He was always there for me, showing compassion when my darkest days had me speaking words I would later regret, and he never once made me feel guilty for them. And the first opportunity I was given to extend that same understanding to him, I failed miserably.

The hushed murmuring of voices grows louder, and the stairs creak under the guards' approaching footsteps. I snap to attention, which inadvertently drives my ass further against Sin's front, and I swear I hear a low groan slip out of him.

"Are you armed?" I ask.

"Always," he answers in a voice that's all grit and teeth.

Not that either of us needs to rely on steel with our magic unhindered, but if the Black Art taught me anything, it was to never rely on one weapon. I didn't remove the dagger from my thigh before going to sleep last night, but the one I usually carry flat under my waistband is next to my bedroll, in the storage room, completely unhelpful to me right now.

"It really is a lovely day outside. Shameful really, to be spending it poking around dusty storage rooms when you ought to be out there taking in Adelphia's light." Gerard's voice is much closer, and the cadence of their footsteps alters. They're on level ground now, in the hall.

Gooseflesh erupts on my arms, and Sin's thumb rubs soothing circles along my bicep, but I sense his growing tension in the alertness of his stance, the subtle shifting of his weight between his feet, and the hand that's still against my stomach clenches slightly.

There are sounds of rummaging from farther away—they're searching the rooms we slept in last night.

"The rays act as a catalyst for the goddess's divine light, you know? The sun has its own energy field, and Adelphia is known to amplify her own blessings by sharing in the sun's. It is a taxing endeavor, even for a goddess, to mold her power into something as powerful as the sun, but nothing is too great a challenge for the goddess of the arcane, oh no. Some may say it is rude to be scrounging through old, empty boxes, a snub to the goddess herself," Gerard rambles.

I furrow my brows, and Sin's head dips behind me, his lips pressed into the hollow of my neck to silence his chuckle. Adelphia may not be my chosen patron, but I have never heard any such stories of the goddess harnessing the power of the sun. The high priest is biding his time, trying to guilt or frighten the guards into leaving before they notice a suspicious tapestry at the end of the hall that most definitely isn't hiding the two most wanted people on the entire isle.

"The kingdom must employ very brave men indeed, I see," he continues. "As a high priest loyal to his station, I am most aware of the goddess's incredible warmth and affinity for acceptance, but I dare say, even I would never dare to snub one of the deities on a day such as this one, where she presents a gift in front of our very eyes. Staying indoors?" Gerard chuckles, and there's a slapping sound as if he smacks his hand to his rounded belly, "I may be close to meeting her, yes, but I think I'll hang on tightly to my final years. Needless to say, I'll be poking my gray head out as soon as all this nonse—" Gerard clears his throat, "erhm, *business,* is taken care of."

The closet doors in each of the rooms open and shut, and there is a sound of boxes sliding across the floor.

"How do we get to the bell tower?" a male voice asks.

Gerard must point to the door leading to the stairwell because a heavy set of footfalls traipse away from us. The door swings open with a screeching creak, and Gerard and the other guard continue chit chatting. Well, *Gerard* continues to speak in nuanced sentences while the guard makes occasional *humpfs* of acknowledgment, his boots thudding against the floor as he slowly paces the hall. The other guard returns a minute later.

"Empty. You sure you haven't seen anything, Priest?" asks the one who returned.

"High Priest, actually, and no, Sir, I'm afraid I have not. I'll be sure to send word should circumstances come to alter themselves."

"You've got quite a few horses out back," the guard continues. "Seems like a lot for one priest."

"Hardly a lot at all when you consider the workload that's been dumped on me," Gerard answers without missing a beat. "Who do you think was responsible for hauling all the furniture and supplies out of here after the fire? I've been making trips to and from the sister church in Emberbourne. The heavier the load, the more horses required." *The priest is clever, I'll give him that.*

An extended pause, then the guards utter a curt dismissal and take their leave.

I continue to breathe through my nose until the main door slams shut. There's a scraping sound from below us, followed by Eldridge and Alistair's muffled voices.

"Well that was closer than I'd like," I say with a sharp exhale.

Sin chuckles softly. "I rather enjoy us being this close."

I whirl around, hand raised to smack his arms off of me, but he catches it. His mouth parts, and he lifts my hand to his face, his expression morphing into something... not angry but... *bestial.*

"What are you doing—let go of me!" I try to yank my arm away, but his grip on my wrist tightens, an iron bracelet.

He turns my hand over so his nose skims the delicate skin along the hollow of my wrist, his nostrils flaring at the pressure point there. I watch him carefully, scrutinizing his reaction, and his eyes drop to my—his—shirt. A wicked smile tugs on his lips, and then realization hits.

Fuck me.

I spin around, this time pulling my hand free from his, but his arm bands around my waist before I can duck through the tapestry. He pulls me against his chest again, and I feel the veins bulging in his forearm as his other hand finds mine again and forces it over my head.

His lips brush the fingers of my right hand. The one I used to pleasure myself with last night.

"Tell me, little witch, how do you expect me not to think of you this way when you're wearing my shirt and touching yourself in it?"

I resist the urge to kick my leg back and plant my boot into his knee. Willing warmth out of my cheeks and emotion from my voice, I answer in a tone sounding almost bored. "What I do with my body is none of your concern, Your Grace."

"Everything between your thighs is my concern, love."

Before I can react, he takes my middle and index fingers and sucks them into his mouth. And for some reason I don't understand, I let him. Just for a moment.

One brutal, agonizing moment.

"You taste like starlight," he murmurs into the juncture of my shoulder and neck. It's not the first time he's said that to me, and my body betrays me by reacting in a way it really, really shouldn't.

It would be impossible to miss the feel of his straining cock against my ass in the too-tight space. My sex clenches in response.

No. He does not get to do this to me. If the Black Art wants to play with fire, let's fucking play.

I spin on my heels and wrap my hand around his cock, only the thin material of his night pants separating us. Sin unleashes a growl—the sound part warning, part needing. His shaft twitches beneath my touch, and goddess above, my pussy weeps with the reminder of his size. It's too dark for me to see his face clearly, which I use to my advantage as I lower my other hand to my thigh.

"Little witch," he rasps, his voice a low and husky thing. It should be illegal for any man's voice to sound that sexy.

One stroke. That's all it takes. One stroke of Sin's stiffened cock and he's distracted enough for me to slip my dagger free of its holster. The blade is under his chin half a second later.

He smiles. *He fucking smiles.*

"I'm getting mixed signals, love."

I angle my knife so the blade skims his jugular, my other hand still wrapped around his erection, which I swear, swells even more now. "Touch me again, and I take it off permanently."

I keep him pinned a moment longer, his narrowed eyes drinking me in like he's just been brought a bottle of the finest mead coin can buy. His lips are still turned up in a facetious smirk, but to his credit, he keeps whatever thoughts he's thinking to himself.

I drop my knife and his dick in the same movement, secure my weapon to my thigh, and leave with my head held high, ignoring the terrible ache between my legs.

CHAPTER 22

O ur fate rests on the candle dancing inside its brass prison. A simple hand lantern resting on a ledge of a church's bell tower—common enough it shouldn't draw attention from the guards, but the location specific enough for Ileana to recognize the summons.

"You think she can see it from this distance?" I ask.

Sin and I lit the candle, now dripping creamy yellow beeswax inside the lantern, while Eldridge and Alistair readied the horses out back. Once Sin convenes with his Hand, the four of us need to vacate the city, leaving no trace we were ever here. Gerard has a wagon he takes into the sister cities south of the capital to stock up on oils and candles for anointing, and a variety of herbs for his practice. The guards know his face as a frequent traveler, and the high priest said they've never checked his cart before.

Sin nods, but it's the only movement he makes, the rest of him as still and rigid as stone. His arms are folded across his flowy white shirt, the fabric pushed up to his elbows, and the warm brown skin of his chest peeking out through the loosened strings of his top. "At this hour and from her vantage point, yes."

It's not yet dawn. The moon bathes the capital in pearly

shadow, the glow of the candle a beacon in the night. She'll see it. She has to.

"And you're sure she'll come?" I ask, not sure why I'm suddenly plagued with doubt. Anxiety. Fear. Because if Ileana doesn't come and Sin doesn't have the chance to explain what's going on, she'll allow Dusaro to lead the entire kingdom army to the Vale.

To my family.

"She'll come," is all he says, but the muscle feathering along his jaw does not escape my notice.

The Black Art is nervous.

I leave him to his thoughts and take a seat on the bench, leaning my weight on one of the arms and propping my chin up with my hand. Seconds feel like minutes, minutes like hours. Realistically, only another half an hour passes before daybreak crests the mountains and the dull yellow lantern gleams with a gilded finish.

Sin begins to pace, his hands stuffed deep in his black trouser pockets, locks of his inky hair billowing in the morning air. When he turns to pace my direction again, the sunlight catches the burnt umber of his cheek, and his green eyes gleam with that familiar golden glow, though this time, from an entirely mundane cause. My breath hitches at the sight of him, but if his transcendent ears take notice, he doesn't show it.

Singard Kilbreth is cold. Calculating. Cruel. But something about him sets a fever raging deep inside me, and there aren't enough medicinal salves in the world to balm that burn.

I notice immediately when his eyes suddenly narrow further, followed by a deep exhale. I spring to my feet, my own sigh of relief falling from my lips as I follow his gaze. Racing down one of the side streets as if she were racing the dawn itself, velvety green cloak fanning out around her, is the Black Hand herself.

Ileana is quiet for a long moment as she makes sense of everything Sin told her. She paces the length of the church, her soft cloak brushing the wood beneath her leather boots, her hands clasped neatly against her waist. Her skepticism was expected, especially towards Sin's confession of his transcendence. It took nothing short of him lengthening his claws and teeth for her to accept it as truth, and then she went silent, musing over what the Black Art has requested of her.

"I am not ignorant to the risk I ask of you, but it is one we must take if we are to avoid war. We cannot afford the distraction with Baelliarah watching from the water—they'll move in as soon as they spot the disturbance. As much as I dislike putting you in this position, I need you, Ileana. *Your people* need you." Sin's tone is gentle with his Hand, but firm.

Ileana turns to face Sin head-on, her hands dropping to her sides. "You needn't question my loyalty, Your Grace, to you or my people. It is not what you ask of me that disturbs me but the fact that you stand here, able-bodied and without magical restraint, and you are *choosing* to return to the elves with your... escorts," she says, her brown eyes meeting each of ours in turn, lingering on mine a second longer than the others.

"I cannot expect you to understand, so I won't ask you to. To put it simply, there is a certain... treasure... in the Vale I cannot have destroyed. I must return to protect it. Please try to understand that, at least."

Eldridge and Alistair share a glance, but I suddenly find fascination in the hem of Ileana's cloak, unable to meet any of the pairs of eyes in this room. I'm quite certain I know what *treasure* the Black Art speaks of, and that knowledge sends my heart pounding mercilessly against its bone cage.

"Your father isn't going to like this," she speaks matter-of-factly, her eyes trained back on Sin.

There's a growl in his voice when he answers. "*My father* isn't ruling in my absence. Protocols are in place for a reason— he bows to you now." He shoves his hand into one of his pockets and pulls out a small, brown leather box. "The high priestess of the elves loaned me this. The ring is enchanted; rub the stone and you'll establish a connection with me. As long as I have something reflective to use as a scrying piece, I'll be able to see through the eye of the jewelry. This way we can stay in contact until we... until we resolve this."

Ileana takes the box and opens it, revealing a silver band sporting a fat, faceted ruby. She slips it onto her finger, the polished metal bright against her slender brown digit. "I see subtly wasn't high on your priority list," she chastises, holding her hand out in front of her. "Your father has called for a public address to be held in the market center this morning. After your bloodhound's stunt on the bridge, he assumes Seraphine and hers have infiltrated the city. Too many civilians saw the bodies... I believe he intends to address the reasoning behind them so everyone will be made aware. More eyes in the city looking for them," she explains.

Sin rubs his hand along the underside of his jaw, then rakes it through his long hair. "To be expected, I suppose." The look he shoots Alistair is laced with poison, and the bloodwitch smirks in response, shrugging his shoulders. "So long as Baelliarah doesn't know, I suppose it doesn't matter if the isle is made aware of my temporary absence."

"Yeah... temporary," Eldridge huffs, running a hand down his braided beard.

Ileana is in front of him a second later, her eyes reduced to slivered points at the corners. She points a finger at Eldridge's chest. "Whether you like it or not, you are still in the presence of your Black Art, and you would be wise to remember that."

If it's possible, Eldridge's chest puffs out farther. "I bow to no Black Art," he says slowly, each word coming out distinct.

"That isn't a choice you get to make," Ileana snaps. "He could break every one of you into tiny pieces with half a thought and you—"

"I do not fear his wrath, female, and neither should you," he interrupts, stepping forward so his chest brushes against her outstretched finger. I have known Eldridge too long to view him as something to be frightened of, but to someone who doesn't know him...

The Black Hand shifts her weight to balance on her toes, but even with the additional height, her forehead only comes to Eldridge's chin. "You may not fear his wrath, but I promise you this, *male*, you will fear mine."

Goddess above, I love her.

To my surprise, Eldridge remains quiet, but a smirk settles on his mouth and excitement flashes in his gray eyes, seemingly finding amusement in her words. Or perhaps he's just impressed that this woman, who weighs a third of his weight, has nerves forged from iron itself.

My friend relinquishes a few inches, and Ileana turns back to Sin. "I'll rub the ring so you can observe the address. And for the love of Adelphia, Singard, do not stir up any more trouble sneaking out of here."

The grin he flashes her is devastating. "Wouldn't dream of it, my Lady."

CHAPTER 23

No one in this odious city can resist the call of a public address it seems; the townsmen and women flock to the market center like unruly geese. The cobblestone streets leading to the event are packed in with bodies, entrances to the small shops blocked with the crowd, and the roads now unsuitable for horse travel.

The four of us watch from inside the belfry, the vantage point granting us a decent view over the attraction, though it is too far to see anyone clearly, and too far for sound to travel, even for Sin and Eldridge. Gerard loaned us a standing mirror from his private quarters, and Eldridge hauled it up here earlier, its glass a perfect surface for scrying.

The mirror appears to be crafted from solid mahogany, polished into a dark glossy brown, and carved vein-ridden leaves run across the top and down the sides. It isn't long before Dusaro takes his place on the center dais, Ileana and Aldred flanking him on either side. I catch glimpses of armored guards mingled throughout the crowd, and more posted at the start of every street leading to and from the event.

Sin hovers his hand above the mirror, and the glass turns frosted. A moment later, the frost dissipates, Sin's magic agitating that in Ileana's ring, and the glass becomes a reflection of everything the Hand sees. Residents crowd the dais, and bodies continue squeezing into the circle from the side streets. It isn't often the kingdom makes public addresses, and especially not on short notice. The city dwellers know something is amiss, and they're starved for new gossip to spread amongst the high-ranking families. Anyone not present will know everything spoken by the end of day, though the facts will likely be delivered in various shades of truth by the time the final rays of sunlight vanish beyond the mountains.

A mane of long, straight hair—as dark and shiny as tumbled obsidian—comes into view. Dusaro. Sin shifts at my side, crossing his arms across his chest, and his mouth twitches as if he's running his tongue across his teeth. I resist the urge to put my hand on his arm, knowing the tumultuous relationship he shares with his father.

The crowd whistles and cheers as Dusaro approaches the lectern, bracing his hands flat on the surface, his arms stiff as boards. Neat braids span either side of his face, his hair spilling down the back of his long, black cloak, gold threading along the seams of the shoulders and wrists. He raises one hand, and the communal roaring silences at once.

Dusaro's voice is thick with authority when he speaks, his words clipped and edged in iron. It isn't difficult to imagine where Sin picked up many of his mannerisms. He's the spitting image of his father, except where Dusaro's heart is frozen through and through, I've seen a faint ember fighting for breath in the depths of Sin's.

"I have no interest in taking more time from any of you than is needed, so I will be quick. I will be blunt," Dusaro addresses the crowd.

I suck in a deep breath. There's no stopping Sin's father

from informing the capital city that their Black Art has been captured. He'll stoke their hatred for transcendents, once again posing them in the darkest light, but this time, blaming them for an act their reputation will never recover from. Dusaro is going to declare war on transcendent-kind, overhauling everything I did to keep Sin from doing the same, and there's not a damn thing I can do about it.

It was a mistake capturing the Black Art.

Sin cared more about protecting his identity than this war. But Dusaro... there is nothing that excites him more than war.

"The Black Art is missing," he says, voice booming.

Gasps and faint mutters of surprise sound from the sea of townsmen and women. The image in the mirror focuses on Dusaro, Ileana shifting her gaze to look at him directly now, and Dusaro's side profile engulfs much of the glass. I dare another look at Sin and find his jaw clenched painfully, his stare so sharp I'm certain it'll shatter the mirror into a thousand glittering fragments. But we knew this was coming.

"He was taken by *beasts*. Men that hide and cower behind the skin of another, whose spirits are too weak to withstand their duties in the flesh and bone they've been given. Adelphia blessed the Black Art with her rich ichor, and it was with this that the Black Art has betrayed her."

No. *No, no, no.* Ileana's vision whips to the crowd, scanning their reactions, some startled, most puzzled, then snaps back to Dusaro. His form grows larger as if she takes a couple steps towards him, but she halts when he stops her with a look. His gaze lingers for only a moment, but it is enough for her to heed his caution. There is nothing but ice in his dark irises, his stare cold, unrelenting, and undeniably a warning.

Alistair and Eldridge mutter something to one another behind me, but my eyes are locked on Sin, who now more closely resembles the *beast* his father speaks of.

"It is my greatest disappointment, as Aegidale's acting Hand, and as a father, to inform you all of this betrayal, but I must uphold my duty with honor." Dusaro pauses, scanning the crowd before condemning our fate. Condemning his son. "Singard Kilbreth is a transcendent. He swore an oath to all of you, to the goddess of the arcane herself, and I regret to tell you his ascension was invalid before it even began. Shifter blood is blasphemous—dirty spillage from the ancient god, Slaine— may he rot without mercy in the next realm—and is not honored within the bindings of kingdom law.

"He abandoned his post to join the revolting things that stalk amongst the Vale, but rest assured neither our beloved Black Hand nor myself had any such knowledge of Singard's cursed magic. Ileana is hereby acting regent of the isle until the next Rite is performed, and within her capable hands, Aegidale can sleep without fear. I bid you all farewell."

As quickly as he emerged, Dusaro steps off the dais with haste, immediately flanked by four guards in heavy armor. Ileana's gaze drops to the large rock on her finger, and I can nearly *feel* her apology, her fear.

The glass streaks with crimson. Ileana's ruby shreds to ribbons, the mirror's surface cracked and fragmented around Sin's fist, blood pouring from his knuckles, but it doesn't stop him from punching the mirror a second time.

I catch his arm before he sinks his fist in a third time and step around him, blocking the mirror with my body. My mouth waters at the scent of his pulp, but I swallow it down, willing the saliva to be enough to satiate my thirst. Eldridge cautions Alistair behind me, the male bloodwitch not as accustomed to denying his appetite.

Sin turns and braces both hands against the wall behind him, his forehead resting on the stone while he collects himself. I whisper his name.

"We need to move. Get Gerard," is his only response.

We don't take time to empty the cart before the four of us squeeze into it. Gerard tethers our horses to the wagon and slams the wooden panel shut after Alistair slips in last, bathing us all in darkness. Sin was first in, leaning his weight against a stack of locked crates, and Eldridge sits on the floor next to him. Alistair is partially sitting on an upturned bucket, his hand combed through his hair, and I'm wedged in between another stack of boxes and Eldridge's jutting knees, which he can't seem to keep in his own space.

The cracking of reins incites the horses to move, and the cart begins to sway with the clip-clopping of hooves against cobblestone.

"Well, we're royally fucked," Eldridge huffs, running a hand down the plait of red hair hanging down his back.

"This wasn't supposed to happen," I murmur, shaking my head. "Why would he do this—*how* could he do this?" I don't ask the questions in earnest, and no one answers them as such.

Dusaro stands mighty and speaks of beasts that prey on the weak, but it was *he* that tossed his only son to the wolves like he was nothing more than spoiled meat. Heat tunnels in my veins, the thought an unwelcome reminder of my own mother ushering me into the street, never to return to the only warmth and security I'd ever known.

"You said you could trust her," Eldridge spits, his hands now dangling off his partially bent knees.

"This wasn't Ileana's doing," I supply before Sin can answer, though his attention is fixed on the floor, and he gives no indication he hears us at all. "She didn't know what Dusaro was planning." I may not know the Hand well, but enough to know she longs for loyalty more than anything else. She wouldn't have betrayed Sin. Not because she's his sworn Hand, but because Sin showed her kindness when so few have.

"Sera's going to be a ray of sunshine when she learns of this. Who wants the privilege of telling her first?" Alistair queries, twirling his loose curls around his finger like satin ribbons.

I turn back to Sin, and my heart sinks into my stomach as I regard the dejection on his face. He doesn't wear the melancholy on his sleeve, but I've studied the Black Art enough to pinpoint the clenched muscles in his jaw, the stiffness in the lines of his neck, the slight raise to his shoulders. Features that may appear incensed to others, but the sorrow in his downturned eyes does not escape my notice.

With everyone huddled around the city's center, the wagon glides along the side streets without pause or disruption, so when Gerard slows the horses and the cart comes to a halt, we know we've reached the gate. I suck in a deep breath, my pulse thrumming erratically in my neck, my ears. Eldridge places a sun-kissed hand on my knee and gives a slight squeeze, undoubtedly hearing the quickening of my heart.

A single set of footsteps approach the wagon, and Gerard and the guard exchange forced pleasantries, the high priest explaining he is heading to Suncove to stock up on a variety of oils, herbs, and beeswax for the church.

"Mind stepping out and popping her open so we can see inside?" asks the guard.

"I can't imagine what for, hardly anything back there aside from some empty trunks for me to haul my supplies back in, and some leather volumes to help me share the goddess's word."

"I apologize for the inconvenience, Priest, but Lord Kilbreth has ordered for every cart to be inspected, or they don't cross the bridge."

"Perhaps Lord Kilbreth has forgotten the church has immunity to such outlandish ordinances. You're young so I won't fault you for your ignorance, son, but I am a *High* Priest, and am under no legal obligation to subject my personal belongings to prying eyes."

"I know the law," the guard snaps. A long pause and then, "Fine, hurry on up through but don't expect—"

"What's the hold up, Evans?" a different male voice calls from farther away, followed by footsteps. "Why haven't you inspected the wagon?"

"He's with the church, Sir," the first guard—Evans —answers.

"No immunity—not anymore, Priest."

I look to Eldridge, then to Sin, sliding my hand to the dagger at my thigh. Eldridge straightens and silently rises to his feet, his hand reaching over his shoulder to rest on the hilt of his blade. Sin tracks both our movements, but makes none of his own as he listens to Gerard arguing with the second voice, the one in charge.

"This is outlandish. You cannot disregard the code because you feel like it—it is the law!"

"And our orders were issued from the law. Now step down and open your cart, or I'm busting it open myself, Priest," the guard spits.

Wood splits to my right, and I whirl around to see Alistair hopping through the gaping hole his magic punched through the cart's back panel, flames licking both his palms.

For the love of Elysande, why can nothing go right on this fucking trip?

I'm following Alistair a second later, my dagger in hand and Eldridge hot on my heels. The whir of metal sliding across its scabbard grazes my ears as Eldridge unsheathes his weapon and sidles up next to me, his knuckles lengthened into claws around the hilt. The guards spring into action, drawing their weapons and ordering for us to drop our own, and Alistair chuckles in response, raising one fire clad palm.

"*Don't.*" Sin's command is weighted with authority as he steps out of the wagon last, his steps slow and deliberate, his attention wholly on the guards in front of us. There are six in total now, four others having joined from their post closer to the gate.

"Traitor," the one in charge shouts, pointing to Sin with the tip of his sword. "On your knees, now!"

I bare my teeth.

Sin raises both hands in a placating gesture. "We are not here to hurt you. I know the lies you've been told, that I abandoned my post, but they are nothing more than that: *lies.*"

"Lord Kilbreth says you're one of them. One of him," he gestures to Eldridge this time who grins back widely, displaying elongated, jagged teeth that rival his lengthened claws for lethality.

"Lord Kilbreth has only spoken a fraction of the truth, and he certainly does not speak for me. I am before you in flesh and spirit, and I am telling you to stand down," Sin growls, his voice restrained, dampening the temper threatening to overcome him at the mention of his father.

The guards look at each other, nervousness making their movements awkward. I scan their armor: heavy plating around their chests, shoulders, and thighs, but the areas under their armpits and the sides of their legs where the plates connect are where they're most vulnerable. There and their stupid, fucking faces. That's where Alistair and I should focus our magic, and Eldridge his blade.

Evans angles himself towards their leader. "Maybe Lord

Kilbreth was wrong, Ackers. I mean, we were told His Grace fled to the Vale and obviously he was wrong about that."

Ackers's eyes narrow, light blue pools stark against his pale white skin and head of black hair that's clipped close to the scalp. His eyes dart between all of us, the tops of his sharp cheekbones twitching as he assesses the threat the four of us pose against them. One known transcendent, one mage with a wicked glimmer in his eye, the Black Art with goddess-blessed magic, and me—the white-tailed fawn surrounded by three wolves—the easiest target.

A slow smile creeps across my face. If only they knew the malignance swelling my veins as I will my collective into my palms, my magic growing hotter as I bring forth nefarious intent. Ackers's attention lingers on me longer than the rest, his eyes flickering between my face, the dagger in my hand, and the fiery orb twitching with hunger in my other.

"As your regent, I am ordering you to stand down *now*," Sin barks, angrier now. The fury twisting his face is evidence enough that the blood of the beast pounds through his veins.

A long pause, and then a subtle nod from Ackers, their leader lowering his weapon to his side and holding his hand out to the others in silent command.

"Let's go. It's time to take our leave," Sin says to the three of us.

Alistair blows out a disappointed sigh but turns to follow Sin back to the wagon. Eldridge hacks up a wad of saliva and spits it in front of Ackers's feet, but concedes, motioning with his head for me to follow him. Still clutching my blade tight, I turn towards the wagon, hastening my steps back to safety.

Instinct tingles my spine, prodding that part of myself that is as primal as the two transcendents at my front.

I don't take time to think. Thinking is hesitating, and hesitating is dying. I'm already turning around when he hollers, "You thought I wouldn't recognize the white-haired witch?"

My ward is up a second later, my knife flying from my hand as I spin on my heels.

The tip lodges into Ackers's throat.

The guard slumps to his knees, his outstretched weapon clanging to the ground, his hands clawing at his ruined neck.

Power storms through me. Scorching and glacial, dark and blinding, heavy and weightless, the ancient magic tunnels into my veins, cording my arms in vining devilry. The others are at my side in an instant, and this time, there is no hesitation between sides. The guards are young, inexperienced, freshly sprung from their homes of comfort in the leading city, assigned to gate duty to earn their place amongst the kingdom guard they mindlessly serve.

Killing them will be easy.

Too easy.

I'm rather in the mood for a good hunt.

Eldridge is a blur of claws, teeth, and steel as he storms towards the others. Evans catches his sword with two of his, but Eldridge's weight carries him forward, pushing the soldier back as he swings his blade with one hand, and swipes with the other, his claws searching for purchase in the guard's face.

Alistair draws power from the blood and kills two others at the same time Eldridge drops the third. That only leaves two—

Wrong.

The gate flies open, and a small brigade comes charging forward, at least fifteen more soldiers that were posted to the bridge, all wearing the same heavy armor. Sin shouts to Gerard to leave, to take the cart and flee while the gate is open. The high priest obeys, the horses and wagon careening in a wobbly frenzy through the guards, sending several of them diving to the side to avoid being trampled by sixteen thunderous hooves.

"Fuck me," Sin growls, suddenly at my side. I don't know where he came from, time passing in meaningless ticks as I appraise the scene before me. Four guards dead, two trembling as they raise their shaky swords, and a legion barreling towards us.

I lick my lips.

What a feast this will be.

Magic pools in my hand, sparking with chaos, the charged flames promising only death and rot. Part of me is aware of the fighting happening around me. Eldridge's wild braid whipping behind him as he overwhelms his targets with mass and speed. Alistair's throaty growls as he inhales their suffering, death flying from his hands faster than a young antelope. Sin running his hand along his sword, coating the blade in a sea of flames as he battles with weapon and magic alike, the dark warlord, reaper of flesh and bone.

I tune it out, all of it, my attention fixed on the barge of soldiers still running towards us. Before I buried my knife in Ackers's throat, my instinct may have been to run, try to take the higher ground before engaging in combat. But not anymore.

I rush towards them.

If the others shout out at me, it is lost in the bone-rattling screech that tears from my chest as I storm the battalion. I drop to my knees, my arms stretching out on either side of me like a tree. Except instead of serene woods, I set the whole damn forest on fire. Magic leaps from my palms in a destructive wake, throwing the guards to either side, scattering them across the ground like tattered dolls.

My collective hums with the hurt from their slashes, slits,

and tears. I rise to my feet, yanking my second dagger free from my waistband holster. I don't need a blade to kill them, not when my magic will do, but magic won't satiate the hunger burning in my gut. I want to *feel* their flesh split as I drag my knife across, their throats bobbing with pleas for mercy.

My boot slams down on the hand of one of the fallen soldiers reaching for his sword that clattered a few feet away from him. The tiny bones in his hand crunch under my foot, and I lick my teeth at the sound.

The person I was before all this—before Cathal and Legion, before Sin and Scarwood... perhaps she would have more regard for clemency.

I slit his throat.

Pressing my dagger to my lips, I drag my tongue up its shaft, and warmth settles low in my belly as I taste his velvet juice. My pussy weeps at the taste of abandon in my mouth.

The others are back on their feet, quickly surrounding me with shields and swords raised, some of their armor punctured by the blast, but most of it intact still. I widen my stance to shoulder width, and raising both hands, I curl my fingers towards myself, a smile as stiff as my joints twisting my lips as I prepare to wring the final drops of their essence from their polluted skins. Weight presses against my back, and the aroma of rain-soaked hyacinths overcomes my senses. A part of me registers that must mean Sin is wounded, if I can scent his blood, but a larger part is glad for it, though I can't make sense of why I would want my ally in a state of disarray.

His mass shifts behind me, and Sin's hands vice around my wrists. He doesn't need to speak; I know what he wants.

I open my veins to him, allowing him to siphon some of the blood magic, stirring it into his goddess-blessed ichor. The whole process takes less than a few seconds, and Sin unleashes a surge of magic that's as dark and ruinous as both our wretched hearts.

Alistair and Eldridge are on the struggling guards instantly. A swipe of claws across jugulars, a blood spear thrusted into pounding, fleshy hearts, the stench of death permeating the air, petting my tongue and caressing my thighs.

Sin drops my hands and turns so he's facing me. My breath hitches. There's a gash on his arm, but it's clean—mending it will be easy. A few more lacerations and scrapes mar the exposed skin of his forearms and hands, but all of it minor. His depthless injuries are not what steals the air from my lungs— it's those fucking forested eyes, ringed with a yellow-hue from the magic.

Beautiful. Devastating.

Lethal.

My ogling is cut short when he suddenly grabs my waist and throws me around his body, forcing me to the ground with his weight. *What the—*

An arrow pierces the ground where I was standing just a second before. My eyes snap to the gates, zeroing in on the emergence of more guards poking their stupid fucking heads out of the watchtower, several with bows aimed towards us. I sprint towards the gate, ignoring Sin's shout for me to stop. I'm too quick for the guards to take aim, and I duck under the overhang of the gate.

Alistair follows, hurtling red-hued orbs towards the towers until he's at my side. Their arrows can't reach us here; they'll be forced to come down, down to where there aren't walls to hide behind from Alistair's and my magics, or Eldridge's deadly blades, both the one in his hand and the ten at the tips of his fingers.

Sin shouts my name again, this time coating the syllable in liquid wrath. I turn to find Eldridge barreling towards us, my feet catching up to my brain not a second too soon as I avoid my lungs taking the brunt force of him crashing into me. His hands still shove into my back, giving me further clearance of the overhang, and the three of us skid to a halt on the opposite side just as two grated gates slam down from the ceiling.

"What the fuck were you thinking, Wren? It's a gods-damned city gate—they have portcullises!" Eldridge shouts, his face as red as the braided beard brushing his chest.

My mouth falls open but no words come out because Sin is still on the other side, now trapped inside the keep, in a city that's just learned of his ancestry. It's me that calls his name this time, but his eyes are glued to the tower above him. Taking in his expression, I'm suddenly not frightened *for* him anymore.

The Black Art is fury incarnate.

I project a ward around the three of us, but the guards in the watchtower aren't looking at us anymore. Their attention is fixed on Sin, who raises his hands and unleashes a roar that's pure beast, pure *transcendent,* and the towers tremble.

"Fuck. Move—move!" Eldridge yells, grabbing my arm and nearly popping my shoulder from its socket as he pulls me after him. Alistair is already gone, having given the gates clearance the second the ground started to quiver.

Arrows fly towards the Black Art, but his shield is already up, reflecting the projectiles without strain. His hands clench and unclench, his face twisted in that monstrous scowl, and he doesn't stop roaring as the foundation buckles and writhes.

Stone cracks and shifts in the center, sending the top careening in on itself in a tempest of rock and sediment. I hear their shouts faintly from the towers, but it's too late—the guards won't survive a jump from that height, and if they survive the crash, it won't be without crippling mutilation.

I call to him again, this time his name a plea on my lips.

And then he's running towards us, diving through the center whose grated gates long since snapped. As soon as he's through, he turns back to Blackreach, his city, his capital.

His home.

With one final shout of anguish, Sin brings down the gate.

CHAPTER 24

"That didn't go as planned," Alistair huffs, wiping the back of his hand across his mouth which only serves to smear the guards' blood further onto his cheeks.

Gerard slows the wagon to a halt, and my feet dig into the wooden planks, holding me steady as the cart careens to an abrupt stop. With the mountain of rubble between us and the kingdom, the four of us quickly caught up to where the high priest waited for our arrival. Eldridge nudges me with his arm to hop out of the cart—my body closest to the gaping hole Alistair blew in it—but I don't budge. My eyes are locked on the bloodwitch's cheeks, his chin, his thin lips made fuller with the vermillion honey lining their seam. My throat burns with want, with need, my nostrils flaring as I inhale the blood splattering my own face, neck, and hands.

"You okay?" Eldridge asks, not able to fully hide the annoyance in his tone, nor does he try hard to. And he shouldn't. I made a poor judgment call, acted impulsively, the spilled blood baiting out my most primal instincts. I give a curt nod in response and head for the opening at the back of the cart just as Gerard pulls the back panel all the way off, making my climb out much easier.

Gerard apologizes profusely to Sin, but the Black Art promptly cuts him off and instead asks if he has accommodations. The high priest cannot return to Blackreach, but he tells Sin he has friends east of The Red Tops that will welcome him with grace and not ask questions. The Black Art sends him off with one of our horses and a saddle bag filled with enough supplies to sustain him for the rest of his journey. I watch as Gerard clutches Sin's arm with one of his wrinkled hands and mutters something to him too low for my ears. Sin nods once, and with a final squeeze of his arm, the high priest releases him and takes off towards the cloud-piercing tips of the towering mountains.

Eldridge and Alistair work on unhitching the three remaining horses from the busted cart, but Sin doesn't move from where the high priest left him, his hands clamped around the back of his head, his elbows splayed out around his head like bat wings. The fabric of his dark shirt cinches around his shoulders as I approach.

I say his name. Again. A third time, and then I reach for his side to turn him towards me, but his body springs into action before my fingers make contact. Sin reels towards me, my breath catching, and for a moment, I wish he hadn't turned around.

The Black Art is *furious*.

"What?" I ask, regretting the dumb question immediately.

"This was not supposed to happen." His words are barely a whisper, but the wrath brimming under them is as clear as daybreak.

"We knew the risks," I start, but his expression promptly cuts me off.

"The risks were that we got caught while out here! Not that I would be exposed to the entire kingdom and ousted by my own people, my own fath—" Now it is himself he cuts off, suddenly driving his stare into the ground by my feet and flicking his tongue across the roof of his mouth.

"Your father shouldn't have done this."

"This isn't my father's doing, Wren!" he yells, *actually yells,* and I can't help my body's natural recoil as his words bite into me. The words sink deeper as he raises his eyes to mine once more, his voice deep and guttural. "It's yours."

"I beg your pardon?" I query, my hand finding my hip. "Why in the gods' names is this my fault? I kept your secret! All this time," I retort, my other hand waving around with a mind of its own.

"But you couldn't stay away. You needed to just fucking stay away, and I would have held up my end of our deal. But you came back, forced us *both* back to a place neither of us should ever have been. Why do you think my father did what he did today? Tell me, why do you think he did it, Wren?"

I do not give space as he steps closer to me, his shoulders low and his head dipped slightly forward, his posture instinctively primed for combat. I'm not sure he asks the question in earnest, but I answer him anyway. "Because your father is a godsdamned monster," I spit.

He's already shaking his head before I finish. "No. Because *you* are. Because you are the very thing my father and my predecessors have sworn to eradicate, and when they had their chance, I chose to protect you instead. *I shifted to protect you!*" he roars. "Do you realize how that would have been perceived to someone like my father? I betrayed my kingdom, my people, the second that arrow pierced my flesh. I cannot blame him for what he did today."

Tears burn in my eyes, but I blink them back, rage flooding my core as I make sense of his words. "I did not ask you to save me," I bite out, voice low.

"I saved a girl who defied every expectation of her. I saved a girl who would rather rip out her own heart than take the life of another. But that," he jabs a finger in the direction of the devastated keep, now far out of eye's view, "I don't know who that was."

"They attacked us first!" I shout, stepping forward so my chest brushes his.

"I don't care that you killed them. I care that you fell prey to the fucking impulses of your kind, and that you were foolish. You almost got yourself trapped in there. They have iron dust, Wren. It wouldn't have been hard to incapacitate you long enough to slit your throat, and you fell right into their hands. And I just brought down the whole godsdamned gate because of it, as if my father didn't have enough reason to lead my army to the Vale already."

Guilt washes through me like liquid fire. How long can Ileana hold her own against Dusaro? By law, she's acting regent, her power absolute. But Ileana is mundane and Dusaro, in addition to his magic, possesses the loyalties of the army that has served under him and Ephraim for longer than I've been alive. If Dusaro chooses to act without Ileana's consent, who is to stop him?

Sin's eyes flick to somewhere behind me, and my spine stiffens as I sense someone approaching, though Eldridge's footfalls are silent.

"You two take a horse. We need to move before they find a way through the wreckage," Sin says, stepping away from us and mounting one of the three steeds. He's off in a flash, not bothering to wait for us before setting course for the Vale, the only safe place left on this isle for someone who's been shunned from it. Alistair takes off behind him, and Eldridge and I hop onto the remaining horse, its hooves kicking up dust as we dive into a gallop as wild and tumultuous as my pounding heart.

CHAPTER 25

Rage burns in the high priestess's stark white irises. Vox remains a statue at her side, his features chiseled into silent perfection, his skin so fair it may very well be crafted from the moon's powdery light. Sera paces the floor before the dais, her eyes barely moving from Sin, and when they do, it's to track Aeverie's staff. I can't help but wonder if Sin's mother has seen the high priestess use it before and if that's why she regards it with caution, especially as she beholds the three of us with judgment.

Three, because Alistair took off as soon as we returned, muttering something about needing to wash away the scent of the dead before losing his sanity. I share in that need, the quick baths I took in the rivers during our trek back to the Vale too rushed to thoroughly cleanse the lingering scent of the guards' suffering from my skin. But that can wait. Right now, I must accept my judgment.

"It would still be unwise for my father to lead the army here with Baelliarah watching from the water. This will have provoked him greatly, but even so, Dusaro is no fool. He won't risk leaving the castle unguarded until the situation with Baelliarah is dealt with."

I clasp my hands at my waist and incline my head. I've

been silent since entering the temple, the high priestess calling for the commander as soon as she beheld us, our expressions surely indicating something had gone awry. Aeverie exchanges a long, pointed glance with Vox, and my heart beats louder with each passing second.

It's the commander that breaks the silence. "I suppose it is time to tell them, Madam Priestess."

Aeverie blinks once, then shifts her glacial gaze to us, flitting between Sin and myself. "I suppose it is. Leave us, wanderer," she says, not needing to specify which transcendent she's referring to.

Eldridge promptly takes his leave, and Aeverie tears her sharp stare away to look at Sera who's still watching Sin as if he may disappear. "And you, wanderer. Leave us."

Sera pauses her pacing and looks to the high priestess with surprise but does not argue. With a slight nod of her head, she leaves the temple. I resist the urge to look at Sin and instead, keep my attention on Aeverie and that staff, swallowing thickly as she steps off the dais towards us.

"Come," she speaks sternly and heads down the dimly lit corridor at the far end of the room. "We have much to discuss, and it is rude to keep the dead waiting."

The room I step into is not what I'm expecting. The small library is surprisingly... *cozy*. Two deep red wing-backed chairs accompany a dark rectangular table in the center, a plush gray patterned rug beneath it all. Shelves carved straight into the sediment line the stone walls, countless leather-bound volumes of reds, browns, and blacks arranged neatly on the ledges with their well-cared for spines peeking out. A wooden rung ladder leans against the farthest shelf.

"A library?" I ask, confusion knitting my brows together.

"A repository," she corrects, bowing at the waist before entering the room after us. "Elves have very long memories, but our magic existed well before the first of our kind were ever born. These are our most archaic records. They detail our culture, rituals, and most importantly, our connection to Source."

I step closer and examine the volumes, the spines all adorned with strange symbols I don't recognize.

"They are all written in the first language," Aeverie supplies, tracking my wandering eyes. "The records are kept for us, no need to transcribe them into the common tongue. But I did not bring you here to gawk at our books. I brought you here for this."

The high priestess paces to the other side of the room where a glass dome rests on top of a small waist-height table. A long silver dagger supported by a steel frame beams at us from inside the dome. Two faceted rubies cap either end of the sweeping crossguard, the cut and style of the gem similar to the one in Ileana's ring, and a third one rounds out the base of the hilt. Another strange symbol is carved into the center of the crossguard, two straight lines intersecting in an X pattern beneath a half-circle. Aeverie lifts the glass dome and carefully collects the sacrificial looking dagger from its stand.

"This blade was crafted for you," she says, turning her snowy gaze towards me.

"For me?"

"For the next blood mage," she clarifies. "It's been nearly a century since one has found themselves inside the Vale. Excluding Alistair, of course, but his appetite for foolishness runs even deeper than his thirst for blood. I do not entertain such costly whims."

I steal a glance at Sin who is watching the high priestess with care, his arms folded with one hand cupping his strong jaw. "Elves can be born as bloodwit—blood *mages?*" he asks.

"I've not seen it, and I am far more ancient than the others here." It's then that I make sense of Aeverie's earlier words. If she's not seen a bloodwitch in nearly a century, just *how old* is the high priestess? "But blood mages and elves have always shared a unique bond, for our magics are tapped from the same supply."

"What you call Source?" I ask.

She nods. "Whereas you," she looks to Sin, "pull your magic from the collective, we take it from the earth. It is why we must tend to the land with thoughtfulness—we do not take without giving in return. The land must be nurtured, sowed, and cared for so we may continue to receive its blessings."

"But I don't pull my magic from the land," I object.

I startle when Aeverie drives the butt of her staff into the floor. "Your magic grows when blood is spilled. What do you think happens to flesh and bone when life no longer inhabits them? They decay, return to the earth and richen the soil. Elves have a direct link to Source always, but blood mages require a channel."

"The blood is my channel?" I query.

"Precisely. Your connection requires a sacrifice, hence why your power deepens when you spill blood. That surge you feel is your mind tapping into Source."

I choke out a laugh, though it is void of humor. "No offense, High Priestess, but your magic is kind of fucked in the mind if it gets its kicks by making me want to slaughter entire cities."

The whites of her eyes grow impossibly colder as she takes a step towards me, dagger clutched in the hand not holding the staff. Somewhere behind me, I hear the sound of boots clapping stone as Sin moves closer to my side. "That much power requires discipline. In order to hone Source and manipulate it into doing what you wish, the wielder must be focused. The frenzy you feel is the magic testing you. Push through the haze, show Source that you are worthy of your claim to its power, and you will regain clarity. Fail in that, and the magic will not bind to you—you'll have created a channel, but if Source does not accept you, you'll be throwing it around with no guidance. Accept your gifts, relinquish the hunger, and the control is yours."

My eyes drop to the dagger in her hand, honing in on the strange symbol at the center. "You said there hasn't been a bloodwitch in the Vale in nearly a century. Was it common for my kind to live amongst yours?"

"To say it was common is to imply that many humans are born with your gifts, which I assure you, they are not. But this was before our lands were scorched, before we were driven back to the Vale. We didn't create the war with humans—his kind did," Aeverie's gaze flits to Sin, then back to me. "Ephraim Whytworthe did more than soil our lands with his vile magic; he created fear between our races. Humans, elves, blood mages, wanderers... Source knows naught of such secular divisions."

"Your *Source* can have a say in such matters when they're here cleaning up the messes your kind makes," Sin growls, now fully at my side.

"Do not take a tone with me in my own temple, Black Art. Or should I call you as you really are—as Source sees you —*Wanderer?*"

"Call me what you wish, Priestess, it does not change our current predicament."

A subtle smile tugs on the elf's lips. "You're right, it doesn't. But she does."

"I don't understand," I start, but quiet when the high priestess turns and leaves the room.

"Follow. There is more to be seen."

Exchanging a glance with Sin, we follow Aeverie back down the corridor and out of the temple. She is quiet while she leads us to the tree line and doesn't stop until we're a few feet within the verdant canopy, which shelters us a bit from the rain now beating the ground into submission.

"You haven't asked why we have allied with blood mages since the beginning of time, or when our kind were first born, whichever came first. But best you didn't because I wouldn't have been able to explain properly until now. You and I are both connected to Source, but if you learned to welcome it into your veins as you absorb the blood magic, you would be infinitely more powerful than myself. The reason for this, is because you are a conduit." Even through the cloudy haze, I can tell Aeverie's eyes are watchful, studying my face as I make sense of her words.

"Take the gems on our weapons, armor, my staff, for example," she continues. "The crystals act as siphons, strengthening our connection to Source. We imbue the stones with its magic so we may call upon it more easily when need arises. The gems—"

"Are conduits," I finish for her, and she nods.

"Exactly that. Elven magic is strong, ancient, but we are still limited by the barriers the land places on us. We are made of flesh, the same as you. In order to penetrate the earth, we need to amplify our magic. We need a catalyst. We need a... conduit," she finishes, and despite her lack of pupils, I feel her careful assessment everywhere on my body.

I run my hand down my braid and twirl the end between my thumb and forefinger, a habit my mother always hated.

"Speak freely," Sin growls. "What does this have to do with all of Aegidale preparing to riot at the Vale's borders?"

"It was your kingdom's doing that brought this plague upon our lands. When Ephraim scorched our forest, he didn't just burn away the trees and grass. He sowed his magic deep beneath the ground, tainting our soil, roots, poisoning the very depths of the crust. This hindered our connection to Source gravely, rendering us unequal against your self-righteous kingdom, but if we restore the land, restore the connection... Why, even Lord Kilbreth would hold no torch to us, *Singard Kilbreth*," she says, her tongue slithering along his name.

"Alright, I'll bite. How do we restore it?" I ask.

Aeverie holds up the dagger. "During our time of peace with the blood mages, they would imbue our land with a blessing. One that would help to nurture the crops, feed the dirt, strengthen the roots for harsh winds, and ensure a bountiful harvest. To unite our prosperous intentions with their magic, it was custom for many of us to make a small sacrifice, an offering to the blood mage and to Source."

My eyes round to small saucers, honing in on the dagger. "This is the blade you used to bleed yourselves in exchange for a bloodwitch's blessing," I say knowingly.

Aeverie nods, and Sin shifts his weight at my side. "It was goddess-blessed magic that rotted our lands, so it is goddess-blessed magic that must restore it. With the help of a conduit, of course," the high priestess continues.

"But how did Ephraim soil your land without the help of a bloodwitch?" I ask.

"The collective you've grown accustomed to pulling magic from is a dangerous thing. All types of energy exist there—the purest, and the vilest. It wasn't just magic your late Black Art used—it was *chaos*. Think of it as suffering a bruise. One hard thwack is enough to purple the skin in a second, but it may take weeks or months to heal. Chaos is a decrepit, savage thing. Easy to wield, difficult to reverse. Now kneel," she commands, lowering her own knees to the soft grass.

I hesitate for a moment but sink to my knees when she jerks her head up to look at me, and a few seconds later, Sin joins me.

"Make a sacrifice to Source, and it will grant you sight like my own, for a moment, at least."

The high priestess hands me the ruby clad dagger, and I will my hand not to shake as I clutch the icy hilt and press it to my palm. She nods to Sin who repeats the action when I pass him the blade.

"Feed it to the earth," she instructs, and both of us turn our hands sideways, our blood dripping onto the tender grass.

Everything is white.

The stark light would be blinding if I still had eyes, but my limbs feel so unbound, so weightless, that I'm not sure my body exists at all anymore. My would-be arms flail around me, and a hand vices around my forearm—Sin's hand—and slides to hold my own, encouraging me to still.

Color bleeds into my vision—blacks and grays, then greens and yellows and browns, and then... red. So much red. Blurs become lines become shapes, human figures taking form behind my eyes, flashes of gold snagging my attention. The kingdom's crest.

Not just human figures—soldiers.

A distant cry wails somewhere behind me, and my own pulse thrums wildly in response, my heart beating viciously against its bone cage as that anguished sob melts into my ears. The distinct sound of steel cleaving through guts and muscle echoes around us, and blood—so much blood—beckons to me.

I hear the crackle of fire before I see it—blazing orange curtains feasting on the trees' dry needles, claiming their wood as its own. Puffs of reddish-brown clouds hover around me, choking my lungs with their heady perfume, and my eyelids sting with smoke and heat. A body slumps to the ground in front of me, a sword plunged into the side of her gut—a dark-skinned woman with distinctly pointed ears—an elf. A very dead elf.

The kingdom soldier withdraws his blade, the woman's face turning towards me, her eyes as open and vacant as the winter sky. I try to scramble backwards, away from her abandoned corpse, but Sin's hand tightens on my arm, reminding me this isn't real.

Except... it is.

The massacre around me isn't happening now, but it did happen. Aeverie's Sight. A memory.

The smoke clears just enough for me to make out another form —a man with a head of graying hair and creases folded into his face —a form I recognize.

Ephraim Whytworthe. Sin's predecessor. The Black Art before Dusaro killed him to gain access to the Rite, where he could claim the throne as his own. But Adelphia denied him, passing him over to bless the Black Hand's only son instead.

The kingdom guard fans out around him, elves and humans engaged in fight while the fire roars and feasts and claims the land, the smoke pushing them farther in, farther into the parts of the Vale that remain unburnt. My vision clears more, and I now make out Ephraim's thin lips moving, mumbling to himself, magic as dark and tumultuous as the Howling Sea vining up his arms, his veins bulging and black.

The magic isn't content to stay in his arms. It expands around him like a swollen storm cloud, suffocating the air around him, charging it with his chaotic current. My body begins to writhe without my consent, my shoulders wracking forward and back as the Sight overwhelms me, and Sin's hand cinches impossibly tighter around mine.

Ephraim drops to his knees, placing a large hand on the ground, and continues uttering words of intention. Elves continue to fall around him, screams and pleas ringing from their mouths, but Ephraim does not halt. Sweat beads across my nape, my pulse pounds wildly in my neck, my wrists, and my fingers curl, my nails digging into flesh, either Sin's or my own, I can't tell. Unable to feel where my body ends and this one begins. All I know is blood.

Blood.

So much blood.

Ephraim's head rips back, his own fingers plunging into the upturned dirt, and a roar louder than the full moon's violent tide pierces this realm and the next. The cloud around him bursts, the chaos splintering into tiny, malignant daggers, arching into the trees, diving beneath the crust, fracturing its roots, its heart, its soul. The ground beneath me trembles and quakes, and I throw my other arm forward, my fingers flattening grass but my body remaining upright. I'm not falling. Not actually, but it's... it's so real. Here. Right fucking here.

Ephraim's body trembles with the expulsion, his entire body vibrating as if he's been struck by lightning, his eyes closed, but his hands now balled into fists, black flames licking his knuckles.

The Black Art opens his eyes.

Chaos explodes.

Breath wheezes from my lungs as my eyelids snap open, my vision returned to present. My chest heaves forward as a strangled breath escapes me, and I place both hands on the ground. I turn to the side and find Sin with both hands combed in his hair, his knuckles clenched, as if pulling his roots a little too hard to keep himself from vomiting from the transition of Aeverie's Sight to our own.

"You could have warned us," I bite, turning my glower to the high priestess whose face remains perfectly calm. The sight of her contentment boils my blood further, and my teeth sink into my tongue.

"You needed to see," she says, planting her staff into the ground to support her weight as she rises to her feet. "Witness the plague Ephraim brought here. Even the crops are sick—our harvests have been slowly dwindling each season since the scorching."

When I'm certain I'm not going to retch, I close the slice in my palm and climb to my feet. Sin copies a moment later, his expression sour as if the motion pains him.

"What say you, Singard Kilbreth, Black Art of Aegidale, of the destruction your kind have caused for my people? Of the elven blood spilled beneath our very feet in pursuit of power?" Aeverie's words slither out, coated in venom. She rests one hand on top of her staff and the other hangs straight at her side, unnaturally still.

Sin slowly tilts his head back to look down at her through long lashes, the sides of his hair curtaining his face. "Ephraim Whytworthe has been dead for nearly two years," he says, an edge in his tone I can't quite place.

"Aye," she agrees. "Precisely why it is time for the next chosen to restore what was taken from us."

"You want me to lift the chaos from your land so you regain access to your Source, granting you access to magic you could use to declare war on me and my people?" Sin asks, raising a dark brow and one side of his mouth pulling up.

"My kind has never been interested in something as mundane as war. We only want what once was ours. Tell me, goddess-blessed, if you do not help us in reclaiming our connection to Source, how do you intend to defeat the army your father leads here? A wanderer he could overlook... a wanderer who chose a blood mage over his kin he cannot."

My mouth pops open, and I yank my gaze away from Sin

before I can register his reaction. Shame burns through me as hot as the fire that blazed before my sight moments before. I should have never fled with Sera. Never taken my family to the Vale. If I hadn't been here, the guard wouldn't have fired that bolt, and Sin... Sin wouldn't have shifted to protect me.

My actions led us to this.

But his did too.

"With all due respect, High Priestess, we just returned from a long journey. I will consider your proposal," he says, his tone giving no indication of his further thoughts on the matter.

"There is time," she says, "but not much. Ephraim's sickness runs deep in the land's veins—the blood mage is strong, but perhaps even her power coupled with yours will not be enough. Our calendars tell us that in three weeks, the moon will be eclipsed. It is then, when the forest is bathed in crimson light and the shadowed sun beams through the blood moon, your magics will be most amplified. That is when the twisted chasm your Black Art created must be closed, and our Source will once again be whole, unbound.

"Our energies mix best when there is no contention between them. I suggest if you wish to not end up on the wrong side of your father's sword, you and the blood mage ease your tensions with one another."

Something close to a laugh rattles free from me. "Don't hold your breath, Madam Priestess. Something tells me the wounds the Black Art and I share run even deeper than your Source."

Aeverie pulls her shoulders back, milky eyes flitting between the two of us. "We shall see."

The high priestess bids us farewell, leaving Sin and me alone with only the trees and the haunting memories of what we just witnessed for company. The rain begins falling harder now, but neither of us moves for more cover. I don't even bother pulling the hood of my cloak up, my hands locked at my sides, and my attention on the ground in front of the Black Art's feet. The air between us is charged, a live current flaring between our chests, daring us to speak the words we've left unspoken for too long.

"We should head back. The storm is rolling in fast," he says, turning his face to the sky. Water drips from his hair and slides down his cheeks, his neck.

My own braid becomes heavy with rain, and I pull it over my shoulder. "Where are you staying?"

"The house I was in before they moved me to the temple. They swapped the chains with a cot," he adds, a touch of dark humor in his tone, but it doesn't meet his eyes which smolder with heat despite the cold rain now pelting us.

"Don't you think we should discuss what the priestess said now? We don't have much time and—"

"It's in both our best interests if we separate for a night," he cuts me off.

"You can be angry with me for what happened in the city, but that doesn't mean we can pretend it didn't happen. Our actions have consequences—big consequences—that we need to prepare for. This isn't just about *our* best interests now."

He yanks a hand through his long hair and blows out a sigh. "I'm only asking for a night, Wren, not a godsdamned vacation. Believe me, I'm well aware there is no undoing your actions."

A hand finds my hip, and my head cocks sharply to the side. "And what about your actions? We wouldn't have even been in Blackreach if not for your father and his impulsiveness!"

"Do not fault me for the crimes of my father," he growls, pinning me in place with a look that turns the rain on my skin to liquid fire. "My father would have never come to the Vale in the first place if you hadn't run off with my mother."

"You didn't exactly leave me much choice, Singard. Where else was I to go?"

"Back to your home! With your family, you didn't have—"

"I couldn't go back there!" I shout. Tears brim in my eyes, and I hope he can't distinguish them from the rain.

"Bullshit, Wren. There was nothing stopping you. You just wanted to hurt me in the worst way you could think of."

"I couldn't trust you!" I roar, closing the distance between us. He straightens as I approach, every muscle snapping to attention, his body rigid as stone. "You knew where I lived! You think I would risk staying there so you could show up and murder us all while we slept?"

"Is that what you think of me?" he asks, angrier now.

"I laid everything I had out for you, and you used it only for your own gains. You lied to me, manipulated me, betrayed me," I tick them off on my fingers, "when all I did was try to help you."

He flicks his head to the side in a movement more beast than man. "Do not stand before me and pretend that you cared a sliver about me. You cared about securing your freedom, which I honored when our deal was through."

"AND I STAYED! I was the one who broke the spell tethering us, Singard, not you. I could have left right then and there, and I should have, but I stayed. I fucking stayed, and it meant nothing to you. None of it meant a godsdamned thing to you." There's no more holding them back, no more disguising my tears as anything but that—fat, ugly tears that he doesn't deserve.

He shifts his weight, his form leaning forward to tower above me, the ends of his wet hair brushing my arms. "You stayed for your sister, you didn't stay for me, and it is low of you to insinuate otherwise."

"Even if that were true, could you blame me? You listened as I poured out my heart to you, terrified of the horrors Cosmina was facing in my name, and you loved it all, didn't you? You loved seeing how much I was willing to risk for her because it meant winning your stupid war—one you caused! You saw where I was broken, and you used it to destroy me," I shout, slamming a finger into his stupid, hard chest. I tear my eyes away from his, furiously blinking to try to clear the tears.

Sin is quiet for a moment, and I wonder if he's going to respond at all when his hand suddenly cups my jaw and steers my face back to his. I try to jerk my chin away, but his fingers clench harder, holding me still. "Look at me," he demands.

Reluctantly, I raise my eyes to his.

"I have never pretended to be something I'm not, Wren, and I won't start now. I am selfish. I am cruel. And I have never struggled hurting others to get what I want. Until you."

His grip on my chin is firm but not painful. Instinct tells me to pull away, shove him for good measure, but my eyes remain trained on his, burning in their liquid green fire.

"What I did to you has haunted me every day since you've left. Every. Single. Day. I know that means nothing to you, and it probably shouldn't, but it does mean something to me that you at least know. If it were anyone but you, I wouldn't hesitate to go back and do it all over again. But you... never you."

His voice is strained, pained even, but his stare is unforgiving. But I've been around the Black Art long enough to notice the creases around his eyes when he forces his expression blank, to mask whatever storm of emotions are rolling through him. I lift my chin out of his hand, gently but firm, and he releases his hold.

"You lied to me." My words are barely more than a whisper.

"I do not trust easily, Singard, and you lied to me. You made me feel used. I sacrificed everything for you, and it still wasn't enough. *I* wasn't..." I trail off, blinking back the salty tears scorching the backs of my eyelids.

His hands are on me again—wrapping around each of my biceps—anchoring me. "You were everything. It is me that is broken, Wren. I will not lie and say I didn't intend to hurt you in the beginning because I did. I would have hurt you, and enjoyed it, because you were everything good and light, and I couldn't stand looking at you and knowing I would never have what you did. But most of all, I knew you would never accept me. Never want me for what I was, what I am, and so when I craved you so intensely, it scared the living hell out of me. By the end of it, I would have thrown myself in front of every Legion sword for you. Bled for you. Died for you. And when you left with... with *her* of all people... you fucking *broke* me."

I raise my chin slightly, the pads of his calloused fingers pressing into my arms. "I'm not sorry for it."

Sin studies me for a moment, eyes flickering between both of mine, before he nods once, mostly to himself. His hands vanish from my skin, and the chilled rain assaults the warmth his touch left on my flesh. "You should go home. The storm is about to hit."

He leaves before I can tell him his words don't make sense. That I left my home months ago, when the horrors of what he'd done chased me to the farthest edge of the isle.

CHAPTER 26

I hate storms.

We're well into summer now, but the tempest that swept through the Vale last night left a violent chill in its wake. I punch my arms into a long-sleeved leather-hide jacket, plush fur peeking out around the hand holes and again at my collar. My leggings aren't thick enough, but the knee-high riding boots I kick on will at least cover half of my legs. I consider adding a hat but decide against it. It is summer after all, and I refuse to allow some isle storm to squander my entire outfit. Plus, it'll likely warm up later in the afternoon.

I'm not scheduled to work in the gardens today, but as I take one last swig of the tea Morrinne brewed and leave the house, that's exactly where I'm headed. The wind rattled the tiny tinctures on the kitchen table all through the night, the hinges on the door groaning well past sundown, the fur skins flapping in the cut-out windows. It is not difficult to imagine the damage it may have done to the gardens. Cosmina is on the roster today, and an extra set of hands dedicated to damage control will ease the workload on everyone.

Eldridge hasn't spoken to me much since our return, and I don't blame him. I make a mental note to find him later and demand his attention. Anxiety stirs in my gut like acid, my mind running rampant with all the things he could say to me, and all the ways he could refuse to talk to me at all.

Except I won't let him.

Eldridge and my relationship has always been complicated, and it doesn't take a genius to note he is hurting.

I have hurt him.

And knowing that sends a pang sharper than any iron bolt straight to my chest.

Several glances are cast my way as I head to the gardens, some curious, others... assessing. Perhaps the elves are questioning the authenticity of the account we told Aeverie of our travel mishaps, studying me for trustworthiness. Or perhaps they're simply amused by my winter attire. Temperature doesn't seem to affect the elves much at all I've noticed, most of them going about in their simple tunics and pants regardless of the air being balmy or frigid. Maybe their bodies have adapted from living outdoors for centuries—millennia, maybe —or perhaps the jewels embroidered into the seams of their clothing are tied to Source, allowing them to self-regulate their body temperatures.

The gardens are in the exact state I expected them to be— disarray. Several of the roots of the leafier plants are exposed, the vibrant greens of their vegetation leaning to one side and flopping over on the upturned soil. Trowels are scattered around the dirt beds, along with containers of gritty, seedy material that serves as food for the crops, and metal pitchers containing water. Several elves and transcendents are scattered about the gardens, working to salvage and nurture the plants, but my attention snags on my sister when I spot her dusting her hands on her linen waist apron. Even though the sun is hidden far beyond our canopy, that ridiculous floppy hat sits on her head, her long dark hair tucked up inside of it.

She's speaking to someone, and I track her gaze, stopping short when—

Bile churns in my stomach as I behold the man who imprisoned and tortured my sister standing mere feet away from her. I stalk towards them, wondering what business the Black Art has with Cosmina, suddenly hating the heavier clothing weighing me down as I traipse across the delicate beds of the garden.

Sin sees me before my sister does, the near-smile disappearing from his face entirely as he angles himself towards me. Cosmina follows his eyes, and part of me expects to see her easy smile plastered on her face, but there is none. Of course there's not. Why would she be happy to be in the presence of the man who caused her so much torment?

Their conversation fades before I'm within hearing distance, and Cosmina bends to collect the shovel at her feet. Sin straightens, clad in a flowy black shirt with a laced neck that's split open, revealing the tanned planes of his sculpted chest beneath. His hair is tousled down his back, the skin beneath his eyes slightly puffy, and I can't help but wonder if it was the isle's storm or the one inside him that caused him a night of fitful sleep.

"What are you doing here?" I don't edit the hostility from my tone.

"I came for you."

I cross my arms. "Here I am."

"Walk with me?" He poses it as a question. "There's something I wish to discuss with you, but it would be wise if we prioritize discretion." He doesn't take his eyes off me, but I'm certain he's hyper aware of every elf and their advanced hearing lingering in close proximity.

I glance to Cosmina who's resting both elbows atop her

shovel handle. She grants me a short nod, but there's something deeper in her eyes I can't place. Something... *knowing*.

I step around Sin without looking at him and call over my shoulder as I start heading away from the gardens. He's at my side a second later, but neither of us speaks, not chancing our voices carrying back towards the gardeners. A few minutes later, we're standing outside a tunneled opening in the rock, and Sin motions with his chin for me to enter before him. I eye him for a moment too long but don't bother reading his collective to deem his intentions with me inside this cave. I was wrong about them before, and should the Black Art wish me harm, he's had every opportunity to chance combat with me before now. Regardless, the weight of my daggers against my thigh and my waist are comforting as I step into the cavern.

Goddess above.

On the other side of the narrow bend in the cave, an oasis awaits us. A large, circular spring occupies the interior of the rock, the water a pale green, reflecting the wall of algae and vining plants climbing the stone to a small opening in the ceiling. Daylight peeks in through the hole, casting a spotlight onto the verdant side of the cave and shrouding the other half in darkness.

"How'd you find this place?" I ask.

"Couldn't sleep last night," is his only reply.

Warmth bleeds into my skin, tendrils of steam wafting from the heated spring, and I shrug out of my jacket, reducing myself to my deep green tunic and dark leggings. I step up to the pool and peer over the ledge, surprised to find bioluminescent plants winking back at me. The green tint to the water isn't just from the reflection of the algae, but the plants sprouting across the floor of the pool are *glowing*.

"I can hardly imagine you brought me here to take a dip, Your Grace."

"Your imagination serves you correctly. Ileana is... calling. The magic in the ring—she is trying to activate it."

She must be rubbing the ruby. I wonder if the magic linking Ileana's ring to Sin elicits the same tug in his core that his tethering spell once did to me. For some reason I don't understand, that thought nips at my chest with jagged teeth, and my fingers curl at my sides.

"You want to use the water to scry?"

Sin nods, stepping up beside me. "The surface is clear, but more importantly, I'd prefer it be only us that hear what she has to say."

"This affects more than just us, you know?"

He turns to meet my gaze head on. "I am not speaking from prejudice when I tell you, do not trust the elves. If it is us they need to restore their Source, there's no telling what they'll do to try to force our hands. We need to maintain leverage, and we'll lose it quickly if we feed them too much too soon. For now, it's me and you."

He studies me until I give a curt nod. He's right. I've never trusted Aeverie or Vox, and especially not after the scheming they planned with Sera, disabling Eldridge and me to capture the Black Art. I have my family to protect, and strangely enough, Singard Kilbreth may be my closest ally right now.

Kneeling on the ledge, he waves a hand across the calm spring, the turquoise water turning milky white for a moment before Ileana appears on the surface. Sinking to my own knees, I peer down at the Black Hand, only the top of her bodice and head visible, her shoulders slumped forward as if she's standing in a cramped closet.

"Took you long enough. Goddess, save me, I was about to chuck this ring into the moat," she scolds, her vexed expression not matching the uncertainty underlining her tone.

"Apologies, my Lady. We needed to find somewhere where our voices would not carry."

"I trust I may speak without restriction, then?" she asks, eyes darting to mine.

Sin nods and murmurs for her to continue.

"I had no idea Dusaro was going to oust you, Your Grace. I swear on my own pyre, I never thought he would expose your secret. Forgive me for not intervening, I—"

"There was nothing you could do once he started," Sin interjects. "Not in the public eye—Black Hand or not—my father does not take well to being questioned in front of others. And certainly not from someone mundane."

Her eyes shut for a brief moment, and when she reopens them, there is relief there. "Do you remember when you told me you'd be discreet when you left the church? Did you think killing our entire watch guard and collapsing the gate was subtle, then?" Annoyance replaces the relief on her face.

Sin glances at me and rolls his bottom lip between his teeth, a hint of something facetious tugging at his mouth. "There was a change of plans. Civility is harder for some of us than others," he drawls, his tone almost bored.

I glower, releasing a sharp breath, and turn back to Ileana. "What is the current call to action? Have troops been discharged?" I ask.

She shakes her head, her long, dark curls bobbing over the curve of her delicate, brown shoulders. "Dusaro is pissed. Like really pissed. But several scouts reported sightings of foreign ships. A pigeon was sent to Baelliarah earlier this week. We reported that a terrible accident had happened, and that Varil's ship was found burning a mile off our coast. We scorched the ship for good measure, but we would be ignorant to think they are content to accept that as an explanation as to why their king and eleven of his men set sail for our isle, and none of them returned. Your father has deployed additional fleets to secure the channel. We cannot afford to send soldiers to the Vale on foot, even if its inhabitants did wreck our keep," Ileana finishes with a chastising grimace.

"And you are well?" Sin asks.

A knowing grin schools her mouth. "Your father would be a fool to lay hands on me, Singard. I may not have magic, but I am equally capable of plunging a dagger into his chest all the same."

"I do not doubt it. But if you are unharmed and my own men aren't being sent to kill me, why the summons?"

Her eyes flit upward, and her lips press into a firm line as she focuses on something in her own distance. "Someone is coming. I have to go," she says quickly. "I called on you to let you know you are safe for now, but you must prepare for your father to come. His respect for me as his superior is superficial. As soon as doors are locked, he issues commands, and it pains me to say it, Singard, but I cannot overcome him. I do not have allies in this place. The guard has served your father for decades, they are loyal to *him*, not me. The moment Dusaro orders your capture, your death even, they'll be gone. You have time, but no telling how much of it."

Her eyes flicker up again, and she tucks a strand of hair behind her ear. "I must go. I think your father senses the magic in the ring; he's been tearing rooms apart convinced there's some kind of scrying device planted inside the castle. He doesn't suspect me yet, but I must stow the ring away for now before he strips me bare looking for the source of it."

Sin bows his head, his long hair curtaining his face. "You have my gratitude, Ileana."

"Singard?" she says, uncertainty creeping back into her tone. "Be careful."

He bids her a final nod before waving his hand, the water

rippling back into a blue-green mirror. Rising to his feet, he runs his hand through his hair, his eyes closing for a moment as he inhales deeply, his chest swelling with relief.

I climb to my feet as well, slapping the tiny specks of loose sediment from my tunic. "Goddess bless us that your father holds out until the eclipse."

Agitation brims his face when he opens his eyes. "You are making the assumption I intend to aid the elves."

"What other choice do we have? If we don't work with the elves, you can be certain they'll rescind our welcome here. Arrange to hand us over to your father, even. We ally with them, or we'll be fighting two wars, not just one."

A short laugh. "You think me so eager to bargain, little witch, but I'm not so easily controlled."

I steel my spine. "Neither am I."

He takes a few steps away from me, his attention drifting to the spring. "Yes, you've made your lack of control well known."

I cross my arms and cock my hip at the accusation in his tone. "Blaming me for our predicament is not going to help us now."

His hands work to further loosen the laces of his black shirt, and he rolls his neck to the side, yielding a sharp crack. "Who would you have me blame?"

"I could name you a plethora of people, Singard, but I'll start with your father. Oh, and then there's your savage predecessor, your entire council, your mother, your guards who failed to protect you from Alistair at the receiving center," I tick off the names on my fingers, "and then there's you. Singard Kilbreth. Charmer of women's hearts before he feasts upon them."

Sin pulls his shirt over his head, revealing his sculpted stomach and muscular arms, his hair falling unevenly over the planes of his chest. I assume he is readying to bathe in the spring, but he pauses before his hands find his pants. I tear my wandering gaze away from his physique, only to find him watching me, leashed anger in his eyes.

"You act so innocent. So righteous in front of Eldridge and Vox and Alistair, but I was *there*. I saw the look in your eyes when you took your first life before Legion. There was no fear when you finally gave in to what you really wanted—what you truly crave. You are no better than me. I just don't hide my desires behind sweet smiles and rounded doe eyes."

Anger lashes behind my chest, my hands trembling with the need to cast. "I *was* that person," I snarl. "Before you. I never wanted to kill anyone, never wanted to lean into that part of myself. You are the reason for my lapse in *civility,* as you like to say, and you are lying to yourself if you see it any other way."

He leans forward, his chest rising and falling faster now, tension charging between us. "You ran off to join them without a second thought. So eager to war with me, Wren! So hungry for my blood, and even now, you won't admit that *this* is you. It's always been you. I may have lit the spark, but you threw yourself onto the pyre. Desperate to burn. Starved for blood, just like you always have been. At least I'm upfront about the kind of monster I am."

I bare my teeth, a snarl slipping free from behind them. "I am nothing like you. You are wicked for the sake of being—"

He rushes me, and my words catch in my throat as his body towers over mine, his face a mask of flames and fury. "If I am so wicked, little witch, why haven't you taken that dagger strapped to your pretty thigh and plunged it into my cold, dead heart?"

His breath is hot on my face, too hot, and I pull my shoulders back, angling my chin up to stare him down. "You'd deserve it," I bite back.

229

Sin's soft laughter is a dark, iniquitous thing, and he nods slowly, his eyes taking their sweet time as they drag themselves up the lines of my neck. "So what are you waiting for?"

I don't give him time to rescind his challenge. In the matter of a second, I swipe the dagger from the back of my waist and hold the blade to the underside of his scruff-peppered chin. Keeping his head perfectly still, his eyes drop to the knife, and a nefarious smile twists his lips upward.

"Bold," he purrs, his voice like silk. "But hesitation will get you killed."

His tongue darts out and drags along the front of his teeth, and he closes in on me further, his bare chest brushing mine and the flesh of his neck sinking into the blade. "Go on then, love. Show me who you really are. Show me just how much you hate me."

My breathing is furious, my heart pounding against its skeletal cage. He's mocking me—forcing me to act on my threats or prove my word is shit—but he wouldn't be this close if he thought himself incapable of defending himself against my blade. My eyes drop to the waist of his black pants and find no weapons holstered there. There's likely a knife or two shoved into his boots, but doubtful he'd be able to draw one fast enough if I decide to bury the tip of my own further into his flesh.

"You're unarmed." The heat from his bare skin burrows into my own, warmth flooding through me and pooling low in my belly.

"I'm quite efficient with my hands. I'd think you'd remember that."

I swallow hard, holding my breath and refusing to allow the sweet, floral scent of his dripping neck beckon me. His blood trickles onto my blade, coating it in a smooth, cherry finish, the sight of it mouthwatering.

And *goddess fucking above.*

My pussy throbs with need at the sight of it. At the sight of him.

I need out of this cavern, need fresh air to swell my lungs and dislodge the scent of him from my nose. Too close. He's too fucking close.

I lower my blade and turn to leave, not caring that I'm proving his point. I just need to get out of this too-tight cave!

Sin's hand collars my neck, and my shoulders slam into the rock behind me, the back of my head bumping into the hand he placed there to stop my head from bashing into the mountain. My blade clatters to the ground, and he kicks it away with a nudge of his boot. His entire body presses against mine, his head tilted down and his long, black hair shrouding me from the rest of the cave, obscuring the *one* exit from my sight.

Leaning forward, his nose skims my cheek, his scent wafting into my nose. "Do I need to remind you what my hands are capable of, little witch?" His voice is raspy, his own control slipping through his calloused fingertips. The pressure on my neck increases slightly, and I can't help the clenching of my sex in response.

It's wrong. I know it's wrong, but my body has never been able to refuse the Black Art's touch, my own demons stirring and reacting to his like ravaging beasts. His question is loaded, taunting me with a threat either laced in violence or desire, but it doesn't matter which. My body reacts all the same, and I suck in a shaky breath under the hand viced around my throat.

"Let go of me," I say through gritted teeth, the words struggling to form under the pressure.

The glint in his eyes is pure beast, and his pupils dilate, shadowing his irises in liquid black. "No," he growls. Then placing his lips at the crown of my ear, "Fight me until your dying breath, but I'm never letting you go."

I jerk my head back, forcing him to meet my eyes, and regret the action immediately. Because as soon as I see the hunger swirling in their depths, craving explodes inside me.

Two breaths. That's all Sin allots me before his mouth claims mine.

Releasing his hold on my neck, he plants his hands on the rock either side of my head, his arms forming a prison around me. His kiss is greedy, desperate, but a moment later, he pulls away, allowing the tiniest bit of space between our mouths.

"It is my actions alone that got us into this mess," he murmurs, "but it does not stop me from blaming you."

"I don't understand," I whisper.

He tilts his head forward, his forehead resting on mine, and his hands drop to sink into my hair, twisting the strands tightly between his fingers. Pain licks at my scalp, and my thighs clench in response.

"I have never stopped thinking about you. Night after night, it was thoughts of you that kept me awake, your voice that chased sleep away. And then you show up, bring me back here, and... and I can't fucking *breathe* around you. You didn't create these problems on your own, but you are the sole cause of my undoing, and for that, I blame you whole-heartedly." His fingers comb through my hair, gripping and twisting and pulling, slowly moving his hands forward to cradle my jaw.

"Do you regret saving me?" The question blurts out before I can stop it, and his hands suddenly freeze.

Dropping one to my waist, he grips my chin between his thumb and forefinger of the other. "I regret many things I've done, but protecting you has never been one of them," he rasps. The hand gripping my waist tugs me closer, his hips pressing into mine. It would be impossible to miss the weight of his swollen cock against my thigh, and I suppress a moan.

Sin's lips graze mine again, gentler this time. "I am sorry... Wren."

My eyes close against his, our mouths barely brushing, his words sinking into my heart. It's not the first time he's apologized, but it is the first time he hasn't hidden it between other inferences, pitter-pattered around what he really meant. His thumb rubs circles along the side of my jaw. "I cannot undo what I've done, but I *can* promise you with every beat of my wicked heart that I will never hurt you again. Forgive me." His voice is barely above a whisper, skating across the seam of his lips, and a single tear leaks from my eye.

I am too lost for words, but I manage a nod of my head. I'm not sure if I intend to accept his apology, or merely acknowledge what he has promised, but a shaky breath rattles free from his chest.

I swallow it whole.

Smashing my mouth to his, I kiss him back. My arms reach up to loop around his neck, my fingers locking into his hair, and his hand drops to my lower spine, crushing my body to his. I arch my back and grind my hips against his, and he unleashes a long groan into my mouth. He's rock hard, his cock throbbing against my thigh, and I'm suddenly all too aware of the clothing separating us.

He's clawing the base of my tunic a second later, balling the fabric into his fists and lifting it up and over my head. Claws extended, he hooks a nail into the ties of my corset and shreds them like silken ribbons, the garment sagging and falling to my feet, baring my chest to him.

An appreciative growl rumbles deep in his chest, and my nipples harden into tight buds at the sound. Gently, he traces one lengthened claw along my throat, between my breasts, and a low moan spills from my lips. And then he's diving for me, sucking my nipple into his mouth, his tongue giving little flicks that shoot heat straight to the juncture of my thighs. His other hand moves to cup my breast, the one his mouth isn't claiming, his thumb rubbing, pinching. My head falls back, and his hands are at my pants, furiously tugging them down, and I step out of them.

A startled laugh escapes me as he wraps his hands around the backs of my thighs and lifts me. My legs immediately wrap around his waist, positioning him between my thighs. Thighs that are soft and full, but muscular from riding horses and spending much of my life hunting and hauling our harvests back to the cabin.

I snake my hand down between us and cup the bulge in his pants, eliciting another groan from him that goes straight to my cunt. My other hand works the fasteners free, and his pants and undergarments fall to his ankles, his cock springing forth. I reach for him immediately, my hand wrapping around his shaft, the tip already slick with need. He growls into my mouth as I stroke, again and again, his dick impossibly thick in my small hand as I work my palm up and down his girth.

Liquid arousal coats my inner thighs, and I grind my hips against his, teasing him with the feel of my wetness against his beading tip. His mouth finds mine again, his tongue entwining with mine, deepening the kiss, and my nails sink into the backs of his shoulders. At some point I noticed the open seam on his neck has closed. I didn't see him heal it, but the sight of the Black Art's mouthwatering cock hasn't exactly allowed me to focus on much else.

And then we're spinning. My shoulders separate from the rough surface of the rock, and Sin pulls me to the ground so I'm straddling him. I lean forward, my braid falling over my shoulder, and my tongue flicks out against the underside of his jaw. And then I'm kissing him everywhere my mouth finds purchase: his neck, his shoulders, the hard planes of his muscled chest. His hand catches my jaw, and he jerks me forward, his head angled so his mouth grazes the crown of my ear. "Bring that needy pussy here so I remember how sweet you taste."

Sin's pupils ring with gold as he watches realization materialize in mine. He wants—*he wants me to sit on his face.*

My limbs spring into action before my mind consents, and I move my way up, Sin's eyes tracking my every movement. His hands wrap around the outsides of my thighs now caging his face, and the ravenous look he shoots me right before he takes his first taste is almost enough to make me come.

"*Fuck*," I moan, rocking my hips as his tongue laps at his feast, hungry and wild and needing. Claws bite into my flesh, the pain setting my nerves on fire, and my head falls back as pleasure washes over me—through me—turning my insides molten. One of his hands slides to cup my ass and the other moves to slip a finger inside me, claw retracted. Another moan falls from my lips as Sin works his finger in and out of my folds, my pussy gripping it for dear life.

My thighs clench around his face, pressure mounting inside me as I ride and ride and ride, Sin's tongue sweeping through my delicate flesh. I startle when a second finger strokes my entrance, and he growls at the sound. "You can take another," he retracts his tongue just long enough to murmur against my thigh. I cry out as he slides the second one in. "Just like that, love. Such a good fucking girl." His voice is a raspy, muted thing. *Goddess, it should be criminal for any man's voice to be so fucking sexy.* "Need to get you ready for me."

I want to tell him I'm ready, that I've *been* ready, but my words are lost in breathy pants as he pumps his fingers in and out of me. And then he lifts me slightly with his other hand, positioning me so his mouth has easier access to my clit, and his teeth lock onto it.

Stars shoot behind my eyes, ecstasy shattering through me like a nova explosion, and I rain down in a thousand glowing pieces. Sin keeps nibbling, giving my clit little tugs with his teeth and flicks from his tongue as I soar to heights greater than the sun.

I'm certain I'd have collapsed if he didn't suddenly sit upright, using his weight to push me on my back as he kneels before me. He nudges my legs open with his knees, and they fall apart without resistance, wrapping around his waist as he leans forward and catches my mouth with his.

My flavor bursts across my tongue, and I arch my hips to brush the tip of his precum slickened cock. He buries himself inside me with a low groan, and my mouth falls open in a silent scream. His hands support most of his weight on either side of my head, but his arms, corded with delicious muscle, tremble as he holds himself here, wrestling with his own self-control as he forces himself to give me time to adjust to his size.

Because *goddess-fucking-dammit,* he's huge, my pussy stretching around his girth in the most painful pleasure I've ever experienced. And I want more. So, so much more.

My hands grab onto his toned ass and pull, pulling him deeper into me as I lift my hips to meet his thrust, and I shatter the last of his restraint. I lean forward and capture his mouth again, matching his rhythm, my hands moving to explore the sides of his stomach, up his chest, around his biceps clenched with flexed muscle. He shifts his weight, dropping onto one forearm and sliding his other hand to grab my ass, leverage to pull himself into me deeper still.

Sin isn't gentle. He isn't kind or tender or merciful as he pounds into me again and again, my pussy coating him in cream. I call out, his name a prayer on my lips, and I lose myself a second time, enraptured by the Black Art, my own personal god.

Teeth sink into the underside of my jaw as his hot seed spurts inside of me, and I wrap my legs impossibly tighter around his waist, milking every last drop out of him. My eyes roll back in my head at the pain in his bite until he releases his primal hold on my jaw, and once again parts my lips with his. My blood is fresh in his mouth, and my tongue darts across his teeth, now lengthened and inhuman. I clench around him farther at the thought of those bestial canines sunken into my throat.

We stay like this for a few moments, allowing our labored breath to slow, until he withdraws from my heat and moves to lay on his side behind me. His cum flows out of me, trickling onto my thighs, and a sound of disapproval rumbles from the Black Art's chest. With a single finger, he forces his seed back inside me, and I look back at him through half-lidded eyes.

"It belongs inside you. *I* belong inside you," he whispers against my collar, and I give an appreciative moan. I sink back against him, allowing him to cradle me in his warmth, and rest my head against the inside of his outstretched arm.

Neither of us moves for a long, long time.

CHAPTER 27

I f my sister wondered where I slipped off to, she doesn't make it known. No one comes looking for us here, and my face heats as I remember the look she gave me before I wandered off with Sin, now musing if Cosmina suspected the storm about to erupt between us. A storm that would prove to be far more *fruitful* than the one that wrecked the gardens the night before. Despite me not being intimate with anyone since Sin, I continued sipping the tonic regularly. A fact that Sin claims he already knew, having glimpsed it in my bag while securing it to my horse during our trek to Blackreach.

I lean further back into his chest, savoring his warmth that burrows straight through my skin like flaming splinters. My hand reaches up to stroke the arm draped across me, his fingers outstretched across my stomach. Heat sparks between my thighs again at the sight of his hand pressed to my stomach, the silent language undoubtedly possessive in nature. I'm not sure how long we've been like this—lying in the scent of our joining—but it's likely at least an hour has passed. We may be dangling on the precipice of war, but right now, the only thing that matters is the Black Art, myself, and the mountain of trust between us that's been shattered and put back together more times than I care to count.

"What were you talking about?" I ask, my fingers tracing lazy circles along his forearm.

"Mm?" he murmurs, voice thick from our coupling still.

"You were talking to my sister when I came to the gardens."

His chest goes still behind me in pregnant pause, and I continue lightly drawing lines into his skin to show I don't intend the question to be hostile. "I was apologizing," he finally answers. Clearing his throat, he adds, "I'm certain it means little to her, but it was owed regardless. Hurting her also hurt you, and for both, I am deeply regretful." His nose skims the hollow of my shoulder, and I work to keep my breathing even in the wake of his transcendent ears.

"What did she say?"

A soft chuckle. "She's nicer than you."

I'm grateful to be facing away as a grin pulls at my lips. His arm snakes around me tighter, pulling me against his solid chest. Putting his lips at the crest of my ear, "It's okay—I prefer my women with more bite," he rasps.

Sin lowers his mouth and kisses the spot he bit along my jaw, his lips a balm to my hurt. His hand vanishes from my stomach, golden light seeping from his fingertips as he raises it to my broken flesh.

I catch his hand with mine. "Don't."

He freezes. "You don't want me to heal my Mark?"

My Mark.

It is custom for transcendents to take a Mate in place of a husband or wife. Zorina had told me that choosing a Mate is never to be done lightly because the vow pledged during the Bonding is an everlasting one. It becomes as vital to your survival as the blood slickening the bones in your flesh, the air swelling the lungs in your chest. Galen was conceived before my sister had sworn herself to his father, and she agreed to the ceremony in hopes it would provide security for her unborn child. In the end, it didn't matter, as Galen's father dismissed her from the pack when she was still with child after he found someone else, a woman that offered him a life not tethered with the responsibilities of caring for young. Morrinne's partner, Garrick, passed long before I came to know her, but the way she has always spoken of him with such adoration in her eyes confirms that the Bond is as strong as my sister claims.

I don't know the full details of what transpires during the Bonding, only that it is considered one of the most sacred vows in transcendent culture, and that the ritual is very *primal*.

I reach up and touch his bite. His Mark. A symbol shared amongst shifter-kind to lay claim to another, a way to show other males this female belongs to them.

More of my arousal leaks onto my thighs.

"Leave it. For now. I can remove it myself later," I finally answer.

His tongue flicks the spot beneath my fingers. "Or you could leave it permanently." His warm breath sends gooseflesh flaring across my bare skin.

I roll towards him. "And have other males thinking I'm not available?" Fire smolders in his eyes, and I'm not too proud to admit that I delight in the jealousy my taunt elicits from him.

"Which males in particular—care to share names?" The hint of a smile tugs on his mouth, but it doesn't meet his eyes.

I purse my lips. "Mm, nope. Can't have you going off and killing all my nighttime company."

He growls, and the sound goes straight to my sex. "Careful, little witch, or I'll pin you down and cover every inch of your body with my Mark. I. Don't. Share." Angling his head, he presses his lips to my throat, his nose skimming the underside of my jaw.

I close my eyes for a moment, relishing in the feel of his

mouth against me. We are playing a dangerous game, the rules messy and unspoken, but for some reason, the wrongness of it arouses me even more. My control is dwindling, and if I don't leave right now, I'm not sure I'll be able to stop myself from climbing on top of him and riding us both into oblivion.

Pulling away, I sit up, but he catches my wrist before I can stand. When I turn and look at him, all amusement has been snuffed from his expression, only the flames of jealousy or wrath or both shadowing his face. "Have you slept with him?"

His question stuns me into silence as I behold the anger brimming behind the mask he's struggling to maintain as he searches my eyes, gauging my reaction. "That's hardly any of your business," I finally say, not needing to ask the *him* he refers to.

"That's not an answer."

"Would it matter if I did?" I ask, ripping my hand free from his grasp and crossing my arms.

His gaze dips to the bite on my neck, then slowly drags back up. "It matters if you have feelings for him."

I laugh without humor. "What good are feelings anyway, Singard, if they don't stop us from hurting the ones we care about?" The blow is low, but I don't regret it. He has no right to waltz back into my life and start asking about Eldridge and me. I rise to my feet and shimmy into my leggings and tunic.

"I didn't mean to... *Fuck*, Wren," he growls, frustrated now. "Can we ever have a halfway decent conversation with one another?" He reaches for his pants and steps into them.

"You're asking me that?" I smooth down the loose hairs jutting out at all angles from my plaited hair.

Sin covers the distance between us in two steps, taking my chin between his thumb and forefinger. He exhales sharply and leans forward to rest his forehead to mine, his other hand scrunching into the braid I just fixed. "I didn't mean to upset you, but I am not above admitting that it drives me... *fucking crazy*... thinking about you being with someone else. I know I have not earned the right to claim you as my own, but that will not stop me from littering the Vale with the bodies of anyone else that tries." His nails lengthen into claws along my chin.

I raise my chin to tilt my head back, forcing him to lift his head and meet my stare. "So possessive for something that isn't yours, Blackheart," I purr, knowing exactly the effect my words will have on him.

He untangles his hold on my hair and cradles my face with both hands, swiping his thumbs across my cheeks. "You have always been mine, little witch. Even if you don't know it yet."

He holds me for an extended beat then slowly releases me, his fingers skirting down the lines of my neck. I slip into a deep curtsy. "Your Grace," I sing, turning and leaving the cave before one of us does something we'll foolishly *not* regret.

⁂

So much for helping Cosmina with the gardens, I think as I watch Eldridge in the distance, pulling my coat tighter around myself as the chill promptly burrows itself back into my bones without the heat of the underground spring to warm me.

I eye the wide, strong body of my friend, the way the muscles in his back clench beneath his tunic as Eldridge swings the ax high above his head and slams it into the log resting sideways on the stump. He would have been an excellent partner, husband. *Mate.* Eldridge longs to provide for others, so much love to give buried beneath his gruff exterior. I don't doubt he will find someone that will treasure and honor him the way he deserves. My heart has always been swollen with unbridled love for my bearish, ginger-haired friend, but the kind of love reserved for companionship. Eldridge deserves to be adored by someone that peers at him with hearts in their eyes and heat in their core.

In another life, that someone may have been me. But fate is a capricious, vicious thing.

Almost as wicked as the man it's destined me to yearn for.

We have enough wood to keep the hearth burning for several more weeks. Knowing Eldridge, he is busying his hands to distract from the thoughts plaguing his daytime hours. I frown to myself, hating that I am likely the source of his blighted mind.

Eldridge brings his ax down once more, the log promptly splitting in two and falling to the forest floor, but he leaves the weapon lodged in the stump, leaning forward to rest his arms on the handle. I made no attempt to quiet my footfalls, knowing he would hear the faintest bend of the tender grass beneath my boots.

"You ought to find a new hobby, Eldridge. At this rate, there won't be any feeling left in your hands in a few years, and then who's going to massage my wrinkly feet when I'm old and gray?"

He turns to face me, running the back of his hand across his slick forehead. "Well fortunately for you, your wrinkly old lady feet came in years ago." His smile is infectious, and for a moment, I almost believe it to be genuine, but his gray eyes remain clouded with the fog of stormy skies.

I approach him, stuffing my hands deep into my coat pockets. "Eldridge, we need to talk."

My ears are human, but even they don't miss the huff of air that blows through his lips as he gathers an armful of split logs and carries them towards the covered shelter outside our house. I follow behind, my legs taking twice as many steps to keep up, even with the added weight in his arms.

"I'm sorry for what I said to you. At Mesa Pointe. I felt like you were judging me for decisions I made, and I couldn't stand the thought of you hating me for what I did. But you must know, I only ever kept Singard's secret to protect you and our family."

He sets the pile of wood down and claps his hands together to shake off the dust as he turns and walks back towards the chopping station. "I understand why you didn't tell us he was one of—a *shifter*," he corrects with a grunt, "but it's more than that. You were fucking the Black Art for Slaine's sake, Wren. How did you expect me to react when I found out?" He picks up another pile of logs and repeats the process of carrying it back to the shelter, me following behind like a lovesick puppy.

"I was ashamed," I admit, my voice coming out meeker than I intend. Willing strength into it, I continue. "It wouldn't have changed anything had I told you before. I knew what he was, the cruelty he was capable of, and I... I fell for him anyway. Please know I am deeply sorry if that feels like a betrayal to you."

He laughs softly to himself, but the sound is laced with something far from humor. Yanking his weapon from the stump, he heaves another log onto the base and proceeds to split it. Another.

And another.

I catch his elbow. "Stop chopping the fucking wood, Eldridge!"

Splitting one more log, he turns towards me, his head giving a slight shake as he beholds me through long, orange lashes. "The crown has wanted my kind dead for as long as either of us have been alive. Not only did you form an alliance to aid them, but you fucked the man who sanctions our slaughter, and now you have the audacity to come to me and say you're sorry *if that feels like a betrayal to me.*"

Tears burn behind my eyes, and I lower them for a moment to collect my thoughts. "I'm sorry. You were too important to me to risk hurting, and by not telling you, I hurt you worse. I don't want to fight anymore. I can't stand the conflict between us. Everything we've been through over the years, us surviving while the isle hunted us like beasts, we've always had each other, and that has forever been my greatest treasure. I'm just so sorry." I can't hold the tears in anymore, and they race down my cheeks in fat, salty rivulets. "I shouldn't have kept it from you, and I value our friendship too much to keep any more secrets from you, which is why I've come here now."

His bushy brows knit together, and he stretches one hand to curl around the ax's handle. To someone else, the action might be interpreted as a threat, but to me, I know it's his way of grounding himself before he hears something he isn't going to like. I flip my braid over my shoulder and pull open my jacket, exposing my neck, bitten and bruised from the Black Art's Mark, and the hold he had on my throat in the cavern.

Eldridge's eyes widen in horror as he beholds my marred flesh, and he drops his hold on the ax as he reaches towards me.

His hand halts mid-air as a mask of fury envelops his face, and he drags his attention from my neck to meet my apologetic stare. "Tell me that isn't what I think it is." His eyes close slowly as if he can't bear to look at me while he hears my truth.

My entire body trembles as I swallow thickly, wishing I could swallow down the words I must voice. "I was with him this morning. I was going to erase it, but it felt like hiding if I did. I don't..." I exhale sharply. "I cannot begin to explain to you the relationship I share with Sin because I don't understand it myself. Just yesterday I was furious with him, this morning even, but then... I cannot explain it. There is good in him, Eldridge. It is deep down, but it is there. I've seen it. Felt it."

"He's a murderer, Wren."

"Yes."

"He captured Cosmina, lied to you, and manipulated you into being his godsdamned whore."

I nod. "Yes." *And no, but now is not the time to argue that point.*

He holds my stare for an excruciating amount of time, not a flicker of emotion crossing his face. Just deadpanned coldness as he searches my expression for something known only to him. "Do you love him?"

Now it's my turn to fix him with a glassed over look of my own.

Love. What a peculiar, wretched thing.

"I know that I no longer harbor the strength to not explore these feelings for him, whatever they may be," I whisper, my heart splintering as the truth of those words hits my chest with the force of the raging sea.

Eldridge nods, mostly to himself, then runs his hand along the length of his braided beard. He bends and throws another log onto the stump, widening his stance once more. "By all means, explore your feelings, Wren. Just don't expect me to stand around and watch while you do it."

His blade bites into the log, the crack of the wood echoing in my ears as his words sink in with equal might.

Tears prick my eyes as I address his back. Perhaps the only part of him I am worthy of anymore. "You deserve to be happy. I appreciate everything you've ever done for me, Eldridge, but I cannot give you what you truly crave, and I am sorry. It was never my intention to hold you back from looking for another, and I was conflicted by my own feelings too. And as low as it may make you think of me, what I feel for the Black Art is something that is so far beyond my comprehension, but the one thing I am certain of, is that every fiber of my being yearns to learn more about it."

"You're setting yourself up to be hurt again, Wren," he growls, replacing the wood.

Crack goes the log under his weapon.

"That may be true. But do not undervalue the sacrifice he made when he shifted in front of his own men. Singard would not be exiled from his own kingdom if he hadn't given up everything to protect me."

"It does not undo what he has done."

"You're right. Nor does my apology reverse the hurt I caused you, but it does not stop me from trying anyway. I love you, Eldridge," I say, stepping back to leave. I linger a moment, grasping my final remnants of strength to finish my thought. "Just not in the same way I might him."

A moment later I'm back inside our house, shrugging off my coat, when a harrowing howl booms across the Vale.

CHAPTER 28

I really hate my sister's sun hat. Cosmina cranes her neck to peer up at me, her view partially blocked by the wide brim. "You need to pull it more taut," she instructs, annoyance feeding into her tone.

I glare at her for the hundredth time, but it's harmless and she knows it. "It's as tight as it'll go without ripping the garland. You need to loop it higher on the trunk. You could see that if you took that bucket off your head," I shoot back, pointing to where the pink-purple fuchsias wrap around the base of the silver barked tree next to her. I'm perched in the tree opposite her, my ability to balance in one far less impressive than my namesake bird, but fortunately, the branches are thick and don't sway an inch under my weight.

A small smile graces her mouth as she adjusts the oversized hat to sit farther back on her head, then works to position the garland higher. The banner constructed of snipped flowers woven and pinned into the vines won't survive long without their roots in the ground, but it will be plenty vibrant for the celebration tonight. I was surprised to learn Aeverie sanctioned the uprooting of so many flowers and plant materials with her respect for nature, to which I was promptly told that the high priestess has long paid her offerings in exchange for the turned earth. *Whatever the goddess that means.*

I haven't seen Sin since our unexpected run-in yesterday morning, but he's in the Vale somewhere. I'm certain he's not slipping out of here undetected with elven guards positioned along the border, but even if he could manage it, I don't think he'd leave. I'm not so naïve as to not recognize that this could all be part of some elaborate ruse Sin had in place with his father before we captured him. Maybe it makes me a damn fool, in fact, I'm positive it does, but I believed him when he told me it wasn't.

Cosmina feeds slack into the garland, and I pull more of the length into my tree, looping it around a few branches then scaling my way down the trunk. I move to the next one, and we repeat the process of my sister stringing the flowery vines across the open center and handing me the ends to thread through the branches.

"Where did you and Singard run off to yesterday? Do you know how many piles of dirt I had to haul on my own, sister?"

She's adjusting the petals in the length between two trees, tucking the deep green leaves behind to showcase the vibrant colors. Aeverie did say she wanted the area around the temple to pop tonight, and she didn't care how many flowers were snipped to achieve it. Apparently several of the other garden elves have been busy preparing for this event for a while, but many of us were only told yesterday about the party planned for tonight. I briefly wondered why that was, but chalked it up to more elven secrecy I didn't need, nor care, to understand.

"He wanted to talk about something... privately," I say, pointing to my ears to indicate I'm wary of any others lingering within elven hearing distance. I wasn't surprised she didn't ask me about it last night when she returned home, her face still shadowed with soil before she bathed. She sensed the contention between Eldridge and me, and true to my sister's considerate nature, she didn't pry about either of my difficult conversations that day. But I'm not surprised she's asking about it now.

Cosmina eyes me with caution, but there's a glitter of something else twinkling in her sky-blue depths. "I see," is all she says. Then, pursing her lips, she adds, "He apologized to me yesterday."

I climb down from my tree and move to the heap of blankets that were dropped off earlier and begin unfolding them, spreading them across the ground outside the temple. I snort in feigned amusement. "And you responded how, dear sister?"

She shrugs her delicate shoulders. "I told him he deserves to rot in the deepest, darkest pits of the earth."

I smile to myself, remembering Sin saying that my sister was nicer than me. If that bathes her in a warm light comparatively, then I can only imagine what the Black Art must think of me.

"Good. He deserves nothing less from you," I say with a note of approval.

"I also told him the demons he'd face in the next realm would be his lowest concern should he ever hurt you again. That the wrath of an overprotective sister who's experienced his violence and cruelty firsthand would be far more painful than anything he'd meet in death."

I shoot her a curious glance. "I'm not accustomed to such ire in you. It's a good look."

She drops her hold on the flowers and spins to face me, her hat falling forward and shielding her eyes before she slides it back again. I reach for another blanket but don't unfold it.

"You must be careful, Wren."

"We're on the brink of war with two armies, both of which outnumber us greatly, and our only saving grace lies in Sin agreeing to work with me to remove the dark magic someone else bled into the land decades ago, which in turn risks the elves harnessing that power to turn and destroy us all. I think we're beyond being careful." I didn't hesitate to fill the others in on the history Aeverie shared with us after I returned to our house two nights ago, wanting no more secrets between us.

"I'm not talking about any of that. You may think I don't see, or maybe you're still clinging to the hope that I won't, but I *do* see the way he looks at you. And more importantly, I see the way you look at him. You needn't hide it out of shame or worry of what any of us might think. It is important to me that you know you can always talk to me. You are a grown woman, Wren, you needn't my or Eldridge or anyone's approval of your choices. I only ask that you proceed with caution. The Black Art's reputation was not simply given—it was earned. You and I have both been on the receiving end of that cruelty, and I do not mean to lecture you, but I think it unwise for you not to proceed with caution."

"I appreciate your concern, but I assure you I will not wear my heart on my sleeve so foolishly this time," I say, shaking out the blanket and laying it on the grass. When she doesn't respond, I turn to her, crossing my arms across my chest. "Why are you staring at me?"

Her blue irises turn to ice as she regards me with newfound coldness. "You already are. Maybe not so plainly for others to see, even him, but you do not hide your affections from me, little sister."

"When have you heard me speak in anything other than hostilities towards him?" I ask, leaning forward to further drive my point.

"It isn't in the words you speak, but rather in how you look when you do. The feelings you hold for him run deep, and it doesn't take shifter eyesight to see that."

I hold her gaze for a long moment, unsure how to respond to her... accusation? Observation, I suppose. Cosmina doesn't miss much—she never has.

"Will you help me with these blankets? I fear there is still much to do."

The Vale always looks ethereal once the moon takes its place above, and no more so than tonight. Cosmina and I finished the decorations just as several other transcendents and elves began bringing in wooden tables to skirt the area set aside for an evening of cheer by firelight. Though, I'm still not sure what there is to be so cheerful about given the precipice we all currently balance upon.

Fire roars and spits in the pit, casting shadows on the furs and blankets strewn across the ground. Decorative cloths sewn from thick fabric adorn the tables, large bowls overflowing with brilliant red apples, oranges with peels nearly split from ripeness, a tossing of garden vegetables amidst dark leafy greens, flaky, fruit-laden pastries, and next to the table, several pigs still on the spit, glazed and dripping with melted butter.

My sister and my efforts do not go to waste. Several others offer their appreciation of the foliage we strung through the trees surrounding the temple, the vibrant pinks of the flowers and the tenderness of the swollen berries a stark comparison to the darkness that looms beyond the border.

Fast-tempo music sung from the strings of fiddles entrance many of us in dance, including, to my surprise, my calm-spirited sister. Cosmina and Blythe frolic amongst a group of transcendents, some gyrating, many drinking, as they lose themselves in the elven music. Lanterns notched on trees shroud the scene in a fiery glow, and through the woods ahead, I can just make out the silhouettes of several shifters leaping and bounding freely in their animal skins. I recognize Theon, his dark gray fur peppered with silver along his maw, and his eyes a deep brown set within his wolfish face.

To my left, Morrinne plates a rock slab for Galen with strips of the tender pork and fresh vegetables, and about three more pastries than Zorina would have permitted. Though something tells me the pure joy on my nephew's face as he beholds the flaky delicacies would soften even his mother's strict guidance.

Speaking of my sister, I spot her sidled up to Cornelius near a group of elves, men and women alike, sparring and wrestling amongst each other. Judging from their lack of discipline as they grapple, not all of them are training under Vox, merely friends joining in on the night of unwarranted festivities.

Cornelius's easy smile dissipates as I approach, and Zorina cranes her neck behind her to follow his gaze. She waves me forward eagerly, her golden hair swishing across the tops of her shoulders. "You and Mina did a sublime job with the decorations," she praises before taking a deep pull of her drink, the elves having brought out an assortment of cups, some crafted from wood, others forged from steel, in place of the hollowed shells they usually drink from.

"Can I get you something to drink, Wren?" Cornelius asks, an edge of caution in his voice.

"You needn't be so wary around me, Langston. It was your brother that tried mounting me like a broken horse, not you."

"A foolish attempt, indeed," he says, the smile reappearing on his face. "I don't know what berries they put in this stuff, but elven wine is divine. I'll be back in a minute." Cornelius hurries off through the crowd.

"What has you all cozied up with a Langston boy?" I ask, perching on the log Cornelius had been sitting on.

Zorina holds her drink close to her as she tucks her head down so her chin brushes her chest and grins like a jester.

"Oh, for Goddess's sake," I groan in feigned annoyance, then grab her knee and give it a shake. "Go on then. Spill."

"He's really nice!" she bursts out, peeking up at me to gauge my reaction. I motion with my hands for her to continue. "I know his brother was a complete and utter ass to you, but Cornelius is anything but to me. He's smart. Disciplined. Kind. And you should see how Galen lights up around him. Cornelius is taking him hunting this week, showing him the ropes. He told him he'll have him putting down game in no time," she says smiling, balancing her chin on the rim of her cup.

"I was away for what—a week? Two? He put the moves on you fast, friend."

"Well, it's been a bit longer than that, actually. You've just been a tad... busy. Distracted. I didn't want to bore you with details about us when you were dealing with your own problems."

"Your *details* are never a bore. Especially when those details involve a handsome man with a goofy-ass grin." I nudge my elbow into her side, eliciting a spurt of laughter from her. "How does it work?" I continue.

She moves a piece of hair that had fallen into her eye. "What do you mean?"

"He's human," I clarify. "Would you guys get married or partake in the Bonding?"

"Goddess, Wren, saddle the horse before you slap it on the ass, would you? It hasn't been *that* long."

I take the drink from her hand and help myself to a generous sip. Blackberry juice bursts across my tongue, tart, but cut with a smooth nectar that rounds out the flavor and coats my tongue in velvet. Cornelius wasn't exaggerating— elven wine really is delicious.

"But if you must know," she huffs in exaggeration, "Cornelius already said he would perform the Bonding if that's what I wanted. He'd need a male to explain the... *process* to him, but like I said, he's smart."

The wine almost spews from my mouth. "So you did talk about it!"

Her cheeks redden, and she gives a sly nod. "What can I say, I'm a planner!" she giggles.

"What happens during the ceremony anyway?"

She takes her drink back and chugs the rest before answering. "A hunt. One the male assumes."

"What do they hunt?"

Her smirk is pure wicked. "You."

Now it's my turn to flush, and I allow my gaze to wander to where a group of transcendents—some shifted, others still in their human skins—form a large circle.

"You wouldn't happen to be asking about human-transcendent relations because of a certain other male, would you?" she asks.

I shoot her an agitated look. "If you're referring to Sin, no. I wouldn't dream of it."

"Of course not. I'm sure you wouldn't dream about ever wearing his Mark then either."

Fire tunnels into my veins, and I stroke the part of my neck that, just yesterday, displayed the Black Art's bite before I healed it. "Eldridge told you!" I don't phrase it as a question.

She gives a dismissive shrug of her shoulders. "He's my brother. He was being all broody, more so than usual, so I pried. It didn't take much; he was pretty riled up and needing to vent. He won't risk losing you as a friend over it... but he'll need time. Eldridge is a pouty one. But I can't say I blame him. I'd have gutted Sin fifty times over by now, and you should have too."

"Your drink, miss Wren," a familiar voice interrupts us. I turn to find the elven commander handing me a steel chalice filled with more of the sweet liquid. "Your friend was swept away so I took it upon myself to hand deliver this. Enjoying the elven wine, then?" Vox asks, raising one pale eyebrow as he takes a sip from a matching chalice. His blond hair is freshly braided, not a lock out of place where the twisted plaits frame his head.

I bring the cup to my nose and give it a pointed sniff.

"You suspect I might poison your drink?" There is no hostility in his tone, just curiosity.

"I didn't suspect you to dump iron into my bloodstream and look where that got me, Commander." The smile I flash him is all teeth.

"I will not attempt to dissuade you from keeping your wits about you, but an elf does not become a commander by slipping belladonna oil into wine." He says it as if the thought offends him.

Shouts from behind me tear away my attention, and I turn in time to catch a shifted transcendent pacing inside the ring they formed minutes earlier. No, not just a transcendent—Eldridge. The circle makes way as another beast stalks into the sparring pit, the onlookers cheering and pumping their fists as the two shifters begin to grapple for sport.

"Well, that's one way to burn off steam," Zorina sighs, standing up. "I ought to go make sure my brother plays by the rules of our game. There are only two, if you didn't know," she says to Vox. "No biting the face and no slapping the sack." She flashes him a coy smile and retreats with a wave of her hand.

I turn back to the commander but angle my body so I

maintain sight of Eldridge and his partner. "Pray tell, how does one become a commander, then?" I ask, continuing our conversation.

"I could tell you it's a title entirely based on merit but it would be a half-truth. Elves pride themselves in their discipline... dedication. In the strength of our bodies, as well as our spirits, to get up and continue even when all seems lost. We are also protective of our lineages. I hail from a very long line of elven blood that's been blessed with both kinds of strength—the ability to ground our hearts in both steel and Source alike. To phrase it more simply, I was destined to take my place as Commander long before I was conceived."

I take a sip of my wine, holding the liquid in my mouth and savoring the smooth mouthfeel before swallowing it down. "Why haven't you had children then? Surely you want to continue your lineage if it is that important to you."

Vox chuckles and glances towards the fighting transcendents for a moment, collecting his thoughts. "Perhaps the stress of the past several decades has aged me, but I'm not that old, blood mage. Not to elves, anyway. You would likely have a very different opinion should you know how long I've walked the earth. There is still plenty of time for me to choose the right partner to ensure that the potency of my family name continues."

Cheering erupts from the shifter ring, and Eldridge runs a victory lap around the inside of the circle, only a cloth covering hanging around his waist. He lets out a howl of laughter as Theon pushes through the crowd, and based on the unison of *"ooohs"* from the crowd, he has a few choice words for his brother before Theon shifts again and gives a playful shake of his furred head.

I study the commander more closely. His alabaster skin is smooth, free from wrinkles or creases despite the stress he spoke of, his fair hair silky and lustrous, and his body honed into that of a warrior's. Nothing about his physical appearance suggests he's much older than myself, a woman in the middle of her second decade, but neither does Aeverie's, and *Goddess knows* how old the high priestess is. "Just how old are you, Vox?"

The commander gives a playful shake of his head, then leans forward, putting his lips at my ear. "Whatever number you're thinking, blood mage, add a century. Or a few."

Surprise doesn't school my face because there is none. I suspected as much. "That many years and you still haven't found the right match? One might think you're just being picky, Commander," I tease.

He takes a pull of his own drink and gives his chalice a swirl. "There's far more to be considered than merely a tolerable personality. The *right match,* as you put it, must also prioritize the betterment of our kind. There are plenty of potential partners in the wings, but I am in no rush if a more... suitable match were to present itself."

I grab a handful of my skirts, a deep purple that compliments my lavender blouse and matching laced bodice, and offer a mock curtsy. "I didn't realize I was standing in the presence of such high elven nobility."

The elf laughs, taking no offense from my teasing. I run a hand through my long hair, turning to watch as Eldridge pins Theon beneath his muscled shoulder, eliciting a bestial yelp of submission from the latter. "That style suits you," Vox interrupts the colorful words I was stringing together at the sight of my friends harming each other for sport.

His near black eyes dip to my outfit, the flowy skirt and form-fitting top a more feminine choice than my usual attire, and rise to rake over my unbound hair.

"Tunics tend to be a better choice when facing enemies, Commander. The blood washes out easier."

"Alright, which one of you ass-sniffers wants to go a round with the Red Wolf next?" Eldridge hollers, slapping his fists against his chest as the lot of onlookers egg him on. *Overgrown cubs, all of them.* Eldridge's stormy eyes snap towards where Vox and I stand in the crowd, and a look of indignation crosses his face. "You," he seethes, pointing a finger in our direction.

It takes me a second to realize he's pointing to someone behind us, and I turn to see the source of his vexation.

Oh, for Goddess's sake.

Clad all in black and looking like darkness incarnate, Sin stands at the edge of the tree line, bathed in shadow. My mouth parts at the sight of him, his vivid eyes already fixed on me, his expression unreadable. Though his clenched jaw has me thinking he's been watching me for a while... me and Vox, that is. Reluctantly, he tears his gaze away to meet Eldridge's.

Before I can yell for Eldridge to knock it off, he's waving Sin forward with increased speed. "What's the matter—cat got your tongue?" He breaks into laughter, and several others follow suit, poking fun at Sin's more feline second skin.

"Choose someone else, Eldridge," I growl, but he doesn't so much as glance in my direction.

"You had no problem forcing your Mark on her, why don't you come leave a few on someone your own size?"

Sin's face is the false calm before a tsunami. "Contrary to what you might believe, *Red Wolf*," he drags out the nickname, "I would never dishonor the only person I ever wish to Mark by not waiting for their *explicit* consent, which I assure you, was in no short supply yesterday."

My breath hitches, and I almost lift my arm to absent-mindedly caress where his bite had been, but I clasp my hands together at the waist of my skirts instead. I dare a glance back to Eldridge who's a pillar of flaming fury as he jerks his head to the side in a movement that's pure shifter. A second later, he jumps and lands on four feet, and the growl that erupts from his bestial form swallows all remnants of my human friend. The bear-sized wolf paces the circle, never taking his eyes off Sin.

"Just walk away, Sin." My whisper is barely audible, but it won't escape his ears. He backs away and disappears into the tree line, and for once, I think he's going to heed my caution.

But when has the dark warlord ever regarded my warnings?

The transcendent that leaps through the brush and stalks towards the ring bears no humanity in its fluid gait. Its shoulders, legs, and back are shaped by thick muscle, its paws wide with yellow-tinged claws already extended, and the faintest glimmers of midnight blue peek out from its ebony coat in the light of the roaring fires. And yet somehow, the predator that slinks into the circle looks more at ease than I've ever seen Sin in his human form. That thought should terrify me.

But it does the opposite.

Where I should feel fear, a spark ignites instead, and a longing so deep it borders on pain settles in the depths of my belly. Vox watches the transcendents circle one another with interest, sipping appreciatively from his chalice, while the crowd of transcendents and elves begin to pump their fists and shout for their chosen champion. My eyes snag on Zorina. Her arms are crossed, and the fire reflects in her extended claws, Cornelius standing at her side. He doesn't touch her, perhaps because they're still taking things slow, or maybe he just has the common sense not to touch her while she resists the urge to shift and intervene. Despite her complaints of Eldridge's behavior, he's still her brother, and Goddess-be-damned before she lets someone hurt him in front of her, especially when that person is the man who has hurt us all in more ways than I care to count.

The two don't waste time circling each other, baiting an attack. Eldridge leaps for him immediately, a move I'm certain the Black Art wasn't expecting, but he dodges to the side with grace. Eldridge skids to a stop and whirls himself around, lunging again, but this time, Sin doesn't skirt the attack.

Sin leaps towards the Red Wolf, and their bodies crash together in a tempest of claws and teeth. The crowd cheers louder, but even it can't drown out the deep snarls rumbling from both the animals' chests. Eldridge is pure bulk and brawn, his shaggy red coat long and soft, his form similar to that of a wolf's, except much larger, and his ears are softly rounded like a bear's. Sin almost matches him in size, but his form is far more cat-like, his black fur shiny and clipped, his ears wider and less rounded than his counterpart's.

The two grapple on hind legs, and Eldridge sinks his teeth into the side of Sin's neck, using his weight to keep himself underfoot. The skin there is thick, but no amount of fur and flesh can keep that jaw-lock from hurting. I step forward, and a hand grabs my forearm. Not painfully, just in warning. I look up at Vox, and he shakes his head. "It is their custom. If they don't let their anger out this way, it will merely fester and bleed out on the battlefield when our attention cannot be divided. Leave them."

I swallow thickly and nod. Vox is right. If we're to war with a kingdom that far outnumbers us in bodies and resources, our loyalties cannot be fractured. A single fault can lose an entire isle to the sea.

Eldridge has weight on him, but Sin's leaner form gives him balance. He swipes one powerful arm into the side of Eldridge's head, again and again, while burying his shoulder into his chest. The Red Wolf growls low and deep over his mouthful of onyx fur but is forced to drop his hold on Sin or fall backwards, twisting his hips and spine at an unnatural angle. As soon as his neck is freed, the Black Art strikes again, using his agility to maneuver half onto Eldridge's back, his own teeth finding purchase in the side of his ginger-tinted fur.

Zorina's brother lets out a guttural snarl, and her fingers flex against her sides. Eldridge dips his large head, trying to buck the cat-like creature off, but Sin's claws have already sunk into the sides of his stomach, giving him too much leverage. The Black Art growls, the sound making every hair on my body snap to attention, and heat pools between my legs. A mix of fear and excitement, a recipe for something as dangerous as it is delectable.

I am an adult capable of making my own decisions, just as Eldridge is responsible for provoking Sin and inviting him into the ring. And right now, watching Sin in a state that is purely *primal,* I want nothing more than to make a plethora of bad decisions with him.

Starting with giving the Black Art a few bites of my own.

Eldridge tosses his weight backwards, causing himself to go sprawling across the ground, but effectively breaking Sin's death grip on him as the Black Art also falls with a loud thump. They both regain their footing immediately, and *now* they circle. Sin's eyes glow brighter than the bioluminescent algae in the spring, ringed with a gold that burns hotter than the fires crackling around us. He dips his head and jerks it to the side, a motion that clearly translates into a challenge. Sin is daring him to strike again.

I glance at Vox who's leaning forward now, his black eyes missing nothing, and his fingers drumming the side of his cup.

"That's enough." I hear Aeverie's voice before I see her. All eyes dart to the ancient elf as the high priestess pushes through the crowd and slams the butt of her staff into the ground.

All except the two transcendents who don't dare take their eyes off each other, nothing shy of bloodshed promised in both of their stares. Eldridge answers with a menacing growl, one Sin matches with his own visceral snarl. And then they're charging, their limbs and snouts entwined in a battle of pent-up rage and unspoken words, each getting in bites around the face and neck while their claws work to shred the other's flesh to ribbons.

My mouth waters at the sight and smell. Eldridge's blood is spicy and woodsy, Sin's floral and sweet. I lock onto that flowery perfume, the scent reminiscent of hyacinths and rain, and I erupt into something far more dangerous than two transcendents struggling to rein in their tempers.

"I SAID ENOUGH!"

A loud boom cracks around us, and I am momentarily blinded by a flash of pale blue light. I shield my eyes with my arm, then lower it to find both shifters slowly regaining their footing several paces away from each other. The high priestess storms between them, the hem of her white dress swishing across the grass. Her skirts must be magicked because despite the wet earth, no stains soil her clothing. Stepping between them, she tucks one hand against her waist while the other keeps a firm grasp on her staff.

"No. Fighting. In. The. Vale." Her voice is pure authority, and despite the heat careening through my veins, a shiver skitters down my spine.

Vox adjusts his stance next to me, and the high priestess whips her head towards him. "Why are rules being broken under your sight, Commander?"

"The wanderers were fighting in jest, Madam Priestess. It is tradition in their culture, as you know."

"And is it tradition for them to nearly rip each other's throats out? This land has drunk enough blood to last many lifetimes, we will not feed it more until it is time. Let the earth parch for vengeance." Her milky stare steers over to mine. "I see the longing in your eyes, blood mage. Are you and Singard Kilbreth ready to pledge your alliance so we may prepare to take back what is ours?"

I catch Sin's head whipping between Aeverie and me in my periphery, but I don't avert my gaze. I was prepared to offer my allegiance two days ago when she showed us the trauma this land experienced, but I cannot commit without Sin. "We are still discussing the matter," I reply.

"Discuss faster. There is no other option. You lift the poison lacing our soil, or you die by the hand of his father. The decision has already been made." Her face betrays no emotion, but something in the cold starkness of her clouded eyes tells me she's already seen the outcome in her Sight. "When you pledge your servitude, an offering will be held in your honor. As a show of good faith, it is custom for our kind to offer a piece of ourselves to the blood mage, to bless your magic with our own." Her attention flickers to the commander at my side, and I notice him tilt his head to look at me from the corner of my eye. I wonder at the meaning of their exchanged glance, but I can't take my eyes off the priestess, ensnared in her sights like a spider in a web.

"By offering, you mean..."

"The purest substance in this realm: elven blood." She turns back towards the shifters. "Cease this act of savagery at once. If it is the blood mage you fight over, perhaps you should redirect your efforts into making those affections more permanent so this nonsensical madness can end. Slaine gifted you with the ability to Mark, I suggest one of you make well of it before the other does."

Sin whips his head around to let out a warning growl, and Eldridge gives a quick shake of his coat, the behavior coming across as almost mocking.

My mouth pops open, and the heat swirling inside me resurfaces, but for an entirely different reason now. I stare at the high priestess in bewilderment, sickened that she speaks on my behalf as if I am unable to myself. She adjusts her grasp on her staff and turns back to me. "Bear in mind that a blood mage is the hardest Mate to conquer. In the end, she must choose who has earned the right to grace her with their brand."

My hands unclench at that, and I drop them to my sides. "The only *brand* I will be wearing is the blood of our enemies when I bring them to their knees before me." Fire blazes in my palms, and I don't miss Vox's quick sidestep that puts distance between us.

My flames reflect in Aeverie's icy depths, and she inclines her head slightly, the motion almost imperceptible. Sin leaps out of the ring, turning his large head towards the priestess as he slinks past her, before leaping into the forest with equal parts grace and lethality.

CHAPTER 29

Goddess, I want to kill someone. Something. Anything. Fury licks at my nerves as I slip through the woods, the sounds of the party dimming as I head in the direction Sin took off. He's long gone by now, but I can't stop myself from traipsing through the forest anyway, needing to be away from the others. As I walk, I reflect on the heat raging to a full-on firestorm in my core, and I wonder if it's not fury at all that stokes those flames.

It's the need to consume. To devour every part of the Black Art, drain him so completely that there is nothing left to feast upon but my arousal on his cold, callused fingertips.

I keep expecting to hear the rustling of trees around me, the snapping of twigs or disturbance of leaves, but an eerie silence blankets the woods tonight. A part of me wished he'd be waiting for me, but I'm not surprised he isn't. I did not miss the wrath radiating from the Black Art when he dipped into these woods. The bites and tears he landed on Eldridge will need tending to immediately, but the Red Wolf has an entire legion of transcendents to clean and heal his lacerations. Sin is out here alone, likely healing his wounds in seclusion where his pride is protected.

I have no doubt that overhearing my conversation with

Vox stoked his anger, and Eldridge's antagonizing remarks sent him spiraling into the reaper the isle has come to fear. The need to mend his wounds isn't the only reason he fled so abruptly. He left so he wouldn't rip Eldridge to pieces. Because as much hate as he may harbor for my friend, Sin knows if he inflicted any real damage Eldridge couldn't recover from, that would forever hinder any affection for him I may return.

I approach a stream and kick off my sandals, letting the water lap at my ankles for a moment before sitting to lean against a tree. Across from me is an outcropping of sediment with mushrooms and algae peeking through the exposed bedrock, and my thoughts drift back to the underground spring and its colorful plant life. The cavern where Sin laid me back and feasted on me like I was his last meal, where he sunk his teeth into my neck and filled me with his seed.

An idea that's as wicked as it is brilliant entices me, and I slide my skirts up so they bunch around my waist.

My hand slips between my thighs.

The Black Art was never shy to boast about how he could smell my arousal. If he's out here lurking somewhere, I'll give him a scent those primal instincts can't resist.

My fingers graze through my slick, and *Goddess above,* slick I am. Just the memory of what we did in that cave, the way Sin looked fighting in the ring, has my pussy weeping for his touch. I slip one finger inside, and my head falls back against the tree as a low moan breaks free, then another, as I gently glide them in and out of my folds. My thumb rubs circles against my clit, pressure mounting inside me as I imagine it is Sin touching me, him feeling each clench of my sex. I yank down my bodice so my full breasts spill free and take one in my hand. I squeeze as I work my fingers faster, my low moans crescendoing into a symphony of desire and madness. Maybe I *am* mad, because right now all that's missing to make me come undone is the taste of the Black Art's ichor coating my tongue and teeth. My legs fall apart wider and—

Sin leaps onto the bedrock with lethal elegance. I hadn't heard him coming, his clawed paws as silent as the death they promise. I admire him appreciatively—his long legs muscled and lithe, his shoulders hunched beneath a coat of midnight fur I yearn to run my hands through. His head dips, and I follow the motion. It's then I notice the absolute fury darkening his already black-furred face.

His pupils are slitted within his glowing yellow-green eyes, his teeth bared, and a nightmarish snarl tears from his chest. He's not just terrifying.

Sin is downright malignant.

The beast isn't directing his posturing towards me. His eyes are trained on the woods around me, his pupils dilating as they search for movement in their shadowy vastness. Sin paces the grassy lip of the bedrock, that snarl never leaving his chest. I speak his name.

Claws sharp as daggers curl over the ledge, the muscles in his feet flexing as if preparing to leap and shred someone to ribbons. Someone he thinks is in these woods...

Someone out here with me.

While I sit half naked with the scent of my need permeating the air.

"It's just me," I whisper.

At that, those wicked eyes finally lock onto mine. I release a breath, relaxing the tension his wrath burrowed into me, and slide my hand to my aching center once more. His snarl finally ceases as he drops those glowing depths to track my hand. I flash him a sweet smile and slip a finger inside, stretching myself. A moan of pure anguish falls from my lips as I add a second, then slowly begin to pump them in and out.

"I didn't know where you went so I wanted... wanted you

to... you to find me," I pant, my fingers glistening with liquid arousal. My other hand cups my breast again, and I squeeze, my toes curling into the tender grass.

Sin leaps off the cliff and stalks towards me, his landing near silent. When he's inches from me, he leans forward and inhales deeply, his nostrils flaring.

His eyes glaze with tormented need.

I allow my knees to drop farther, inciting another growl. And then he's gone. Bounding into the woods to my right, his feline form dissipating into the shadows. A part of me wonders where he's going, but I can't call out for him to stop. Can't do anything but grind against my hand as I bring myself closer and closer to the edge. I cry out as I remember the taste of Sin's blood between my teeth, the feel of his thick length gliding inside me. *Goddess above*, I'm going to fucking come...

A hand closes over my mouth, and his lips are at my ear before I can react. "Such pretty little sounds you make," Sin rasps. He lowers his hand and winds his arm across my chest, forcing my throat into the crook of his elbow. Replacing my muzzle with a collar. I moan at the pressure against my jugular, and his arm tightens further, promptly silencing me. His grip isn't snug enough to restrict air, but any more and I'll be seeing stars. "You're close?" he asks, his nose skimming my hair.

I nod, my head brushing his bare chest. My eyes dip just enough to see he's wearing pants, and I curse him for being prepared with a change of clothes. Ever the strategist, even while stalking through the woods and hunting whatever comes lurking too close.

And right now, I desperately want to be his prey.

He groans his appreciation. "Then keep touching yourself, love. But you better savor it because it's going to be the last time you ever come for anyone but me."

I slide my hand back to my heat and plunge my fingers deep, then let out a strangled cry as his arm tightens around my throat, and he tugs my hair back with the other. The sting goes straight to my cunt. "Do you understand me?"

I nod, and he growls, the sound raw and feral in my ear. "Tell me. Say you understand that no one touches this pretty pussy but me."

"I understand," I whisper. Tears sting my eyes, a reaction to the pressure in my airway. "No one but you. Only you."

The pressure eases slightly, and he releases my hair, sliding that hand to hold my jaw instead. "Good girl," he murmurs in my ear. "Now make yourself come one last time."

He told me to savor it, but all control slips right through my fingers as I ride them into release, calling Sin's name in both prayer and plea. Stars burst across my vision, having nothing to do with Sin's chokehold and everything to do with the earth-shattering orgasm that barrels through me. I sink against his chest, feeling his own heart thumping against my spine.

He relaxes his grip and catches my hand with his. Lifting it over my head, he takes my two fingers between his lips and sucks, pulling them out slowly as he tastes my nectar on his tongue. I turn in his arms and tilt my head up to look at him. "You're a rather devious thing, do you know that?"

His grin is utterly indecent. "How else would I please such a salacious creature?"

I palm the underside of his jaw and gently press my lips to his. "*Exactly*... like that, Your Grace." I'm not gentle as I rake my nails down his chest, then rise to my feet. Making a cup with my hands, I palm some water from the stream and quench my sudden thirst. I trace my damp fingertips across my collarbones, needing to cool the burn Sin's body left on mine. He rises then, stretching his arms above his head which causes the

THE BONDS THAT BREAK US

muscles along his stomach and triceps to flex. My pack family often did the same after shifting, the transition between forms usually leaving their bodies tiresome and achy immediately after. I scan him for signs of injury and find none.

"Did you have any trouble healing?" I ask.

Whatever warmth was on his face vanishes. "No."

I study him curiously. "When you came for me... you didn't think I was alone?"

Sin stands taller, his chin tilted up as he stares down at me with those brilliant yellow-green eyes. There is no denying the Black Art is beautiful, but in the pearl glow of the moonlight, he is nothing short of devastating. "I scented you," is all he says, as if that was answer enough.

My plan to bait him to me with the smell of my arousal worked, but his initial reaction when he found me sends a pang of hurt to my chest. "And you thought I was with him." I don't need to speak his name. Sin's violent posturing when he leaped onto the bedrock was enough to show he thought I'd run off with Eldridge after the fight.

The face of death corrupts his features, the Sin that gave up his identity to protect me replaced with the reaper his subjects fear. His jaw clenches, and his lips twitch as if he's running his tongue across the front of his teeth. He doesn't speak, but his expression tells all.

"You think that low of me? That I would be with you just yesterday, then run off with someone else tonight?" Anger licks my veins as I give voice to my thoughts.

"You were content to entertain the commander well enough."

I take a step towards him, and he adjusts his stance instinctually. Ever primed to defend himself, as if the need to has become so second-nature to him that his body shifts of its own accord. "It's called a conversation, Your Grace. Perhaps you should try having one once in a while. And you have no right to eavesdrop on me anyway."

"It was hard to miss him spouting off about looking for the best woman to bury his seed into."

My mouth pops open before I promptly close it, and I shake my head, fury rising in me. I want to shout at him, pound my fists into his chest, but I turn to walk away instead. "You always do this. Anytime I try to get close to you, you throw up a godsdamned fortress around you! It's inspiring that after everything, you think so highly of me, Your Grace." I storm off before tears have the chance to well in my eyes.

He catches my wrist as I pass but doesn't turn towards me. In fact, he doesn't say anything. I tilt my head down to watch him in my periphery and find his stance unbearably tense, his attention on the ground, but I think his eyes are closed. I wait a moment, then tug my wrist free. He releases it, but his whisper keeps my feet planted. "Don't go." Not a command. A plea.

"Stop making me."

He seems to deliberate on that for a moment, then slowly turns to face me.

Torment.

That's the only word to describe the scrunch in his brows, the feathering in his jaw, the resentment gleaming behind his vivid eyes. Not towards me, but inward. "That's not an easy feat for me, love."

"And you think it has been for me? I was ousted by my birth parents, near starving to death on the streets under the kingdom's rule, forced to hide what I am, and then must watch as my family stifles their nature everyday to exist within the laws you've been content to uphold. You're not the only one that struggles with trust, Singard."

Anger eclipses the sorrow on his face. "I will never deny your struggle nor the role I played in it. But at least you had people that took you in as one of their own. My own mother abandoned me to that godsforsaken castle, and my father just publicly outed me in front of my capital. You have a family, Wren. I have subjects. Or at least, I did."

I pause as his words sink in and twist themselves into my gut. Shame burns through me as understanding rises. But it does not excuse his behavior. "Our families don't have to be whom we are bound to in blood. Those bonds will *break* us if we grant them that leverage. I have been many things, Your Grace, but broken has never been a hat I've been content to wear."

He studies me closely. "You fault me for being resentful towards those I share blood with?"

"Never. I fault you for not giving a chance to those you do not." My fingers curl at my sides, and I avert my gaze for a moment to collect my thoughts. Words stack on my tongue, but I hesitate, knowing there is no return once I utter them. "It hurts me for you to suggest that I would have entertained an offer from Vox even if he had made one. And worse that you'd think I'd have run off with Eldridge after I told you I wasn't involved with him."

"You never told me that. You refused to answer when I asked you. What do you expect me to think when you toy with me like that?" he demands, angling away from me as he runs both hands through his hair.

"I expect you to respect my privacy while I figure out what I want."

A sinister laugh has him shaking his head and his hands clenching at his sides. "I can't do that, Wren."

"Respect me?" I scoff.

Sin whips around, unleashing the full might of that bestial gaze on me. "Share you," he growls.

A second later I'm backed against the tree, his arms a cage

on either side of my head. Not threatening, but as if his hands need to find purchase in something before they tear the forest apart. My pulse pounds wildly in my neck, a song of desire and fear. Not fear of him, but fear of our elaborate game of cat and mouse finally arriving at its end. "I never asked you to," I whisper. "But I have spent my whole life being pushed away by others. I cannot be with someone who does the same."

He leans forward, using his arms to support himself as he levels his head with mine. "And I cannot share that kind of trust with someone who will never be able to give themselves to me completely."

"That kind of relationship is earned."

Sin cants his head to the side, a lock of hair hanging over one eye. "You'll never be able to look at me without remembering what I did to you. I see it on your face every time, and every time it drives a fucking blade through my heart." His right hand slams into the trunk, but I don't move an inch. A moment later, he drops his arms to his sides as if he doesn't trust himself not to shift.

"I see the way he looks at you, and it takes every ounce of control I have left not to tear his fucking head off when he does," he snarls, his knuckles lengthening into claws. Tension rolls off him, charging the air between us, and his arms tremble as if it's taking everything he has not to let his beast out. "I know I haven't earned the right to your heart, but you stole mine long ago."

I struggle to calm my racing heart, my breathing uneven and shaky. I want to be collected. Poised. But like the gates to his capital city, the Black Art is collapsing my walls, piece by broken piece. "Why are you saying all this now?"

Fury flashes in his eyes, but I don't have time to wonder what I said before his claws punch into the tree around my head. "Because I can't stand the thought of you giving your heart to someone else when yours is all I think about." He leans forward and rests his forehead against mine, taking deliberate breaths to tame his beast. I grant him the silence he doesn't ask for. After a moment, he drops one hand and takes hold of my jaw, forcing me to meet his eyes. This time, his hold on me is gentle, tender even. "I love you, Wren. And I think I have for a very long time."

My breath hitches, and I go deadly still in his grip.

"I would face a thousand brutal deaths before I ever see that look on your face again. Knowing I betrayed you. I do not deserve it, but I am asking you to make a choice anyway."

Sin sinks to his knees before me.

"Forgive me. Tell me there is the faintest chance you might one day feel something similar for me. Or tell me to get out of your life permanently. I will respect your choice, but I cannot have half of you."

I school my features into granite as I behold the mighty warlord. The king who kneels for no one but is on his knees before me. He watches me intensely, his monstrous, glowing eyes trained on my every movement.

"You wish to know if I might one day love you?" I ask in a voice as cold and unforgiving as death herself.

He nods once, short and curt.

"No."

Half a second. That's all the time it takes for his mask to falter and reveal the face of a burning man before he wills his expression to stone, then goes to rise.

I slam my foot onto his shoulder, halting his climb. "I cannot promise to give you what you stripped from me long ago. You stole my heart many moons ago, and as hard as I tried to wrench it back, you kept it in your clutches. It is yours for now, Blackheart, but wrong me again, and it'll be yours I devour."

CHAPTER 30

The Black Art had been staring at me with smoldering regret forged straight from the heart of Elysande herself. But slowly, my words sink in, chipping away the ice encasing his cold, black heart. Caution overwhelms the hope on his face, like I might fade from his life altogether and leave it littered in ash and dust as he wakes in his bedchambers, his castle and kingdom and subjects bending to his every whim and will. Back when the dark mage had everything.

Except me.

The one flicker of light in his all-black world.

He's on his feet faster than I can track the movement, a phantom of war and need, his lips crashing into mine with more force than the might of his armies combined. I part my mouth for his, and our tongues battle for victory, the pounding of our hearts our personal war drums as we fight for an uncertain future. One that doesn't see us on opposite sides of the battlefield. One where the lineages of our magics are appreciated, one where our differences inspire growth instead of pain.

I bite his lower lip, and he groans into my mouth, the sound going straight to my aching center. His hands are everywhere, sliding down my neck, my arms, his fingers digging into the divots of my hips. I arch against him and moan at the feel of him stiffening against my belly. My fingers twist into his hair, and I kiss him greedily, showing him my love where my words often fail me. I trace the peaks and valleys of his biceps, across the planes of his sculpted pectorals, making my way down his rippling abdominals to where his trousers hug his trim waist. He doesn't pull away when I break our kiss.

"You promise to safe-guard my heart?" I whisper against his lips.

He trails a finger down the side of my face. "My most sacred vow, my Lady."

I grab his finger and take it into my mouth, pulling it back out slowly though my lips. "And you want me to be yours?"

Sin's eyes dip to where his finger now grazes my lower lip. "It would be my greatest honor," he murmurs, his words a caress to both my heart and sex.

"Then show me. Show me I'm yours."

He doesn't hesitate, dropping his mouth to my neck and kissing a trail to my shoulders, his hands unthreading the ties of my bodice and yanking the sleeves off my arms so it falls in a heap of fabric at my feet. He growls appreciatively at the sight of my nipples, tight and hardened as they ache to feel his mouth on them. Dipping his head, he sucks one into his mouth, thumbing the other as he cups and squeezes my full breast. My head falls back against the tree, and my pussy throbs so hard I think I might explode from the pressure. His hands drop to grab my ass and he begins to lower to his knees.

"Stop," I demand.

He does immediately, looking at me with bemusement.

"Allow me to make myself more clear." Not breaking eye contact, I unfasten the buttons of his trousers and sink to my knees, lowering his pants along with me. Something perverse and wicked flashes in his eyes. "Show me," I repeat. "And I swear to every god in this realm and the next, I'll leave if you hold back even a little. I want it all." We both know he's too big for me to take all of him, but I want him to try anyway. I want to feel. I want to *hurt.*

Sin reaches down to cradle my jaw. "Filthy words for such a pretty mouth, little witch." I smile, elated he's shifting his demeanor to play with me some more. "Someone needs to teach it a lesson." His other hand grasps his swollen cock, and he begins to pump.

I finally let my eyes drop to admire him, and my pussy weeps at the sight of him taking his own pleasure, his gaze trained on my mouth. "Not someone—only you. Show me who I belong to."

His stare turns downright predatory as the hand cupping my jaw moves to the back of my head, and he slides himself between my lips. He utters an impressive curse, then begins rocking his hips. Slowly.

Too slowly.

I shoot him a look that he interprets immediately. *Don't hold back.* Tonight, I don't want the man willing to go to his knees to beg my forgiveness. I want the warlord that takes what he wants without remorse.

The Black Art hears my silent plea, and my sex clenches as his features mold into his mask of ice and wrath. He pulls out of me and tugs my hair back so I'm forced to expose my neck. His other hand thumbs over my lips, then strokes a lengthened claw down the front of my throat, sending shivers pebbling my entire body. "A wicked little thing, you are," he rasps, teasing my flesh with the sharp edge of his claw. "There are three things you're going to learn tonight, little witch. One, I'm the only one that touches your sweet pussy. Two, death will find anyone that ever tries to touch what I am about to claim. And three," he moves his hand to grab my jaw, "you're going to learn just how long you can hold your breath."

Sin plunges his cock into my mouth.

He's anything but gentle this time as the hand in my hair tugs and twists, my jaw straining to open wide enough to welcome his girth. I never lower my eyes from his, watching as he drops the hand on my face to his side, his stance slightly reclined as he guides my mouth up and down his shaft. I raise a hand to wrap around him, but it halts mid-air. Half a second later, both my arms are swept behind my back, and a pair of phantom manacles bind my wrists, anchored into the tree behind me.

A devious smile blooms across his face as he takes in the realization on mine, undoubtedly noting the scent of my arousal deepening with the awareness that I am now at his mercy.

The Black Art is known for many things, but mercy has never been one of them. His cock grows impossibly larger as he beholds me on my knees before him, my breasts heaving with faltered breath. His thrusts deepen, seating himself all the way until his tip touches my throat, again and again. "Just like that, love. You're so beautiful with my cock in your mouth."

Tears prick my eyes, and one trails down my cheek, my jaw aching as he pumps into me. He wipes the tear with a finger of his free hand and licks it. If it's possible, I grow even wetter, my thighs drenched with my own slick. And then he's not looking at me anymore, his head tilted towards the heavens while he mouth fucks me to a song that's anything but holy. His grunts fill me with deep pleasure of my own, contrasting the pang of emptiness that spreads through me as need heightens my senses to something painful.

Sin pulls out of me with a curse, the hand entangled in my hair keeping my head from moving an inch while he collects himself, keeping his human form intact while his instincts plead for him to shift and rut into me that way.

The manacles release, and my hands fall limp. I slowly rise to my feet, prey trapped in the predator's sight. Sin wraps his arms around my waist as he pulls me in and kisses me deeply, my gums seasoned with his salty precum. "Turn around," he barks, dropping his hold.

He doesn't spin me himself, forcing me to be the one to choose to give myself to him so completely. I turn.

"Hands on the tree and spread those beautiful fucking legs for me."

I do as I'm told.

He grunts as he sheathes himself inside of me, and it's the most glorious sound I've ever heard. The warlord wrings my own cries of pleasure from my lips as he fucks me without remorse, fulfilling my demand that he show me who I belong to in mind, heart, and body. I grind my hips back against him, my pussy stretching around his thickness, but I'm too wet for it to hurt anymore. I want him. Every tortured, cruel part of him, I want it all.

I shatter. Again and again and again as I rock against him, ecstasy chasing through my limbs, my core, my heart. I turn to look at him over my shoulder. "Let me feel your love," I whisper.

The Black Art comes with a roar, filling me with his hot seed, his promise, his... *his love*. I clench around him, milking him dry as his cum trickles out around us and drips down my thighs. His arms band around me, crushing me to his chest, his nose pressed into my hair. We remain here a few moments, and I turn to face him when he finally withdraws himself.

I pull him against me and twist one hand into his hair, gently guiding his mouth towards mine. "Look at me." His feline eyes lock onto mine, and my heart somersaults in my chest. I stroke his cheek with one hand, admiring his beauty and the devastating way he's looking at me right now. "You may have taught me three things tonight, but there's one thing I need to tell you too," I whisper. His expression turns curious as he waits for me to continue. "I love you, Singard. More than the stars in the sky and the breath in my lungs, I love you. I have for a very long time."

CHAPTER 31

It feels strange not fighting. Like at any moment, the Black Art and I will rip off the masks of civility we wear, draw our weapons, and compete to be the first to deliver the blow that will finally end the games we play once and for all.

That would be a pity, indeed. I rather enjoy our games.

It's been a week since we made this forest our personal bedchamber, and relations have been eerily pleasant since we've agreed to stop trying to kill each other and explore the deep-seated feelings we both confessed to having. I'm tempted to believe it's been the best week of my life.

"You're going to scare all the fish away if you keep clomping around like that," I scold, my own spear primed over the rushing river.

Sin shoots me a half-grin and makes a show of lifting his feet very high and slowly so as to not frighten the fish. I can't suppress the giggle—actual *giggle*—that follows. It has been almost comforting to discover one skill Sin hasn't already honed into masterful perfection. He was quick to remind me there was never a need for him to spear his own fish when he had an entire kitchen staff dedicated to preparing meals, though he did say he used to sneak down to the shorelines when he was younger and try his hand at it for leisure. I had wondered if Bennett Langston, the Black Art's longtime childhood friend, accompanied him during these trips before he shredded his throat to tattered flesh, but I didn't ask.

For once, I don't desire to provoke him.

A glimmer of olive-green scales catches my attention, and I angle the prongs of my spear. The thick canopy above prevents the sunlight from distorting the fish in the water, and my weapon slices through the bass's belly like melted butter. I hold it up, admiring the deep greens and muted browns of its scales, when a pair of hands vine around my waist.

"My vicious, little killer," he whispers in my ear, tugging my lobe between his teeth.

There's that airy laugh again, the one that feels so strange coming from my throat, and I turn out of his grasp to add my catch to the bucket. There are eleven fish now, ten of them caught by me.

"You want an equal, right? It's only fair that I catch up." I flash him a smile that's all tease, and he mirrors with one of his own. I told him about killing Varil's guard—the one Vox and Aeverie were going to allow to return to Baelliarah with a message. I didn't leave out the part where I delighted in the feel of my blade slipping into his neck, and even more at the sight of his blood trickling down his throat like a macabre waterfall. Sin never once recoiled as I described my perverse appetite for the scarlet syrup that sustains us all. He merely listened, and I loved him all the more for it.

"Did you know Cornelius is bedding my sister?" I ask, wiping the small bone splinters fastened to each prong of my spear with a tattered rag.

"How do you feel about that?"

I roll my eyes at his lack of surprise. I should have known Sin would be keeping a close eye on the whereabouts of his closest... enemies? A few months ago, the eldest Langston earned himself a top spot on the Black Art's long list of them, having been the one to escort my limping sister to me when he rescued Cosmina from her cell in Sin's dungeon. Relations between the elves and transcendents have been rocky, especially with the added discourse circulating that the only possibility of the Vale winning this war is to place trust in the man who, up to this point, did everything in his power to harm their kinds. But Sin isn't our enemy anymore.

Or, he isn't mine, at least. The others may need more convincing.

"Zorina seems happy and that's all that matters to me. Cornelius has only ever been on our side. Well, sort of," I amend. "I suppose none of us were on the same side in the beginning, but things are different now. Cosmina and Blythe seem happy too. It appears my entire family is pairing off in human-transcendent relations." I wink at him.

Sin strikes, and his spear lands dead center in the belly of dinner. He chucks it into the bucket, then rinses his hands in the river. "I'd hardly consider you human, *blood mage*," he recites in his best impression of Aeverie. "If the rest of the humans were half as ferocious as you, my kind would have lost this war long ago."

I stare up at him, and he raises a dark brow, seemingly not catching his slip up. Tossing my weapon aside, I sit and pat the grass next to me, and he joins me a second later. Tilting my head back, I soak up all the warmth I can from the summer air. The sky is streaked with wisps of clouds, only part of it visible through the latticework of interlocking tree limbs high above our heads. The weather has finally settled into the heart of summer when the air is balmiest and the storms the calmest.

"That's the first I've heard you refer to transcendents as your kind," I say softly.

He's quiet for a while, and when I steal a glance, he appears deep in thought. I almost wonder if he hadn't heard me at all when he finally speaks. "It's harder now." I angle myself towards him and stroke his hand with mine, waiting for him to continue when he's ready. "Being a transcendent is more than just being able to shift forms. It's in my blood always. The instincts... the need. All my senses are heightened like that of an animal's, and when certain emotions rile up, I'm primed to react in certain ways. I've repressed those instincts my entire life, and only shifted when the need was so strong I risked madness.

"Being around other shifters heightens those reactions even more. We're pack animals by nature, and I've always been alone. Here... surrounded by so many of my kind... I've been shifting a lot more. For no reason other than to run and experience the woods through eyes I was forced to blind for a long time." He is thoughtful when he speaks, and my chest warms at seeing the glimmer of something new in his eyes. Not quite happy, but... content.

"What is it like?" I trace lazy circles up and down his forearm while he considers.

His lips purse, then flatten while he stares into the trees opposite the river bank. "It's like being weightless and infinitely powerful at the same time. Like nothing can hold me back anymore—not my kingdom or the law or my..." he swallows, "or my father. It's like breaking the surface of the water when you've spent a lifetime under the sea." He turns to look at me, his expression thoughtful. "It's the third greatest feeling I've ever experienced. Right behind making love with you."

I cock my head and shoot him an expression of mock hurt.

"Oh really? And pray tell, what feeling is so great it tops seeing me naked?"

"When you tell me you love me."

Warmth starbursts inside my chest, spreading through every limb and careening into my fingers and toes. I lean forward and brush my lips against his shoulder. "I love you." I kiss the base of his neck. "Every," I whisper, skimming my nose up the column of his throat, "wicked," then teasing my lips against the corner of his, "part." My mouth crashes into his, tasting every villainous piece of him and craving more. He parts my lips with his, and our tongues exchange blows, each of us rushing to taste as much of the other as possible before I need to leave to get ready for the blood offering tonight.

For as steadfast as she was about us making a decision, Aeverie didn't utter a single word of gratitude when Sin and I agreed to lift the ruinous magic out of their land during the forthcoming blood moon. *As the gods have shown* was all she said before explaining that Vox will offer the most blood so my magic will be blessed with that of their strongest warrior. A tradition that Sin bared his teeth about every time we discussed the ceremony this week. Sin's goddess-blessed power will supply the foundation of the land's restoration, but it is my ability to amplify it that will do the heavy-lifting.

I break our kiss and lean back on my elbows, the end of my braid curling over my forearm. "You made the right choice. Agreeing to help them."

Ire simmers in his eyes, and he leans forward, resting an elbow on top of his bent knee. "I cannot take my kingdom back alone with my own armies conditioned to attack me on sight, and I refuse to allow my people to be subjected to my father's rule. If restoring the elves their power is the price I must pay, then I will. And with the elven army at my rear, I swear to

Adelphia herself I will stop at nothing before I am back on my throne."

"You make getting what you want sound so simple," I say.

The glimmer in his eye is as sinful as his name. "It is when you burn everything and everyone that gets in your way, love."

CHAPTER 32

"Is gold truly the color we want me wearing the night I'm supposed to be gorged on blood?" I ask, peering at myself in the full-length mirror.

Zorina snickers. "Perhaps the high priestess has a matching gold bib you can borrow," she says, making a show of pretending to wrap a bib around her neck and holding up invisible eating utensils.

I give her a wry smile in the mirror. "Is that derisive humor what swept Cornelius off his feet, sister?"

She mock curtsies, fanning out her skirts. "Mr. Langston finds me very charming indeed." Her response bleeds into laughter the rest of us share.

Morrinne steps forward from where she's been quietly observing in the corner of the room and adjusts my crown woven from branches and dried purple dewberries. She drops her gaze to assess me head to toe, taking in the flowy gold dress with a gauzy train. A trail of blood-red rubies decorates the center seam of the bodice, and more adorn the fabric that collars my neck all the way to my chin. The sleeves are over-sized and translucent like the gossamer wings of a butterfly, and a bronze sash sits just above my hips.

The dress is gorgeous.

And completely ridiculous for some glorified bloodletting ceremony.

My mother tips my chin up with one finger, calloused from decades of weaving and knitting. "You're happier lately," she says, not commenting on my attire at all.

I pull her in for a hug and bury my nose in her silver-streaked hair. Lavender and chamomile tease my nose, and I inhale deeply. I've missed the scent of my mother's favorite blend of tea and wish I could bottle her comforting aroma and carry it in my pocket forever. "Our family is whole again. Of course I'm happier now," I agree.

"You were a miserable goose before you dragged the Black Art back here."

"Mama!" Zorina scolds.

"I'm your mother, I can speak freely if I choose," she snips.

I look to Cosmina for help, but she offers none, merely smiling to herself as she places the brushes and little pots of cosmetics she used to paint my face back into the basket on the table.

"It is complicated," I say.

Morrinne scoffs. "You have that right." I can't read her tone to determine if she is criticizing my relationship with Sin, or simply hinting that she is privy to the increased time we've been spending together, as our schedules permit. I've returned to my work in the gardens, and Sin has been integrating into the elven army, learning their weapons, armors, and tactics, and in exchange, schooling them in the kingdom's disposition of troops and the common maneuvers they rehearse in training.

I *am* happier since the Black Art and I decided to explore the current that's pulsed between us since the day we met—a fickle, dangerous thing, but one we can deny no longer. Blythe enters the room, a vacant space in the temple Aeverie has allowed us to use for readying ourselves, and offers me a complimentary note on my hair which my sisters twisted into a crown braid, my diadem pinned carefully behind it. She bids Cosmina a brief kiss, then announces that the high priestess has summoned us.

The blood ceremony is about to begin.

The temple is more crowded than I've ever seen it, and outside are more elves already enjoying the festivities set up for after the celebration. The lectern has been pushed to the side next to a long, rectangular table with a vermillion cloth running down the center. A few goblets with etchings of symbols I don't recognize sit on the table, alongside a slender bottle of the elves' signature wine. And in the center, propped in its metal stand inside the glass dome, is the ruby adorned dagger Aeverie showed us before, the one that was used in these ceremonies in the past.

Twelve elves clad in ebony robes, minus Aeverie who wears her usual white ones, line the far end of the temple. Six male, six female, with the high priestess and Vox at their center. They face the stone dais, now covered by a red carpet beneath a wing-backed chair with the softest-looking gold cushions, more rubies imbued into the arms of the seat.

All twelve pairs of eyes snap to me as I approach from the hall, and a hush falls across the room.

"Sit where we may honor you," Aeverie instructs, stepping aside so I may breach the wall the elves formed, separating the rest of the room from the dais steps.

The cushions groan softly as I settle into the chair, placing my arms on the rests. Firelight flickers from the wall sconces, bathing the House of Worship in a warm, ember glow. I find my family near the front of the room, their expressions stoic as they wait for me to partake of the forbidden wine. Eldridge catches my eye and gives me a slight nod in silent encouragement. My heart swells at the gesture, and I return it with a subtle incline of my own.

Aeverie's white robes swish across the floor as she retrieves the dagger from its holder, grabs one of the chalices, and walks to the foot of the dais. "For centuries, our kinds have joined to ensure our magic remains potent and our harvests fruitful. Soon the blood moon will eclipse the morning star, and when it does, our connection to Source will be at its strongest. As my Sight has already shown me, the blood of the goddess-blessed will feed our land, and the blood mage will direct it through this wretched chasm and into its heart. As a show of good faith and to bless your magic with his strength, the commander will make an offering for your indulgence. But first, the council will bless this union with our own."

Aeverie ascends the steps, slides the dagger across her palm, and presses the flat side of the blade across my lips like she does with the juice of the berries during the weekly service. My throat tingles with thirst, but I swallow it down, breathing through my mouth only. She mutters something in the ancient tongue, then hands the blade and cup to the elf farthest to my left. The woman slices her palm and tilts her hand to drain into the ornate goblet, murmuring something that sounds similar to what Aeverie said. One by one, the cup and dagger make their way down the line, the goblet growing fuller and fuller with each new set of hands. When the last elf's palm has given its juice to the cup, the high priestess collects the chalice and presents it to me.

"Please accept our offering. With this drink, may our blessing aid your magic to serve us all."

I accept the cup, and with a dip of her head, she returns to the foot of the platform. Despite the throng of bodies watching from the far end, the room is near silent. Everyone's attention trained on me and the sacred wine in my hand, as if they truly believe I am to be their salvation.

I feel his heat before I see him.

Standing near the side of the room, arms folded tight across his chest, Sin watches me intensely, his eyes feverish enough to melt this tulle dress to golden ash at my feet. Half of his hair is pulled up in a top knot, the rest neatly combed well past his shoulders. A flowy white shirt laced partially open compliments the rich color of his sepia skin, and his black pants, despite being borrowed, conform to his muscular thighs in all the right places. Here, I thought I was the one looking like Elysande's gift to mortal men, but Sin is devastating in his own right too.

I return my gaze to Aeverie, bring the cup to my mouth, and down its contents in one deep pull. My eyes close, savoring the creaminess of their collected ichor, the convoluting flavors competing for my tongue's attention. Most of them bright and citrusy, but a few deeper flavors like birch and cedar cut the tartness with an earthy finish. I drag my tongue across my teeth, lapping up all remnants of the dark wine.

My collective hums in my veins, itching to be unleashed, but I keep it tethered. Now is not the time, especially when I still have Vox's blood to drink. My magic obeys without struggle. I didn't shed the blood myself, so my beast remains mostly unprovoked for now.

Aeverie collects my cup and summons Vox, who comes forward, the sacred dagger now clutched in his hand. His blond hair is startlingly bright against black robes that obscure most of his clothing, his braids freshly plaited and twisted against the sides of his head. He gives my attire an appreciative sweep, then lowers to one knee.

I lean forward, one eyebrow raised.

Vox reaches for my hand and gently brushes a kiss against the backs of my knuckles. "It is my honor to be the final offering. With my blood, Wren, I gift you strength in mind, body, and heart."

Vox rises and slices his palm, crimson creeping across his hand where it drips to the matching carpet. I make the mistake of inhaling and have to fight to keep my eyes from rolling back into my head. He smells delicious, especially with my senses heightened from the fill I already drank. I wait for him to bleed himself into the goblet, but he leans forward instead, his hand tilted sideways.

My breath hitches.

He... he means for me to drink from him directly.

I bid him a silent question, looking pointedly between him and the hand he hovers near my mouth. "It is tradition for the final offering to be consumed directly. There is an ancient saying in our tongue, it translates loosely to 'the strongest of magic herein lies in the flesh.'"

The temperature in the room plummets.

"She will drink from the cup." I don't need to peer around Vox to place the voice; I would recognize Sin's guttural snarl anywhere.

Vox straightens but doesn't turn around. "It is in the best interest for all of us if the blood mage accepts the offering from the pulse."

"And it is in *your* best interest to not suggest it again. The cup, Commander," Sin warns in a voice colder than winter's breath.

I angle myself to look around him and find Sin standing directly behind the elven council. Gone is the playful lover from earlier today. Tonight he is the warlord, the dark mage, the reaper whose blood is rumored to be as black as his frigid heart.

Something stirs inside me, and I cross my legs, leaning back in the elegant chair. A muscle feathers in Vox's jaw, and he curls and uncurls his marred hand before meeting my gaze. "The offering is in your honor, blood mage. Your blessing, your choice."

I grin sweetly, some perverse part of me enjoying the bickering between the two. "The cup would be most splendid, Commander. Thank you."

"Very well." Aeverie passes him the chalice, and he bleeds himself into it.

I accept the drink with a curt smile, and Vox returns to the line of robed elves. My eyes lock onto Sin's, and I don't look away as I tip the goblet, Vox's ichor coating my throat in a velvet finish.

Lemon and cream bursts across my tongue. The flavor reminiscent of the pudding that was a staple in our kitchen during the late winter months when the fruit was ripe and swollen. I'm decent with mashing berries into jams and pestling herbs into seasoning, but anything that requires the patience of cutting tart flavors with the perfect balance of sugar and cream was best suited to Morrinne. If she were the head baker for every kingdom, I'm certain all fighting would have ceased long ago.

I swallow the last of it while never taking my eyes off Sin, wanting him to know that just because it's Vox's blood I'm drinking, it's him I'm wholly focused on. Something yellow snags my periphery, and I note that his claws have extended. He's pissed. But to his credit, he's leashing his anger well. Perhaps I'll reward him for that later.

Aeverie offers me a cloth napkin which I use to dab my

mouth, then uncross my legs as the high priestess addresses the spectators. In unison, each elf in the temple places a fist over their hearts and mutters a word in their native tongue. A moment later, the crowd begins to disperse outside to the celebration, the flower garlands Cosmina and I hung still alive and vibrant. In hindsight, Aeverie wanted them strung up for the party last week because she knew that the flowers would serve as decorations for the celebration tonight. One she knew would occur, courtesy of her so-called Sight supposedly assuring her Sin and I would agree to her terms. One final offering to the blood mage, this one from nature herself.

I rise from my chair and head for the room I dressed in, giving a little extra sway to my hips as I'm certain Sin watches me until I'm out of view. I strip the sash and gown first, relieved I somehow managed to keep any blood from spilling onto the light-colored fabric. I pull on my change of clothes in its stead: a simple deep blue dress under my leather bodice, the fabric fanning out around my hips. My crown braid and headpiece are next to go, and my hair falls in loose waves down my back. With the swash of gold on my eyelids and the color of murder on my lips, I leave the room feeling good.

Really fucking good.

Holding my head just a little higher, I waltz outside to the party and find Theon, Cosmina, and Blythe laughing and enjoying drinks. A group of young elven girls are frolicking around handing out crowns woven from blue and white flowers, two of which already sit on the heads of Blythe and my sister.

"I would have poured you a drink, Wren, but I'm sorry to say I forgot my dagger at home," Theon says with a wink, raising his cup in a mock toast.

I scrunch my face and stick my tongue out at him. "Ha-ha, yes, Wren drinks blood, laugh it up."

He wraps an arm around me and pulls me against him, tousling my hair with his other hand until it's a tangled mess. I swat him away, laughing as I pry away the pieces clinging to my cheeks. Dropping my hands to my sides, I—

The sight of him stops me short.

A lone storm cloud amidst a bright sky, Sin's colder, rigid demeanor stands out against the circlet of cheer. I motion with my chin for him to come over, and he raises a brow, to which I then use my hands to furiously wave him over to us.

Blythe takes a sip of her drink and looks to Cosmina nervously, but my sister's expression remains unchanged. A hand slides into place on the small of my back, just a hint of possessiveness as Sin sidles up to me, all trace of the bemusement he wore from across the field now absent from his face.

I reach down and slip my hand into his. If my public display of affection surprises him, he doesn't let it show, curling his fingers around mine.

"While I know you technically met before, it was under false pretenses," I say, feeling a twinge of guilt still for having led my family to believe my traveling companion was a guard named Roarke sent to escort me by the Black Art himself. "I'd like you to meet my pack brother, Theon. And this is Blythe. She's a part of my sister's life, so as far as I'm concerned, she's an honorary member of our familial pack."

Blythe returns in kind, and Theon dips his head. "Word in the brush is you collapsed your own gate—watchtowers and all," he says.

Sin might as well be a wall at my side, all hard lines and edges. "Improvisation," he replies, his tone underlined with dark amusement.

"By that, he means Wren was a royal pain in our asses and sent our plan careening into shit."

I spin so quickly at the sound of Eldridge's voice I'm

lucky to not twist an ankle. He grabs Theon's drink from him and takes a deep pull. "Mind if I have a sip of that, brother?" he says, shoving the now empty cup into Theon's chest. The two exchange a series of mock blows and side steps, making ridiculous grunts and looking like simpletons.

My heart doubles in size at the sight of it.

Movement from my periphery snags my attention, and I turn in time to see Cosmina giving Sin a subtle nod. The action is simple but feels weighted—like I missed some exchange between them while focused on the idiots wrestling at my side. I glance at Sin and swear there's the tiniest hint of relief etched into his features.

"Wren, have you decided what you're making for Morrinne for her birthday?" Cosmina asks, perhaps to dissuade me from asking about the shared look.

"Yes, actually, and I need your help keeping her occupied so I can use the kitchen. I'm making her soap—well, as close to soap as I can with the few oils and herbs I have—and I doubt the others want me using the joint kitchen for my personal use."

"Consider it done. Will you be joining us, Singard? Her birthday is in a few days. Don't tell anyone I told you, but it's kind of a big one," she says with a wry grin.

"My lips are sealed, my Lady. And I won't insert myself where I'm not wanted."

"I wouldn't have invited you had I not wished you to accept it. We all have skeletons in our closets, Your Grace. You just so happen to have a preference for keeping them in your dungeon."

My eyes widen at my sister's boldness—out of character for her timid nature, but her smile is wide and playful. "It is far from my wish for you to be in my sister's life, but that is not for me to decide. It is your choice, but don't not come because you think my invitation was disingenuous."

Sin opens his mouth to speak but he... *hesitates*. Possibly the first time I've ever seen the Black Art, smugness incarnate, struggle for words. He settles for a nod and a forced smile, but Cosmina seems pleased enough.

"What about you overgrown dogs?" I steer my voice towards my brothers who get in a few last shoves, snickering like two pre-pubescent boys.

"Are you saying my presence isn't enough to please the old broad?" Eldridge says, his grin lopsided and toothy. He speaks in jest. Eldridge's relationship with his birth mother is strained, and I know how deep his respect for his chosen one runs. I deadpan him, and his howl of laughter in return turns my blood to gold. "Alright, alright, so maybe I've secretly been making her a new box to store all those things she's always using." He makes a motion of knitting with his hands. "It's been a real bitch and a half too. The wood here isn't easy to cut —too fucking wet, and it collapses like you just damn told it its puppy died or something."

"Are you being bested by some logs, Eldridge?" my brother asks, eliciting a chuckle from all of us except Sin.

It also earns him a vulgar gesture, but Eldridge's eyes are alight with warmth as he rattles off an insult of his own, but I don't hear it, my focus going to the hand tugging me a few steps back. Sin's lips are at my ear before I can turn. "Meet me in our cavern tonight?" His breath is hot on my neck, and I want to inhale every bit of the peppery scent clinging to him.

"I wouldn't say it's *our* cavern," I say, leaning back into his chest.

"I'm pretty sure the scent of what we did in there will keep others from disturbing us. And if it doesn't, your screams certainly will."

It takes everything I have not to turn around, wrap my legs around his hips, and beg him to take me right here. "Are you threatening me, Your Grace?"

He drops his voice lower and whispers directly into my ear. "Does it make you wet if I am?"

Goddess have mercy. Poof a bed under us right now.

"Immensely."

It's his beast that replies in a voice more raw and graveled than the craggiest river bed. "Then I promise you, you'll be spending your night begging for mercy from the torture I'm going to put you through. Enjoy your party, love. When you've had your fill here, come find me. And then I'll show you just how much fuller you can be."

CHAPTER 33

It turns out that parties aren't nearly as fun when you know a beautiful man is waiting to torture you afterwards. I tried to put it out of my mind, wanting to enjoy this time with my family. I danced and drank and ate, but not even the sweet elven wine could satiate the ache deep in my belly. Every fiber of my being calls out for him like a siren in a bone-chilling storm, my body desperate for his touch, his warmth.

His *torture*.

I make it one hour before I excuse myself and head for the cavern beyond the gardens. The entrance is an all-black mouth at this hour, and I use my hands to guide my way towards the bend that spills into the larger opening with the hot spring. Light flickers in the narrow tunnel, illuminating the asperous rock on either side of my head. The breach in the darkness allows me to move faster, following the light like a lantern at sea until I reach the final turn.

An oasis greets me.

Candles adorn the cavern floor, bathing everything in a warm, romantic light. Several red pillows are thrown tastefully about, and plush furs are spread along the far side, more pillows and a gold blanket stashed next to them. A slender bottle of wine and two goblets sit at the edge of the spring, the heat coming off it warming my skin from here. A kaleidoscope of colors reflects from the bioluminescent plant life in the bottom of the pool—greens and pinks and purples striating the rock ceiling in our own personal aurora.

The cavern has been transformed into a haven of beauty, but it's not the dazzling scenery I can't look away from. It's the gorgeous male waiting for me, looking like he was carved from bronze itself. The laces of his flowy shirt have been loosened, showing more of the sculpted planes of his chest, his hair now unbound, and he's barefoot.

"Don't tell me the feared Black Art is a helpless romantic at heart," I say, going to him and placing my palms against the bare skin of his chest.

Sin palms my lower back and leans forward to skim his nose against mine. His peppery scent overwhelms me, and my lips part to taste it on my tongue, my thighs dampening as the aroma teases me like a seductive enchantress. I blame the blood.

"It pains me to say it, my Lady, but I can be quite charming —" My breath whooshes out of me when he suddenly dips me back like lovers in a dance, lifting my thigh around his hip while his mouth skims my collarbone. "When I'm not trying to kill you." He kisses the hollows of my shoulders and across my chest, his lips leaving a trail of fire in their wake.

I reach up and curl a hand into his long hair. "To what do I owe the sentiment then, Your Grace?"

"You deserve nothing less every single day of your life, and I have a lot of lost time to make up for. Join me for a swim?"

I slowly strip away my dress and bodice, devouring the raw hunger that flares in his eyes. My body brushes his as I walk around him, putting a little extra swing in my hips. "And here I thought I was to be tortured tonight." I ease into the spring, and a deep sigh falls from my lips as the warmth wraps itself around me like the coziest hug I've ever been given. Water splashes behind me, and muscular arms band around my waist from behind.

"There is plenty of time for me to make you scream later, little witch." He tugs my ear between his teeth. "But I intend to make you beg first."

He nuzzles my neck, his hands gliding up and down my arms and squeezing, working my aching muscles. I let out a low moan, months of tension unwinding itself from my knotted shoulders. "How are you feeling? You handled the ceremony well," he says.

You didn't go feral with bloodlust and kill everyone.

"Everything's heightened still, but I'm fine. Elven blood is different. Brighter. Like sucking on a lemon." I omit the part where the lemon is dusted in powdered sugar and served on a bed of cream.

Sin grows stiff behind me and not in the way I want him to. "Does it bother you?" I ask, my nails grazing his corded forearms. "To watch me drink from another?"

His grip tightens. "Blood is an aphrodisiac for you. Of course it bothers me," he snarls. "I would have ripped his fucking head off if he had gotten anywhere near your mouth."

I replay the moment he intervened and forced Vox to use the chalice, sending heat tunneling straight to the juncture of my thighs. "Easy, Blackheart. I want only you," I say, putting on my best sultry voice and leaning back to rest my head on his chest.

He remains rigid. I wait a moment for him to respond, almost losing patience and asking him what's wrong when he finally speaks. "Does that want run deep enough that you'd be willing to make a commitment?"

My brows knit together as I turn over his words, trying to

make sense of them. I spin in his arms so I'm facing him, and he releases me. I instantly miss his touch but don't want to appear needy if I move his hands back to their rightful places. On me.

"Are you asking me to go exclusive, Your Grace?" I ask, my tone highlighted in tease.

He doesn't return my smile, and for a second, I think that isn't what he meant at all, and I've just made a gigantic fool of myself.

"It's extremely selfish, but I'm asking for a lot more than that."

Now it's my turn to make like a corpse and go deadly still. "I don't understand."

"Do you remember earlier when you asked me what it's like—being a transcendent?" He continues when I nod. "It's a part of myself that is becoming increasingly harder to deny, some parts especially. My entire being is wired by instincts, and being around you..." He closes his eyes and water splashes at my side. I'm certain his claws just extended. He blows out a breath to steady himself, then looks at me again. "It's like being at war all the time. Every part of me aches with the need to Mark you, to claim you as mine. It takes every bit of self-control I have to not take you in front of everyone and bite that pretty neck so they know who you belong to. Every day it kills me to watch you talking to other males without my scent attached to yours."

I search his face for any sign he's teasing me, but there is only possessiveness brimming there. "I'm around you all the time. Surely your scent is mingled with mine."

"It's a different scent after the... after the Bonding." He watches me carefully, assessing my reaction.

My heart pounds furiously against its skeletal cage as I try to rearrange his words, to find a different meaning to them.

There is still much I'm unclear on when it comes to Bonding, but from what I've gathered from my family, receiving a Mark during a Bonding ritual is different than merely being bitten. Blessed by Slaine, the shifter god, the Mark is imbued with a magic that tethers the participants souls and binds them in flesh, heart, and spirit.

Is Sin asking me to Bond with him? A month ago, I was fantasizing about all the ways I might kill him. All the ways I could make him suffer for what he did to me. My family. The countless other transcendent deaths he sanctioned in the name of dominion. The man that tossed me in his dungeon where I nearly died from infection, coerced me into doing his bidding while he chased power... the brute warrior that made me fall deeply, madly, and irrevocably in love with him.

The reaper of hearts and death incarnate is asking me to Bond with him.

"You would take me as your Mate?" I query.

He sweeps a lock of damp hair behind my ear. "There is nothing I desire more. I mistook you for a spy when you first surrendered to the crown, a mistake that for anyone else —*anyone else*— would have meant I killed them and not spared a second thought. But you haunted me. Something about you called to me, stirred some deep, primal part of myself, and I didn't understand it for a long time.

"When you left..." He wraps his hand around my nape and leans forward to rest his forehead to mine. "When you left because of what *I* had done," his voice is pained, "you took half of me with you. I wanted to forget you because I knew I could never take back the pain I caused you, and I didn't deserve your forgiveness even if I could. The thought of facing you on the battlefield drove me mad. If we ever make it back to Scarwood, don't ask River how many rooms I destroyed in the time we were apart," he chuckles, lifting his head again and wiping the single tear that leapt from my eye.

"I had no right to blame you for any of this. Not for my father's declaration or the destruction of the gate. None of it mattered anyway because I would have brought down my entire kingdom and burned them all before I let them get anywhere near you. I may be warring for the loss of my throne, but nothing will ever compare to what it felt like to lose you. I have a lot of regrets for mistakes I've made, and I know I'll make more, but having you as a Mate would never be one of them. You may think my heart to be dead, but every part of it belongs to you."

I don't bother trying to hold the tears back now. He raises his hand again and wipes the salty liquid away with his thumbs, his expression more earnest and genuine than I've ever seen him. I place my hand on the back of his, holding it to my cheek. "I love you," I whisper. "I was afraid to admit that for a long time, but I'm through with shaping my heart to fit the mold of others. I love you, Sin. I always have."

He searches both my eyes, the ends of his mouth turning down slightly as he spots the uncertainty there. The answer I left unspoken. "There is a difference between loving someone and taking them as your Mate, and I do not fault you for not being able to accept my proposal. Nor do I expect you to be satisfied with only pledging our union through transcendent culture to satiate my... *needs*. We could have a wedding too, if that is something you find you desire."

I shake my head. "It isn't that. And it certainly isn't because I don't want you, either. It's just... it's a lot, Sin. With so much at stake right now, I'm not sure it's wise to make that kind of decision when our emotions are running so high. I need time is all. You should take the time too to make sure I am what you really want. Who you really want."

"You deserve to take all the time you need. But you needn't question my loyalty ever. I choose you, Wren. Every. Single. Part." His words are barely above a whisper, and I swallow them all, crushing my mouth to his in a fervent kiss.

Sin comes alive beneath me, the rigidness in his shoulders easing only to emerge again in his cock. His hands slide down my arms and pass over the curve of my hips, moving to cup my ass under the water. I drag my tongue across the seam of his lips, and he opens for me, letting me taste the promises he just swore. His cock throbs against my belly, and he groans into my mouth when I wrap my hand around him and begin to stroke.

His skin is like molten steel against my own, hands warm and callused as they clamp onto my upper thighs and hoist me up. My legs wrap around his hips, and I moan as his crown brushes my sex, but his grip tightens, keeping me from sheathing him in my heat. Sin walks us backwards until I'm perched on the ledge of the cavern floor, my calves still dangling in the spring. Leaning forward, he kisses me once more before reaching for one of the pillows within reach and tucking it under my ass.

My breath stutters as he tugs my hips forward and forces my knees to part. If I held any reservations about being so bare before him, they're immediately dissolved as his eyes glaze with unbridled lust as he beholds me beneath him. His touch doesn't match the urgency on his face, his fingers featherlight as they trace up and down my thighs, his thumb inching closer to my aching center with each passing sweep. I arch my hips forward, and he growls in approval.

My head falls back as he obeys my silent demand, gliding two fingers through my folds. Lightning cracks through me, every nerve a live current, as he slips a finger inside and curls it just right. Sin shoots me a wolfish grin before dipping his head and lapping at my cunt like it's filled with the sweetest honeyed wine.

I moan deeply as he flattens his tongue against me, taking his time tasting me, savoring his feast. The Black Art groans his own pleasure as he swirls his tongue through my apex, the kind of pleasure one only receives when making their partner feel like they've just ascended to the heavens.

My thighs snap together as he slips a second finger inside, the pressure too much, too fucking good. I *feel* his lips part in a smile, and when he looks up at me from between my legs, looking like a god of war and strength, I vow to never pray to another false idol again. I worship him now, in this realm and the next, and the one after that.

He forces my legs apart again, and I let out a yelp as he tugs my clit between his teeth and bites down a fraction. "Tell me what you want, love."

My thighs are drenched in my own slick, my breathing labored, and if he doesn't fuck me right now, I'm certain I'll combust into a thousand pieces. "I need to come," I rasp. "Don't make me wait."

His laughter is soft and menacing at the same time, and I swear I'm going to punch that smirk right off his face if he denies me this. "Beg," he murmurs, then pulls my clit between his teeth again, sending pleasure coursing through me, all the way down to where my toes curl with need.

My thighs clench so tight I'm certain I give him a concussion. "Please. Please, Sin. Let me come."

His growl that follows is almost enough to shove me over the edge. "Tell me who's allowed to make this pussy come."

"You. Just you. Only you. Sin, *please*," I mewl.

"That's right, little witch," he murmurs against my center, his breath there sending a shockwave down my legs. "Now you're going to be a good girl and make a mess on my face."

Sin curls his fingers and pumps them faster, dragging his tongue through my slickened flesh as he works me in measured strokes. And when his teeth find my clit once more, stars explode across my vision, and I shatter, shouting his name in both a curse and prayer. He doesn't stop lapping as I ride out my ecstasy, holding true to his vow that I'd *make a mess* on him. And even then, when the last of my climax fades, he doesn't relent.

The Black Art grabs the backs of my thighs and carries us out of the water to the furs in the corner. Pinning me on my back, he thrusts inside of me, my moans and his grunts a symphony of pain and pleasure. I ache as I stretch around him, his cock stiff and thick as he ruts into me with carnal need. My legs tighten around him as I grind my hips against his, needing him deeper, harder. His lips skim my neck and pain pricks the skin there as his teeth graze my tender flesh.

Sin pumps into me without mercy, and when he growls my name into the hollow of my shoulder, I come undone all over again. His grunts turn savage, his cock swelling impossibly larger, stuffing me until I am fuller than I knew was possible. I almost whimper when he suddenly slows his pace and twists his hand into my hair, the slight pain making me clench tighter around him still. "Let me Mark you."

I hear the question in his words, even if he doesn't phrase it as such. Spoken in the way his muscles tremble as he supports himself above me, forcing himself to slow. Waiting for my consent.

Consent I'm all too eager to give. Because I am done denying what I've always known to be true. That some primal part of me has always longed for the Black Art to lay claim to my body, to belong to him and him alone.

"Yes," I breathe.

My words call forth his beast, and he parts his lips again,

his teeth hovering just above the underside of my jaw. *"You. Are. Mine."* His teeth sink into my flesh at the same time he spills hot ropes inside of me, claiming me there too. My legs cinch around his waist, tethering us together as I milk every last drop of his love. I comb my hand through his hair and lock my mouth to his as I clench around him, tasting myself on his tongue.

When we pull apart for air, Sin beams down at me with a yearning that burns hotter than all of Elysande's rage.

But it's not just my body he's longing for.

It's my heart.

And it is undeniably his.

CHAPTER 34

I've never before wept over a bar of soap. Infused with a blend of dried chamomile, lavender, and rosehips, the buttery soft bar smells exactly like my mother's hair and clothing. Adding it to the stack of the other two bars I crafted this week, I wrap a purple ribbon around the pile, cinch, and tie it off in a delicate bow. The oils I used, along with the nutrients in the flowers, will add moisture to Morrinne's aging skin, but that wasn't the only reason I decided to spend the last couple days pestling flowers, mixing oil into submission, and pouring them with care.

"Are you crying?"

I startle at Sin's voice but relax when he winds his arms around me from behind, and he props his chin on my shoulder. I slept in his quarters last night, no longer hiding the hours I spend with the Black Art from my family. The empty stone house where I once found him kneeled and shackled to the supports has been updated. The manacles have since disappeared, a bed that isn't large enough for the two of us brought in, along with a single chair in the corner, and a table pushed against the wall. The one currently holding my stack of tear-stained soaps. It isn't much, the elves not having a large reserve of self-crafted furniture that's not being used somewhere, but it offers some privacy as the Black Art and I explore and test the inner workings of our relationship. The relationship he desires to make permanent through the Bonding.

"Your horse once shattered my rib, and I didn't shed a single tear. I'm allowed to cry over some soap," I manage to choke out through a snotty laugh.

Sin moves to lean against the table and watches me thoughtfully. "She means a lot to you." He doesn't phrase it as a question.

I wipe my face with the back of my hand and nod. "I owe her for so much. Morrinne took me in when I had nothing, when I was no one. Just an unwanted girl, starving and filthy on the street. She could have left me as Cosmina's problem, but she opened her home to both of us instead. And Eldridge and Zorina too.

"She saved all of us, and I should be giving her the world, but until I learn how to do that, this measly soap will have to do. It smells like her, you know."

He does know. Because I'm certain I've mentioned it fifty times this morning alone.

But Sin doesn't remind me of that. Instead, he lifts my chin with the tip of his finger and looks at me in a way that has me wondering if my skin has blanched so much that my soul is bare before him. "Please do not ever let me hear you referring to yourself as no one. Starving and filthy maybe, but you have never been no one."

"This isle is hardly forgiving for women that were in my predicament. If Cosmina hadn't seen something in me, I would have likely found my way to a brothel eventually, where I'm sure I'd have long since revealed what I am the first time a man tried to make me do something I didn't want to. And then I suppose you're right. I wouldn't have been no one at all, rather the *white-haired witch*, wanted dead or alive."

"You needn't carry such worries any longer, my love. There are only a few days left until the blood moon. We will fix this. *I* will fix this."

"How are you so sure they'll follow you? If we restore the land, why would the elves fight with us if they have the means to protect the Vale?"

Wrath shadows his face, and a claw pricks my chin. He drops his hand before it can bite into my skin, crossing his arms across his chest instead. "Because my father will never stop. I'm not such a fool as to believe the elves to be the pacifistic earth-huggers they claim to be. I've seen the commander in training, felt the ire in his sword. He is as hungry for vengeance as I am, and the high priestess more so than all of us combined. Granted, they won't overthrow one kingdom just for me to begin another, but that's a predicament for a later day. For now, we focus on one threat at a time."

"And if your father doesn't kneel before you?" I ask.

His pupils dilate, darkening his eyes to liquid black. "Then he will die before me."

⁂

We're the last to arrive. Morrinne is stirring some kind of stew now bubbling in her cauldron, the fire licking the sides of the metal pot. My stomach grumbles at the smell of tender meat and savory spices, my mouth watering from the yeasty aroma of bread permeating the quaint house. On the couch, Theon plays the fiddle softly, likely trying to drown out the sibling bickering happening between Eldridge and Zorina as they argue over which one of them Galen resembles more.

My nephew abandons his small collection of wooden horses on the living room floor to shatter my ribs in one of his signature hugs. I comb my hand through his golden curls and give them a good ruffle. "Who do you think I look more like, Wren?" Galen asks.

"I am inclined to say you look like your mother. And be grateful for it," I say, winking at Eldridge.

Galen makes an irritated screech, more and more wolf bleeding into his voice each day. "That's not fair! I want to be like the Red Wolf!" he shouts, flexing his arms in a downward pose, then proceeding to scream while he runs laps around the couch, Eldridge hot on his tail and Theon grinning over the strings of his fiddle.

Zorina shakes her head at me, but the light in her eyes is pure bliss. Cornelius appears over her shoulder and hands her a steaming mug, gives me an appreciative smile, and shifts his eyes to Sin at my side, his expression growing wary for a second before he schools his features back to marble. I don't miss the subtle nod Sin gives him from my periphery, and a bit of tension seems to relax from the eldest Langston's shoulders.

A lifetime of alliance, betrayal, and misjudgment does not vanish overnight, but this is a start. Even Eldridge has stopped the seething glances in Sin's direction. It's not perfect, but we are all trying, the beginnings of a scab creeping across my heart.

"Dare I ask, why is it that today is Morrinne's birthday and she's left to do the cooking?" I say, heading to where my mother is still stirring the stew.

"She needed something to distract herself from thoughts of her sweet, innocent Wren being late to her party because she was being deflowered, isn't that right, Mama?" Zorina calls after us.

I shoot her a vulgar gesture over my head, and she snorts in return. "You sit, let me finish this," I say, reaching for the ladle.

Morrinne swats my hand. "Nonsense. You're going to go sit

down and spend time with your family and let me make this for you all."

"It's your birthday. Please get off your feet."

"What's this—I turn one year older and suddenly my legs don't work? It brings me peace. Plus, you don't know how to stir it right. You have to start along the edges, you see, and stir it clockwise, moving closer to the center each turn. Melts the flavors together better."

I cock my hip and cross my arms. "Oh really? Why, I've never heard of such a thing, Mother."

"Well now you have. Now get." Her elbow is unforgiving in my ribs as she nudges me towards the couch.

A mock roll of my eyes and I head back towards the others, Cosmina and Blythe appearing from one of the bedrooms. Blythe suggests we move outside, and we all follow Galen who barrels through the door, still making animal grunts and now occasionally throwing his head back and howling.

Chaos is the lot of us. And I love every single part of it.

There's a long table set up along the side of the house, draped with a lavender cloth and displaying a small spread of refreshments. Tall pitchers of lemonade with floating pink flowers, a plate of flaky pastries with a dollop of creamy berry filling, butter for the freshly baked bread, and a few flower crowns leftover from the blood ceremony. Zorina and Cornelius help carry out the bowls of stew and place one in front of each of us.

My stomach somersaults at the smell of tender meat infused with rosemary and sage on top of a bed of fire-roasted potatoes and carrots. The bread is crusty and warm, and beneath a layer of smooth butter, is utter decadence in my mouth. Cosmina places one of the floral crowns on our mother's graying hair, and the rest of us dig into our feast.

Conversation flows easily enough. Even so, I don't miss the

few exchanged glances between Sin and Cornelius, but both men hold their tongues. Even Eldridge chimes in on Sin's commentary about the elves' unique weaponry and fighting styles, sharing in the Black Art's fascination, though he doesn't engage with Sin directly, and I don't blame him. After the hurt he inflicted upon us all, I doubt I will ever see the day my family forgives Sin. Welcoming him into their home for my sake is one thing, welcoming him into their hearts is another.

Morrinne opens her gifts after the meal, and the lot of us admire Eldridge's craftsmanship, the tiered wooden box he carved for her smooth and polished, complete with a feather-like design etched into the drawers. Cosmina and Blythe knitted her a cozy sweater, fitting since the woman claims to always be freezing regardless how torrid the temperature may be. Zorina and Cornelius planted a pale blue hydrangea in a clay pot they painted together, and Sin and I gifted her the soap, wrapped in ribbon and tucked inside the basket Sin wove for her.

I had poked fun that the almighty warlord struggled to spear a fish, but could weave grass, reeds, and honeysuckle together with a proficiency far past my own. River had taught him when he was a boy, he told me. Before Sin was the Black Art and had a kingdom to lead, he would weave mini pouches, tea towels, and wall hangings with the housekeeper—a reminiscing that had shadowed his face with great fondness. There is no denying the bond between them runs deep, and my heart aches for him, knowing how difficult it must be for Sin to have lost her during this.

It isn't permanent, I had reminded him. None of this is. In just a few days, the blood moon will thin the veil separating us from Source, and there won't be a single corner for Ephraim's chaos to flee to. We'll restore what was taken from the elves, and then we'll seize what was taken from the rest of us. The balance is shifting, and I can't wait for their prejudiced walls to crumble and fall, burying them in their own hateful rubble.

I bring in the last of the dishes to the kitchen, Morrinne hot on my heels despite me insisting she stay outside with the others and enjoy some of the pastries by the fire. I dump them into the wash basin and turn towards my mother who is following so close she nearly walks right into me.

"You're not cleaning up the meal *you* cooked on *your* birthday."

"It's my house, and I'll do as I please, young lady. But the dishes can wait. You were missing for months, and every night that I sat up worrying myself sick, you know what I didn't think one single time? *Goddess, if only those dishes were done.* So sit your rear down, and I want you to answer something for me. The soaps were lovely, but the only thing I want from you today is some honesty."

I eye her warily but take a seat on the green cushioned couch. She refills her mug with a ladle of the hot water and perches next to me. She studies me over the brim while she takes a sip, bobbing the small pouch containing a mix of loose herbs with her other hand.

"Sin is the one that personally imprisoned you after you sought refuge at the outpost?"

That was... unexpected. "Yes," I answer hesitantly, unsure where she is going with this.

"Then he coerced you into leading him to our cabin under the guise that he was a stranger, forcing you to lie to us, and knowing you'd discover Cosmina was missing."

I blow out a breath. "You know he did, so what are you really asking?"

"He betrayed you, Wren."

I push off the couch. "I am well aware of that, Mother. Do

you believe I allowed him to just waltz back into my life as if none of it happened?"

She remains seated, but her brown eyes track me, their usual warmth stamped out. "I'm certain you did not. You are no ignorant girl, Wren, but he has forced your hand before, and it is my responsibility to make sure he is not doing it again. Just because he hasn't forced you to drink some silly little cocktail to alter your appearance this time doesn't mean he's not manipulating you."

"Sin isn't manipulating me into anything. I went and captured him, remember! All of this is my bloody fault, so if you want to point a finger at someone, start with me." I pace the room, my hands finding the divots of my hips.

There's a long pause as Morrinne blows on her tea before taking another sip. "Do you love him?" she asks, voice wooden.

I stop pacing. That's not judgment in her eyes, but it's a far cry from the unbridled joy a daughter might hope to see on her mother's face when she tells her she's found the love of her life. I suppose I knew this conversation was coming. As much as I'd like to avoid the topic with her, the least I owe Morrinne is my honesty. "Yes." I forge the word from the strongest steel, willing it to remain steady.

"Child!" She slams her cup onto the table with more force than necessary and rises from the couch. "I know I did not hear you correctly because it sounded a whole lot like you just said you love that wicked man. The same one that stowed Mina away in some dank cellar to be forgotten, and ran you around like his personal errand boy. The same one that—"

"I know what he did, Morrinne," I interject. "Do you think I have forgotten the pain he's caused me—caused all of us? But I also know what he is doing for us now. He saved my life, Mother. He threw it all away to save *me*," my voice cracks around the word, "and I have forgiven him. Perhaps one day, when all this is done, you might too."

"Bah—you'll never see that day from me, young lady. He's lucky I didn't slip something into his stew."

"I don't know what to tell you, Mama. The others are trying to make peace. Zorina and Theon, even Cosmina of all people! If she can find it in her heart to at least give him a chance, then I don't understand why you cannot at least attempt to—"

"HE TOOK MY DAUGHTERS!" she shouts, her face coloring to a deep red. "For months—MONTHS—I grieved you girls. Worried sick about what might be happening to you. Not knowing if you would ever come home, or if you were even alive. Cosmina is young, she doesn't have children, and neither do you. Do not mistake Zorina's cordiality as anything but a means to not lose you again. She's the only one in this entire house that has a semblance of understanding of what I felt. Imagine if someone took Galen, and you had to sit here every day knowing he was out there having gods-know-what happening to him. So do not wag your finger at me and tell me that I should ever forgive that monster for what he has done to my family."

I open my eyes, not having realized I'd closed them while she was talking. I blot my now tear-stained cheeks, wiping my fingers on my shirt and dampening the fabric, and cross my arms. Morrinne releases a long exhale and turns her back on me, heading towards the dishes in the basin.

"I'm sorry," I whisper. Then louder, "Forgive me. I know what he did, Mama. I know what he did, and I don't want to love him, I don't, but I *can't stop.*" The tears overwhelm my willpower and flood my ducts, now freely soaking my cheeks and running over my lips.

I must have closed my eyes again because suddenly her

arms are around me, clutching my bent head against her shoulder, her fingers massaging my scalp. "Hush now, child."

"I'm so sorry. I'm just so sorry," I sob.

"Look at me. Ah, ah, none of that. Enough with the tears. Look at me," she repeats, and so I do.

Her hands move to my shoulders, and she presses down gently. I collect my breath as she does, the pressure grounding me. "I am not angry with you. There is nothing you could do— nothing, my child—that would lessen my love for you." A deep breath, followed by a long pause. "The heart is a cruel, evil thing, but rarely does it lead us astray. I have always hoped for all of you to find something as special as Garrick and I had. You are a light, Wren. You deserve someone that will keep you burning bright, not someone who will snuff out your flame."

"I know it doesn't mean anything to you, but he is deeply regretful of his actions."

"I did not say I doubt his feelings for you. I may be half blind these days, but I can see a love sick fool from a mile away. But that wickedness still lies in his heart, even if it may be dormant for now."

"There are times I think my heart may be wicked too, Mama. And that is partly why I am so drawn to him," I admit, sniffing loudly to clear my nose.

Morrinne tsks softly and shakes her head. "Your heart is pure, sweet child. That is why *he* is so drawn to *you*."

I throw my arms around her, crushing her against me. She returns the hug, then wiggles her shoulders to buck me off. "Easy, easy, you're going to grind my bones to dust, you keep squeezing me like that."

I pull out of the hug and grasp her arm to steady her. "I am sorry about Garrick."

She smiles, her thin lips pressed together. "He would have

taken a great liking to you. Garrick always did favor the lasses with the sharp tongues."

"Then it's no surprise he was so drawn to you," I choke through my tears.

"Not a day goes by that I don't miss him, but do not pity me. We had many joyous years together, and I would bear the pain of losing him again and again if it meant I also got to relive those moments of happiness." A moment of silence, then, "Be happy, Wren. That is the greatest gift you may ever give me. Now," she says, smacking me with the end of a tea towel she swiped from the counter, "dry up those tears before you ruin that pretty paint on your face, and go outside with the others. But send Sin in here when you do."

That catches my attention. "You want to speak with him alone?"

"That's what I said, is it not? Goddess help me, you're looking at me like you think I'm about to whip the damn boy. Send him in here."

The look I shoot her is one that confirms that is *exactly* what I fear Morrinne might do. But who am I to argue with a woman on her damn birthday?

"Alright, but you better return him to me in one piece."

"Mhmm," is all she says.

⁂

The Black Art wears many expressions, fear rarely one of them. But when I tell Sin my mother is requesting a word in private, something very, *very* close to it crosses his face, as if I just presented him with the most arduous of tasks. It is there and gone in a moment, before he merely nods, crosses the lawn, and enters the house without so much as a glance behind himself. Whatever is waiting for him on the other side, he deserves every lick of it. And he knows it.

"Your boyfriend in trouble?" Eldridge asks around a pipe he pulled from somewhere, clouds of cottony smoke puffing from the bowl.

I grab one of the flower crowns from the table and plop it on his head. "We shall see."

He folds his hands under his chin and flashes me a smile that's all teeth while batting a curtain of red lashes. "How do I look, ladies?"

"Someone send for a painter quick. I need to commission a portrait of this so everyone can bear witness to the mighty Red Wolf in the peak of his glory," Theon says around a bite of pastry, a dollop of berry smeared on his chin.

"Don't tease him—he's very sensitive," Cosmina chimes in from where she rests her head on Blythe's shoulder.

I giggle and plop down next to him, elbowing him in the gut. The others take to conversing, but something hovers around the two of us like we're in our own private bubble. Eldridge rolls a stick between his thumb and forefinger, the other end crackling in the fire as its final breaths are suffocated by the flames.

"I've missed you," I say, my voice barely an octave above the spitting embers.

The corners of his mouth perk up, and he slants his head towards me. "Is your old lady vision coming in to match your granny feet? I've not gone anywhere."

I shoot him a wry grin. "You know what I mean."

He flattens his palms on either side of the stick and rolls it between them. "I do," he says, softer now. "And I'm sorry. I've been an ass and a half, haven't I?"

"I've not exactly been a ray of sunshine either. But you have always been an important part of my life and one of my favorite people in this entire fucked up realm we live in. I never want that to change."

Eldridge tosses the stick in the fire and throws one of his bear-sized arms around my shoulders, tucking me against his side. "Then it seems we may agree on one thing after all. I know things have always teetered on the *what ifs* with us, and maybe in another life, but I understand if this isn't the one for that. Perhaps in the next."

I wrap my hands around his neck and bury my face in his chest, savoring his scent of cedar and worn-in leather. Comfortable. Familiar.

Home.

"Thank you," I whisper. I don't need to elaborate. Eldridge knows.

He always has.

"I hate to interrupt this sentimental bullshit thing we have going on here, but your boyfriend is waiting for you, and trying really hard to make it look like he's not eavesdropping."

I look over my shoulder and sure enough, Sin's slowly making his way back to us, his usual stride replaced with a laid-back saunter, buying us time before his presence punctures our bubble.

I meet him halfway, and he slips my hand in his, guiding me around the house and out of view from the others.

"How was your chat? Did you two sit down, drink tea together, and gossip like little old ladies?" I ask.

Sin's answering smile sends my stomach into a flurry, a tiny thousand snowflakes whipping around in a blustering night. "Something like that."

I tug at the laces of his shirt. "No really—what did she want to talk about?"

"Morrinne had... valid concerns she wanted to address, and I respect her for them. She is looking out for you."

"Did she threaten to beat you up if you broke my heart?"

His soft chuckle turns my bones to butter. "Something like that," he repeats. He backs us up so my shoulders brush the house and ensnares my mouth with his, kissing me deeply. I wind my hands around his neck, and his own find their way to my hips, tracing the curves there. I groan, interlocking my fingers behind his head to keep my hands from traveling to where they long to be, but not here. Not with the others lingering in earshot.

"One day very soon, when I take back my throne, you will know comfort and pleasure like you've never experienced. You will only sleep in the softest bedding, bathe with the finest of oils, and dress in the silkiest of nightgowns. You will yearn for nothing. Whatever you desire, I will personally deliver it to you."

"And if I don't care about silken sheets or lacey night things? If all I desire is to receive unyielding pleasure, will you personally deliver that also, Your Grace?"

He rolls his bottom lip between his teeth and leans forward, his hips grinding into mine. "Then I will live out the rest of my days in my favorite place—kneeling between these gorgeous fucking thighs."

He claims my mouth again, his tongue parting my lips and entwining with mine. I don't care that someone could walk around the corner and see us, I drop my hand and wrap it around his cock, now straining for dear life against the confines of his fitted trousers. Sin groans into my mouth, but a moment later, pulls out of our kiss. "Careful, little witch. Unless you want me to carry you into these woods and have everyone hearing how pretty you sing."

I capture my bottom lip, far too enticed by his offer. "Or we could just go back to your house, or slip away to our secret cavern."

He thumbs my lips, then drags an extended claw down my neck. "As much as I want to take you away and have you all to myself, you should spend the night with your family. They are important to you, and I don't wish to carry forth past hurts into our future."

Warmth spreads through my chest like I just swallowed the biggest gulp of honeyed wine. "I like the way that sounds: *our* future."

"You are my salvation, Wren. And one day you will wear my Mark."

"Are you certain of that, Blackheart?"

He flattens his hand against my chest, the tips of his fingers gently grazing my throat. "I know I am not worthy of you, but I will stop at nothing to claim you as my own. My love. My wife. My *Mate.*"

Tears burn behind my eyes, my heart swelling with a love that surpasses time itself. I nod, a single tear rolling down my cheek. He kisses me one last time, wipes that tear away with his thumb, and vanishes into the night.

CHAPTER 35

I dream of Eldridge's pipe. The smell of smoking mugwort and calendula flowers drifting in and out of my nighttime fantasies like ghosts, lulling me to the deep kind of sleep I've left uninhabited for months. Images flash through my mind's eye like lightning. Eldridge's mouth closing around the lip, a gentle inhale, puffs of gray clouds floating from the chamber like bundles of silver bush. It's comforting. The burning herbs a boon to my stimulated nerves, stress melting off me like heaps of butter in the sun, the smoke invading my mouth...

Too much. Like choking on hearth-warmed socks. An aggressive cough sends me spiraling into consciousness with a mighty shove, and I sit up in bed.

Decay stirs in my mouth.

I rip back the fur flap covering the window next to my bed.

Red and orange variegate the Vale in a blistering aurora. I hear it then—the crackling of bark and leaves as flames feast on the forest. The sound is distant still, but the thick perfume is already seeping into our house.

No. *This wasn't supposed to happen.*

"FIRE! Get up, get up!" I spring out of bed, shoving my legs into pants, then into boots. There is clattering from my brothers' room, and my sisters, their beds farther from the window and smoke, sit up with a start, their hands quickly rubbing the sleep from their eyes.

"What in the Goddess?" Cosmina says, bolting past me to stick her head out the window and behold the orange lights winking in the distance.

Zorina shouts for Galen and gallops to the other room, returning with her son and brothers a moment later. My tunic is already on, and I shove clothes at Cosmina, not knowing if they're hers or mine. "Hurry!"

"Where's my mother?" Theon demands, sticking his head out the window and calling for her.

That's when we all scan the house, our eyes darting from one abandoned corner to the next. No Morrinne.

"Mama!" Zorina calls, ducking her head into her brothers' room again despite them having just come from there.

Eldridge storms to the door, waving his hand frantically. "We'll find her. First, everyone out now. We need to get that fucking fire out before it reaches the houses."

The blood moon is in two days. If they had just waited two more fucking days! I grab my daggers, strapping one to my thigh and slipping the other into my waist, then follow the others out the door.

Morrinne stands in the yard, clutching her black velvet cloak around her despite the smoldering heat, staring towards the rising inferno. "What are you doing out here alone?" Theon demands, running to his mother. When she turns towards us, her eyes rival the flames for threat. My sisters flock her on either side, while Eldridge lingers near me, his hand on Galen's shoulder.

"They've come to take it," Morrinne seethes. "They've come to take it all."

"They're not taking anything," I growl, my hands itching

326

for my daggers as if they're going to miraculously put out the flames. They can't, but I know what might.

"I need to get closer and help the others," I bite out, my magic already flickering to life in my palms.

"I'm going with her. The rest of you follow them," Cosmina says, pointing to the others now pouring from their houses all across the Vale's heart. They're fleeing west, the direction of the temple, and farther from the perimeter.

Eldridge's hand vices around my bicep before I can take off. Neither of us speaks, but in the silence, we share everything. All of this is too familiar. It was just months ago I woke to an untamable combustion—except this time, it isn't castle stone that feeds the beast's bottomless stomach. It's the verdant life of the Vale.

Cosmina and I need to get to the border, do our part in joining the elven mages to douse the flames before they can spread too far. Transcendents are masters of transmutation, not destruction. My family is best suited to hunker down with the others while us mages meet it head on and promptly suffo-cate it. The elves are strong; the flames will have no choice but to bow to us. They will.

They must.

Still, I've known Eldridge long enough to recognize that determined set of his jaw. He's coming with us, and it's not worth trying to dissuade him.

I nod, and the three of us take off, sprinting towards the burning horizon. I don't dare mention the thought that hasn't left my mind since first glimpsing the flames. What if it's alchemist fire, like before? What if the only master it obeys is the one that created it?

"We need to find Sin!" I shout, whipping my head to either side as I scan the throng of transcendents and elves, finding no sign of the long-haired regent.

"He was farther inland, he's fine. He's probably heading this way already," Cosmina replies, breathing heavy as we push onward.

She's right. The fire started on the opposite end from the tiny house he was staying in—*he's safe,* I tell myself. I don't miss the silent question in Eldridge's eyes. The one that asks if I'm certain Sin isn't the one behind this. I steer my attention straight ahead and pound the ground faster, adrenaline pumping my legs with more speed than I'm accustomed to.

Sin wouldn't do this. He wouldn't betray me. Not again.

I'm sure of it.

The smoke thickens as we approach the part of the forest nearest the perimeter. Elven mages form a border against the flames, their own vermillion light radiating from their outstretched palms in unison, forming a wall against the fire. Non magic wielders chuck basins upon basins of river water into the conflagration, and slowly, the flames yield, little by little. I catch a bob of black hair and moonbeam skin—Sera is among the water throwers, her jaw set in determination and her eyes unforgiving. It's no secret who's behind this attack.

Her husband.

I just can't wrap my head around Dusaro actually doing this—leading an attack against his own son. His own civilians. Especially with the known threat of Baelliarah circling our shores like sharks, waiting for the faintest twinge of blood in the air to move inland.

Where in Elysande's name were our scouts? Taken out before they could return and alert the Vale obviously, but how? *They were trained for this.*

"I'm going to help the others," Eldridge hollers, taking off towards the river.

I grab Cosmina's hand and pull her towards the elves. "Come on!"

I find Alistair at the end of the line, and I grab his hand, Cosmina's in my other. My collective already humming in my veins, I call it forth, merging it with the swell of elven magic they called forth from their Source.

A tree splits to my right, and shouts ring out as men and women scramble to avoid the falling branches that crash to the ground with an earth-trembling *thud*. Fire races to claim the surrounding floor, the tender grasses igniting in a blazing orange carpet.

"Fuck me," Alistair grumbles, ripping his hand from mine. "GET BACK!" he shouts, my sister and I already retreating with the swarm of elves who race away from the tunneling flames, some climbing into the unburnt trees and leaping from branch to branch.

An ear-splitting scream pierces the woods, snapping every hair on my body to a rigid point. I whip around, trying to locate who is injured, but it must have been farther off. It's hard to gauge with the sea of flames swallowing up all noise that isn't the spitting of cherry embers.

"Move back!" Sera yells to no one in particular. "Everyone move bac—"

An explosion rends the air.

My feet go out from under me. Or maybe my top half goes careening forward. I can't tell as the world turns upside down, the soil thundering under my bruised ribs like the heartbeat of a ravenous demon who's just laid eyes on dinner.

Earth seasons my mouth. My lips are sweet with blood where my teeth sunk into the pink flesh, and my limbs ache from impact. Sound swirls in and out of my ears for a few seconds, slowly growing louder as the whooshing fades from them, distorting into something loud, heavy...

Footsteps. A whole fucking lot of them.

I roll to the side, nearly avoiding being trampled by

another mage, and rise to my feet, ignoring the searing pain in my side as I do. There's a large depression in the ground—where we just stood a minute ago—bodies lying crumbled around it, limbs contorted at unnatural angles.

What the fuck was that?

I scream for Cosmina, spinning as I run, searching for a swish of dark hair amidst the red haze, but it's impossible to make anything out in the stampede of bodies sprinting towards cover. I dart back the way we came, about to dive into the section of woods that remains unburnt for now.

Another crash to my right has the ground quaking beneath my feet, and I whip towards the sound. A tree a few segments away has a gaping hole the size of a large iron pot in its trunk. Two elves that had scaled it moments prior lay at its fractured base on pillows of liquid crimson, their eyes vacant, their bodies lifeless. My attention snags on a craggy surface behind them.

Dread washes through me.

They're launching iron balls.

"COSMINA!" I holler again, pounding the forest floor as I hurtle through the wooded labyrinth, not knowing where I'm going other than that it's opposite from where the kingdom is launching giant packed stones at our heads. "ELDRIDGE!" I'm nearly knocked over several times, bony wrists and armored plates shoving into my shoulders, my calves and ankles taking a beating from jagged sticks. I'm farther from the scorching earth, but my lungs are heavier, the smoke closing in on all sides.

My sleeves don't do much to block the toxic vapor from entering my nose and mouth, my tunic much too thin and the smoke too thick. The heat is overwhelming, and I resist the urge to pull the stupid clothing over my head just to remove a layer. The dense canopy of the Vale is great at keeping the damaging sun away from the plants that thrive in shade. Contrarily, it is also good at trapping the torrid heat in here with us.

How far did the rest of my family get? Did they find somewhere safe to hunker down? Of course not. No where is safe when they're lobbing packed sediment overhead, burning the fucking forest down, and smoking us out. Where in the Goddess's name is Sin?

We have minutes before this fire spreads through half the Vale, and so long as they keep driving us back with projectiles, we're not putting it out. We need more power, a way to douse the flames quickly before being plummeted into the earth by another hunk of stone. Think Wren, *think!*

Goddess help me, the bodies!

I skid to a stop and hurtle myself around, throwing my arms up to shield my head from the assault of fleeing elves. Weaving through them like vines through latticework, I race back to the tree that had been blown open by the iron ball. Pain lances through my jaw as a shoulder connects with it, blood coating my gums as my teeth bite into my bottom lip. *Faster, Wren.*

A whooshing sound has me diving to the ground and tucking my head as another stone arcs above us, this one launching farther into the woods at my rear. Screams of horror follow, cut with the kind of cries that are only produced when one watches a loved one fall to tragedy at their side and being utterly helpless to do anything to save them.

Dropping low was a mistake.

My arms and ribs take a beating as I try to right myself, my jaw being kicked repeatedly as my feet struggle to find enough purchase in the dirt to stand. I don't feel the pain. I refuse to.

The smoke draws closer, a blanket of spun cotton dyed to the darkest gray, choking out all air that's not already infused with its heady incense. "Out of the way!" I shout as I make use of my own elbows, maneuvering them like oars to cut through the mass of panicked bodies. A millennium might pass before I'm back to the fractured tree, or maybe a few minutes. There's no telling.

Fire laps at the splintered wood now, the fallen elves crisping into ash, the stench of charred flesh violating my nose. *Goddess, grant them peace.*

I stand a few segments away and throw out my hand, flinging my collective out to latch onto theirs like a phantom spiderweb. Their auras are slippery, what remains of their life-force like the shiny side of a glacier. I push harder, willing my nails to bite into the ice, but it chips beneath my curling finger-tips. Maybe I'm too far.

Braving the heat and the raging inferno, I dare a few more steps and try again. Willing their blood to obey and serve me as its master. A sacrifice to the blood mage, the white-haired witch, the feared.

My fingers scrape against the surface, not an inch of give for me to strong-arm my way in. I search for the song of their blood, the lullaby that calls to my dark power like an enchanting temptress of lust and damnation, but all I hear are the cries of abandon, anguish fluttering from their broken hearts as if they were moths and me the waxing moon.

I plead with the gods. The ones I know and the ones I don't.

I beg for their blood to curdle, to clot in my web so their deaths aren't wasted in vain, but it continues to drip without mercy between my mental fingers, coating the ground in waste and desolation.

Blood cannot obey when it's been dried to ash and dust.

I'm too late. The fire already feasted on their ichor, leaving their bodies as sunken, hollowed husks. I am a wielder of blood and torment, not bones and grit. Slowly, my arm returns to my side, and I stand in a final salute of solidarity, converting their sacrifice to memory. I bid them a parting promise. One I can't guarantee we'll see fulfilled today. Or tomorrow. Or even the next. But one day... one day...

We will burn them all. Until their very souls melt from their flesh and there is nothing left for the heavens, they will burn.

This portion of the Vale is evacuated now, the fleeing crowd well into the woods. I turn to sprint back after them, covering my mouth and nose with my sleeves once again. I need to draw blood from someone living, just enough to swell my veins with the malignance that's lying dormant in my heart.

And then I'm flying.

I didn't see it land, but I heard the cracking of the earth as another iron ball shattered into a thousand splintered edges, spritzing the air with needled rain.

The wake of the crash flattens me into rock, then sends me sliding down a slope hewn from barbed stone, and I tumble into a bed of serrated knives. Stars burst across my vision, flashes of red and gray winking in the distance, consciousness fading in and out like an arrhythmic heartbeat.

My hands regain feeling first. The honed end of a stone bites into my palm as I plant my hands on either side and push up. My ribs holler in protest, and I yelp, pain lancing through my sides and down my thighs. I landed on my back, my tailbone absorbing much of the shock and leaving my legs feeling like they've been injected with lead.

I am surrounded by rock.

A ravine. The opening is craggy and narrow, the width of a few bodies, and the depression about fifteen feet deep. I leap onto the side, my hands searching for purchase as loose rocks and pebbles clatter to the bottom, my feet slipping from their footing as the material gives out.

No. *No, no, no.*

This can't be happening.

Cupping my mouth, I scream for help, hoping someone is still within earshot and praying their elven hearing is acute enough to hear my shouts over the spitting fire that's growing dangerously near. Sweat beads across my nape, slithering down my spine in sticky demise as I will the remains of my strength into my voice.

A head of dark hair peers over the opening. It takes my eyes a second to adjust, to make out his alabaster skin against the bloody dawn.

Alistair.

"Grab my hand!" He must be on his stomach because his shoulders are flush with the ground, his spindly arm straining towards me. The bloodwitch is tall, but there's still a few feet of distance between our outstretched hands. I need to jump and pray he's strong enough to support my weight one-handed.

Fire rears up behind him like a bucking stallion. Alistair glances over his shoulder, and when he looks back down at me, fear corrupts his features. My mouth goes dry. There are many motivators in life, but I've found few to be more effective than fear. I need to act now.

Breath rushes from my lungs the same time my feet leave the ground. Alistair's hand vices around my wrist, and for the briefest of seconds, relief washes through me.

And then it's gone.

I'm slipping, my weight too much for him to support from his disadvantaged angle. I try to swing my other arm up to clasp his forearm, but it ends up windmilling at my side—not enough momentum. I need his other hand but can't risk him falling in too.

"Anchor yourself!" I call up to him. "You need to make a tether, then haul me up!"

Smoke peeks over the ravine, a malicious smile swirled in its charcoal haze as it beholds its next meal. The bloodwitch's pale cheeks darken in natural blush as if the heat reached out and grazed a rotting, blistered finger across his face. "Now! Do it now!" I bellow.

His gaze flickers between the fire and smoke and then back to me in the hole, lines creasing his forehead and his skin glossy with a sheen of sweat. And then the lines in his head smooth, his fear vanishing as he pushes up to his knees. Rage hotter than Elysande's molten heart ignites through me, every nerve sparking with rancor. "Don't you fucking leave me here! Alistair! ALISTAIR!"

If there's remorse on his face, it blinks away before it has time to fully register. "I'm sorry, Wren," he says, his voice wooden. And then he's gone.

I have no more energy to waste on screaming. I launch myself at the dirt wall instead, shoving my nails so deep into the packed sediment they flatten and break. My collective scales the side and pushes against the limits of its confines, searching for something to latch onto. Anything I might be able to anchor into enough to hoist myself out of here.

Nothing.

The blast tossed me like I was a woven doll, the ravine too far from the trees for me to form any kind of fastener to one. Red stains my sight. I slide down the wall, again and again, the rock too unstable and the mud too slippery to gain any kind of foothold.

I'm going to burn alive in this hole. Buried with the nefarious magic that sprouted lethal roots and choked the very life from this Vale.

My eyes close, and I plead with Elysande one final time. I beg the goddess of war and vengeance to protect my family, to hone their weapons to barbs and their hearts to steel. Do not let this suffering be wasted; remember this day of parchedness and flood the realm with rains of retribution.

I swallow thickly and will my breath to slow, forcing my final moments to not be spent in panic. Profane delight spreads through me as I imagine the day when all this is shattered, and the only gods left to rule this battered isle will be the corpses of us all.

Perhaps it was ignorant of me to think that someone who has spilled as much blood as I would be welcomed into the heavens. Have a place of comfort under Elysande's reign. But the growl that sounds from above me has me thinking my heart too wicked for even the goddess of war to overlook. Perhaps it's for the best that I stalk amongst the fiends and demons. I always did feel most at home when I unleashed my creature.

I open my eyes to the jaws of a beast.

Leaping with lithe and savage grace, a devil himself dives to the bottom of the pit in a flash of midnight fur and muscled limbs. He lowers so his stomach brushes the ground and whips his head towards me, his ethereal eyes like a gilded forest. He snarls, a sound denoting imminence, not aggression, and I throw a leg over his hind quarters and curl my fingers into his silky fur. A warning growl rumbles from his chest, one that clearly translates to *hold on tight,* and I clench my thighs around his sides, leaning forward to slide my hands under his neck.

Sin leaps out of the ravine like a dark, winged god.

And then he's sprinting, me clinging to his back as his

paws beat the ground into submission. Perhaps I imagine it, but I swear a roar bellows out from the incandescence, one as hellish as the men who unleashed it. The sound a haunting, ugly thing.

I don't look back.

CHAPTER 36

We don't stop until we reach the temple. The interior of the House of Worship is as packed as the surrounding courtyard, as if somehow an open-air structure is going to protect them if another iron ball comes barreling this way. Aeverie orders for the crowd to part as she storms towards us, the ruby-embedded knife from the night of the blood offering clutched beneath her blanched knuckles. "We must do it now. Outside—come now, make haste!" she commands.

"The blood moon is still two days away. Will this even work?" I ask.

Sin darts behind the dais to shift and returns wearing a loose-fitting pair of borrowed trousers. A nasty gash splits his cheek, and the skin around one of his eyes is bruised and swollen. His arms bear a maze of lacerations, and his right shoulder is darkening into a deep shade of garnet. The limp in his gait does not escape my notice either. He suffered an impact somewhere and somehow managed to shift through it, leap into that ravine, and carry us both out of the fire's path at the speed of lightning.

Aeverie's robes billow behind her as she rushes me, grabbing my arm and dragging me behind her. Sin is at my side before we take more than a few steps. "It will work. I have seen it," she says. "To the grass, where the earth can harvest your sacrifice. Quickly!"

Theon calls my name as I step off the last stair, and I find him huddled with the rest of our family, minus Zorina and Eldridge. I let out a shaky breath at the sight of them, and relief thrums through me as I lay eyes on Cosmina. She bears her own marring, a series of cuts and tears along her cheeks, jaw, and neck—likely taking a fall similar to my own, or maybe several. Nothing that can't be healed with a little time and a lot of magic. Worry stirs in my gut at Eldridge and Zorina's absence, but I know the others wouldn't be standing here if they weren't accounted for. Somewhere.

Aeverie shoves the dagger at me, and I wrap my hand around the cold hilt, my palms clammy from sweat. "Focus. Feed the blood of the goddess-blessed to Source. Close the wound scourging the land, and in turn, awaken the eye that has been closed to us. Do it now, blood mage. Our time is dwindling."

Sin moves to stand in front of me, worry set deep in his eyes, but something tells me it's not because he's frightened for *him*. This isn't right—it wasn't supposed to happen like this. "What if it doesn't work? Without the blood moon amplifying it?" I blurt out.

"It will work. I have seen it already. But you must do it now, or that fire will claim us all and everything we've ever known right along with it."

I work to steady my breathing and lock eyes with Sin as he presents his forearm, palm exposed. His other hand cups my face, and his thumb strokes my jaw in reassurance. "You are strong, little witch. Be strong for me now, okay?"

Tears well in my eyes and fall without restraint, ignoring my attempts to blink them back. I'm about to inflict pain upon him, and he is focused on comforting *me*. I don't look away from Sin, but I feel my family hovering around us, joining the others waiting with baited breath as they pray to gods I don't know, pleading for us to be their saving grace.

I need to do this. For them. For all of us.

To give us a fighting chance against the men that try to reap us.

I clutch his arm and slide the blade across.

To his credit, Sin doesn't make a sound. Pain shadows his face for a mere second before he schools his features back to slate, searching my face as my collective latches onto his with whetted talons.

His blood is thick as it drips over my fingers. I close my eyes, focusing on the connection humming between us as our magics merge. There is no flirting between our seams this time, his opening to mine like a trusty book. A firebolt cracks across my chest as Sin tears down all barriers, inviting me into his collective, his mind, his soul.

He is magnificent.

My power blooms with new growth—his ice and my fire swirling in a frost-tipped inferno that swells my veins with the need to consume. I grip the underside of his arm tighter, holding my blade still against the steady flow of his wound, the blood rain that will drip into the soil and sink well into its bowels. His collective entwines with mine, and I wrap my own around his, layer after layer, Sin allowing himself to be caught prey inside my sticky nest. I pause, testing its strength. And when I'm certain his magic is fully bound to my own, not a single chink in our twin armors, I apply more pressure to the knife and plunge us both into ruined depths.

My lips curl instinctively, the smell of rain-soaked hyacinths wafting into my nose and trailing a finger across my greedy tongue. Power surges through me, my magic like lightning and Sin's blood the ocean, agitating together in a ravenous storm. My lungs turn to fire pokers, the smoke swelling my chest, my breath growing labored as I wrestle to control his magic, to snake it through the earth and latch onto Ephraim's chaos.

Ephraim's magic is feral. An untamed beast, bucking and writhing in my white-knuckled grip. Sin's magic is greedy, lapping it up like cream from every dark, forgotten corner of the crust. My hands are trembling so badly it takes me a couple minutes longer than it should to register that the shaking isn't coming from my body alone.

I open my eyes and nearly drop my hold on him, both physically and in our mental entanglement under the rock.

Something is very wrong with the Black Art.

His eyes are still trained on mine, but the light behind them is dimming. A lantern caught behind a rising wave, just the faintest glimmer as its reflection catches on the foam. My breath hitches, and I try to yank the knife away, but his hand catches mine before I can act, caging it over the hilt. *What are you doing,* I want to scream at him. To tell him to *let me go, that something isn't right,* but the words are lost in my throat. Unable to breach the surface of that tidal storm, the waves cresting in my throat and choking out my voice.

My focus drops to where Sin's blood is pooling faster now. A syrup redder than rubies, ladling over my hand and fingers. Thick and honeyed, it calls to my darkness with its enticing song, his demons beckoning my own to share in a dance as wild and free as autumn wheat. His arm quivers beneath the blade, but it's not his shaking that snags my attention.

It's the black vines climbing his body.

This time I force enough will behind my voice to call out his name, but I don't look up, unable to tear my gaze away from the intricate maze of lines creeping up the muscular curves and dips of his arms and inching towards his neck and chest. His usual warm, umber skin blanches to a stark paleness beneath the black contouring, frost replacing the embers in his coloring. They crawl across his clavicle, the dips of his collarbones hollowing into deep, bony depressions.

I call his name again, but this time, it's a plea. To drop his hold on me so I can lift the dagger, stop the bleeding. His hand tightens around mine in response, and I cry out, using all my might to pull at his arm with my other. He doesn't budge, channeling what remains of his power to bind his strength onto my hand clutching the knife, to lock us here in this prison.

Stop, stop, stop! I don't know if I scream the words out loud or not. I'm not sure it matters. Time hovers around us like an unwelcome guest, peering down its nose at our sacrifice.

His sacrifice.

"The dagger." My voice is barely above a whisper. I repeat it, louder this time.

I eye the dagger again, this time with scrutiny, taking in the slender blade sharpened to a lethal point, the sweeping crossguard, the ruby siphons on either end. The gems that are supposed to siphon from Source, to assist me in my role as conduit to draw out the bruise left in the battered earth. But as I behold Sin, the warlord honed to muscle and vigor, withering to sunken flesh and bone...

"Sin, you have to let me go! The blade isn't drawing from Source; it's taking from you. Sin... SIN!"

I should be stronger than him. His blood should be feeding my beast, fueling my adrenaline, and I *should* be able to rip my arm from his. His jaw is clenched, strained so tightly I can see every muscle feathering along his cheeks, his neck. I feel the wall between us now. He's holding out on me, barring me from slipping deeper and taking the rest of his magic, the remnants he channels solely into his banded grip on me.

But it's not Sin's unyielding hold that frightens me most.

It's not the wretched dagger, or Aeverie's deception, or the kingdom soldiers burning down the Vale.

It's the way he's looking at me.

I shake my head. I shake and shake and shake, salty tears stinging my eyes as they fall in fat rivulets down my cheeks. As much as I try to refuse it, Sin's magic continues to bleed into me, his power, his goddess-blessed ichor, his life source.

"It will kill you," I choke out, the words half-strangled in my throat. "Sin, stop. Let me go. Stop. *Stop,*" I plead, my voice fading as my vision begins to blur, a dull ache hammering into my forehead. It's too much, his collective bound to mine, swelling a body not fit to contain that of the Black Art's.

I plunge it deep. Past where the heart of this wicked world beats in rhythmic cadence in its core, past the roots of Source magic and my own, past the beginning of time and matter and man. All the while he watches me with an expression that will haunt me forever, both in my waking hours and the ones spent in nightmares.

Sin watches as I slowly kill him with chilling serenity. Acceptance. Consent. I study him through bleary eyes, my lips trembling as they struggle to form words. "Please," is all I manage.

The black vines snake up his neck, slithering around the column to his chin. If they hurt him, he doesn't show it. Doesn't display any emotion other than sheer grit as his teeth grind together, and he swallows thickly, his eyes locking mine in a death grip of their own. He tilts his chin up as if outrunning the strangling vines. "Listen to me," he says, his voice far too calm for a man teetering on the cold precipice of death. "I have brought pain and hurt to this world. It cannot continue. Not for you. Not for them." He doesn't need to specify the *them*. It's not the elves he's doing this for. It's my family. "I need to do this. Let me do this, Wren. Let me go."

I'm shaking my head before he finishes, hardly able to see him through the globs of tears sticking to my lashes. "No," I repeat over and over, still trying to pull my arm away. If I can just hold out until the last of his strength fades, I can let go and heal him. I can fix him. I have to. I have to fix him.

"Wren," he whispers my name, and spiderwebs crack across my heart. I'm certain it's the most beautiful sound I've ever heard. One I'll never hear again if he doesn't let me fucking go right now.

"Please," I beg. "Please let me go. Let me fix this. I can fix this. I can fix it, Sin. You just have to let me go, okay?"

His eyes are gentle as he watches me, not matching the strength he pours into his hand. He shakes his head softly, uncaring of the labyrinth of black-tipped shards winding up his throat. "You can't. But I can."

Something shifts in his eyes, something that turns my lungs to ice and my heart to granite. Now it's me who tightens my grip on him, desperate to cling to him as if he is about to shatter into dust. If I just hold tight enough, outlast his dwindling magic...

"I love you, Wren. I wish I could have been more for you, but you have always been my salvation."

For a split second, he releases his hold on me, and for that split second, I almost feel the breath of relief on my neck.

And then his arms band around my waist, and he pulls me against him, plunging the blade deep into his heart.

CHAPTER 37

Inch by brutal inch, the dagger slips into his meaty flesh.

The Black Art is dying. I am killing him.

I want to scream. I want to shove out of his grip, yank the knife from his chest, and pump his heart until it beats again. Hold his hand while the gaping chasm in his organ heals and closes, stroke his cheek while I tell him it will all be over soon.

But I don't do any of that. My body—this suit of flesh and bone—doesn't belong to me. Not anymore. The rest of Sin's goddess-blessed power bleeds into my own, turning my blood to molten vengeance. I tremble and shake, unable to move, unable to speak. Unable to holler for help. If the others are still near us, I don't see them. Don't hear them.

All I see is him. My Blackheart. My most beloved sin.

And then I see the blood. Coating the front of my tunic in hot, sticky tar. The knife protruding from his chest, the blade velveted in harrowing regret. Sin's hands fall from my waist, his knees slumping to the ground, my fallen god.

Everything goes black.

I don't know if I closed my eyes, or my vision failed me, but all sight evades me. My body convulses like the Howling Sea rocks through it, waves of power and fury washing through each limb, cresting into my fingers and toes. Crystals of ice bloom down my spine, frosty tendrils caress my cheeks, and my bones bury in a heap of heavy snow. My very marrow solidifies to glittering diamonds, and my own legs surrender.

I fall to my knees and place my hands on Sin's too-still chest. His skin is bleached, the onyx vines having choked the last of his magic, his strength, his life. And I weep. Sobs tear from the depths of my barbed heart, the spiderwebbed cracks deepening and stretching to every grisly corner.

For years, I shushed my beast. Sedated her with images of what would happen if I unleashed that part of myself, the violence and pain and horror that would become the world if she fled her leash. But now, as my head falls back and a cry of anguish rends the dawn, I snap that tether, along with the final fraying strand of my morality.

They took Sin from me. My love. My Bonded-to-be.

I scream.

And with that scream, I take *everything*.

CHAPTER 38

I'm falling.

Down, down, down, deep beyond the crust, well past the earth's heart.

Except... I'm not falling at all.

I'm rooting.

My limbs are weightless things, this suit of meat and bone but a costume slung over unyielding light. A light so blinding, so ethereal, it can only be divine. And then I feel it. Sludge. A sticky, molten substance splattered on the rock, speckling it with toxic ruin. It provides but a second of resistance before I'm punching through it—no, annihilating it—and I flood everything beyond it with unforgiving heat. Heat that tunnels through my swollen veins, threatening to char my flesh to blistered leather.

And then I hear her. A voice so gentle in my ear, a caress to my essence as she whispers in a tone that's almost sultry. "To ashes and dust they shall return. Now breathe, my darling witch. Breathe, and when you wake, the earth shall know nothing but blood hazed eyes and blackened teeth. Breathe. And when you do, you must take."

I stir in the crust. Sediment flying outward as I stampede onward, chasing the warm, red light that shines through my chest, guiding my way. No. Not light. The inexorable rush of Elysande's heat, her vengeance, her wrathful, unbeating heart.

My celestial beacon in this sacrilegious realm.

"That's it, darling witch. Take it all."

And with that, the final sutures piecing me together split with a mighty rip, and I fill every abandoned corner with my damning song.

Another voice. This one higher-pitched, and the rise in her tone as she mutters something too far away for me to decipher, indicating panic. I almost turn to search for the cause of her distress, but I exist beyond the measures of direction and realm. I push farther, fracturing the earth with all that I am, and all that I am yet to become.

Somewhere behind me, in the pocket of earth I leave behind, the woman unleashes a wail as woeful as the ones I yearn to devour.

"Very good," the first voice purrs. "Take. Take, darling witch. Take it all."

And so I do.

I was always taught that death was a peaceful, tranquil thing. That our fears dissipate as we ascend from our borrowed skins and enter into the next realm. No worries, no affliction, no despair following us like a lurking lone wolf.

Death is not any of those things.

I must have made it to Elysande's domain after all if the fire incinerating my chest is any tell. I'm too still, too stiff. My bones like stripped bark that's been laid out in the arid season, my muscles stiffened and bound into tight knots. I wiggle my fingers, then my toes, pain lancing up my legs when I do, and a low groan slips from my mouth.

Someone calls my name. Distanced.

Again. Closer.

"Wren!" This time, in my ear.

My eyes flutter, the lashes sticking together before finally parting. Morrinne leans over the bed I'm lying in, her hands hovering over my body like she's not sure what to do with them. Her usual bound hair hangs loose and limp over her shoulders, the ends frayed and in desperate need of a washing. An air of sorrow clings to her eyes as she stares down at me, the corners of her lips tugging upward, but it doesn't match the rest of her creased face, wrinkles splitting her forehead. I try to sit up, to chase away whatever nightmares are plaguing her, but I stop short as the meat in my arms and sides ache with protest, like someone charred my muscles to blackened crisps then stuffed them back into my body.

"No—stop, stop," she murmurs, gently pushing my shoulders back onto the bed. "Your injuries aren't nearly mended. The healers said they could do much more once you were awake, but they didn't want to stress your body while it was recovering from your..." she trails off, her fingers drumming the sheets and her lips smashing down into a firm line.

Oh.

It all comes flooding back with vigor: the Vale burning, the ravine, Aeverie handing me the dagger, Sin's blood seeping through my fingers, our bodies chest to chest as his heart wept into mine. His body failing as the elven blade siphoned him dry until nothing was left but rot and decay.

I was certain my heart had shattered when the Black Art crumpled to my feet. I wish it had so there would be nothing left to feel the anguish twisting in my chest, deeper and sharper than any wretched blade. My heart did not shatter. It's right here, thumping in my chest, a thousand tiny thorns piercing it like some kind of macabre rose sculpture. I want to cry, longing for release, but my eyes remain parched, refusing to grant me even that.

It doesn't stop the tremors from wracking through me

though, my shoulders rocking not of their own volition against the soft sheets. Too soft. I don't deserve such comfort. I couldn't save him. Morrinne's hands find my shoulders again, pressing them more firmly against the bedding to hold them in place. "Shh, shh, none of this," she says, even though I haven't uttered a sound. "You'll reopen your stitches."

It's then I notice the bandages adorning my arms, and another on my right hand. I'm wearing a simple lilac night-gown, the color reminding me of dusk on evenings spent in our cabin, when my life held some measure of happiness. A quick pat down of my sides confirms the nagging itchiness along the sides of my stomach are a few more bandages, likely where I experienced the brunt of my fall into the ravine.

"Aeverie told us she could personally heal you if—*when*—you woke up," she says.

More pain pangs my chest, but this wave is reserved for the horror Morrinne must have experienced when she thought she might lose me for a third time. This one final. "What happened to me? I don't remember after Sin... after he fell and..." I trail off, trying to blink memories I don't possess back into my mind.

"You collapsed, honey. One minute you were crying, and then you grabbed a hold of Singard and screamed," she shud-ders, as if recounting my wail was enough to raise gooseflesh along her back, "and the next thing any of us knew, you were unconscious. We didn't know if you were going to come back to us, sweet girl. The damn priestess kept saying you would, but I wasn't so sure."

The mention of said priestess turns my tongue to lead. "She lied to us."

Morrinne nods. "I know. She explained everything after. Didn't have much choice unless she wanted the lot of us whooping her ass with that damn staff of hers. Sin most of all.

I knew he was a wicked, wayward man, but not even your Elysande could compare to the god of wrath he became. I about—"

"Wait—what?" I interrupt her, pushing up on my elbows and ignoring the pain and Morrinne's disapproving snicker that both follow. "Sin is... alive?" I swallow around the last word, hardly able to choke it out.

Her eyes soften, and she smooths the hair on the top of my head with a gentle rub of her palm. "Yes, honey. He's alive."

Now, I'm crying. No—sobbing. So many questions wrestle for my attention, but I speak none. Fortunately, Morrinne seems to pluck them from my mind, one by one. "That dagger was enchanted to act as a vessel. When you used it on Singard, it created a direct link for the elves to drain his magic into it. Since you were still the wielder of the blade and already joined your collective with his, his magic was yours to channel. And it damn nearly killed you. I didn't know if Singard was dead or a hairbreadth away from it; the priestess had a ward up, keeping everyone back so no one could intervene."

I shake my head furiously, trying to will sense into her words. "I don't understand."

"Sin was goddess-blessed. You, while one of my greatest blessings, are not. There was a chance you wouldn't survive that transferal. A fraction of it, sure, but that blade took *all* of his power, and in turn, you wielded it completely. Something no mage should have endured, let alone recover from. But you stared death down and punted her right between the legs. When you screamed, it was like Elysande herself was ripping the veil between our realms apart. There was light—so much light, it was blinding—but it didn't hurt anyone. Your hands were on his heart; that's where the light was coming from. And then as fast as it all happened, your eyes closed, and you sagged right off him. I thought you had joined him in peace."

Morrinne wipes wetness from her cheeks with the back of her frayed, tan sweater. I sit up and carefully maneuver so my legs hang off the side of the bed, and I hug her waist. Her necklace, a bunch of shells from the sandbars strung together—dangles in my face, and I turn my head so my cheek presses against her belly. She combs her hand through my hair.

"You saved him, sweet girl. He's only alive because of you."

A part of me wonders if she wishes I hadn't, but I will it away. Of course she does. How could she not?

I pull away, and she sits next to me on the bed. "Earlier you said that Sin *was* goddess-blessed. As in, he no longer is?" I ask hesitantly, turning the words over in my mind as I speak them out loud.

"No. He's not. The ritual took it all."

"Aeverie... the elves... they wanted his power? They wanted us to do the ritual so they could have his magic for themselves?" I shake my head. That doesn't make sense. The elves weren't interested in our magics, only in restoring Source. Unless that was also a lie.

"The elves have no interest in using the magic they stole. It's stored in the dagger, and it's remained there since. You've been out for several days, honey," she supplies. "Their kind don't believe in our gods, apparently. They don't discredit their existence—in fact, quite the opposite. But they don't believe Adelphia is the goddess of the arcane. That magic is something that belongs to those who Source forms a connection with, not something that can be bestowed through an arbitrary Rite. Aeverie said it is unnatural for any one person to wield the power of a deity. That it belongs to the earth, and it is not up to us to determine who it is shared with. At least, I think that's the gist of what that damn priestess was saying. I could hardly stand to look at her.

"But they did not bind Singard's magic for their own use,"

she continues. "They did it because as long as Adelphia's magic is bound to this realm through that dagger, she cannot choose another Black Art. Rendering the goddess of the arcane nothing more than a construct."

I chew on my bottom lip, rolling it between my teeth as I mull over everything she's told me. It makes sense that the elves wouldn't want man to wield the power of the gods. Look at what the last Black Art did with such a blessing: Ephraim scorched their lands and fractured their very connection to its magic.

"Did it even work? Did we draw out the chaos? And what about the blood moon?"

Morrinne rakes her blunt nails down the fronts of her legs, the fingers usually wrapped around a steaming mug itching for something to do. "Yes. Whatever you and Singard did before helped," she waves her hand, "but call it mother's intuition, that light that beamed out of you is what did the trick. I'm certain of it. It's only been days and already there is new life in the Vale. Many of the trees that were burnt have new growth, the bark is moistening, there is new grass sprouting, even the wildlife has been abundant, like something is drawing them near.

"The blood moon was supposed to alleviate some of the strain. Since the celestial energy would have made the entire process quicker and more efficient, Singard had a greater chance of surviving. It wasn't Aeverie's wish for him, or either of you, to die."

"But they knew it was a possibility," I say, grinding my jaw.

"And a damn good one. If it weren't for Theon, I would have ripped that woman to shreds. I don't care if she is some kind of priestess, I'd like to see her magic stop the wrath of a mother."

I harbor no doubt that Aeverie could kill Morrinne with

nothing more than a fleeting glance, but I keep my comments to myself.

"The others will be overjoyed. They've all been by your side every day, sleeping in shifts. All except Singard that is."

My heart sinks to my gut. "How badly is he injured?"

To my surprise, Morrinne chuckles. "Oh honey, that man woke up looking like a damn god. You used a fragment of Adelphia's magic to heal him; there wasn't a scratch left when he came to. Only took a few hours after you collapsed for him to revive."

I breathe a sigh of relief but then knit my brows. Morrinne notices, and her smile vanishes immediately. "He hasn't come to see you because he's been locked away. Singard was very... well, to be blunt, he was a downright menace. He would have killed Aeverie, or died trying, I'm sure of it. The blond fellow with the braids—"

"Vox."

"Yes, that was his name. It took him and several other burly ones to get Sin shoved behind a threshold Aeverie could seal. I've not hidden my feelings for him, but I found it in my heart to visit him in light of what he tried to do for us. His temper seems to cool for a bit when I'm there, so I've taken to frequenting him a few times a day. All he ever wants to know is if you've woken. He's been terrified you wouldn't. We all were. Speaking of such, I need to tell your sisters, Theon and Eldrid —" My mother blanches as she cuts herself off, and my heart lodges in my throat as tears brim in her eyes.

"What happened? What happened to Eldridge?" I demand, panic hastening my voice. Morrinne sucks in a sharp breath, and quickly wipes the salty tears from the tops of her cheekbones. "The others got away unscathed, but Eldridge..."

"What happened, Mama?" I shout the words now, resisting the urge to shake her until her own rattle free.

"His arm, honey. One of the explosions, he was hanging back, trying to help where he could, but one of those damn projectiles came down so close to him. He was fast enough to avoid the hit, but no one could outrun the debris. Severed him at the elbow."

No. *Gods, no.* "Oh Eldridge," I whisper, my hand covering my mouth instinctually.

"He's alive, child. That is... I want to be so furious, but I can't even bring it forth in me. I'm just so grateful he's alive." And that's when my mother's mask finally falters and the pain that has been festering inside her, the kind of pain only a mother can experience when she fears for her children, lashes across her face.

"How is he?" I ask.

"How do you figure? You know Eldridge. He equates his brawn with his worth and has never been able to see just how much more he is than that. He's distraught." She purses her lips as if searching for how to elaborate and coming up short. There's no need for her to say more. My heart aches with the pain he must be in. For the trepidation he must be feeling for how this will affect us all, so soon.

"Knowing you've woken will ease his spirits," she adds.

I nod. "I'll go to him right away."

Morrinne goes to stand, but I catch her forearm. She looks at me, one eyebrow cocked.

"May I... may I go see *him* first?" I yearn to visit Eldridge, but my stomach is so twisted in knots with the need to see Sin in the flesh, to know he really, truly is okay.

Her cheeks lift in a close-lipped smile. "He's just down the hall. The rooms have been magicked to not let sound pass, so you'll want to be careful when you enter. He won't be expecting you, and like I said, he's been itching to get his hands on Aeverie, or any of the elves for that matter."

I nod. "I'll announce myself."

She leads us out of the room and motions towards a door a few segments down. "I'll go let the others know and give you some privacy. You know where to find us." She envelopes my hand in both of hers before turning and heading down the hall.

As soon as I hear the echo of her first footsteps on the stairs, I sprint for the door.

CHAPTER 39

I don't announce myself. Even a simple knock is one obstacle too many, delaying me from being with him, and I will have none of it. Nothing—*nothing*—will keep us apart again. I throw open the door and rush inside.

He's on me immediately.

If he had meant to attack me on instinct, I wouldn't have been fast enough to stop him. But there is nothing but warmth and love bleeding from his in-tact chest into mine, his arm banded around my waist as he crushes me against him. His other hand cups the back of my head, tucking it against his collarbone, and he leans down, his lips pressing to the crown of my hair.

I sob.

All the tears I couldn't form earlier pour out of me, soaking the front of his laced, white shirt. Sin runs his hand through my hair, over and over, saying nothing while I weep with relief. I don't think he could speak if he wanted to. His own body is a board beneath me, and I can *feel* the emotion seeping out of him, in the tightness of his muscles, his grip in my hair. The torment that has held him captive for days, trapped in this room while he waited to hear if my injuries overcame me. Not the ones I received physically, but the internal shock and devastation my insides took as I wielded divine power.

I pull away and quickly wipe my tear-stained face, knowing I look like a drowned cat washed up on the river bank. Sin waits patiently, his gaze raking me over and lingering on every bandage, even seemingly taking note of the ones hidden beneath my nightgown. Wrath licks his eyes, and a muscle feathers along his tight jaw. I watch as he clenches his hands at his sides, reining in his beast, and I step forward, placing both hands on his chest.

"Hi," I whisper.

Warmth spreads through me at the slight upward tug of his lips. "Hi, beautiful. You came back to me."

"Always."

But then as I remember what he did, the fear *I* had felt, my relief turns to liquid ire, and I drop my hands. "How could you have done that to me? I thought you were dead."

"Maybe I was," he murmurs. He doesn't touch me, granting me privacy to sort through these feelings. "I'm sorry, Wren." His voice is like honey, and so low, so soft. "It was the only way I could protect you. We couldn't win against whoever attacked us, not without better preparation, and a lot of it. I will not ask your forgiveness because I do not regret it. I would die a thousand times over, each death more brutal than the last, if it meant keeping you safe."

It's then I notice the disarray of the room. Deep gouges in sets of five curved lines mar the stone walls, the tousled bedding is shredded, and the table in the corner is overturned, partially blocking a shattered vase. It wasn't Sin the high priestess kept caged—it was his beast.

I turn back towards him, unable to bear the distance even if I am still peeved. Because in truth, I'm not angry. I never was—not at him anyway. I was just so, so frightened. I throw my arms around him and crush my mouth to his, my hands twirling in his long hair. Sin parts my lips with his, deepening our kiss, our bodies pressed so tightly together it's impossible to tell where I end and he begins.

There is lust in the kiss, but so much more than that too. I taste his love in every sweep of his tongue, every squeeze of my waist, every thump of his heart against mine. My lips are swollen when we part.

"I love you," I murmur. "You don't get to leave me. Not now, not ever."

He rests his forehead against mine. "I'm not the one that's been battling death for the past three days," he reminds me. "If the magic didn't kill me, waiting for you to wake up from your cat nap nearly did. *Never* do that to me again."

"I'll consider your request."

He cocks an eyebrow at my taunt and flicks his tongue across the front of his teeth. "It's no wonder you came back. I imagine you looked death in the eye and spat in her face."

I shrug my shoulders. "Something like that." He smiles at my use of his words from last ni—well, several nights ago, I suppose. More serious, I ask, "Your power... it's really gone?"

"The part of it that belonged to Adelphia, yes. I'm still a mage, my magic is still there. It's just now I'm only three times as deadly as any normal male, instead of five times." His light-hearted wink eases some of the tension in my chest. I stroke his cheek. I know having this stolen from him is much harder than he's letting on, masking his anger for my sake. Before Sin ascended in the Rite, I was acquainted with the rumor of his power. It was well-known Sin's destruction magic was advanced, a dangerous thing, especially since his allegiance was to the crown, and he was Dusaro Kilbreth's son.

"You don't have to hide from me. It's okay to be furious. It's okay to *feel*."

He places his hand on the back of my own, still caressing the skin of his cheek which has restored to its normal reddish-brown, warm and lively. His eyes turn molten. "I am going to burn them all for what they did to you. They will not know mercy. They will not know peace. Because even in death, I will haunt them."

Something flutters low in my belly at his words, but it's not the time or place. And I don't want to open the stitches temporarily holding me together until the healers tend to me. "We will get it back. The dagger. Your magic. If that's what you want."

"You are what I want. What I need. The rest is secondary always."

I step away from him, needing a sliver of space, now *really* at risk of opening my stitches. "Earlier you said we wouldn't win against whoever attacked us. As if you weren't sure of the perpetuator. Do you doubt your father's involvement?" Incredulousness heightens my tone.

"Not at all. But we don't have those kinds of weapons. Ballistas sure, but they are very tedious to move. It was challenging to maneuver them around Blackreach in preparation for Legion. Moving them across the isle would have been near impossible."

"Who else would possibly have that kind of weaponry?" I ask, rubbing my arms at the memory of the iron balls flying overhead and shattering into the ground around us. The bodies that lay fallen as we traipsed across them, desperate to outrun the lethal rain.

"With great waters come great sharks."

Both of us stiffen at Aeverie's voice floating in from the door I left open. Well, *I* stiffen. Sin is at the threshold before I can track the movement, his arms caged on either side as he leans forward. Aeverie doesn't so much as flinch at Sin's bared teeth hovering an inch from her face, the phantom barrier providing a shield between them. "I imagine you both have a few questions, and far more than a few choice words you'd like to say to me. You deserve the opportunity for both, but first, I come with news. A letter arrived by pigeon this morning. Your first question will be answered when you read it." She pulls a rolled-up piece of parchment from one of her inner robe pockets, the gold wax seal already split.

"Second, I apologize for the risks we took. It was never my hope that either of you should perish, and the celestial event was our greatest hope in preventing that, as it would have aided the blood mage in absorbing the goddess's power. It was unfortunate circumstances outside our control that prevented us from relying on that resource.

"Thirdly, you have our gratitude. On behalf of my entire race, I thank you for restoring our connection to Source. The Vale is already beginning to thrive—something you will see for yourselves as soon as you leave my temple. Which you will do, including you, Singard Kilbreth, because I will remove the boundary spell when I am finished. You may be adults by your race, but to mine, you are still young, foolish, and impulsive. My magic is far more mature than yours. Do not mistake that, Singard Kilbreth or Wren the blood mage, or you will regret it. My appreciation for what you have done for us runs deep, but not more so than my desire to protect my people and our home. A trait I'm certain we all share."

Sin's body is a current, the tension rolling off him enough to choke the air from the room. The muscles in his arms flex as he grips the sides of the doorframe, his chest rising and falling in even breaths, each one promising a death swifter than the last. He snarls when I press a hand to his arm, but promptly silences it when he recognizes it's my touch.

"If we are to be working together, you will need to rein in

those instincts," Aeverie says, nodding to where my hand provoked Sin's redirected aggression. "The more you shift, wanderer, the easier it will be to control the beast. Your blood mage's life may depend on that yet."

"*Do not* speak of her," Sin growls in a voice like gravel. "You will have her tended to at once. And Aeverie," he says, leaning forward a hair's width more before the barrier stops him, "if I ever find a mark on her from elven hands again, it will be the last mark their hands ever make. *You* would be wise to remember that."

The priestess regards him blankly but does not antagonize him further. Perhaps her age has instilled some wisdom after all.

I clear my throat and swallow down the shadows that seemed to slip off Sin. "Did you know? Before I used the dagger, I asked you if it would work and you said yes because you had seen it. Did you see that we'd survive it too?"

Aeverie's stare moves to behold me where I stand just behind Sin. It's impossible to tell what thoughts are behind her milky eyes, and not a hair on her body moves out of place at my question. She holds up the rolled-up parchment and extends it towards Sin, not diverting her gaze. "Read this at once. You may think we are your enemies, and perhaps in a way, we are. Our war may be next, blood mage, wanderer, but it is not the one we fight now."

As soon as Sin snatches the end of the letter poking through the invisible barrier, Aeverie turns and retreats down the hall. I move to sit on the bed, tossing the shredded bedding to the side, and wave Sin to sit next to me.

The golden parchment crinkles like decaying leaves as he unrolls it, revealing a note penned in black ink.

Did you enjoy our gift? It was with great pride that we displayed a small portion of our treasures. I do apologize for the death of your scouts. Perhaps it can serve as a reminder to never assume your known enemy is also your sole one.

I am woeful to learn our efforts to exterminate the white-haired witch were not fruitful. We will take great care to ensure that does not happen again. A word of advice from your neighbor: the wayward wolf does not warrant the death of the pack. Give us the white-haired witch, and we will offer you clemency in return.

Safeguard her, and we will offer only ruin.

Sincerely,

King Torin

Son of the late King Varil

"The letterhead?" I ask, my finger lazily grazing over the *L* that's been stamped onto the top of the page.

"Langston," Sin snarls. A second later, his claws shred the letter to ribbons, the pieces falling to the ground like grim confetti. Stalking to the wall, he punches both sets of nails into the stone, his head hanging low between his raised shoulders.

I follow after him but grant him a moment of autonomy to tame his creature. "Baelliarah attacked us? Weren't the waterways being watched?"

A low growl rumbles from somewhere deep in his chest. "Vox deployed them all out to The Red Tops to watch for my— for *Dusaro's* men. They must have docked on the far side of the Vale and moved in during the night. Brought the weapons over on a ship. Now we know where they found the coin to do it."

"If Sterling has allied with Baelliarah, do you think your father has also?"

Sin shakes his head, the ends of his hair mingling with the loose strings of his shirt. "I do not know. It would be unlike him to trust a nation we've warred with before, and there isn't anything on the letter to symbolize himself, so I'm inclined to say I doubt it. But one thing is for certain, we need to find out. And before that, we need to plan."

"How does one begin to plan for a war against three parties intent on killing them?"

Sin turns, unleashing the full heat of his gaze on me. A promise in his eyes that would make anyone else fall to their knees at once, a plea of mercy already on their lips. "With a whole lot of weapons, love."

I let his words sink in, mulling them over and considering what this means. For me. My family. For us. Ice capped talons find their way back to my chest, their jagged ends puncturing my heart as I remember what it felt like to lose him. Like the breath had been ripped from my lungs and my soul from my flesh. Torn in half, never to be whole again.

I step towards him. Sin watches me carefully, noting the sudden change in my expression. "Ask me again," I whisper, my voice a honeyed breath. "Ask me to Bond with you. To be your Mate. If that's still what you want."

I wish I could bottle the softening of his features and tuck it away forever. Because no matter how hard I try, my memory will never be able to conjure the details of how his cheeks lift with rosy bliss and stars burst across his eyes. A nova that sparks a new kind of flame, one infinitely more possessive, as he takes a measured step forward and cups my jaw. He towers above me, tilting my head back to look at him. As if I would want to look anywhere other than at the devastating man studying me like I am the rarest treasure he's ever laid eyes on. "There is nothing I desire more than to take you as my Mate, so I may love you in this life and the next, and every one that comes after. Will you Bond with me, my vicious, little witch?"

A single tear leaks from my eye and lazily rolls down my cheek. I don't wipe it away. "Yes," I whisper. "It would be my honor."

The kiss that follows is selfish. Greedy. His need to claim me coating his mouth in a covetous finish.

And I want to give him everything. All that I am and more, over and over, until he feels the love festering in my chest.

He breaks our kiss to murmur against my lips. "You will be my equal. My Bonded. My *Mate*." Sin grins with his newfound favorite word.

"And when you retake the crown?" I ask, reaching up to twirl a lock of his hair around my finger. I speak the words with confidence, not willing to consider the possibility that we may fail. Not yet. Not right now.

My question fans the flames in his eyes, and his returning smile is as sinful as his name. "You will be devastating on the throne, my love. Her Black Grace. It suits you."

I capture his mouth with mine, tasting the truth in his words and the devotion on his tongue. Tonight is reserved for me to experience one night of passion with my Bonded-to-be. Tomorrow is for the woman I must become, consort to the Black Art.

The dark queen.

Her Black Grace.

To be continued...

Wren and Sin's story will continue in The Beasts That Bleed Us.

ACKNOWLEDGMENTS

For someone who calls themselves a writer, I am terrible at finding the right words to express how I feel towards everyone who continues to support me and make all of this possible, but none more so than my readers.

My darling readers: thank you. Thank you for taking a chance on me and on these characters. I know they can be hard to love at times, but they have enraptured my heart so completely, and it means so much for me to be able to share them with you. For as long as I can remember, I've wanted to write and share stories, and none of this would have come to fruition without your love and support. This series has gotten so much more love than I could have dreamed possible, and it's all because of you. Thank you for hyping these books up on Booktok and Bookstagram (and anywhere else!), for engaging with me on socials, and most importantly, for simply reading them. My gratitude runs far deeper than I can possibly express in something as mundane as words.

My ridiculously talented writing friends: thank you for all the early morning and late-night laughs. I need them, probably more so than I let on most of the time. This writing thing is hard, and I'd be so lost without your encouragement, wisdom, and most importantly, your friendship. You all are such super-stars, and I'm so honored to know you, let alone call you my friends. You know who you are.

Brittany, Bryan, and the entire team at Lake Country Press:

thank you for seeing something in that very first version of The Blood That Binds Us. That story went through one heck of a revision, but you saw a glimmer of what it could be. Thank you for taking a chance on me and TBTBU, and I'm so thrilled to publish this next installment of Sin and Wren's story with you.

Everett: thank you for showing me I am worth far more than the number of words I can type onto a page on any given day. I love you so very much, little bear.

And lastly, my incredible husband, Ian: I don't know who or what I made a deal with to have you as my partner, but I would give anything to be your person in this life and every one that comes after. Thank you for your endless encouragement, for all the afternoons you solo parented so I could have time to write, and for your unyielding support. You are the sunshine to my grumpy, the blood to my heart. Writing has allowed me to journey to so many places, but you have always been my greatest and most treasured adventure. Love you forever.

About the Author

Erin is a lover of all things fantasy and more than a little obsessed with morally gray characters. She holds a degree in Film and Media Studies but has shifted her focus to her one true love—writing novels set in fantastical places with dark, twisty romance. A self-proclaimed iced coffee enthusiast, you can often find Erin writing in local cafes, poorly singing along to the radio in a Starbucks drive-through, or rewatching The Vampire Diaries with a cold brew in tow. An avid traveler, Erin has lived all over the country, but Alaska and the Pacific Northwest have a special place in her heart. The Bonds That Break Us is her second novel, and she looks forward to writing more stories where the "villain" gets the girl.

Also by Erin Mainord

The Blood That Binds Us